GATE OF DEATH

First Published in Great Britain 2020 by Mirador Publishing

First edition: 2020

A copy of this work is available through the British Library.

ISBN: 978-1-913833-12-1

Mirador Publishing
10 Greenbrook Terrace
Taunton
Somerset
UK
TA1 1UT

GATE OF DEATH

By

Chris DeSantis

DEDICATION

TO:

GPE

ETERNAL THANKS

ACKNOWLEDGEMENT

A profound thanks to the following for their input and encouragement:

Sarah Luddington and the team at Mirador Publishing
Irene Pavitt
Adele Brinkley
Kevin Daulong
Dimitrios Moscholeas
Ian Kaplan
Victoria Jensen
Eileen Provost

It is now generally acknowledged that the Egyptians, of all the ancient peoples, were the most learned in the Occult Sciences of Nature. . . Thales, Solon, Pythagoras, and Plato journeyed from Greece to the delta of the Nile in quest of knowledge. Upon returning to their own country, these illumined men acknowledged the Egyptians to be the wisest of mortals and the Egyptian temples to be the repositories of the most sublime doctrines concerning the history of the Gods and the regeneration of men.

~~ Manly P. Hall, 33rd Degree Mason

If I tell you one of the sayings he spoke to me, you will pick up rocks and stone me, and fire will come from the rocks and devour you.

~~ Thomas the Apostle

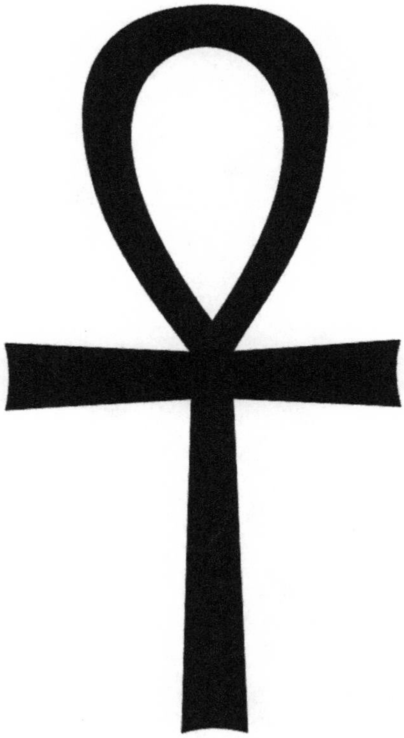

CHAPTER 1

AT THE HEIGHT OF ITS POPULARITY, upward of 40,000 visitors a day streamed through the doors of the Metropolitan Museum of Art. As the director of security for the museum, Anthony Leonardi kept abreast of the numbers. He also made a point of stopping in the atrium in the museum's Egyptian Wing when doing his daily rounds. The two-story, glass-enclosed atrium was bright and airy and never overly congested. The desert-rose marble wall at the rear of the ancient Temple of Dendur mimicked the steep cliffs along the banks of the Nile. A granite crocodile chiseled by the hands of humans who had lived when B.C. turned to A.D. lurked alongside the upward-cupped, green leaves of a blue lotus plant in the opaque water of the large reflecting pool designed to resemble the Nile. A small plaque explained the role of the crocodile in the cult of Isis and Serapis.

Role in the cult of Isis and Serapis? he often asked himself.

Continuing his rounds, Anthony shuddered at the thought that countless ancient Egyptians met their demise in the powerful jaws of the giant Nile crocodiles. He stopped in front of a pair of colossal statues of Amenhotep III seated on the royal throne and gazed between the twin representations of Tutankhamun's grandfather and into the Temple of Dendur, momentarily allowing his imagination to travel back in time.

"Don't look now," he heard with a tap on his shoulder.

Anthony spun. "You know I hate it when you sneak up on me."

"Thought you'd like to know that the old guy who's always in here is headed your way," Vicki said, subtly pointing to an elderly man.

1

Anthony didn't bother to look. "Jörg Miller?" he said and frowned. "I bumped into him last week and he nearly talked my ear off."

"Well, I'm pretty sure that he spotted you because he's headed this way."

"I may need an out," Anthony said.

Vicki inched closer to her boss. "Just give me the sign."

The elderly man neared, grinning as he approached.

Anthony extended his hand with a cordial smile. "Nice to see you here again, Mr. Miller," he said as he clasped hands. The old man's hand felt breakable, cold, the proverbial dead fish.

"Herr Doktor Leonardi. What a pleasant surprise. Our paths cross once again. Ah, but you can certainly forgive this old man's longing to spend so much time in here," Jörg Miller remarked with a wearied Teutonic charisma while making a sweeping gesture with his trembling hand. "This wing is filled with so many extraordinary and glorious objects, all revealing the hidden mysteries of the ancients. It's as though the dead come to life in here."

Anthony and Vicki exchanged quick glances.

Miller slowly shifted his gaze, head shaking, and stared at the Temple of Dendur in a trance-like state. "I want to tell you something very important, Doktor Leonardi," he said, faintly. A slight but discernable inflection indicated a Bavarian or Austrian accent. "The word *Tod* in German means 'death'. Do you know what else the letters *TOD* stand for?"

"No," Anthony replied, discreetly wiping his hand on his pants.

"Temple of Dendur." Miller stared at the ancient temple.

Anthony raised his silver-and-gold Santos de Cartier watch toward his face, and kept it there until Miller noticed the gesture. "Well, if you'll excuse me, Mr. Miller, I'm running a little behind schedule for a meeting."

"Please, say no more, Inspector. I know you're terribly busy."

Anthony stared through the bifocal lenses of Miller's glasses and into his rheumy eyes. Thin blood vessels streaked the more transparent white areas of his watery eyes. "It's been many years, Mr. Miller, since I left my job with the police department for my position here."

Vicki stepped between the men. "You don't want to be late to the meeting."

Anthony grinned. "Enjoy your visit today, Mr. Miller."

CHAPTER 2

Rome. One Week Before the Heliacal Rising of Sirius.
40°C (104°F).

THE THREE MEN MET IN THE depths of the massive basilica where the Egyptian obelisk had stood for fifteen centuries before relocating to St. Peter's Square. During Roman times, the obelisk had served as the centerpiece for Caligula's Circus, an open-air venue used for an array of gory events until the slaughter of Christians became a popular pastime.

The choice of location wasn't random.

"I fear we are faced with little choice in this matter," remarked the Superiore Generale. He spoke in English instead of Spanish or Italian to avoid any suggestion of superiority.

The Worshipful Master assented with a complaisant nod and then gently tugged at the canary-diamond-studded cuffs of his custom-tailored suit. He went by the name Puppet Master and Egyptian Cobra to a select few chosen to form a tight band of brothers at the core of an Italian secret society.

The head of the third man remained bowed in silent obeisance.

The three slowly exited what remained of the outer walls of the Circus and stopped short of a corridor that traced the ancient Via Cornelia, a paved Roman road that once connected the blood-stained arena to a Roman pagan cemetery, the present-day site of the Vatican Necropolis.

The Worshipful Master removed a silk handkerchief from his suit pocket and wiped his forehead. "How do we proceed?" he asked.

3

"The scrolls *must* be destroyed once and for all," the Superiore Generale stated. "Heaven and hell will collide if they are deciphered."

The Master wiped his brow again and pocketed the handkerchief. The pause in conversation allowed for a quiet meditation in the dim setting until dark eyes reconnected. "You have my word that the scrolls will be found and destroyed, Generale, but we mustn't stop there. My association can do much more. The group in New York has become too powerful."

The suggestion of elimination was clear.

"That would be unwise," the pious leader softly remarked after a short, but intended, pause in conversation.

"If they're not stopped soon," the Master cautioned, dread in his voice, "they'll succeed in their ultimate goal of controlling all three pillars of power. They will be unstoppable in their pursuit of world supremacy."

Clerics, kings, tyrants, and maniacal heads of state throughout history had long sought to solidify control over the three pillars of power – political, monetary, and ecclesiastical. Systematic control of all three pillars in the hands of groups that already controlled the world's global alliances, the Worshipful Master feared, would result in the total collapse of everything established over the past two millennia. He knew only one way to handle the growing monopolization of global wealth and political power.

The Master pressed the matter. Too much was at stake.

"My organization has stopped them when they tried to impose their ideology and policies on this continent and others. We can do it again."

Darkness marred the more drawn parts of the Superiore Generale's gaunt face as he slumped and reflected on the handful of groups who dictated the course of humanity. Most people had never learned who pulled the strings behind the scenes, he knew. After all, the groups themselves owned all the outlets that decided what the public should and shouldn't know. Control of world economic and political power by the elite, however, didn't concern him as much as the enduring failure to find and destroy the ancient scrolls.

He mulled over the hiding places of the scrolls.

Surreptitiously removed from Memphis when Persian and Greek armies advanced on Egypt in 343 B.C., the scrolls remained hidden in Alexandria until the city was sacked by the Romans. With all routes out of Egypt blocked, the scrolls were concealed underneath the emperor's nose in Egypt's

Roman city of Antinopolis. There, it's believed, they remained for nearly two millennia, but were relocated when European missionaries arrived in Antinopolis in 1708 in search of them. As Napoleon poised to take control of the Mediterranean, the scrolls were secreted away to the New World.

MEMPHIS → ALEXANDRIA → ANTINOPOLIS → ? → NEW YORK.

"Bloodshed would only bring unwanted attention," the Superiore Generale answered. "We must find the scrolls and quietly dispose of them."

The Worshipful Master had anticipated the resistance to his plan to deal with the rogue group in New York City, but he also knew that he could get the necessary backing elsewhere at a moment's notice. He bowed his head as a show of deference to the Generale's jurisdiction over such matters.

"What will his cover be?" the Master asked, turning to the third man.

"A meeting will be arranged to negotiate the return of a painting at the Metropolitan Museum of Art that rightfully belongs here. While in New York," the Generale added, gently resting his hand on the burly shoulder of the third man, "you are to find and destroy those scrolls."

The man remained silent out of respect for his superiors. The tranquil expression confirmed his immunity from the searing heat of the catacombs. Fabrizio Armata offered no response as he received his orders.

CHAPTER 3

BEFORE THE END OF HER SHIFT, Victoria Lange received a text message from a friend in the Conservation Department informing her that someone had taken two items out of storage and moved them to the trustees' conference room without following the proper museum procedures. Over the years, Vicki had worked with various museum conservators to implement a protocol for the movement of items into and out of storage, so the unauthorized removal of a museum object was a particular bugaboo for her.

She had to investigate, but only after doing a little research.

The volume on the two-way radio clipped to her nylon duty belt was lowered as Vicki passed the reference desk in the museum's library. She pulled back her long, brown hair and tied it into a bun. Three years earlier, Vicki had made a vow to herself to cut her hair upon turning thirty, thinking that short hair would make her appear more professional. But on the day of her thirtieth birthday, she looked into the bathroom mirror and had a sudden change of mind. Parting with her long hair wasn't an option.

She quickly found the museum website for the first item, an oil painting from 1803 titled *The American Star*, honoring George Washington as a soldier, statesman, and Freemason. Washington's portrait hung above a marble podium. His epitaph – *First in War. First in Peace. First in defence of our Country* – was inscribed on a Masonic royal sash draped around the front of the podium. A star dangled above Washington's head. The star, Vicki discovered, had various meanings, but all hinted at a guiding light.

The second item was a sketch by Salvator Rosa.

In the background, a man wearing a hooded, clerical robe and holding a rosary appeared to be engaged in a dispute with another man with a long Socrates-like beard and garbed in a toga. A third man drawn in the middle of the two debaters contemplated in the position of Auguste Rodin's *Thinker*.

Intentional dichotomy? Vicki asked herself.

A young man dressed in aristocratic clothing and with a dog engaged the only woman in the sketch. The staff held by the young man formed a curious angle with the woman's staff. Rosa even portrayed the movement of the young man's staff to suggest temporal duality of past and present.

Below a half-drawn man in the foreground of the sketch was Rosa's signature, followed by the word *ducatour*.

After printing a copy of each image, Vicki proceeded directly to the locker room used by the female security staff and changed out of her uniform for the day. She placed the two printouts on the shelf in her locker. She'd further investigate first thing in the morning.

* ~ * ~ *

ANTHONY FINISHED THE dry ham-and-cheese sandwich purchased from the vending machine in the employee cafeteria and slipped on his Brooks Brothers pinstriped jacket. He looked at his reflection in the Plexiglas and smoothed his hair, pleased that it was more peppery than salty. There was no denying the gray in his five o'clock shadow.

He was on his way to the final of his many appointments for the day, this one with Cy Hetford, head curator in the museum's Egyptian Arts Department.

His phone vibrated as he rode the escalator up to the Egyptian galleries. The caller ID displayed the name of his ex-wife, Carla. The two had separated when Anthony was a captain with the NYPD, and Carla obtained primary custody of their two daughters. That stung. But the spare time provided the opportunity for Anthony to finish the dissertation that he'd been working on for his PhD in criminology, which opened the way for his rise up two ranks to inspector and into the top echelon of the NYPD, alongside the deputy chiefs, chiefs, and chief of the department—the highest-ranking uniformed officers.

At the top of the short escalator, Anthony found himself face to face with Cy Hetford, who was standing in a posture that announced his irritation.

"I was starting to wonder if you were going to show up."

Anthony pocketed his phone. "Sorry, I couldn't escape my last meeting."

"What's more important than what happened in the temple today?" Cy crossed his arms. His lowered eyebrows connected on the bony bridge of his nose. "Are you aware that the Temple of Dendur is the *only* Egyptian temple in the Western Hemisphere?"

It was too late in the day to engage Cy. He could be impossibly unreasonable at times. Most times, in fact. Anthony knew a way out.

"If not mistaken, the temple was built when Egypt was under Roman rule."

"It's very unique in that respect," Cy maintained as they walked side by side into the Egyptian Wing atrium. "It was commissioned by Emperor Augustus in 10 B.C."

"Augustus, that's right. Wasn't he the first Roman emperor?"

"As the founder of the Empire, I should certainly think so."

Anthony had grown immune to the customary condescension from the crustier curators. He peered at the reflection of the gallery light off Cy's shiny bald head. At six feet, three inches, Anthony had a higher perspective than most museum employees.

Cy ascended several stairs and crossed the marble platform built to support the bulky temple. Tall columns at the entrance to the temple shaped like papyrus stalks accentuated his slight stature. Turning back, he said, "Only pharaohs and high priests were allowed to enter temples. Before entering a temple, the priest was required to chant, 'I have come to perform the ritual. I have not come to do what should not be done'."

Anthony scanned the sandstone walls of the temple, all covered with carvings of gods, pharaohs, and their servants. Male figures were portrayed with sinewy shoulders and taut torsos. The women had slight shoulders, large breasts, and curvy hips covered by tight-fitting dresses. Some figures, male and female alike, wore conical hats.

He turned his attention to one of the many European names shamelessly engraved into the walls of the temple. "Who were these people?" he asked, facing Cy.

Cy lowered his bifocals. Annoyance showed in his sharp, blue eyes.

"I beg your pardon?"

Anthony read the name and date aloud. "Doretta 1816. Who was this guy?"

Cy huffed before speaking. "Bernardino Drovetti was an Italian who fought under Napoleon. He also served as French consul-general of Egypt when Napoleon sent a team of experts to Egypt in search of relics."

"And this guy?" Anthony asked, pointing to 'Girolamo Segato'.

"Let's not waste any more time than necessary," Cy insisted as he moved the flimsy security stanchion used to prevent visitors from walking beyond the *pronaos* and into the antechamber. He guided Anthony into the back room, the crypt, where both men stood in front of the rear wall incised with a time-dulled relief of two young boys paying homage to the Egyptian gods Osiris and Isis. Above the gods, a solar disk was chiseled into the sandstone wall, flanked by outstretched wings with flawlessly carved feathers.

"Where are the markings?" Anthony asked, looking around the crypt.

Cy pointed. "On the lintel above the door."

Anthony moved closer to the large, horizontal block above the door. To the untrained eye, the markings appeared similar to the other hieroglyphics inside the temple.

"Do these markings mean something?" he asked.

"The first symbol represents the word 'gate'." Cy positioned himself alongside the door of the burial chamber. "The marking to the right is the symbol for death."

"What about the third symbol carved above the words 'gate' and 'death?' The carving that looks like a man with a dog's head?"

"That's Anubis, the jackal-headed god of mummification and death. Most early Egyptians believed that Anubis guided the deceased through the gates of the underworld, but he was eventually replaced by Osiris as the lord of the afterlife."

Anthony strained to hold back a yawn before speaking.

"What do you make of this?" he asked.

Cy's slender shoulders rose, nearly connecting with his stretched, wrinkled earlobes. "I haven't the foggiest idea. I mean, read together, the carvings could connote a few things, depending on how you read it. But these markings aren't written in a standard Egyptian fashion. Hieroglyphics are read from left to right or vice versa. Even downward when in a column, but these symbols are etched in a triangular or pyramidal shape. That suggests they are not hieroglyphics, but they are hierogrammatics."

Anthony stepped back. "What the heck is a hierogrammatic?"

"Hierogrammatics," Cy repeated, making it clear that he was correcting Anthony's pronunciation, "are arrangements of symbols, or hierograms, and are used by certain groups as codes or messages that can be interpreted only by those groups."

Anthony held up his iPhone and snapped a picture of the carvings. "More often than not," he said between shots, "these types of things are done by employees."

Cy held his arms akimbo, hands fastened at the hip bones. His baby blue cardigan sagged over his narrow shoulders in a grandfatherly way.

"No one in my department would do such a thing."

"Could be someone from any department," Anthony replied, evenly, turning to exit the temple. "I'll check the feed from the cameras first thing in the morning."

"Now wait one minute!" Cy bellowed, trailing Anthony as he exited through the antechamber and onto the *pronaos*, the outside porch of the temple. "Those types of markings are usually associated with the practice of certain rituals. Rituals performed by some dastardly people. I can assure you that those marks weren't made by just anyone."

Anthony gazed through the glass wall facing Central Park. Dusk had set. Despite the uncomfortable evening heat, the park was teeming with runners, bikers, or couples out for an evening stroll.

"Real Egyptologists don't delve into such rituals," Cy insisted, "but I can provide the names of two people who could provide more information."

Anthony patted his shirt pocket for a pen. "Just tell me the names."

"David Graham, for one. He's not an actual Egyptologist, but he knows a great deal about the occult. I have his phone number. I'll send it to you."

"And the other?" Anthony grudgingly asked.

"Jörg Miller helped reconstruct the temple when it was moved here from Egypt, so he might have some insight into the vandalism."

The stoic expression on Anthony's face concealed his surprise. "Jörg Miller? I didn't know that Mr. Miller worked here at the museum."

"He didn't officially work for the museum. He simply supervised the team that relocated the temple from Egypt to the museum."

"Okay, I'll look into this situation first thing in the morning."

CHAPTER 4

FABRIZIO ARMATA EXITED ST. PETER'S BASILICA through the *Porta Sancta*. He studied the sixteen bronze panels on the doors, each carved with religious scenes of sin and redemption. The tips of his fingers grazed the shiny pink-and-white marble doorframe as he stared at his favorite panel illustrating the biblical story of the conversion of Saul. He contemplated the many centuries during which the holy door had opened for Jubilee to allow pilgrims to enter St. Peter's Basilica and seek remission for their sins. The irony of using the entryway as an exit forced a split-second rise at the ends of his lips.

He moved through the metal gate affixed to the imperial columns and stepped onto Piazza Retta, the trapezoidal section of St. Peter's Square. Two well-groomed Swiss Guards stood outside the basilica and held long halberds with sharp, steely points rising above the red-dyed, ostrich feather plumes of their headdress. Their puffy, tri-colored uniforms peacocked bold blue, red, and yellow stripes from gaiters to collars.

Hard to fathom that the same man who painted the masterpiece on the ceiling of the Sistine Chapel designed those uniforms, he thought, again.

He loosened his tie and unbuttoned the first two buttons of his shirt while staring at the gilt-bronze cross on top of the soaring Egyptian obelisk symbolizing the triumph of Christianity over paganism. Most of the visitors milling about the square, he noticed, overlooked the eight-pointed-star below the cross. Fewer knew the meaning.

The beatified stone faces of 140 saints standing on top of the four-columns deep Tuscan colonnades encircling the square looked in different directions as Fabrizio passed underneath and exited the Vatican limits. A Maserati screeched to a curbside stop, and Fabrizio jumped into the car. He was on his way to Leonardo da Vinci–Fiumicino Airport, where a Gulfstream jet was chartered to take him to Zurich and then to Teterboro Airport.

* ~ * ~ *

AS A SPECIAL officer, Vicki wasn't pinned down to a particular gallery or to one of the museum's two entranceways, as were the hundreds of other Met security employees. Special officers were handpicked by Anthony and were authorized by the New York City Police Commissioner to carry a firearm, along with the power to make arrests.

On her morning break, Vicki decided to browse the Old Masters galleries with the intention of examining paintings containing esoteric messages. While familiar with the majority of paintings in the Met's collection, Vicki also wanted to talk with an expert.

Sibyl Forest had become a security guard at the Met after earning her MFA from Columbia University's School of the Arts fifteen years earlier. Like other security guards at the museum, Sibyl was a gifted artist. And like many truly gifted artists, she was anything but ordinary. She also knew that most people perceived her as different, and that only fueled an even greater desire to keep her bleached blonde hair utterly tousled.

At 10:45, Sibyl would be posted in a Baroque period gallery, most likely, and standing in a slightly slouched pose as she envisioned her next painting.

Vicki exited the elevator in the rear of the Old Masters galleries and admired the huge Peter Paul Rubens and Anthony Van Dyck paintings as she passed through the Flemish paintings section. The world's largest collection of Vermeers momentarily came into focus in a connecting Dutch gallery, where she turned and entered a room filled with home furnishings that adorned the houses of wealthy Dutch merchants. Vicki gazed through a half-moon-shaped window at the European Sculpture Court one floor below. Sunlight streamed through the triangular skylights of the court. She was now standing over what was once the main entrance to the museum over a century earlier, and every now and then, Vicki liked to imagine what it had been like to arrive at the museum when the entrance was located in Central Park. She had seen the black-and-white pictures of nineteenth-century women wearing bonnets, clad in elegant, flowing Victorian-era dresses, and brought to the museum by coachmen wearing top hats and livery waistcoats sitting atop stylish horse-drawn carriages. It seemed so much more romantic, more natural, than arriving by modern means. In an inexplicable, wistful way she felt a strange relatedness to the simpler times – an almost personal knowledge, of sorts.

Then again, she reconsidered as she turned and continued walking through the museum's Old Masters galleries, on insufferably hot and humid days—like the muggy days of the past three-week-long heat wave that had transformed Manhattan into a boiling cauldron of cement-and-steel soup—life back then was no bed of roses.

"You're not paid to think," Vicki said as she approached Sibyl from behind.

Sibyl shimmied, turned, and then giggled. She stepped back and raised her thick glasses to the top of her head, giving Vicki the once-over with a big smile. "I've said it before, Vick, and I'll say it again. You look so chic in your uniform."

"What's so great about this uniform?" Vicki asked, knowing that all the guards in the museum thought that Special Officers wore the coolest uniforms.

"We have to wear these uniforms," Sibyl crooned, raising her left foot in front of her right knee, and extending her arms to the side in the style of a *retiré devant* ballet pose, allowing her to model her uniform with satirical panache. Her ballet skills weren't what they once were, so she nixed the idea of doing a pirouette. "But you get the slick jacket, cargo pants stylish enough to wear to a club, the cool utility belt, the handcuffs."

Vicki straightened Sibyl's red clip-on tie, thinking she was right. The standard security uniform was designed to project a sense of authority, but it looked more like a glorified bellhop outfit. She placed her hand on Sibyl's shoulder in an encouraging manner. "Why don't you wear the uniform pants instead of the skirt?"

"Are you serious? As uncomfortable as this is," Sibyl replied, pulling on her skirt, "it's better than the pants issued to low-level guards. The pants make my ass look fat."

Vicki unfolded the printout of Salvator Rosa's sketch and pointed to the staffs. "What do you make of the angles of these staffs?" she asked in a more sober voice, handing the printout to Sibyl.

Sibyl eyeballed it at arm's-length, lowering her glasses. She wasn't familiar with the print, but instantly recognized Rosa's gifted hand. "The staffs could form a golden ratio," Sibyl stated with a tone of uncertainty. "Though the use of golden ratios wasn't common in Rosa's day."

Vicki closed the distance.

"What about the odd signature?"

"*Ducatour*? That's Latin. It's used by some groups as a way to indicate some kind of leadership or guide position." Sibyl raised the sketch up to the light and inspected the signature closer. "As I expected. There's a watermark below the word *Ducatour*. It's barely noticeable on this photocopy, but it appears to be his usual secret-society mark."

Vicki slanted, vacantly staring with uncertainty in her eyes. "Why would there be a secret society watermark on a Rosa print?"

Sibyl snorted and led Vicki into an adjoining gallery. She stopped in front of a self-portrait of Rosa writing the Greek words ἠνί ποῖ ποτέ on a skull.

"Salvator Rosa was an interesting fellow, to say the least. He was a polymath – a painter, a printmaker, a poet, an actor who rarely took commissions for his paintings, most of which he signed with strange signatures. Many of his paintings also flaunted his fascination with death. Those ancient Greek words painted on the skull," Sibyl said, pointing to the lower left of Rosa's painting, "translate as *behold, whither, when.*"

"That sounds pretty ghoulish." Vicki leaned closer to the large painting, careful not to set off the motion-detection alarm, as she studied the Greek words on the top of the human skull painted gold. "Wasn't ancient Greek a dead language hundreds of years before Rosa's time?" she asked.

"More like a thousand years." Sibyl returned the printout to Vicki. "But I don't think Rosa thought of death in the way you may think. Let me ask you something. Are you familiar with his painting of Pythagoras?"

"I'm not sure," Vicki admitted.

"On first blush, you'd think the painting is another Baroque-era biblical scene, but it's Pythagoras whom Rosa depicts returning from the dead."

"Is the painting here at the Met?"

Sibyl surveyed the adjoining galleries. A small group of Japanese tourists

15

exited the gallery directly ahead. A French couple with well-mannered children passed through an adjacent gallery to the left. There was little activity in the Old Masters paintings gallery. The majority of the day's visitors were still standing in line or were loitering in the Great Hall, examining maps or brochures with titles like, 'What's On Today' or 'What's On This Season', planning their itineraries for the next few hours. The initial hour of tranquility in the galleries was virtually as consistent as the faint, ammonia-like smell from the past day's human traffic. Subtly, Sibyl shuffled closer to Vicki's side. "No, but in light of Rosa's associations, some believe that his painting of Pythagoras shows his connection to the Rosicrucians."

Intrigue twinkled in Vicki's indigo eyes.

"Are there any paintings here in the museum associated with the Rosicrucian Order?" she asked, enthusiastically.

"More than you'd think." Sybil pointed to an adjacent gallery. "Do you see that Rembrandt on the far wall? The man in the painting has never been positively identified by the experts, but many believe that he is Comte de St. Germain, master Rosicrucian and illuminist."

Vicki fixated on the seventeenth-century painting in the adjoining gallery. From a distance, the background appeared murky and accentuated the man on the white horse in the foreground. The red cap, stylish riding coat, unusual red trousers, and calf-high leather boots all hinted at nobility. But it wasn't the man's attire that grabbed Vicki's attention. The dashing, young man appeared more poised, more transcendent than Rembrandt's usual studies.

"You say St. Germain was an illuminist?"

"A genius," Sibyl replied as she and Vicki strolled into the adjoining gallery and stopped in front of the large painting. Up close, the evocative, nocturnal landscape, though gloomy, somehow imparted a hospitable feeling. "Some believe that St. Germain discovered the secret of immortality. Others think he had taken on a dozen personalities during his lifetime."

Vicki studied the painting, looking for the "seven elements of art" that artists use to communicate their message. Something unusual caught her eye. "What's that obscured structure in the background?" she asked. "It looks like some type of building or temple from ancient Greece or Rome."

Sibyl shook her head. "No one knows for sure. It's a complete mystery, but do you see that saber hanging from St. Germain's side?"

"You mean the sword?" Vicki asked.

"For some reason, it's called a saber. We have a similar one in the Arms and Armor collection. It's so razor-sharp, I'm told by people familiar with the weapon, that you wouldn't feel being stabbed by it."

"Really? I don't think I know it."

"I really should get back to my post, but there are a few other things you may find interesting about some of the items that the museum owns," Sibyl stated, followed with an impish grin. "I'll tell you at lunch."

CHAPTER 5

THE MET CLOISTERS WAS BUILT ON the northern tip of Manhattan, eight miles north of the Metropolitan Museum as the crow flies, on a craggy summit up to that time owned by a wealthy industrialist, along with the adjoining Fort Tryon Park. John D. Rockefeller Jr. purchased the land and the existing medieval art museum on the site and determined that the museum would be more authentic if rebuilt using segments of actual European abbeys. He ordered his men to scour Europe in search of the most well-preserved edifices. Crews swiftly disassembled five abbeys in France and Spain, brick by brick, shipped the segments to New York City, and reconfigured them as one contiguous building. Rockefeller then made the museum a branch of the Metropolitan Museum of Art.

At lunch, Sibyl provided Vicki with a contact at The Cloisters.

Vicki had changed out of her uniform and left the museum after lunch, but not before doing some research on some of the things that Sibyl had mentioned. Pythagoras, she knew, was a great mathematician. She had even heard fanciful tales about his transhistorical abilities. But a quick Internet search had revealed that Pythagoras also spent forty years traveling to locations throughout the Mediterranean, Near East, and Egypt to study various academic disciplines, religion, and philosophy before becoming a master of metempsychosis – transformation of the soul after death.

IN SPITE OF the stifling heat, Vicki walked through Central Park, along the south side of the vast Jacqueline Kennedy Onassis Reservoir. It was the same route she took each day to get to and from work; the same grounds she had stomped as a girl growing up on the Upper West Side. She stopped and leaned against the iron fence that encircles the one-and-a-half-mile perimeter of the reservoir as she rubbed SPF 30 sunscreen on her face and stared at the sixty-foot-high arching spray of the fountain in the reservoir. The falling water droplets refracted the intense sunlight in such a way that the fountain produced a multicolored rainbow. Two rainbows, actually. One rainbow appeared in the mist of the fountain, which reflected in the water below.

With just enough time to get to The Cloisters before it closed for the day, Vicki exited the park on Central Park West and entered the Eighth Avenue Line using the 88th Street entrance instead of the main entrance at 86th Street. She cringed as she descended the stairs. Since the removal of the ticketing agent, the subway entrance doubled as a public bathroom. The sweltering summer heat intensified the smell of the urine.

In one fluent motion, Vicki removed her MetroCard from her purse, swiped it in the turnstile slot, and returned it to her purse. An express train zipped through the station with a piercing, metallic shrill as she walked onto the platform. A construction crew wearing orange and yellow vests and welding helmets were working on a rail. She unfolded the printout of Rosa's sketch and examined it until a blinding flash diverted her attention.

A sensation of jelly legs forced Vicki's knees to buckle inward at the same instant that she caught sight of a man on the platform. She looked at the turnstile, wondering why she hadn't heard the clicking sound as he passed through. The few passengers waiting for the train were on the far side of the platform. A C local train roared into the station.

Vicki scooted closer to the tracks, eyesight still splotchy from the bright light, but she knew exactly where to stand on the platform to enter either the first or second car of the train.

The man appeared in Vicki's peripheral vision as he inched forward.

As the very-much outmoded, 'Brightliner' train rumbled to a raucous stop, the man moved toward the second car. Vicki entered the front car and walked to the middle. With no one else inside the first car, she selected a seat that appeared less filthy than the others. "Stand clear of the closing doors, please," incoherently sounded through the speakers. Vicki reclined, removed a paperback from her purse, and opened it to the dog-eared page. The air conditioning inside the car was less than substandard, though still a welcome relief from the elevated-level of heat inside the subway station. With the poor lighting inside the half-century-old train, and her sight a bit blurry from the flash, she closed her book, raised her head, and beheld the image of the man from the platform. He was seated on the opposite end of the subway car. Vicki flinched with a hiccup-like spasm. She quickly turned away.

With a barely discernible motion, Vicki grazed her shirt where it puffed above her belt. Vicki never took her museum-issued Glock 19 out of the museum, but often carried her KelTec P-3AT while still on duty and outside the museum. The small pistol was easily concealable, and for a lightweight semi-automatic, it packed a wallop.

Returning the book to her purse, she craned her neck and peered out the window as the train came to a stop at the next station. A handful of straphangers rushed through the doors and raced for the end seats. Vicki surveyed the car. The man had exited.

CHAPTER 6

SIBYL'S CONTACT CAME TO MIND AS Vicki entered through the Postern Gate entrance at the rear of The Cloisters and ascended the winding stairs in the long entryway corridor. Margarita Abran was in her mid-forties, a generation ahead of both Vicki and Sibyl. Margarita and Sibyl had worked in the same galleries for several years before Margarita was transferred to The Cloisters. Vicki recalled Margarita's gregarious and often exuberant demeanor, and she hadn't seen Margarita for some time, so she was looking forward to catching up. She flashed her museum ID at the admission desk.

"Hi, I'm looking for a guard named Margarita Abran."

"You work at the Met," the dapperly dressed young man at the desk politely remarked, followed by a kiss-ass grin. "Go right in, please."

"Thank you," Vicki said to be courteous and professional, and then rephrased the question. "Do you know a guard here named Margarita Abran?"

"Sorry, I'm new here. You can ask the guard over there." He pointed to the uniformed guard standing in front of the pointed Gothic Hall entrance. Vicki eyed the guard but decided to enter through the rounded entrance of the Romanesque Hall, where her surroundings were initially absorbed by her sense of hearing. Inharmonious Gregorian chants resonated throughout the Romanesque Hall. She stopped and marveled at the thousand-year-old Spanish fresco of a muscular lion, wondering how something so old, so fragile, had made it across the Atlantic Ocean on a steamship without breaking into thousands of pieces.

A small group led by a docent examined the smooth, pink-marble columns that delimited the hall from the main cloister – a large garden, open to the sky, surrounded by four covered walkways with a center decorative fountain – that was originally the center of a Benedictine monastery built in the French Pyrenees. The docent pointed to a worn face carved into the arched capitals, explaining that it remained unknown why someone carved the humorous, though slightly frightening, face into pink-marble capitals. A geeky-looking man in a suit raised his hand and suggested that the carving was a representation of one of the creatures that haunted the depths of hell. Unsympathetic to the man's theory, the docent shook her head.

Vicki peeked into the Fuentidueña Chapel, a consecrated vestige of the twelfth-century church of San Martín from the Spanish village of its namesake. The bare apse at the front of the chapel – the liturgical end – lacked an altar. The usual statuary was conspicuously missing. Unrecognizable human figures carved into the topmost portion of the chapel's columns told stories unknown to the annals of time. Spurred by the sight of the stark chapel, feelings of awe and consternation arose. Even the life-size Christ on the cross seemed somewhat unsettling.

Vicki spotted Margarita standing watch in the apse of the adjoining Langon Chapel. Margarita's curly, brunette hair looked several shades darker than it had years ago. *Clearly dyed*, Vicki instantly realized, noticing that Margarita was also a bit more buxom than she had remembered, but concluded that Margarita filled out her uniform quite nicely.

Entering the Langon Chapel, Vicki gaped at the human heads carved into the top section of the stone entrance. Below, two life-size statues standing at either side of the entrance were representations of the first Christian kings of the Franks, Clovis and his son Chlothar. Sunlight filled the chapel. Tiny pieces of quartz in the white-limestone walls glimmered and danced in Vicki's peripheral vision as she approached the front.

"Margarita?" Vicki called as she approached The Cloisters guard.

"Yes," Margarita indifferently responded as she slowly turned around. An elongated *hiiiiiii* hung in the air until Margarita's expression finally showed recognition. "What are you doing here?" she asked, aware that Vicki wouldn't be at The Cloisters simply for a leisurely visit.

The two hugged, their shoulders barely touching.

"Let's wait until these visitors move on, and I'll tell you why I'm here. In the meantime, maybe you can help me wrap my head around the arrangement of the collection here."

"What do you mean?" Margarita's head twitched, uneasily.

"Every time I'm here, I wonder why this chapel looks so festive and why the Spanish chapel looks so spooky. This chapel looks almost Christmassy."

"Oh, that? That's just the way each chapel is represented." Margarita led Vicki to the altar. "Objects you describe as festive are really pagan symbols. We associate certain things like wreaths, garlands, and holly with the holidays, but all these things were pagan symbols long before the rise of Christianity. See that sheaf of wheat in the corner of the transept?" Margarita pointed to the narrow but empty area that once separated the nave from the apse. "A sheaf of wheat is also a pagan symbol. It symbolized death and rebirth of life, although it eventually became an integral part of the nativity scene."

Vicki scanned her surroundings to make sure the chapel was free of visitors before she spoke. The ghostly, milk-white faces of Henry II of England and his queen consort, Eleanor of Aquitaine, carved into the chapel's capital, seemingly eavesdropped with nosy expressions of interest.

"Sibyl suggested that I talk to you about this." Vicki unfolded the printout of the Rosa sketch. "See the signature at the bottom? Sibyl thinks that watermark is used by secret societies, and you'd know something about it."

A devilish smile crossed Margarita's face.

"Come with me."

Vicki followed as Margarita traversed the Cuxa Cloister, then through the Early Gothic Hall – filled with thirteenth-century paintings, sculptures, and stained-glass windows all from places like Paris, Strasbourg, and Canterbury – and descended the narrow, winding stone staircase to the lower section of the Gothic Chapel, an area known to The Cloisters's employees as the 'Tombs'. As they descended the staircase, Margarita informed Vicki that many of the guards refused to work in the Tombs during evening hours, swearing up and down that they had seen ghosts and supernatural aberrations.

The space was cold, like a drab basement. It smelled of masonry.

Vicki regarded the six limestone sarcophagi in the chapel, arranged in the pattern of a cross. All the coffins displayed effigies of the deceased. Double-lancet, stained-glass windows at the far end of the Tombs hyped apostles, saints, and scenes from the life of Christ in dark vitreous paint. The panel scenes in the windows diffused light. The faces on the four statues, two male and two female, directly below the windows, were barely visible, but Vicki recognized the statue of St. Margaret by the dragon at her feet.

"Over here," Margarita directed, moving to the center of the Tombs.

Vicki followed, taking in the dark setting.

Margarita abruptly stopped in front of the most imposing effigy sarcophagus in the hallowed chapel. She looked about. No one else was around. "I'm going to let you in on a secret." She inched closer to Vicki, owl-eyed, and bursting with intrigue. "I first learned of St. Germain's connection to The Cloisters not long after I began working here."

"Connection?" Vicki said, amazed. "What connection?"

"St. Germain was many things to many people. Some say Germain was the founder of the Rosicrucians," Margarita asserted, now casting her animated, brown eyes down toward the ornate sarcophagus. Its placement in the center of the chapel suggested its importance. "Others say he was the son of the Imperial Prince of Transylvania, and that Germain had discovered hidden secrets of mysticism in a crypt in an Egyptian burial ground."

"And now you are going to tell me that this coffin belongs to St. Germain?" Vicki said cynically as she gazed down at the polished tomb effigy on the sarcophagus. The stone likeness was of a Frenchman with his hands folded in piety, long hair, and ruminative eyes. He was heavily garbed in full armor, complete with a long-sleeved chain-mail shirt. His hood was lowered at the shoulders, his belt hooked from the weight of his hefty sword. The large, triangular shield covered the entire length of his lower body.

Vicki looked closer at the mars and dings on the limestone shield. Most of the markings, she assumed correctly, were made to replicate genuine lacerations received in battle. Then she noticed something peculiar. She lowered her head for a closer look. It was the pattern of an eight-petaled flower inscribed in a perfectly etched circle.

"It's a flower!" Vicki yelled and then covered her mouth.

"Meet Mr. Jean d'Alluye, a crusader and a Knight Templar. It's said that three generations of d'Alluyes went to the Holy Land to redeem their souls. Jean returned in 1248 with an actual piece of the True Cross." Margarita pointed to the conspicuously etched flower petals. "Some say that's the

24

Templar Rose. Others like myself think the flower bears a striking resemblance to da Vinci's Flower of Life. But that," she said, now pointing to the sword beneath the shield, "is the most mysterious thing on this tomb."

Head skewed, Vicki asked, "What's so interesting about the sword?"

"I'm told it's not a replica of a Templar sword. In fact, it's not even a European sword. D'Alluye carried a unique sword forged in Asia Minor."

Vicki thought about the special sword, or saber, in Rembrandt's painting of St. Germain. "But what about St. Germain?" she asked.

"I'm getting to that part. You see, d'Alluye was buried in the very same chapel where St. Germain later conducted his rituals. And here's the most interesting part, so listen closely. You're standing in that chapel right now."

"Really?" Goose bumps ascended Vicki's back.

"This particular chapel was disassembled in the Bordeaux region of France. Everything was brought here to New York at the behest of those in charge at the time, including important ritual items."

"Hey, Margarita," a guard said from above. "It's almost closing time. Are you working overtime today?" The guard appeared at the top of the stairs.

"Sorry, I lost track of the time, Pete. We'll be up in a minute." Margarita led Vicki to the rear of the Tombs. "I really should show you something else that you'll find interesting. Can you come up again on Friday after work?"

"What's going on here on Friday night?"

"I'm doing a double shift Friday. Getting some overtime in by working a private concert, so we will have the place to ourselves."

"What time is the concert?" Vicki asked.

"Seven, but it's better if you come at least a half hour earlier."

CHAPTER 7

"I WANT THIS SECTION SEALED OFF!" Anthony shouted while dashing through the Ptolemaic corridor of the museum's Egyptian Wing. Paul McDonough was running alongside Anthony. They stopped at the entrance to the atrium for the temple.

"I want guards posted on the east side of the atrium and the security manager of this section posted at the rear exit," Anthony commanded loud enough so that everyone in earshot could hear his instructions. "No one but the president is to come into this atrium. Is that clear?"

"Got it, Tony." Paul was the only person at the museum who was close enough to Anthony to use the shortened name.

An unsettling mix of anger and disbelief took hold as Anthony entered the bright atrium built to house the ancient Temple of Dendur. Nothing this bad had occurred in the museum's 150-year-history.

Anthony and Paul hastened around the Nile reflecting pool and rushed up the stairs of the platform and stopped in front of the Temple of Dendur.

"Is it someone from the night-shift?" Anthony asked, sheer disbelief in his voice. His heart palpitations were near-audible.

Winded, Paul said, "It's the old German guy who's always here."

"Jörg Miller!" Anthony roared. He stepped onto the *pronaos* of the temple and stopped. "Jesus. What was he doing in the museum after closing?"

Paul's broad shoulders rose. "He was found this morning."

Anthony looked at the temple. The ancient shrine seemed less august than usual. "I want to speak to the security manager of this section."

"But you just told me to send him to the rear exit." Paul's deep-set eyes looked more distant from his copper-colored eyebrows than usual. Uncertainty showed on his ruddy, freckled face, but he knew not to press the matter. He whistled with his index and middle fingers and gestured *come here* to a security manager wearing a formal suit.

The morning rays of sun filtering through the slits in the ceiling of the fifteen-feet-high temple lit the inside. The invisible effluvium of death infused the crypt. Anthony entered and knelt alongside Miller's prone body and put the tips of his index and middle finger on the carotid artery. The body, covered by a long purple robe, was on the warm side and not stiff, so the death, it seemed clear, had occurred not more than three hours earlier. The open mouth confirmed the onset of rigor mortis. He rose and circled the body, examining it closely. No signs of struggle. No blood. No visible wounds.

Hesitating at the rear door of the sanctuary, the security manager leaned into the burial chamber, making sure that he didn't rub against either side of the narrow doorway. "You wanted to talk to me?"

Anthony exited the temple without a response. Outside the temple, he calmly asked, "What time did you get here this morning?"

"I clocked in around 8:50, and changed into my suit. I got a cup of joe in the cafeteria, came up here, and did my rounds. There was no one in sight this morning, strangely. The entire Egyptian Wing was completely empty."

Paul approached and broke in. "How do we handle the visitors, Tony?"

Without hesitation, Anthony said, "Get private-concert signs from the Concert and Lectures Department and place them at all three entrances. Then seal-off the entrances with a curtain or whatever you can find so that no one can see in here." Anthony ran his hand through his hair as he contemplated the possibility of covering the enormous glass wall fronting Central Park. "What the hell?" he barked, fixing his sights on a man in the park walking away and holding a tripod attached to a camera and long lens. It was clear that the man was looking out of the corner of his eye. "Did he take a picture of this?"

Paul stormed toward the glass wall. "Do you want me to go out there and question this freakin' guy?" His forehead was furrowed, his fists were clenched. He held up his phone and snapped a picture through the glass.

"I'll handle it. I've had a run-in with this guy before."

Paul turned and uttered something that confirmed his confusion. "Well, do you want me to contact the Central Park Precinct?"

Anthony unhooked the Motorola two-way radio from his belt and turned up the volume. "Contact police headquarters directly and tell the chief that we'll need the Manhattan Evidence Collection Team. I want them to be the first on the scene." He pointed to an inconspicuous glass door at the rear of the Egyptian atrium. "Have them enter through this emergency exit. I don't want to alarm visitors waiting on line in the front of the building."

Paul snapped into a ready front position. "Anything else?"

"Send someone you trust to the north sentry entrance to direct the Crime Scene Unit truck to the loading dock inside. Under no circumstances should the CSU truck be parked outside the museum. Clear?" Anthony didn't wait for an answer. "Have Operations set up screens in front of the glass wall at once, so that people in the park don't see the detectives in their Tyveks."

No further clarification was required. Be as discreet as possible.

ANTHONY EXITED THE building at the rear and radioed the museum's security command center with instructions to ignore the emergency exit alarm. He wiped the perspiration from his brow, disgusted that it was so hot so early in the day. It would take the Evidence Collection Team ten to fifteen minutes to get to the museum. Anthony would use the time to question the man with the camera he had seen only minutes earlier.

Adjusting his prescription sunglasses, he followed the paved path leading into the core of the park. A saxophonist performed at the entrance to the tunnel running under Central Park Drive, one of twenty or so tunnels constructed throughout the park to allow nineteenth-century parkgoers a horse-poop-free passage into the park. The tunnel was fronted by the pointed Greywacke Arch, designed to resemble the Saracenic architectural style of the people who lived in and around desert areas of the Roman Empire.

The musician was blowing 'Over the Rainbow'. An open saxophone case was placed in front of the performer. It was too early in the day for handouts, so the few dollar bills in the man's case served more as a visual suggestion.

Anthony stared into the darkened underpass. Immediately, he recognized the man in the shadows. Bob White. Anthony was assigned to crowd control while working with the NYPD, and Bob had led a spirited demonstration in front of a ritzy apartment building on Fifth Avenue to protest the destruction of a large hawk's nest built on the façade.

Anthony took an indirect approach. "Did you get any good pictures today?" he asked, smiling as he neared White.

Devoid of expression, Bob peered over the nearly three-foot-long, fifteen-thousand-dollar Canon 400mm lens at Anthony. The narrowing of the eyes showed recognition. And discontentment. He twisted the lens cap shut.

"Nothing in particular," he replied, detaching the camera from his Manfrotto 055 aluminum tripod.

Anthony stepped closer. "Are you still taking pictures of that bird?"

"It's a Red-tailed Hawk."

Anthony acknowledged with a single nod.

"I'd like to ask you a question, if you don't mind?"

Bob lifted his tripod and began to walk. "You already asked a few."

"This will just take a minute, I promise," Anthony insisted, trailing Bob as he exited the west side of the tunnel.

Bob stopped on the Greywacke Knoll outside the tunnel, removed his Galaxy phone from his camouflage pants, and checked the most recent updates on a rare bird alert site. With no new posts, he scanned the tree canopy until he spotted a Baltimore Oriole warbling its song next to its sock-like nest. He spread open the legs of the long tripod and set up his camera on the cement path in front of the stairs leading up to the platform for Cleopatra's Needle. The nearly seventy-foot-tall, granite Egyptian obelisk ascended from its twenty-foot-tall pedestal and soared above the leafy magnolia and Japanese cherry trees planted around the perimeter of the knoll.

"You know," Bob remarked casually, pointing to the large monolith, "this Egyptian obelisk is much more valuable than any of the art in the museum."

Anthony gazed at the obelisk. "What makes you say that?"

"I read about it in a book by David Graham."

"Did you say David Graham?" Anthony questioned, tilting back and recalling that Cy had also mentioned the same name. "Why were you taking pictures of the museum a few minutes ago?"

"I was taking pictures of a gorgeous American Kestrel that was perched on top of the museum," Bob replied, aiming his camera and then snapping pictures of the colorful oriole in rapid succession.

Anthony removed his glasses. "See anything else?"

Bob hesitated, clearly annoyed, and then swiveled the Canon 7D camera on top of the five-foot-high tripod so that Anthony could view the pictures on the camera's LCD monitor.

"Do you want to see the pictures I took today?" he asked.

Anthony stared into Bob's brown eyes, trying to detect the telltale signs of deception but half-smiled. "I don't suppose that'll be necessary."

Bob pointed toward the museum, emitting a scoff of disapproval. "The Temple of Dendur is supposed to be visible up close at all hours," he said irritably, "but the museum closed the grassy area outside the atrium?"

Bob was right. The museum had assured the Egyptian government that the temple would be visible 24-7. But Anthony's attention was already diverted by Paul's radio message that the Evidence Collection Team was entering the north side of the museum. The highly-specialized ECT officers handled celebrity or other sensitive cases that were likely to make national headlines. They specialized in discreetness. They had also arrived faster than Anthony had expected. He raised his radio to his face. "I'll be there in two minutes," he told Paul. He grinned at Bob. "Thank you for your time."

CHAPTER 8

ON THE FIRST OF SEVERAL OF the Met's subterranean levels, a room like no other room existed. It looked similar to a mechanic's garage or, more fittingly, a high-school metal shop. It reeked of grease. Hefty lathes, metal cabinets, and an iron anvil cluttered the room. Screws and bolts filled the drawers of metal cabinets. Javelins and halberds were banded together and propped in the corner. Antique flintlock rifles and pistols hung on the wall, and half-completed suits of armor stood upright on skeletal wooden racks.

Most museum employees considered Albert Bennington, head curator of the Arms and Armor Department, as somewhat of a recluse, a hermit, someone who spent too much time toiling around in his underground workroom like a mole ceaselessly burrowing beneath ground. Albert, actually, was a social person. He just needed a little coaxing to break out of his shell, so Vicki asked Albert to meet her in the Medieval Hall after he had agreed to take her to the Arms and Armor collection to view the saber.

She steered Albert through the medieval arts galleries and into the American Wing courtyard, where the cream-and-white-swirled marble floor gleamed from the sunlight beaming through the glass ceiling. Silvery machines in the corner café sparkled and perfumed the air with the aroma of freshly brewed espresso. In the center of the courtyard, the gilt bronze statue of Diana, the Roman goddess of the hunt, presided over a collection of statues. Her drawn arrow directed visitors to the wing's interior.

Vicki paused in front of *Garden Landscape*, a stunning, Byzantine-inspired tile-mosaic mural fountain crafted with thousands of pieces of tesserae and made by the famed Art Nouveau artist, Louis Comfort Tiffany.

"I love this fountain." The sun reflected with a glaring oscillation off the tiles, making Vicki's indigo eyes more purple than variants of violet and blue.

"It's neat," Albert remarked. "I'll grant you that."

"Neat." Vicki silently laughed at the use of the dated word. "The mosaic mural always reminds me of van Gogh's *Wheat Field with Cypresses.*"

Albert gasped. "Wasn't that meant to be his suicide note?"

"That's *Wheatfield with Crows*. And that theory isn't supported by any solid evidence. But I'll tell you a secret about *Wheat Field with Cypresses*. When van Gogh painted it, grain seeds got stuck to the canvas."

Albert's mouth opened with an inhale. "Doesn't that ruin the painting?"

"Apparently not." Vicki noticed that she had captured his interest. She leaned closer to Albert's side and whispered the purchase price of van Gogh's painting in his ear. Purchase prices of the museum's art were top secret, never to be disclosed to the public.

The top half of Albert's body angled away from Vicki as he eyeballed her over the top of his horned-rimmed glasses. Near speechless, he puffed and shook his head as he began toward the Arms and Armor galleries. "Mind boggling," he uttered as he walked to the exit of the courtyard.

"I honestly don't know how I've overlooked the sword all these years," Vicki remarked as they walked through the swinging glass doors leading into the adjacent Arms and Armor collection.

"Sword?" Albert stopped. "When you called me –"

"Excuse me, Albert. I meant saber."

"There's a considerable difference between the two weapons," Albert contended with a note of rising bravado. "A saber is a type of sword that has a curved, single-edged blade, which can be easily wielded with one hand. Sabers are used for ceremonial purposes, mostly."

They exited the darker side galleries and entered the bright equestrian court. Multihued flags representing banners of the Knights of the Round Table dangled motionless high above a fearsome and life-size brigade of fully armored crusading knights on horseback.

"So, those aren't sabers?" Vicki asked, pointing to the long swords hanging from the daunting knights' sides.

"Knights in armor wouldn't carry sabers, Vicki. Sabers are, well, let me show you," he said as they sauntered around the display of mounted knights.

Two teenage girls were standing in front of the armored suit made for King Henry VIII. The girls were giggling hysterically, spastically. One pointed to the groin area of the steely suit. "How did the king pee when he had to go?" she asked. "Through the mesh?"

Both girls broke out into a frenzied laughter.

Entering a side gallery, Albert pointed and said, "There she is."

"Is that it?" The gallery lighting was dim, but the radiance inside the glass case displaying the saber made the blade sparkle in an enchanted way. Wonderstruck, Vicki's eyes widened as she moved closer. "Wow. It's gorgeous. It's like the Aladdin's Lamp of swords, I mean sabers, and it's covered in so many beautiful jewels. This thing must cost a fortune."

"You can't put a price on something like this, Vicki. This saber is essentially priceless." Albert was beaming with pride.

"Is this sheath really gold?"

"The cover is called a scabbard. And, yes, it's 100 percent gold."

"Those lovely strings of pearls. All those rose-cut diamonds. There must be hundreds of glistening diamonds on the scabbard," Vicki gushed, astonished by the bejeweled weapon. She marveled at the beautiful gold and diamond pattern running the length of the blade, interspersed with Arabic words or symbols. "Is it true that the blade is so sharp that if someone were stabbed by it, he wouldn't feel it entering his body?" she asked.

An almost maniacal grin stretched from ear to ear on Albert's face.

"Sharp?" A note of hubris sounded in Albert's breathy laugh. "That blade is so sharp that it can cut through human skin like a hot knife through butter."

"And those huge green stones. Are those emeralds?"

Albert nodded, smiling from ear-to-ear. "Aren't they exquisite? The emeralds and gold scabbard were assembled by a court jeweler in Turkey when this saber was presented to the only Ottoman sultan to be a member of the Grand Lodge of Free and Accepted Masons of Turkey."

Vicki recalled that holy crusader, Jean d'Alluye, carried a sword from Asia Minor, though decided not to bring up the connection, fearing Albert might stir up some unnecessary scrutiny. Instead, she said, "The top emerald seems to act as a cover for a little chamber."

"You certainly have a keen eye, Vicki. To be honest, no one knew the gold mounts encasing the emeralds flipped opened when we acquired this piece. It wasn't until a few decades ago that we discovered tiny hinges attached to the mounts. When we pried the mounts open, secret compartments were found underneath all three emeralds. The middle compartment has tiny words on the inside in an unknown, ancient language. To this day, we haven't deciphered those words, so we open only the top or bottom mount."

Vicki grinned. "You have been very helpful, Albert."

CHAPTER 9

A MILE NORTH OF THE METROPOLITAN Museum of Art in a neighborhood once known as Italian Harlem, Fabrizio Francesco Armata stood on the corner of 114th Street and Pleasant Avenue and watched as a horde of sweaty men struggled to transport the towering *giglio* down Pleasant Avenue to the Church of Our Lady of Mount Carmel.

The *giglio*, an eighty-foot-tall wood-and-papier-mâché steeple, adorned with flowers, was supported on the husky shoulders of a dozen men as part of an annual tradition in honor of St. Anthony known as the Dance of the *Giglio*, the main event of a festival dating back one hundred years in Harlem and many more centuries in Italy.

Fabrizio reread the missive in his hand, perplexed by the unexpected change in the orders. He knew the Superiore Generale would not have sanctioned the change.

Was he deposed? the burly Italian wondered.

The two swarthy men at Fabrizio's side held back the exuberant crowd – most wearing tank tops and shorts – with little more than the right facial expression. The designer suits broadcast their status. The suits also suggested that it was best to keep a safe distance away, even for the inexperienced flatfoot assigned to crowd control. Fabrizio signaled after the parade passed, and the three men made their way to one of the few remaining Italian restaurants in East Harlem, an establishment with a reputation for superb Italian cuisine, but where few were permitted to dine. Reservations were not accepted. Tables were set aside for the well connected for undisclosed amounts.

The three men were seated at a corner table alongside two South American associates in the small, but stylishly decorated, restaurant. Sharply dressed waiters promptly served signature dishes with the utmost etiquette, beginning with roasted red peppers and pine nuts, followed by oversized meatballs, then main dishes of mouthwatering orecchiette with broccoli rabe and sausage, and several large trays of chicken piccata.

With the *olio, pane di casa,* and entrees spread out on the table, chianti-filled glasses clinked together with a round of *"cin-cin"* and *"salud."* The four men at the table alongside Fabrizio were all brothers in the Worshipful Master's organization, handling New York and South American operations. The secret society was considered by many as a state within a state, a shadow government, grand maestros of governmental upheavals.

Passing around a picture of a painting commissioned for the Church of the Gesù in Rome, which hung at the Met, Fabrizio informed the others that he would use his credentials to reclaim the painting. While doing so, he was now instructed to get a better understanding of the museum leadership and its patrons. He unfolded the message from the Worshipful Master, placed it on the tabletop, and showed the title to the others.

OPERACIÓN BANDERA FALSA/OPERAZIONE BANDIERA FALSA/OPERATION FALSE FLAG.

Leaning forward, Fabrizio quietly explained how they would proceed with the new orders. The South American contingent, experts in the elimination of ideological and religious threats, was assigned the immediate work, then were ordered to return home. He and the New York associates would handle the larger problem, and the deception.

* ~ * ~ *

"WHAT DID THE police have to say?" Vicki asked. She and Anthony were sitting on a marble bench at the edge of the museum's rooftop café, which had closed for the day. Anthony took a long hard breath and hesitantly said, "The one upside, as far as the museum is concerned, was reporting the time of Mr. Miller's death as 10:15 A.M."

"Why did you request that?"

Anthony shook his head. "The request came from the executive offices."

Vicki stood and gazed out over Central Park, taking in the view, first emotionally, then intellectually. The carroty radiance produced by the setting sun had transfigured the leafy treetops of the park into evocative shades of an oriental rug. She visualized the expansive scene in front of her as an enormous landscape painting. The luxury apartment buildings around the perimeter of the park would assimilate well with a Barbizon-style frame for a painting depicting an aerial view of the park. In the foreground, Cleopatra's Needle would soar over the treetops. The Romanesque-style Belvedere Castle would cast an evening shadow over the far end of Turtle Pond directly below, forming green and fuchsia shading on the lizard tail and blue flag iris plants.

"It'd make a nice painting," she said aloud.

Anthony sat up. "What did you say?"

"So, they're saying the old man died during operating hours." Vicki spun around and stared with a grave expression. "Do you think we are dealing with a murder?"

Glossy-green leaves rustled as a sudden gust of wind spread across the park and over the top of the museum. The buzzing sound of a swarm of cicadas rattling their exoskeletons in unison high in the treetops abruptly stopped, then rose again.

"Nothing adds up. Why was Mr. Miller in the museum? Why was he wearing a royal-purple robe? Hopefully, the autopsy will reveal something."

"Didn't Mr. Miller say something about death?"

"That occurred to me, too. I'm not sure what to make of it, but Cy Hetford also told me that Jörg had helped set up the temple when it arrived at the museum, so I asked a friend at police headquarters to run a background check. Seems Miller also gave private tours of the Temple of Dendur when it was in Egypt. And to some very wealthy people."

Vicki steepled her fingertips. "What's the next move?"

"There's a meeting in the director of communication's office tomorrow. A strategy will be discussed on how to prevent the death from going public."

"I was planning to go to The Cloisters tomorrow, if that's okay? I've been following a lead. It may be a dead end, but I have a hunch it'll pay off."

Briefly, Anthony wondered what Vicki was up to, but he also knew that Vicki's hunches usually paid off. He twisted his forearm and looked at his watch. "Let's go," he said softly. "The roof alarm will activate in a few minutes." He stood. "I want a detailed report of this scavenger hunt of yours on my desk by the end of the week."

CHAPTER 10

THE INTENSE RAYS OF THE MORNING sun rising in the eastern sky irradiated the museum's majestic Beaux-Arts façade.

Fabrizio stood in front of the museum and inspected the six medallion reliefs chiseled into the white limestone above the entrance. He approved the choices of the artists depicted in the medallions—Michelangelo, Raphael, Dürer, Rembrandt, and Velázquez—but he was surprised to see Donato Bramante alongside the celebrated artists.

He questioned why the architect of the great St. Peter's Basilica was displayed, but his thoughts drifted to the day when he had become an *uomo d'onore*.

Blindfolded, he had entered a room where the *caporegimes*, some familiar, some not, sat at a horseshoe-shaped table. Guns were out. A skull had been painted on the table, the ceremonial knife placed over the skull. Without uttering a word, a chosen *capo* sliced the tip of Fabrizio's trigger finger with the ritualistic gladius, a short sword used by Roman foot soldiers in pre-Christian times, his blood dripping onto the skull.

A card-sized picture of a saint was lit and placed in Fabrizio's hand.

The blood meant family.

The burning of the saint signified priority of loyalty.

Fabrizio was reborn.

His reflected on his orders, thinking that false-flag operations required absolute secrecy, and even greater deception. The covert tactic had required the utmost secrecy ever since pillaging pirates lowered their skull-and-bones flags and deceptively raised the flags of the countries or outposts that they were about to ambush and plunder.

Would the omertà, the time-honored code of silence, be upheld? Fabrizio knew one could never be too sure who is sided with whom.

MUSEUM GUARDS WEARING decorated uniforms announcing their authority opened the entrance doors, and the long line began to move, slowly at first, then noticeably faster.

Fabrizio patiently walked through the doors of the museum, loosening his handmade silk tie as he entered. His single-breasted Brioni suit, like all his formal clothes, ran a full size big in an attempt to mask the contours of his brawny physique.

He stopped at the information desk in the center of the Great Hall.

"*Scusi, Signora.* You have *la mappa* in *italiano?*" he asked, intentionally using broken English. He spoke four languages better than the average speaker.

The woman behind the counter stared into Fabrizio's darkly lashed, jade eyes in disregard of her training, which was to always make eye contact but never stare. She handed him a maroon-colored map with the word *CIAO* in bold letters on the front. "Are you looking for something in particular?" she asked beaming extendedly.

"You have a painting here by Scipione Pulzone," Fabrizio said exactly as he had rehearsed using a more English-sounding pronunciation of the artist's name.

"Il Gaetano," she remarked, hoping to come off as knowledgeable.

"*The Lamentation.*" He nodded. "Where do I find that?"

"You'd find that in Gallery 601 in our Baroque galleries. Get your ticket and go up these steps," she said pointing to the Grand Staircase. "It's the second gallery after you enter the European Paintings suite of galleries."

He showed his Vatican Bank credentials.

"Oh, then, you get in for free. Give me a few seconds to print a ticket."

With a passionate focus, Fabrizio's photographic memory internalized the museum's one thousand galleries even before the woman returned.

"Here you are." The woman behind the desk handed Fabrizio a sticker. "Just peel off the top part of the sticker and put it on your jacket."

The right corner of his lip curled slightly with an acknowledging expression as he turned, slowly walked around the information desk, and entered the museum's main entrance. Large plaques announcing the names of those who donated tens of millions of dollars to the museum were bolted to the wall. The lists were arranged in chronological order, starting with the earliest donors to the most recent. Fabrizio read the names on the first plaque with the Roman numerals MDCCCLXX – MCMXX.

JOHN JACOB ASTOR

ANDREW CARNEGIE

CORNELIUS VANDERBILT II

DAVID ROCKEFELLER

Impressive list, but dead people were of no interest. He'd inconspicuously snap pictures of the plaques with the names of the more recent donors on his way out.

Ascending the Grand Staircase, Fabrizio removed the jacket of his Brioni suit. Summer in New York City was not much better than in Rome.

He entered the Old Masters galleries, taking note of the cameras in the ceiling while crossing the first gallery, then stopped in front of Pulzone's nearly ten-foot-tall painting. It was simple. It was classical. The lamentation scene not only would serve as the model for numerous future lamentation scenes, but the depiction would sear into the minds of all who laid eyes on it. In the foreground, Joseph held up Jesus's body. To his side, John the Apostle held the crown of thorns. Tears streamed down the Virgin Mary's cheek as Mary Magdalene knelt at Jesus's feet. The painting exuded devoutness; it broadcasted adherence to the Counter-Reformation of Pulzone's day while projecting a *bella senza tempo*, or beautiful timelessness. The underlying message, the more hidden meaning, however, must never be deciphered. Iconoclasm in art must be rejected.

* ~ * ~ *

THE ONE AREA of Manhattan that Anthony always found perplexing was David Graham's neighborhood. There was no Broadway, but a disparate East Broadway. It wasn't Madison Avenue, lined with boutiques, but Madison Street, bordered by housing projects. The leafy trees that ornamented Park Avenue were nowhere to be found on Park Row, a two-

41

way street that intersected David's neighborhood. There were few trees in David's neighborhood, other than several slender ginkgos that shed autumn berries collected by Chinese residents before rotting and emitting a vomit-like odor.

Anthony hesitated in front of David's building and took off his sunglasses. He hoped David could provide some useful information for his investigation, but he couldn't shake the skepticism. He read the reviews for David's books on Amazon. He had also watched an online video of a lecture given by David at an international conference. Neither left an impression. He pressed the button for David's apartment.

"Who is it?" sounded through the perforated circle resembling a speaker.

"It's Anthony Leonardi. We spoke on the phone."

A crackly, almost inaudible, "Okay," sounded, followed by a buzzing.

Pushing open the first door, Anthony didn't move fast enough to make it through the vestibule between the outside and inside doors before the buzzing stopped. The small area between the two doors felt like a steam sauna. He pressed the inside button with the same apartment number but didn't get a response. Wiping the sweat beads forming on his eyebrow, he pushed the same button again, this time harder.

"Who is it?" The voice sounded as staticky as before.

"Who is it?" Anthony repeated. *Who the hell does he think it is?* Anthony moved his face closer to the speaker. "It's still Anthony!" he shouted.

A buzz rebounded in the vestibule as Anthony opened the door.

He braced himself for the five-story walkup. The seventy or so step climb wouldn't prove backbreaking, but Anthony was aware that he had grown a little softer, a bit out of shape, since he had moved into a luxury building several decades earlier.

"IT'S UNLOCKED," ANTHONY heard after knocking.

The hinges squeaked as he pushed the door open and peered into the apartment. "Whoa," he uttered. The skunky smell of marijuana filled the apartment.

"In here!" David yelled from another room.

Anthony followed the voice and smell of pot into the second room, where pictures and maps of ancient civilizations covered the walls of David's railroad apartment. Oversize books randomly littered the coffee table in front of the couch where David sat. He was a thin man, wearing smart-looking, rectangular glasses. He was also well groomed, which surprised Anthony because he associated marijuana with long hair. But David belonged to the new generation of smokers – smokers who worked as lawyers, doctors, law-enforcement officials, and even politicians who denied inhaling.

The computer on the left side of the room defaulted to screensaver mode. A sphinx bounced about the screen in an unsystematic order. The room was bright, filled with natural light from the large windows that faced east toward Brooklyn.

"Thank you for meeting with me," Anthony said, nearing David, hand extended.

David remained seated, holding up his index finger as an indication, and then slowly released a mist of smoke from his mouth. "Sorry for the smoke," he said, half standing and extending his hand. "Glaucoma. If it bothers you, I'll put the bong away."

Hoping to bypass any awkwardness, Anthony replied, "Not at all."

David rested the bong on the top of the coffee table and reclined on the couch.

"As I explained on the phone, I met Jörg Miller several times on a few of my trips to Egypt, but I don't know anything about his death."

"Well, I'm not here to discuss that. I just have a few questions about rituals associated with Egyptology."

"Egyptology," David said while making air quotes with his index and middle fingers. "That's for people who refuse to accept the truth about the past."

Anthony rubbed his sticky neck. He was in no mood for games. He needed to cool down. "You wrote a book on ancient Egypt, if I'm not mistaken?"

David pointed to a hardcover book on the coffee table. "My books are not accepted in scholarly circles. I'm sure the Met doesn't sell my books in its bookshop. They'd blow the top off everything the museum says about the ancient Egyptians."

Anthony sensed the hostility. To break the unease, he said, "That's a fascinating depiction," referring to a large poster on the wall that resembled an unfinished puzzle.

"It's a print of the Turin Erotic Papyrus."

Anthony stepped closer to the bizarre poster. Up close, he could make out the patchy images, in particular that of a short, bald man with an enormous penis about to enter a woman with her legs pointed up in the air. Next to the amorous couple, another well-endowed man was taking a woman from behind. Below, a large-breasted woman with dark, thick pubic hair and exaggerated labia inserted a vessel into her vagina.

His face reddened.

David giggled. "Archaeologists concealed that papyrus from the public for over a century and not because of the lurid sex scenes, but because the so-called experts know if people saw this papyrus, they'd realize that life in ancient Egypt was different from what we're told."

David rose from the couch, walked with a slightly unsteady gait to his desk, and took out a file from the bottom drawer. He shuffled through the pictures in the file until he found the one he wanted.

"Let's see how well you know the history of the Met. Do you recognize the fellow in the middle of this picture?" he asked, returning to the couch, and handing Anthony a frayed, black-and-white photograph.

Anthony put on his glasses and studied the worn picture, shaking his head. "I don't think so. Should I? It appears to be an old picture."

"It was taken in 1870, but I'd still think someone in your position would know the history of the museum better. The guy in the middle with the mutton chops is John Taylor Johnston, the Met's first president."

"That isn't Central Park in the background."

"Far from it." David softly laughed. "This picture was taken in Aswan, Egypt. Do you have any idea what Johnston was doing in Aswan?"

Anthony shrugged. "Collecting objects for the museum?"

"Collecting objects," David repeated. His forced laughter filled the room.

"What's so funny?"

"Johnston had a very different mission," David stated and unfurled a big grin. "Have a seat. What I'm about to tell you will blow your mind."

CHAPTER 11

VICKI PROCEEDED TO THE CLOISTERS BY taking a shortcut that traversed the center of Fort Tryon Park, then ran under a thicket of trees, and eventually reconnected with the main road a few hundred yards before the museum. Delays on the subway had her running behind schedule. The elevator at the station was out, again, and that meant a steep, four-story climb in the hot stairwell. The heat was equally gross outside.

I need air-conditioning as soon as possible, Vicki thought more than once as she sluggishly trekked in the direction of The Cloisters. The stifling heat was catching up to her. A headache was coming on, even a slight wooziness. Her surroundings looked surprisingly unfamiliar, even though she had taken the same path dozens of times.

The waning sun floated over the vertical cliffs of the New Jersey Palisades on the far side of the Hudson River, stubbornly refusing to set for the day. From an imperceptible place in the dark woods, hauntingly unforgettable chants sounded, putting Vicki on high alert. She shuddered, looking around, recalling the first time she had heard similar sounds. The incident had occurred in the North Woods of Central Park. From a tree-lined glade, the eerie sound of an assemblage of people chanting something in the Lucumí dialect elevated to a bone-chilling climax. A distressed chicken balked, then silence. She hadn't stuck around to find out what was happening, but returned the next day and found liquor bottles, used needles, and a headless chicken. The practice of Santería thrived in New York City.

A shady-looking man emerged from the trees.

Vicki stared at the man, attempting to assess his motives as he moved closer, staggering as he walked. His Yankees cap shaded his ashen pallor. Sweat formed darkened circles in his shirt under the arms. Sagging jeans exposed defined abdominals, framed by protuberant oblique muscles ending with suggestive, fleshy barbs that announced his pelvis.

No gun, she said to herself.

The crazed man advanced, shaking his head as if he had lost his senses. Enlarged pupils looked like Ping-Pong balls bulging from his skull.

Vicki placed her hand on her KelTec. "Stand back!" she said forcibly.

The sound of sticks crackling underneath a shoe triggered an unnatural twist of the man's head as he stopped and gaped in terror at a second man who emerged from the woods and advanced. All at once, the scene playing out around Vicki obscured.

"What the fuck?" she faintly heard the first man garble. His arms were raised. His head gyrated with looming fear. "Where the hell did you –?" he uttered before beating a hasty retreat into the trees.

Vicki locked eyes with the second man, assessing his intention. His eyes were sharp, crystal clear. They glowed as if he had never ingested a toxin in his life. The way eyes much have appeared in the past. A scream sounded from the woods. Vicki shaded her eyes as she scanned the copse of trees lining the grassy area to the side of the path. Somewhere in the park, a dog barked restively. A police helicopter hovered overhead, followed by blaring sirens.

Vicki tried to take in everything happening in that moment, but the heat was taking its toll. She pushed forward, toward The Cloisters, desperately seeking relief from the mugginess, befuddled, and thinking that she'd just witnessed something bizarre, though nothing too out of the ordinary for that area of the city. She stopped with the realization that the second man was the same man from the subway on her trip to The Cloisters earlier in the week. She hadn't noticed the calf-high leather boots during the last encounter. She looked over her shoulder, but he was nowhere in sight.

THE STENCH OF the pot smoke was nauseating. The small window air conditioner did little to cool David's apartment. The hands on Anthony's watch seemed rusted in place, but David's unexpected query into the museum's past had sparked his interest, so he examined the picture closer. "Where did you get this picture?" Anthony asked.

"In the historical database at the New York Public Library."

"Why did you copy it?" Anthony asked directly.

David disregarded the question. "It was a rainy day in 1869 when *they*," David stressed, peering almost crossed-eyed through the lenses of his glasses, "secretly convened behind closed doors at the Union League Club and chose John Taylor Johnston as the first president of the Met."

Anthony rested the picture on the table. "Union League Club?"

"America's first private club for the rich and influential. Anyway, it just so happens that Johnston had chartered a steamer in Egypt that very same week and went up the Nile to engage in negotiations with the people who lived along the banks."

Anthony's eyebrows arched. "Why are you telling me this?"

"Johnston's mission was to plan the construction of a dam. He was the perfect guy for the job. He had made a fortune building railroads and bridges, and he and his rich cohorts at the Union League Club knew that if the Nile was dammed at Aswan, the banks would flood over, and ancient artifacts would need to be relocated." David took a life-resuscitating inhale and slowly exhaled. "Not just any artifacts, but sacred objects like the Temple of Dendur. And nothing was going to stop the construction of that dam."

CHAPTER 12

VICKI STOOD IN THE DISTANCE AND observed the spectacle playing out in front of The Cloisters. Several dozen limousines idled in a row short of the rear entrance. Black Cadillac Escalade SUVs were at the front and rear of the line of cars. Six men in black uniforms and berets with sniffer dogs checked the surrounding area. Two men with coiled tubes extending from their suits and into their ears were combing a patch of trees, while several other men investigated the rocky ramparts that supported Fort Tryon and The Cloisters on the sheer cliffs rising hundreds of feet above the Hudson River.

The all-clear sign was given with a whirl of a wrist, and one-by-one, polished limousines stopped in front of the entrance. Drivers held doors open and then sped off to allow the next limousine to pull up. Women alighted robed in flowing evening gowns, white gloves, and showy jewelry. The men wore black tuxedoes with black bow ties.

Vicki read the text message from Margarita as the last couple walked through the doors of the museum. 'Meet me in the ladies' room on the lower level'.

As Vicki neared the Postern Gate entranceway at the rear of The Cloisters, she recalled that postern doors were used as concealed entrances in castles or as fortifications to medieval city walls. *Still putting the door to good use*, she mused as she tried to pull the door open. It was locked. She stepped back, thinking it was too hot to walk around the building to the staff entrance. She banged on the door with the palm of her hand until the heavy door swung open and she was face-to-face with a large man dressed in a formal suit. He was the size of an Olympic heavyweight wrestler. She showed her ID.

"This is a private event."

His deep voice reverberated in the foyer like a strike on a hollow drum.

More agitated by the simmering heat than intimidated, she unclipped her ID from her belt, firmly holding her gaze on the man. "I guess you didn't see my ID badge," she remarked, raising the badge. "See the words in capitals that read FULL ACCESS? Only a handful of security employees at the Met have this level of clearance. No one here at The Cloisters has this clearance," she made quite clear, shaking her head. She clasped her ID back onto her belt, pushing back her shirt and revealing the gun on her belt.

Nothing more was said.

MARGARITA USHERED VICKI to a bathroom mirror where the light was brightest.

"I asked you to meet down here because I want to show you something in private and didn't want to take the chance of being overheard."

"What if someone comes down to use the restroom?"

"Not a chance," Margarita countered. "The women here tonight wouldn't even consider using a public restroom. They use the employee restroom upstairs."

Vicki gently wiped her face using several multifold paper towels. "It's so nice to be inside," she said, taking in the cool air from the building's AC. She heard rumbling a flight up, from the group that had entered the museum. "Fancy group upstairs."

"Yeah, you know, the usual rich people who come here for events from time to time." Margarita leaned over the porcelain sink. The shiny, gold cross dangling from her neck redirected light from above and into the mirror, reflecting it into her likeness. She checked to make sure her eyeliner was still intact. Margarita had mastered the cat-eye technique. She loved how the style amplified the smokiness of her Andalusian eyes.

"*Ah, péter plus haut que son cul,*" Vicki said, looking at Margarita's reflection.

Margarita's left eyebrow rose higher than her right. Lips parted as she contemplated Vicki's statement. She stood upright. "What did you say?"

"Literally translated, it means to fart higher than one's ass. It's a funny French way of saying someone is a snob."

Margarita giggled while pulling out a rolled-up, soft-cover booklet from her pocketbook. "I totally forgot that you lived in France. And speaking of foreign countries, this is what I wanted to show you. Someone left it behind after the last concert here. I planned to find the owner, but I was so intrigued with it that I —"

Vicki grabbed hold of the booklet and flipped through the pages.

"What did you find so intriguing?" she asked.

"Toward the end, there's a picture of the cover of the *Crata Repoa*, an initiation document that details Egyptian rituals performed by St. Germain."

Vicki's mouth slowly opened as she examined the facsimile of the cover of the *Crata Repoa*, showing an intentionally blurry image of apparitional-like initiates, perhaps a half dozen or more, all walking through enormous sandstone columns and toward a golden light radiating from the inside of an ancient temple. Below the temple it read:

'THE CONCEPTS AND THE BELIEF IN THE IDEA OF A PARTICULAR TYPE OF INITIATION SYSTEM, OR THE MYSTERIES, WERE FIRST FORMED BY THIS TEXT.'

"Did you tell anyone about this?" Vicki asked.

"Just Darrel. The cutie working the door."

Vicki grinned and thought back to the large African-American man at the entry who tried to prevent her from entering. "Are you guys dating?"

"More like having a little fun." There was excitement in Margarita's voice. "Anyway, listen, Vicki, I think the actual *Crata Repoa* is here."

"That's right. You said St. Germain carried out rituals in the Tombs."

Pointing up, Margarita cried out, "To the Tombs!"

CHAPTER 13

OFFICIAL MET EXCAVATIONS IN EGYPT BEGAN at the dawn of the twentieth century. No expense was spared. J. P. Morgan, grasping the presidential reins of the museum, personally funded the Egyptian excavations. His third and final trip to Egypt, in 1913, began with a stopover at the Vatican, where he convened with Pope Pius X and Wilhelm II, the last emperor of Germany and the king of Prussia. The meeting wasn't made public.

Morgan then dashed off to Egypt in pursuit of objects buried in an ancient cemetery, desperate to understand the secrets of the Egyptians. But the trip proved to be a fatal blunder for the financier, who spent the majority of his fortune acquiring ancient relics. He took ill while on the Nile, and his condition declined swiftly. His crew rushed him back to Italy for treatment, but it was too late. It was reported that Morgan died from a high fever caused by malaria or one of the other illnesses used to cover up the demise of those who exploited sacred burial grounds.

His last words were an Egyptian prayer.

Many similar tales echoed through the ages.

What neither Anthony nor David knew was that Met personnel had recently returned to Egypt to engage in further archaeological excavation.

* ~ * ~ *

THE MUFFLED SOUND of the opening movement of Mozart's *Requiem Mass in D Minor* sounded through the thick oak doors of the Langon Chapel as

51

Margarita and Vicki dashed from the top of the stairs, passed the chapel, and entered the Cuxa Cloister.

Vicki gazed back at the massive doors of the chapel.

"Why are you stopping?" Margarita said, in a whisper.

Vicki examined the Langon Chapel's arched doors, strapped with horizontal black-iron bands made to withstand battering rams. A tinge of red radiance seeped through the crack between the two halves of the door. She looked at Margarita and said, "Just a second. I want to see if I can look through the separation in the doors."

"No, Vicki," Margarita cautioned. "We'll get caught."

"They won't hear me, I promise."

Familiar Mortzartian chords sounded from within the chapel as Vicki silently approached. The narrow space between the two wood doors didn't allow for much of a visual inside the chapel, so she bent down until she found a marginally wider gap. The view was still limited to a small sliver inside the chapel. The room was dark, but light enough to see that the people were no longer dressed in their expensive attire, or perhaps they were wearing dark gowns over their clothes. It was too murky to tell.

Vicki jumped backward when she felt the hand on her shoulder.

"Vicki, this is crazy."

"What kind of concert is this? Everyone is standing."

"C'mon," Margarita said in hushed tones. "You'll get us both in trouble."

Noticing the terrified look on Margarita's face, Vicki nodded with consent and shadowed Margarita as she scurried through the ambulatory boarding the east arcade of the Saint-Michel-de-Cuxa, the main Cuxa Cloister, and through the pointed, ornamental door to the Early Gothic Hall. Margarita lit her halogen flashlight and led the way down the steep, winding stairs into the Tombs. It was immediately clear to Vicki why the employees at The Cloisters refused to work in that section at night.

"Ouch!" Vicki shrieked, and covered her mouth with her hand.

Margarita redirected her light onto Vicki. "Are you okay?"

"I just stubbed my toe on this tomb."

"That's the sarcophagus of Lady Margaret of Gloucester." Margarita crossed herself, then shined her flashlight on the limestone effigy of the woman on the top of the coffin, dressed in a thirteenth-century aristocratic gown. Her hands were clasped in prayer on her waist; her head and chin covered by a veil and a wimple.

"Whose coffin is that against the wall?" Vicki asked, moving toward the coffin.

"That's the sarcophagus of Ermengol VII, Count of Urgell. He was an extremely wealthy Spaniard who lived in the fourteenth century."

Vicki paced the dark chapel, thinking that it looked similar to the other gothic chapels she had seen in Europe. The large sculptures in the apse were barely detectable because of the lack of light secreted through the stained-glass windows in the evening hours. A feeling of being watched forced a shiver, but she realized that she was just being paranoid. There were no cameras in the Tombs, nothing paranormal. Her gaze shifted to the limestone bricks making up the two sidewalls. She guessed there were about thirty rows of one-foot-wide bricks extending from the floor to the high-arched ceiling.

She scanned the smaller, outer row of stones that outlined the chapel's pointed, rib-vaulted ceiling. The stone rib pattern mimicked a spider with long legs. A round keystone served as the centerpiece of the ceiling. Vicki moved beneath the keystone of the rib vault, where a rosy-colored light pierced the darkness with ray-like precision. The beam pointed to the effigy tomb of the Holy Crusader, Jean d'Alluye.

"Have you seen the inside of d'Alluye's tomb?" she asked.

Margarita stiffened. "I was here when a team of French conservators did a conservation treatment on the tombs a few years ago. I got to look inside all of them. They're all completely empty."

Vicki scrutinized the dark chapel, looking for any irregularities. The numerous funerary relics inside the Tombs in some spooky way synced well, particularly well, with the portal shape of the space.

"How come there's no placard for d'Alluye's tomb?"

"It's over there." Margarita pointed with her flashlight to the wall. "The stand for the placard kept getting knocked over by visitors when it was in the center of the chapel."

Vicki approached the wall and read the placard.

"It says the base for the sarcophagus isn't authentic. I never knew that."

"The bases for the tombs stayed in Europe, along with any remains."

Margarita crossed herself again. "These bases were made here and are designed to replicate the real bases, though not made of real stone."

"Hand me your flashlight, Margarita."

Margarita passed the flashlight to Vicki. "What are you looking for?"

"I'm not sure, to be honest."

Vicki grazed her fingertips against the base of d'Alluye's effigy tomb and detected a rut in the front section six or eight inches from the corner. Another groove delineated the corner. "I think I hit on something. This small section of the base below Monsieur d'Alluye's left foot may be removable."

"Where the odd sword points," Margarita observed, astutely. "Of course."

Vicki gently jiggled the segment.

"It's loose. Looks like this section comes out."

Margarita clutched Vicki's shoulder and quivered with unrestrained elation. "I can't even tell you how excited I am right now, Vicki. I knew you'd be able to find something."

Delicately, Vicki slid the segment out of the base. She laid flat on the floor and aimed the flashlight into the gap in the base. "I think I see something in there," she said, trying to hold the flashlight at the right angle to see under the tomb. She scooted on her belly closer to the tomb and reached into the empty space underneath, grunting as she stretched her arm.

"Can you reach it?" Margarita asked, unable to stand still.

"Got it." Vicki pulled a package out from underneath the tomb, wrapped in what felt like vellum and tied together by a red ribbon. She handed the package and flashlight to Margarita and promptly stood.

Margarita untied the ribbon. Carefully, she unwrapped the package, removed a document, and placed it on d'Alluye's shield. She compared the cover of the document with the cover of the copy of the *Crata Repoa* in her booklet. The images were identical. "It's the actual *Crata Repoa*," Margarita whispered sotto voce. Her mouth opened; a glint of mischievousness exuded from her dark eyes. "Darrel is going to freak out when I show him this!"

Vicki grabbed the document. "I should bring this to Anthony Leonardi."

"Director Leonardi?" The elation in Margarita's expression quickly wilted. "Why would you bring this to the Met? It belongs here at The Cloisters."

Vicki knew the real reason for Margarita's objection.

"I know that you had some issues with Anthony in the past, Margarita, but whoever put this document here may be doing things that he should know about. I have no choice but to bring it to him."

Margarita conceded with a soft sigh. "Okay, but it really does belong here with d'Alluye's tomb. See what you can do about getting it back here as soon as possible."

"I'll let you know what Anthony says," Vicki promised. "Let's clean up this mess and put everything back in its proper place."

CHAPTER 14

THE SOUND OF BUBBLING FILLED THE room as David inhaled and then held his breath until the smoke seeped from his mouth. Anthony stared out of one of the two windows in David's apartment and watched as the cars on the Manhattan Bridge moved at a swift pace while the cars on the Brooklyn Bridge inched forward. Even with the window closed, the sounds of the city could be heard: police sirens, Doppler reverberation made by the speeding cars on the FDR Drive below, the horns of cars driven by people with no self-control. Anthony was eager to leave David's apartment, but he needed to probe a bit further. "Can you explain to me how any of this information is pertinent to my investigation?"

"Can you explain why Cleopatra's Needle arrived in New York immediately following Johnston's trip to Egypt and was erected behind the museum?"

"I . . . I'm not sure," Anthony stammered.

"The heliacal rising of Sirius occurred on the night of the death in your museum," David remarked, rising from the couch. He sparked his lighter and held the bong to his mouth, but instead of inhaling, he spoke. "The Egyptians associated Sirius with the goddess Isis, consort of Osiris, both still idolized, if you will, by secret societies, so it's entirely possible that there was some kind of ritual taking place inside the temple."

Anthony rose from the couch, ready to make his departure.

David detected the skepticism in Anthony's slitted eyes.

"It'd behoove you to keep an open mind if you wish to get to the bottom of this," he averred, but in a way that suggested that he didn't care if Anthony accepted the information or not. "There's a good reason why Met officials chose to take a temple from Aswan, of all places in Egypt, or anywhere else in the world for that matter. In fact, the choice of location is obvious to anyone with knowledge of history and astronomy."

Anthony growled inwardly, then played along.

"What are you talking about?"

"Aswan has the geographical distinction of lying on the Tropic of Cancer. The sun reaches its greatest declination as it passes directly over the Tropic of Cancer on the summer solstice. That also means," David said, now more eager to talk than take another hit, "that the sun is directly below Aswan on the winter solstice, December 21, at the Tropic of Capricorn. As you may or may not know, the Roman writer, Macrobius, and even Plato, spoke of portals, or gates that appeared in the galaxy when the sun and the earth lined up with the elliptical path of those tropical signs. And it is during these such astronomical events that souls are allowed to pass through the gates."

"You're suggesting the museum acquired the Temple of Dendur because it came from some place that aligns with an abstract sphere in the solar system?" Anthony probed further. "And just where do you think these traveling souls ultimately end up?"

"Where we came from, the galaxy, though some reach the Eighth Sphere."

Anthony exhaled and stared at David's book on the coffee table titled *Giza Necropolis*. The cover displayed a picture of the three main pyramids of Giza rising from the desert sand to a backdrop of a darkening sky. Stars twinkled in the upper portion of the book cover where the sky was darkest. Three stars were precisely aligned with the three pyramids.

An irrepressible cynicism sounded in Anthony's voice when he spoke.

"Even if the heliacal rising of Sirius occurred on the night of the death in the museum, that event occurs later in the summer than the summer solstice."

"That's correct. At least by today's measurements. But because of the precession of the equinoxes, that is, the rotation of the heavens, the gates nowadays open at different times."

Anthony folded his arms. "It took a major effort, not to mention exorbitant costs, to move the Temple of Dendur to the Met. Government officials were involved. International organizations had a hand in the relocation, along with many influential people who took part in the negotiations."

"Of course. Who else could do such a thing?" David took a long, gratifying hit from his bong.

Straight away, Anthony felt check-mated, though not sure why.

"Just how do you suppose these people get into the museum?" he asked, almost angrily. His postural positioning was more revealing.

David slowly let the smoke seep out of his mouth. Glassy-eyed, he said, "That sounds like something in your area of expertise, I'd say, but you may want to start with Humming Tombstone. Some say there's a tunnel underneath it that leads to the museum."

"Humming Tombstone?"

"You never heard of Humming Tombstone?" David snapped his head back theatrically. "I thought that everyone in New York City knew about the tombstone. It's behind the museum, directly across from Cleopatra's Needle."

Anthony rotated his wrist and checked his watch. He was running behind schedule, and street congestion would only get worse with the evening traffic. "Thank you for your time," he politely said and exited the smoke-filled apartment.

CHAPTER 15

ANTHONY WAS ON THE FIFTH FLOOR of the Met in a meeting with the museum president. As always, it was his least favorite way to start the day.

Lane Merrill touted a prestigious career in high-profile positions. Before her appointment as the president of the Met, Lane was listed by *Forbes* as one of the top five institutional fund-raisers in the United States. Courted by various foundations and universities worldwide for top-level jobs, Lane rebuffed corporate life and opted for a path of less stress and summers on Martha's Vineyard when she signed on as chief executive administrator at the Museum of Fine Arts in Boston, where she had developed a reputation for having a Midas touch. Several salary bumps later, she jumped at the opportunity to double her salary and accepted the top position at the Met.

Lane was nothing short of formal. She never addressed museum employees by their first names, and Anthony could never quite put his finger on her exact intentions whenever he was summoned to her office. Today's meeting was no different.

"I presume you remember the expense and legal battle the museum encountered before we, let's just say, repatriated the antiquities to Turkey."

Anthony straightened. "The Lydian objects illegally excavated?"

"We prefer not to use such terms," Lane insisted. She picked up a pen from the top of her antique desk and rolled it between her fingers. "Suffice it to say, that little cause célèbre paled in comparison with the media circus surrounding the Italian items."

The direction of the conversation was already beginning to trouble

Anthony. "You mean, the vase we recently returned to Italy?" he said anxiously.

"You know, Mr. Leonardi, I was offered the job here at the Met because of the way in which I discreetly handled the return of the Greek silverware at the MFA."

Anthony didn't know what to say. Only an "Oh?" emitted from his mouth. He lowered his head and forced himself to sip the coffee prepared by Lane's secretary. It was too fancy for his taste. He added two packets of brown sugar.

Lane rose from her chair and tied her jet-black hair into a taut, samurai-like knot as she positioned herself alongside a window in her office, raised the blinds, and squinted at the sight of the sunny park five stories below. She shook her head and closed the blinds.

"That horrid sun is determined to freckle my skin," she remarked, running a finger down the blinds in a gratifying way and making sure each slat was tightly closed.

Anthony glanced, perhaps longer than he intended, at Lane's pointed, python-skinned boots, knowing that there wasn't an employee at the museum who didn't talk about her boots at close quarters. He dismissed the gossip as cattiness, unsure if it was true that Lane was hanging on to a fashion statement that didn't fly during its time. He didn't know one way or the other.

Lane turned, but Anthony had already looked away from the boots.

"I asked you to meet with me because the museum received a request to return something else," she said flatly, but with a discernible contralto-pitch. She fluffed the Hermès silk scarf draped over the lapels of her tight-fitting, charcoal-colored pantsuit and returned to her desk. "A painting in our Old Masters collection."

Surprised, Anthony asked, "Who made the request?"

"The request came from Rome." Lane sat at her desk. "It was also requested that we keep this matter confidential, which I trust you will." She tore off a piece of paper from a notepad illustrated with the Met's artwork and wrote the name Len Lee and a phone number. "Mr. Lee was kind enough to offer a private forum for discussion."

She pushed the paper toward Anthony.

"The Legal Department handles these matters," Anthony said, staring at the paper and masking his irritation.

"Our lawyers are called upon only when there's a legitimate claim," she remarked, leaning back in her chair and tapping the armrest. "There's little reason to involve them or anyone else, for that matter, in this situation, but that's completely beside the point. I don't want you to engage in actual negotiations. My word, no! You are scarcely trained for such matters. I want you to welcome the representative from Rome and feel out the situation," Lane insisted, knowing Anthony had myriad investigative resources at his fingertips, but not officially suggesting that he use them. "Find out who he is. What he expects, generally speaking, and what he is offering us in return."

Anthony swallowed his discontent. "I'll schedule an appointment."

"Might I suggest, Mr. Leonardi, that you put this at the top of your list."

CHAPTER 16

THE BLAZE FROM THE AFTERNOON SUN passing overhead baked the museum's plaza. Long lines extended from both entranceway doors, queued with people seeking relief from the unrelenting sun. Less heliophobic individuals had assembled on the steps to the entrance. Most visitors were chatting; some sitting and examining maps of New York City. A few showed an interest in the men who regularly regaled the crowd with classics like 'Under the Boardwalk' and 'The Lion Sleeps Tonight'.

Vicki skipped lunch to familiarize herself with the *Crata Repoa* before bringing it to Anthony's attention at the end of the day. She placed a bottle of water on a ledge on the museum's façade and searched the Internet for information on the document on her laptop. The document, she discovered, was written in the eighteenth century and detailed initiatory rites that dated back to ancient Egypt. Certain groups, she further read, referred to the *Crata Repoa* as the *Initiations into the Ancient, Secret Society of the Egyptian Priests*. It was translated from German and into French, then into English, and was circulated among secret societies. Since it was leaked, various versions, some unadulterated, some phony, were offered for sale on Amazon and numerous other websites, mainly those that hyped alternative history. Vicki read the ritual headings:

PREPARATION

FIRST GRADE – PASTOPHORIS

SECOND GRADE – NEOCORIS

THIRD GRADE – THE GATE OF DEATH

63

FOURTH GRADE – CHISTOPHORIS
FIFTH GRADE – BALAHATE
SIXTH GRADE – ASTRONOMER BEFORE THE GATE OF THE GODS
SEVENTH GRADE – SAPHENATH PANCAH

She scrolled back to the top of the page and read the 'Preparation' section:

WHEN AN ASPIRANT DESIRED TO LEARN THE ANCIENT MYSTERIES OF THE CRATA REPOA, HE HAD TO BE RECOMMENDED BY INITIATES. HAVING APPLIED AT HELIOPOLIS, THE ASPIRANT WAS SENT TO MEMPHIS, AND THEN SENT ON TO THEBES. THERE HE WAS CIRCUMCISED.

Vicki raised her head, astounded. She scanned the museum's plaza. The size of the horde loitering outside the museum had grown incrementally as people streamed out of several coach buses parked curbside and filled the plaza. A familiar-looking face appeared, then disappeared in the gathering, but Vicki's thoughts were focused squarely on the initiation document.

She skimmed the First and Second Grades, slowing her pace as she reached the Third Grade, astonished to learn that initiates were blindfolded and escorted through subterranean tunnels and passages and into temples, where the long-held secrets of the Egyptian Mystery School were revealed. Acquiring the knowledge passed down from ancient times equipped the initiate to traverse to an 'unknown country', what Vicki determined had to be secret code for the afterlife. Those who failed the rites of the Third Grade failed to understand the true source of the light.

Vicki's jaw dropped as she continued reading:

Through much learning and the manifest exhibiting of high moral conduct, the Initiate of this Grade was ready to receive the name Melanephoris. He was led by the Thesmophores from the pronaos into an antechamber. The room was filled with various mummies and coffins of high priests; similarly themed designs decorated the walls. This was where the Neophyte found Paraskistes. There the Melanephoris was also read the terms of the Crata Repoa, which he had to accept.

He was then blindfolded and brought to the Sanctuary. Above the entrance of the room was written, 'Gate of Death'. This was surely a place of death. The Heroi was found here, as was the tomb of the recently murdered King Osiris, surrounded by the crimson blood of the fresh wounds. The Melanephoris was asked repeatedly if he had taken any part in the assassination of his Master. After denying the charges, two Tapixeytes, those who inter the dead, took possession of him. They threw the Initiate to the ground and bound him. His fellow brethren cried out for his safety. Thunder and lightning filled the room. The Worshipful Master cried out "Vengeance" and placed the tip of his blade against the back of the neck of the Melanephoris.

"Oh my God," Vicki said sitting up. Another realization hit her. She may have just seen the man from the subway and Fort Tryon Park, but he was no longer in sight.

* ~ * ~ *

ANTHONY ENTERED CENTRAL Park on the paved path just south of the 79th Street transverse. Children frolicked around a fountain alongside a large statue known as *Group of Bears* while parents wiped the moisture from their faces as they chatted on benches. The saxophone player delivered another recital inside the Greywacke Arch.

As a show of gratitude for enduring the past twenty-four days of scorching heat, Anthony dropped several dollars into the musician's open saxophone case.

The man grinned and blew, 'What a Wonderful World'.

Exiting the west side of the tunnel, Anthony searched the bushy area south of the Greywacke Knoll until he located the upright, box-like object that David Graham called Humming Tombstone. Whatever the object was, it clearly appeared to be out of place amid the undergrowth of flowering plants and verdant rhododendron bushes. The double doors in the front of the box were large enough for a person to pass through but were locked with a rusted padlock. He'd return later in the day with tools.

Ascending the granite stairs of the Greywacke Knoll, Anthony stopped on the red-brick, octagonal platform for Cleopatra's Needle, wiped the sweat, and gazed at the soaring, 3,600-year-old obelisk sitting on its foundation in the exact same way it had stood in Egypt. He marveled at the colossal monument, knowing that it took a huge team of horses and one hundred and twelve days to move the obelisk from the East River to its spot on the Greywacke Knoll. Slowly, he circled the massive four-sided monolith. All

65

four sides were inscribed with hieroglyphics in the form of characters, pictures, and symbols. Many of the carvings had faded with time, but Anthony took note of the same dog-headed man who was carved on the inside wall of the Temple of Dendur—Anubis, the first god of the underworld. The plaque below the obelisk's pedestal read:

This obelisk was erected first at Heliopolis in Egypt, in 1600 B.C. It was removed to Alexandria in 12 B.C. by the Romans. Presented by the Khedive of Egypt to the City of New York, it was erected here on February 22, 1881, through the generosity of William H. Vanderbilt.

Above the granite pedestal, the Romans had inserted four gigantic bronze crabs under the four corners of the obelisk to prevent the tapering pillar from toppling over. Latin words were inscribed into the left claws. Greek letters into the right ones. A small plaque explained that Emperor Augustus had the obelisk moved to Alexandria.

Augustus, Anthony recalled, had commissioned the Temple of Dendur.

~~*

AFTER THE MUSEUM closed for the day, Vicki and Sibyl met in the women's locker room, alongside other excited guards who couldn't wait to get out of their uniforms and into their regular clothes after the long, twelve-hour Saturday shift.

"Those are scanty panties," Vicki mused.

"What'd you expect? I'm an artist, not a lawyer." Sibyl took a pair of worn denim jeans out of her locker. "Besides, you're one to talk. What about that tat?"

"This?" Vicki pointed to a faded tattoo of the letter *S* on her hip.

"Yeah, the one you got when you were dating that guy."

Vicki laughed. "This stupid thing was his idea from the start. He said I always sneaked up on him, so he kept pushing me to get a tattoo of the word 'Stealth'. I eventually gave in, but only agreed to get this *S*."

"Josh, right? Whatever happened to him?"

Vicki puffed indifferently while neatly folding her uniform. "Haven't heard from him since we broke up last year."

"And you've dated few times since. What's going on, Vick?" Sibyl asked as she put on her thick glasses, then tousled her hair into the style she liked. "A lot of the guys around here are crazy about you."

Vicki felt the moment was right, so she confessed. "Who says I'm not involved with someone? You know I am not the type to kiss and tell."

Sibyl froze in place. "And you didn't say anything?"

Vicki smiled coyly and hung her uniform in her locker.

"Well," Sibyl eagerly pushed, leaning closer to Vicki, "is it someone at the museum? Oh, I know who it is. It's that cute guy in the Membership department that you talk to all the time. Or more likely, it's someone in security," she conjectured, getting ahead of herself. "The guys in security are nuts about you. I hear what they say when you're not around."

"I didn't want to say anything too soon. That's the number-one rule of dating a co-worker. And for the record," Vicki clarified, "he's an artist in his own right. That reminds me, are you entering a painting in the employee art show this year?"

"Oh, very clever, Vick. Change the subject just like that." Sibyl laughed inwardly and grabbed the tie-dyed shirt that she'd painted and draped it over her locker door. She inspected the shirt for any color bleeding from the dyes extracted from knotweed, goldenrod, avocado peels, and coffee grounds. The vinegar rise used to prevent running seemed to be holding. She hung her uniform shirt on a metal hanger and placed it inside her locker. "Every time I bring up relationships, you sidetrack the conversation."

"That's not true, Sibyl. I just haven't dated anyone lately worth discussing." Vicki zipped her pants. "You're lucky to have found your soul mate."

"Hold on. It's not all sunny skies. Some days Claire can be so uptight when she comes home from work. It can take her hours to unwind."

"What does she do again?"

"She's a lawyer." Sibyl tittered. "How do you think I know they're so uptight?"

Subtly, Vicki removed the *Crata Repoa* from her locker, looking around. "Check out what Margarita and I found at The Cloisters. We literally struck gold."

"What is it?" Sibyl pushed up her glasses. Hazel-green eyes enlarged.

Vicki made sure that none of the other guards were looking her way as she handed the document to Sibyl. "Something called the *Crata Repoa*."

"Is this the *actual* initiation book?" Sibyl asked, lowering her glasses.

"Can you believe it? I'm bringing it up to Anthony's office now." Vicki put her hand on her locker door. "You know what? I think I'll keep the document here in my locker and bring up my laptop and show him a copy I downloaded earlier. He said he may have to leave early today, and I don't want to come back down here to lock it up."

"Smart move. Just be sure not to mention Margarita to Anthony."

"What choice do I have?" Vicki shrugged. "I have to tell him everything."

"You know he accused Margarita of tampering with her time-card?"

"It was more than that," Vicki said, but held her tongue.

Sibyl closed the door to her locker and locked it. "If I recall, the *Crata Repoa* contains rituals that inspired hermetic, cabbalistic, and gnostic traditions. It may be worthwhile to check the Greek and Roman galleries for something related."

CHAPTER 17

VICKI HELD HER ID NEXT TO the scanner box and pushed open the secure door to the museum's security command center. Dubbed C3, the high-tech command and communications center was revamped when Anthony was hired and was equipped with the latest security technology, designed to thwart even the most unanticipated of crimes. Dozens of multi-display LCD monitors – each screen divided into nine screen views – flashed images of nearly every inch of the inside of the museum as well as the entirety of the outside perimeter and roof. An elongated, slanted control panel displayed an array of colored lights alongside dials that regulated devices connected to motion detection, heat detection, and even gas, chemical, and radiation detection. A dedicated phone line connected the command center with the Central Park Police Precinct, and should a more critical situation arise, encrypted lines connected the command center directly to the New York office of the FBI and the Department of Homeland Security.

Anthony was at the rear of C3 talking to Paul McDonough.

"Hey, what do you know?" Paul said as Vicki approached. "I don't think I've ever seen you in here this late in the day, Vicki."

"My job requires me to be on the floor, not in here. I'm sure you know that." Vicki pressed her lips together and turned to Anthony. "Can I see you in your office?" *Alone*, she mouthed to Anthony.

Paul shook his head. "Everything is always so secretive with you."

Anthony nodded and walked with Vicki to his office. "What's so private that Paul couldn't hear?" he asked as he closed the door to his office.

Vicki sat. "I thought it would be better if I showed this to you in private." She placed her laptop on Anthony's desk and powered it up. "Did you get the autopsy report from the medical examiner yet?" she asked as her computer booted.

"It's odd. According to the report, the only thing suspect on Miller's body was a slight penetration through the right occipital, just as the CSU team determined." .

"He didn't have a stroke or heart attack?"

"Not according to the autopsy. And what's more bizarre is that the ME's report also notes that in many cases people have survived similar incisions to that region of the head. Some have even miraculously survived when an object goes all the way through the skull, if the puncture in the occipital is not too intrusive."

Vicki contemplated for several seconds, then asked, "So the stab through the back of the neck was or was not the cause of Mr. Miller's death?"

"That's just it. It's still not clear if the injury to the back of the neck was the actual cause of death, so this matter is not being considered a homicide at this point. In all my years on the force, I've never encountered anything like this." Anthony raised his cup to his mouth, but the coffee was too hot to drink with any grace, so he slurped it.

Vicki gazed with astonishment. "Do you ever sleep?"

Anthony added a packet of sugar to his coffee while feigning the sound of a yawn. "Not since I took this job." He stirred his coffee. "I'm sorry. Would you like a cup?"

"Very funny. You know I don't drink coffee."

"Oh, that's right. Your addiction theory." Anthony shook his head. "Both coffee and cocaine come from plants from South America, and both have the same effect on the reward pathway in the brain," he said. But Anthony had worked the mean streets of New York in the 1970s, when the Big Apple was rotten to the core and drug addiction was rampant. Not once had he seen someone strung out from coffee withdrawal.

Vicki clicked on a download icon on her laptop screen and turned it toward Anthony. "Can you see this document? It's called the *Crata Repoa.*"

Anthony swiveled in his chair and squinted as he looked at the screen.

"It contains ancient secret rituals performed in places like Heliopolis,

Memphis, and Thebes," she informed her boss. "I have the real document in my locker. I wasn't sure if you'd be in your office, so I kept it locked up."

"Real document?" Heliopolis spurred Anthony's second thought, but the ringing sound of his phone diverted his attention. "Even at this hour, the calls just keep coming," he said and pressed the round speaker button. "Yes." Anthony moved his face closer to his phone as his assistant's voice came through the speaker with the message that the president asked if he had scheduled a meeting with Len Lee. Anthony's face tensed. "Good lord," he remarked, turning his annoyed gaze to Vicki, but making sure his assistant heard his voice. "Can you please call her on Monday and tell her that I'm meeting with Mr. Lee first thing Tuesday morning."

Vicki pushed her laptop closer to Anthony after the call. "Look at this part," she said, highlighting a section of the *Crata Repoa* that read, *placed the tip of his blade against the back of the neck.*

Anthony leaned back in his chair and pinched the bridge of his nose, eyes closed. His nostrils flared as he deliberated until he returned to a vertical position. "Are you suggesting that I base the theory of the death in the Temple of Dendur on this document?"

"I can't prove this explains what happened, but —"

His sigh muted Vicki. "Let's just say for argument's sake that there was a secret ceremony going on in the museum. I can't see how," Anthony added, "but you're the third person to make the suggestion, so let's talk it through. People aren't supposed to die during ritual ceremonies. In fact, it even says in this document that a knife was placed to the neck. You just said so."

"No," Vicki retorted, "it specifically says that a blade was placed *against* the back of the neck. For argument's sake, to use your phrase." Vicki smiled cheekily to abate any possible tincture of disrespect, and then set forth her strongest point. "Let's say the blade was a sharp blade, one that could cut into a person like a hot knife through butter."

"Can you scroll up?" Anthony asked, eyes fixed on Vicki's laptop and rolling his chair closer to the edge of his desk. "Does this say, 'Gate of Death' in this section?"

"That's the title of the Third Grade of this document."

"'Gate' and 'Death' are the words carved into the wall, I mean lintel, inside the Temple of Dendur. Cy called the carvings hierogrammatics, or something like that." Confusion registered in Anthony's brown eyes. "Where'd you get this document?"

"The Cloisters." Vicki tensed.

"What was this doing there?"

"No idea, that's why I'm showing it to you. I'd suggest we contact one of the medieval curators," Vicki suggested, "but we should also talk with Albert Bennington about a saber in the Arms and Armor collection."

"Saber?" Anthony repeated, showing no trace of a surge of alarm that shot through his very core, thinking that few people in the museum knew that the display case for the saber concealed one of the museum's dirty, little secrets—behind the scenes goings on known only to the upper echelons and described as "the biggest scandals in the history of the museum." To the day, Anthony had never spoken a word about what was behind that display case.

"There's another connection," Vicki remarked, pointing to the initiation document on her laptop. "The *Crata Repoa* was first written in German. Mr. Miller was German, right? And didn't you tell me he was doing something in the temple when it was in Egypt?"

Anthony exhaled. "Schedule something with Albert Tuesday evening, but bring me this document first thing Monday morning, before the preparations for the party begin. I'll also need a detailed report."

"Is everything set for the gala on Monday?" Vicki knew Anthony wouldn't be pleased with the question, but she had a hard time suppressing her excitement when it came to the museum's yearly Costume Institute Gala.

Anthony combed his hand through his hair and squeezed the tension from his stiff trapezoids at the base of his neck. "Someone died in the Temple of Dendur earlier in the week, and the biggest fashion party in the country is happening on Monday."

"This may be a bad time to ask, but can I go into the party this year?"

Anthony noted a puckish twinkle in Vicki's eyes. "You know the rules. The only people allowed into the gala are the chosen celebrities, personally invited guests, and the museum executives."

"I'm bored with watching the gala from the sidelines."

"Remind me again why I promoted you?" Anthony said, wryly.

CHAPTER 18

DESCRIBED AS THE 'SUPER BOWL OF the fashion world', the Met's fashion gala served as the most elaborate fashion show in New York City. For Anthony, it was a throbbing headache.

He stood at the museum entry. Several hours earlier, he had changed into his most fashionable Brooks Brothers suit, made of wool sharkskin, well aware that his suit would be considered uncouth compared with the suits worn by the men attending the gala.

The celebrity tent set up hours earlier extended from the museum's entrance down to the street. The red carpet covering the stairs was railed on both sides by tall, lush boxwood hedges, put in place to keep invited photographers and sneaky paparazzi a comfortable distance from the people hand-picked to attend the fête at the Met.

The day began with a steady rain that produced patches of vaporous steam that rose from the hot concrete streets, but tapered into a temperate, gray mist by afternoon.

Anthony looked through the haze at the heightened NYPD security presence in front of the museum. The city's two elite police squads had assembled hours earlier. The Critical Response Command team formed a military line in front of two armored trucks parked a strategic distance from the entrance to the celebrity tent. The Strategic Response Group took up a position on the opposite side of the street. The officers in both squads wore bulky, bullet-resistant vests and combat-style helmets, fastened by thick chinstraps. Index fingers remained fixed to triggers on machine guns held to the side.

"Everything all set?" Vicki asked as she tapped Anthony on the shoulder.

"Damn it!" Anthony turned. "How many times do I have to tell you?"

Vicki grinned. "Sorry, I'm just so excited."

Anthony scanned the Great Hall for any lingering employees. Few employees were allowed inside the museum on the day of the gala. The vast majority were required to depart the building hours before the event started and invitees arrived to display their expensive outfits like runway models on the catwalk. "All the employees out of the museum?" he asked.

"Paul is taking care of that now."

"He does a good job clearing employees from the museum."

"And scaring the hell out of people," Vicki asserted while leaning to the side and looking beyond Anthony and out the entrance door, hoping to see someone famous.

Anthony crossed his arms, irked by Vicki's statement.

"That's not nice, Vicki. You know, when Paul and I were in the service together, the guys in the platoon constantly teased him about his appearance. They called him things like the Red Hulk or the Jolly Red Giant because of his size and his scraggly red hair." Anthony gazed at the marble floor, recalling the teasing. 'Ho Ho, Red Giant'. That was usually followed by: 'Don't get him angry. You wouldn't like him when he's angry'. Anthony raised his head. "The flushed complexion didn't help matters."

"So you've said, but I'm not talking about his appearance. There's just something else. Anyway," Vicki began with a more animated tone, "have you seen the decorations inside? They're incredible. I don't even recognize some of the galleries."

Anthony unfolded his arms and pointed out the door.

"I've been working with the police since I saw you earlier."

"You have to see the American Wing atrium. The entire atrium has been transformed into an elaborate banquet room. Flowers, at least ten feet long, dangle around the perimeter of the ceiling. They're spirally and are purple and white and lavender. I think they're wisteria," Vicki said, peeking out the entranceway doors again. "And the tables have the loveliest settings. I wonder who will sit at the dais this year."

"C'mon." Anthony turned and entered the museum. "This is going to start any minute. Let's go up to the balcony and watch people enter from there."

Crossing the Great Hall, Anthony and Vicki stopped in front of the twenty-foot-tall representation of Tullio Lombardo's *Adam* that soared above the information desk at the center of the hall. 'Renaissance & Resurgence in Fashion' was the theme of the gala, and Lombardo's marble statue of Adam, one of the great sculptural works of the High Renaissance, served as the gala's emblem. The plaster cast mimicked the contours of Lombardo's *Adam* and was covered with over 200,000 white-rose petals.

Anthony examined the floral display. "I can't get over how the museum's artists made this look so much like the real statue in gallery 504."

"The artisans who did the flower placement used a darker shade of white rose for Adam's fig leaf and hair," Vicki remarked as she walked around the statue and observed Adam's rear. "But this is nothing compared with what's in the Medieval Hall, where they're having the reception tonight. Mona Lisa's face is spread out across the Spanish choir screen with a combination of nearly a million different flowers."

"Who told you that?"

"I have my sources."

"And who might that be?"

"Friends who work in the Costume Institute."

Anthony looked up at the representation of *Adam*. "Well, they do a hell of a job, that's for sure. It's incredible how they get this stuff up overnight."

"It's too bad visitors never get to see the beautiful gala decorations. Then again, how many people can afford to pay the $35,000 price of the gala ticket?"

The red carpet put in place for the gala extended from the museum's entrance, through the Great Hall, and into the Byzantine galleries, but Anthony and Vicki climbed the Grand Staircase. They sat on a marble bench and waited for the celebrities to make their entrance. The Great Hall one level below was unusually quiet. It was the calm before the storm.

Anthony put his hand on his knee and winced.

"It's the wet weather, isn't it?" Vicki said with a pitying expression.

"It's not unusual for my leg to act up on humid days like this."

Vicki knew the gunshot wound that Anthony had received during a raid on a heroin syndicate operating out of Brooklyn never properly healed and pained him on wet days. "Look at it this way," she said supportively. "Your time on sabbatical provided you a great opportunity to go to Europe and get the training for your job here."

"Well, that's half true. There were no written guarantees, but I was told that Carabinieri Art Squad training would put me on the top of the list."

"I'll always treasure the time I spent in France."

Anthony angled his body into a more sympathetic position next to Vicki. "I know your dream is to become a professor, but you have a future here."

Vicki reflected on her passion for art history. It ran through her blood since she had vacationed in Paris with her family as a girl. The Louvre was enchanting, but she was awe-struck by the Impressionist paintings at the Musée d'Orsay and the Musée de l'Orangerie. She couldn't see enough. Monet, Manet, Cézanne, Renoir, Seurat, Degas, and van Gogh. It was her first encounter with Impressionist paintings, and she felt sensations she had never felt before. There was a stirring, an unexpected awakening. She recalled crying when her parents forced her to leave, but she knew then that she'd pursue her passion for Impressionist paintings. She studied art history in college and received a scholarship to the Sorbonne. After earning her graduate degree, she was offered a position as a teacher's assistant at a university in the south of France, but returned to New York not long after to help her mother after her father passed. She accepted the job at the Met over decade ago with the expectation of returning to France one day, but the right opportunity to return to France never presented itself. *C'est la vie.*

Contemplative-eyed, she said, "We'll see."

The sound of cameras clicking preceded the *oohs* and *ahhs* as the celebrities from the worlds of fashion, stage, television, and even politics alighted from stretch limousines and stepped onto the red carpet. Anyone who was someone yearned to be seen at the Met gala, and not a second was wasted before countless camera flashes flickered as shabbily dressed photographers yelled out names and asked for poses, while reporters with extended microphones shouted questions that were conceived to elicit personal information to serve as toxic hobgoblin for modern minds.

Bright flashes of light accompanied the attendees through the entrance.

"Here they come!" Vicki jumped to her feet and leaned on the swirled ivory-and-green marble balustrade surrounding the balcony. She pointed to the singer, actress walking through the entrance wearing a Renaissance, haute couture–styled gown modeled on the opulent outfit worn by Catherine de' Medici on her wedding day. The meticulously woven ashen-and-metallic-gold brocade dress puffed royally around her shoulders and erupted at the neck with a silken fabric intended to imitate the feathers of the exotic European ruff. Tight-fitting French sleeves hugged the arms down to the wrists. The skirt flared with an avant-garde elegance at the bottom. Sultry, flower-clad girls held up the extended train flashing spurious smiles.

"She's this year's queen of the gala." Vicki looked over her shoulder at Anthony. "Do you have any idea how much her dress cost?"

Anthony shook his head, unenthusiastically. "I don't think I want to know." He wasn't impressed by the pomp and circumstance. But he didn't wish to spoil Vicki's excitement. "That's too much," he said looking at the next woman entering the museum. "I mean too little."

Vicki sat, admiring the pop singer's button-down, leather Versace jacket ending at the midriff and allowing for a full visual of the nearly see-through lace ensemble covering her waist.

"Don't be such a stick in the mud. Those types of outfits are typical for these types of events. You should see what she wears in concert."

"I'll pass, thank you."

"What's the problem? I thought men liked that kind of stuff."

"I have daughters the same age." Anthony's mumbled statement was inaudible over the mounting chatter of the excited invitees one flight below.

"Oh, lighten up. She wears that outfit so elegantly. She's simply sensational. And look at those platform boots. Twelve inches, at least!"

Anthony didn't bother to look at the pop singer's boots, but instead kept his gaze fixed on the queen of the gala wearing the Catherine de' Medici outfit. "Did you know that Catherine de' Medici invented high heels?"

"See, I knew you had an interest in fashion."

"The only reason I know that is because she wore the heels at her wedding to Henry II of France, who started the War of 1551, aka, the Last Italian War." Anthony surveyed the museum's Great Hall, astounded by the sheer pomp and circumstance of the Met's annual gala. The cast of glitterati filled the entrance. Confetti floated in the air. It was incredible, he reflected with a change of mind. For one day, the Met transformed from one of the world's great institutions of art and enlightenment into a glitzy, star-studded venue.

He felt a sense of pride in his job. An even prouder feeling surfaced with the thought of his decision to mentor Vicki. He saw great things for her future.

Paul's voice came through the two-way radio.

"Did Paul just say that there are people having oral sex in gallery 501?" Vicki's jaw dropped. "They just got here like five minutes ago."

"Relax, this type of stuff happens every year."

"I can't believe it."

"You'd think they'd learn, but we usually catch three or four people fooling around or smoking every year." Anthony shook his head. "They just don't seem to comprehend that we can see the entire museum on camera."

"What are you going to do about it?"

"You mean, what are *you* going to do about it?" he said while pointing at Vicki. Anthony stood. "Here's your chance to get into the party."

CHAPTER 19

LEN LEE SQUEEZED INTO HIS JACKET, tightened his tie, and gazed out a window of his office on the forty-first floor of the sleek skyscraper on Madison Avenue. He could feel the pulsing in his forehead as he massaged his temples and gazed downward at the congested midtown streets nearly five hundred feet below, bustling with people spilling out in an endless torrent from the various Grand Central passageway exits like ants from nests. In a few minutes, he'd meet a new client. A worrisome client. A client that most financial institutions around the world stopped doing business with years ago.

He reflected on his life growing up in Queens, in a household where Mandarin was the sole language. He scored in the top-ten percentile on the New York City Specialized High Schools Admissions Test and was courted by counselors at a dozen top city high schools. College was a breeze. Obtaining an MBA was even less of a challenge. He landed a high-paying job at a premiere investment bank and swiftly ascended to vice president. But Len didn't fit the bank's profile for managing director, so he took a job with another investment bank where he was asked to take on clients that most investment banks around the globe had severed ties with long ago.

ANTHONY'S DRIVER DOUBLE-PARKED alongside the normal morning line of company cars and taxis dropping off employees at the bank. He exited the car and entered the skyscraper built on a combination of hubris and countless underhanded deals. Stock prices flashed incessantly in familiar blue lights on the back wall as Anthony approached the welcome desk and smiled at the guard in the corporate security uniform.

"Good morning. I'm here to see Mr. Len Lee."

The security guard turned away from his phone and regarded Anthony with a blasé expression. "Do you have an appointment with Mr. Lee?"

"At 8:30, I believe."

"Believe," the guard remarked, condescension evident. "Your name?"

Anthony provided his driver's license and waited for the usual response as the guard typed in his name. "You're scheduled to see Mr. Lee at –" the guard stated and then fell silent after discovering Anthony's identity as the Met's director of security. He looked up with a half-grin. "8:30 is correct, sir," he said, handing back the license and a temporary ID sticker. "You're right on time. Take the elevator to the forty-first floor."

THE HANDSOME FACIAL features of the man in Len's office weren't offset by the kind of jowly cheeks portrayed on subjects painted during the Renaissance – *grandi mascelle*, as the Italians pointedly say. A broad platysma muscle stretched from his cheeks to the bottom of his neck, then covered by the tight-fitting collar of his Ermenegildo Zegna shirt.

Len thanked his assistant and shook Anthony's hand.

"Mr. Armata is a representative of IOR," Len informed Anthony, making the introductions. "My company is honored to have him here with us today."

"Istituto per le Opere di Religione," Fabrizio stated, remaining seated.

"The Vatican Bank," Len clarified to resolve any confusion.

Fabrizio turned from Len with a vacant smile, sipped his sparkling water, and gently returned the glass to the coffee table. "Signor Leonardi, I am informed that you're a busy man, so let me get to the point, but first let me commend you on your long and distinguished career. I understand that you served with distinction as a commander in the American military, then worked your way up in the ranks with the New York City police department." A sense of approval almost showed in Fabrizio's expression before he continued speaking. "I believe you even came to my country and worked with the Comando Carabinieri Tutela Patrimonio Culturale. *Bravissimo*! We at the Vatican Bank, I can assure you, are grateful to all those who assist with the sacred task of safekeeping of art and antiquities."

Anthony grinned and sat. Silence was the best option, especially since he didn't have the time to do the background research on Fabrizio. Nor was it his job to investigate every Tom, Dick and Harry who claimed that the museum had wrongfully possessed something that belonged to them.

Fabrizio's accent shifted from standard Italian to a Romanesco-dialect. "There are similarities in our lines of work, Signore. The Vatican Bank was founded with the crucial mission of preserving great works of religious art."

Len interjected. "And now they wish to reclaim the painting."

"Which painting are we talking about?" Anthony asked, wondering why there seemed to be deliberate omission of the name of the painting at issue.

Fabrizio stood and crossed Len's office with measured paces as he spoke.

"*La Pietà*," he said using the Italian description of the biblical scene in which Mary holds her son's body, "was commissioned for a special church in Roma. Tell me, Signore, are you familiar with the Church of the Gesù?"

"I've only seen pictures," Anthony responded.

Fabrizio placed himself alongside one of three tinted windows in Len's office designed to temper the intense rays of the sun. At that hour, the glare off the chrome-colored window trim bested the tint. "The Church of the Gesù is the mother church for the Jesuit Order, as you may be aware. Pulzone painted the lamentation scene to serve as an altarpiece in the Cappella della Passione, one of several grand chapels in the church."

"How did it end up in New York?" Anthony asked, focused.

Fabrizio gazed out the window, fixing his sights on the pyramidal roof of the Helmsley Building, several blocks south as he spoke. "I'm afraid I cannot answer that question. When it was taken from the church is not clear."

Anthony's face contoured crossly as he checked his watch.

"This will be the first of several meetings, I'm sure," Len stated sensing some friction. "I think it would be constructive if we can walk away today with a simple meeting of the minds on the fundamentals of the transaction. Of course, there's a great degree of discretion in this matter," Len added.

Anthony nodded in agreement. "I'll be sure to relay your interest in the painting to the appropriate people at the museum, Mr. Armata. What exactly did you have in mind, that is, regarding the terms of the return?"

Fabrizio adjusted his tie and walked back to the center of Len's office.

"Who at the museum makes these such decision?" he asked.

It was a probing question, and Anthony saw right through it, but the answer wasn't confidential information, so he answered.

"It wouldn't be just one person, but a number of people would be involved in the decision before it was brought up to the Board of Trustees for approval, I believe. But I'd have to get verification on that."

"Would you happen to know the names of these trustees?"

Anthony didn't hesitate with a reply. "Not off hand, sorry."

"You can get that information from the Met's Annual Report, Mr. Armata," Len readily offered. "It's on the museum's website."

Assessing eyes connected, fixed for a moment in time.

"It's the most prestigious board in New York. Correct me if I am wrong, Mr. Leonardi, but the big wigs on the board pay ten million for their seats."

Icy-green irises tinged with hazel flashed with an unexpected sensation of incredulity. Americans were naively forthcoming with information, Fabrizo sensed. The Holy See wasn't as accommodating.

"I would very much appreciate if you can see to it that this matter is expedited, Signore. I must return to Rome immediately."

Wishing to push the subject tactfully, Anthony said, "You'll have to excuse my ignorance, but are you talking about paying for the painting?"

"I don't see why a payment is necessary in order to return the painting to its rightful place. Please understand, *Signore*, Pulzone painted the altarpiece with no intention of having it removed." Fabrizio turned to Len. "Still, I suppose an honorarium could be arranged. I will see what I can do about transferring some discretionary funds, shall we say, to Mr. Lee's bank."

Anthony rose and took out his wallet. He heard all he needed. "Here's my business card, Mr. Armata. Why don't you talk to the people on your end about the best way to handle this," he remarked, now with a better understanding of why he was asked to be involved in the negotiations. "I'll get clarification on my end, then we can discuss the matter further."

Fabrizio extended his hand, his content expression hidden with a bow. "*Grazie*, Signore. I look forward to hearing from you as soon as possible."

"Oh, one last question, Mr. Armata," Anthony added, smiling and waiting until he had clear eye contact. He purposely withheld the question to the end. "Has the Italian Cultural Ministry been informed of this matter?"

Fabrizio leered at Len as he spoke. "At this juncture, there's no reason to involve government officials or anyone who'd possibly make this public."

"Of course." Anthony grinned and walked out of the office.

* ~ * ~ *

VICKI DESCENDED A flight of stairs and paced the main galleries of the Greek and Roman collections. She examined the garland wreaths carved on a Roman sarcophagus, the very first item in the Met's collection, recalling what Margarita had said about the pagan use of garlands. A more ornate sarcophagus to the side displayed a likeness of Dionysus, patron god of the arts and figurehead for an ancient sect that paid homage to the arts. Vicki knew of Dionysus's association with art, but it wasn't until she began working at the Met that she learned about the Dionysus sect that had become known for its advancements in the science of architecture. Utilizing time-honored secrets, the Dionysiac Architects engineered many of the great temples of antiquity. Their knowledge was passed down, mouth to ear, and was later used in constructing the great cathedrals of Europe. Each cathedral was uniquely ornamented with symbols and scenes of secret esoteric initiations. A millennium later, few have deciphered the iconography.

"Hi, Vicki!"

The security manager of the Greek and Roman galleries rose from his desk. "Something wrong?" he asked. A toadying smile followed.

"Nothing wrong, Steve." Vicki knew Steve was a bit of a busybody. "I'm here on a personal matter. It's kind of silly, so I don't want to trouble you."

Steve stroked his downy mustache. "Please, how can I help?"

Vicki scanned the large Greek and Roman peristyle sculpture court. Natural light poured through large skylights in the vaulted ceiling, warming an army of life-size statues of gods, goddesses, and notable historical figures. Turning back to Steve, Vicki said, "I'm trying to find something in this collection with any type of connection to Egypt."

Steve pointed. "There's a bust over there alongside the wall of a Greek man who visited Egypt, I believe."

"Thanks, Steve. I'll take a look."

She grinned and glided across the shiny black-and-white mosaic-tile floor of the open court, passing a large bronze statue of Hermes-Thoth without realizing the importance of the Greco-Egyptian god. Hermes Trismegistusas, a small placard explained, was an Egyptian philosopher and founder of the Ancient Mystery School. Like all gods with psychopompic abilities, he was revered as a sovereign guide into the afterlife. Many ancients viewed him as the founder of all religion and some as the foreseer of Christianity.

Vicki stopped in front of a row of Greek busts on tall podiums.

"At the end!" Steve hollered.

She identified the piece Steve indicated and read the accompanying plaque, which suggested that the marble bust was likely the cast representation of a Greek man named Solon, but little else.

Noticing that Steve was engaged with a visitor, Vicki quietly exited the Greek and Roman galleries and entered the museum library. She sat in front of a computer, clicked on the museum's electronic catalog system, and searched the vast database with missionary intensity until she discovered that Solon was a sixth-century B.C. Athenian statesman and the sole descendant of the last king of Athens. He was also considered one of the Seven Sages of Greece, statesmen celebrated for their exceptional wisdom.

Her search results also brought up Plato's dialogue with Critias, recounting the fabled battle between Atlantis and Athens, a story once forgotten, but preserved by the Egyptians. Solon brought the epic tale back to Greece after he journeyed to the temple of the Egyptian goddess of war, Neith, located in the town of Sais in the Western Nile Delta.

Curious, Vicki ran a search for secret societies and sculptures. The first hit referenced the bust of Benjamin Franklin by French sculptor Jean-Antoine Houdon. Apparently, both artist and subject were Rosicrucians and Freemasons. The search also brought up results showing Franklin laying the cornerstone in Philadelphia's Independence Hall in full Masonic garb. The website led to another site showing George Washington leading the ritual ceremony during the placement of the cornerstone in the United States Capitol. The secrets of the Old World had made it to America.

CHAPTER 20

ANTHONY SCUTTLED THROUGH THE MUSEUM, WONDERING if his job was to oversee security or if he was actually being paid to bounce from meeting to meeting. He was on his way to his third meeting of the day, and it was barely noon.

Anthony ran into Cy Hetford in the elevator on his way to the patrons lounge, the Met's posh restaurant that catered only to wealthy members and high-ranking museum officials. They were shown to a table in the first of the lounge's two rooms, the main dining space, which accommodated only a handful of diners at a given time. The small but bright room, lavishly decorated with tasteful, antique furniture, was embellished with a handful of masterpieces, selected from the Met's extensive collection.

The lounge had taken on the midday scent of eau de haute couture.

A staff member pulled out mahogany armchairs from beneath the polished mahogany table. Table and chairs were Rococo-styled.

The waiter served baked cheese twists and water. He placed two prix fixe menus on the table, removed a pen and pad from the pocket of his white serving jacket, and smiled readily. Both men knew the choices by heart. Anthony ordered the pan-seared breast of chicken and asked for a salad in place of the potatoes. He declined the desert. Cy settled for the sautéed fillet of salmon and stressed a glass of his usual white wine.

"This is my second time up here today," Anthony informed Cy as the waiter collected the menus and departed. "I was in a real yawner across the hall in the trustees' conference room this morning."

"Board of Trustees, huh?" Cy remarked with a contemptuous sneer. "Was it the full board, or did you meet with the Executive Committee?"

Anthony ducked the question. "I'm not sure, to be honest. I've been in so many meetings lately. It's hard to remember one from the other."

Cy slouched into the plush cushioning of the leather seat, placing his arms on the armrests. "I called the security office several times, but I couldn't get through to you. Frankly, it's quite infuriating. And no one in your office would give me a straight answer regarding what the security footage showed concerning the atrocities happening in the temple."

Anthony leisurely unfolded his napkin and placed it on his lap, mentally preparing himself for his reply. He knew it would not go over well.

He gazed at the dark walnut bookshelf that partially covered the wall on the north side of the lounge. Next to the bookshelf, two well-dressed, white-haired women sat on a pillowy sofa with their legs crossed in the same direction. Both wore red shoes. Another woman with a shawl around her shoulders and a man in a suit that appeared to fit too tightly sat on plush recliners flanking the couch. The four Patrons sipped tea from porcelain teacups with the utmost show of etiquette. A similar furniture arrangement abutted the rear wall, accommodating a similar set of people. Tall, stylish lamps bounded sofas like bookends, but the large skylight provided more than enough light for the room. Anthony turned his attention back to Cy.

"It seems there's a problem with some of the cameras in the Egyptian galleries. A glitch of some sort, so we didn't get any playback."

"Glitch?" Cy sat up and removed his glasses. "Are you telling me that the cameras weren't working on the night of Miller's death?"

"I'm afraid it's true." Anthony sipped his water.

"Someone must be held accountable!" Cy declared, hitting the table to punctuate his statement. The undeviating stare made it clear who he meant. "Has the president been apprised of this situation?"

"She's aware," Anthony said evenly and altered the direction of the conversation. "I met with David Graham the other day. He has the most bizarre replica of an erotic scene from Egypt on his apartment wall."

"You met David in his apartment?" Cy leaned forward and selected a cheese twist. "Ah, yes, the Turin Erotic Papyrus, known, of course, in more vulgar circles as the first men's magazine." He bit into the pastry, and continued as he chewed. "I'm sure David gave you an earful on that papyrus. I can hear it now. He probably told you that the papyrus was hidden from public view for years, and plenty of other outrageous things. The Turin Papyrus has been on display in the Turin Museum since it was discovered."

Anthony felt a tightening with a realization. "Is that why it's called the Turin Erotic Papyrus? Because the papyrus is owned by the Turin Museum?"

"The Museo Egizio in Turin, Italy, owns the largest collection of Egyptian papyri outside Cairo, thanks to the pillaging by Bernardino Drovetti." Cy averted his stare, fixing his sight on the far wall. "That's strange. I don't think I've ever noticed that Renoir on the wall over there."

Anthony didn't bother to look at the painting.

"When we were in the temple last week, you seemed reluctant to talk about the names carved into the walls. Do you mind telling me why?"

The sun flared like pointed, white flames in the flatware as Cy began. "Some say that Drovetti and the others who chiseled their names inside the Temple of Dendur," he confessed, "used the temple to conduct rituals when it was still in Egypt. But that's simply out of the question."

"Why is that?" Anthony probed.

"Girolamo Segato, the other person who you asked about, was a distinguished Egyptologist, so it's highly unlikely that he'd engage in such profane ceremonies. Egyptologists are trained to take a very orthodox approach to ancient beliefs and customs."

"What was Segato best known for?"

Anthony knew the answer. He had Paul McDonough look into the names carved into the temple and he was astonished by what Paul uncovered.

Cy placed his glasses on the table. He leaned back in his chair, hesitated before speaking, then said, "Segato discovered many things, but he's best known for mastering the process of perfectly preserving the human body, a process that some claim Segato learned while he was in Egypt."

Anthony placed his elbows on the table, and clasped his hands together. Doubt reflected in his brown eyes. "You're telling me that Drovetti, Segato, and all the other people who carved their names into the walls of the Temple of Dendur in the nineteenth century were just leaving their mark?"

"Carving names on a shrine was as common several centuries ago as two teenagers carving names into a tree today. It was an acceptable thing to do, unfortunately." Cy raised his hand, index finger pointed up. "Now, inscribing hierogrammatics in a temple is another story altogether. That's a bad sign. An omen of things to come. Bad things. I can't stress that enough, Anthony."

The upward eye movement that accompanied Cy's statement spoke volumes. As a police officer, Anthony had assessed the credibility of suspects' statements by using the Reid Technique—a questioning technique used by law enforcement—and he knew that Cy's eye movement indicated that he wasn't being forthcoming with the facts.

The waiter returned, used his table crumber in front of Cy, and placed a tall, Waterford crystal, wine glass on the table. With a practiced smile, he stood erect, uncorked the bottle, and offered a sniff. With no response, he maintained his smile and poured the Chardonnay into the glass.

"Of course, the Egyptians conducted rituals in temples." Cy swirled his wine. The tears were to his liking. "Don't get me wrong. We own a small statue of Pharaoh Nectanebo II, the very last Egyptian pharaoh, who engaged in some rather outlandish rituals inside temples."

A generous sip of wine resulted in a slightly calmer voice.

"Can I assume that you are unaware that the Met is the only museum in the world to own a complete representation of pharaoh Nectanebo II?"

Anthony didn't answer, forcing an awkward pause.

"It's a crying shame that so many employees here know so little about the museum's collection. You'd think they'd take advantage while working here. I'd strongly suggest that you take a look at the piece. Nectanebo was a fascinating pharaoh. Of course, he had to move around a lot because Egypt was under constant siege by the Persian and the Greek armies during his reign, so shrines dedicated to him have been found in numerous places, like Heliopolis and Karnak, though he spent most of his time in Memphis."

"Memphis, Egypt?"

Anthony instantly wished he could retract the question.

Cy gulped his wine, relishing his next statement. "I suppose many Americans don't know the location of the original Memphis, or that it served as the first capital of Egypt." He laughed and waved what was left of the cheese twist like a magic wand as he spoke. "As I was saying, some say Nectanebo moved to Nubia. Others claim that he traveled to Macedonia disguised as a magician while Philip II was at war and he seduced Philip's wife. Nine months later, none other than Alexander the Great was born."

The sunlight in the lounge made Cy's cornflower-blue eyes appear distinctly more steely-blue. Despite the high-handedness, the difficult personality, and even the tiresome condescension, Anthony respected Cy for his knowledge of the ancient world. He was admired by most at the museum for the advancements that he had made in the field of Egyptology. But Anthony also knew the smart ones masked their secrets well.

* ~ * ~ *

VICKI ENTERED THE elevator on the north side of the building and placed her special access RFID-encrypted ID next to the scanner. When the light flashed red, she pressed the S2 button. All Met employees had access to the first of several lower levels of the museum, but only a few had clearance to descend to the lowest levels. Most employees had no inkling that there were lower levels. But two floors below ground level was the museum's concealed gun range, an antiquated remnant from the days when carrying a gun in New York City was commonplace. The museum kept the range open for its employees who were licensed to carry a gun and required by New York State law to prove they met strict, state marksmanship requirements.

Vicki took the time during her lunch break to use the range. Her encounter with the men in Fort Tryon Park was still weighing on her mind.

She exited the elevator and stepped out into a hushed hallway.

What a difference two floors make, she thought. Upstairs, the museum bustled with thousands of visitors and employees, all stirring up an energy and noise concoction that pulsed daily throughout the museum. Two floors below, a dropped pin resounded.

She placed her ID against the scanner on the side of the door. The lock clicked open, and Vicki pushed open the soundproof door, cringing as she absorbed the noise of gunshots and lead dust inside the firing range.

"Taking care of your state qualification?" the guard at the desk asked. "Keep in mind, Vicki, it doesn't hurt to work on your gun skills more than twice a year."

"I'll take that under advisement, Gene."

Vicki filled out the qualification card and returned it to Gene.

"See you in another six months," she said with a departing smile.

At the locker alcove, Vicki unfastened the magnetic closure on her pistol range bag and removed her shooting gear and KelTec semi-automatic. She stuffed the bag into a locker and 'doubled up' on the way to the firing line by putting in earplugs and then securing noise-canceling earmuffs. Safety glasses secured, Vicki positioned herself while racking the slide and emptied the Glock's magazine with dead-on precision. She holstered the gun, removed her KelTec tucked into her belt, and fired a second round.

CHAPTER 21

THE HALLWAY WAS GHOSTLY SILENT.

Vicki unclipped her ID from her belt when she reached the elevator and held it up to the scanner until the red light flashed. She pressed the elevator button and gazed at the floor indication as she waited, thinking that her gun skills were up to par.

Before her brain processed the startling noise, her body had already jolted. Her head swiveled as her eyes darted about, tracking the noise with her senses.

"Is that you, Gene?" she said aloud. No one answered.

A minute passed. Then two as Vicki observed the lit numbers above the elevator. It was stuck on a floor above, and Vicki knew what that meant. That particular elevator was four times the size of a normal elevator, designed for the movement of larger museum items. Someone was using it to move something in the collection. That meant a long wait, and she was in no mood to linger. The lead dust inside the firing range had irritated her eyes; the gunshots had pierced her gear and her ears were still ringing.

Another noisy clamor. This time closer. Now, she had to investigate.

Vicki homed in on the noise, turning a corner at the end of the hallway, but didn't see anyone. She raced down a connecting hallway that stretched another two hundred feet or so and was also vacant. The bizarre noise abruptly stopped, but Vicki was now determined to find out who or what was responsible for making such a racket in a highly-restricted area. But there were endless hallways underneath the museum, half she had never explored. The hallways leading to the museum's electrical power plant was the first thought that entered her mind. Perhaps head north to the main boiler room under the Greek and Roman collection? Or the museum's fire station? The fire warden was bound to be there, and he may have seen someone.

Another clash, and Vicki's head jerked. She rushed toward the sound, where she spotted someone. He was exiting the only door in the hallway.

She contemplated yelling out *Hello* to get him to turn, but she decided against the idea. She didn't have a good reason to engage him.

The man hightailed in the opposite direction with brisk strides. His head was down and partially covered by a red cap.

Vicki advanced, making sure he remained in sight.

Before rounding a corner, the man looked over his shoulder and smiled.

Vicki halted in her tracks. *Is that the same guy from the subway and from Fort Tryon Park?* He was too far away to tell for sure. Besides, she just now realized, she never got a good look at his face either time.

"Hey!" she shouted, rushing down the hallway and rounding the corner. The connecting corridor was empty – as was the next hallway, which terminated with a stairwell. She entered and stilled, hoping to hear footsteps.

Silence settled in the stairwell. Vicki took a halting step up, then stopped.

"Command Center, come in," she said raising her radio to her face, but there was no reception that far underground. Vicki quickly backtracked.

As she passed the door where the man had emerged, she stopped, unlocked the door, and peeked inside the room. A peculiar radiance at the rear of the room gave her pause, sparking her curiosity. Amber light with hues of orange and variants of yellow projected through aligned gaps between items stacked on shelves, marking a distinctive path.

Unfamiliar with the room, Vicki entered.

Aside from Katsushika Hokusai's woodblock print, popularly known as *The Great Wave*, all the shelved items looked unfamiliar. She unhooked her flashlight from her utility belt and pointed it in all directions. A spiral staircase that appeared to be as old as the museum itself corkscrewed one flight up in the corner. Vicki guessed that she was now directly below the Registrar's Office, the most restricted and secured area of the museum, where priceless items were moved into and out of the collection.

A level smile accompanied the realization that she had discovered the room that served as the conduit to move museum items while circumventing security protocols. She drew her attention away from the dimly lit surroundings and recalled the two items that had been improperly moved to the trustees' conference room—Salvator Rosa's sketch with the secret society watermark and the painting of George Washington as a Freemason.

I'm on to you people, she said to herself.

A shelf held a Tiffany lamp with a floral shade. A manuscript with a captivating cover twinkled from the radiance of the softly-lite lamp. Slipping on latex gloves, Vicki picked up the manuscript despite herself. She knew that she should be in pursuit of the man she just saw in the hallway, but she sensed that she was on to something bigger.

On the cover, LA TRÈS SAINTE TRINOSOPHIE was written inside a golden circle in the center. The style of the script suggested that the document was old, likely rare. Bordering the circle, or what had the appearance of some sort of void or portal, were twelve smaller multihued plates. Each plate contained esoteric symbols, suggestive of an antiquitous zodiac. Some of the plates contained Egyptian symbolism, like the multicolored falcon on the top left-hand corner or the adjacent pyramid inside what appeared to be the radiant sun. Another plate contained a palm tree and water vessel. A plate on the right side of the cover displayed a man wearing a conical hat and engaging in a ritual.

She flipped the cover page and read the name signed on the flyleaf.

Count Hompesch

The placement of the manuscript may or may not have been intentional, but two things were certain. The manuscript did not belong in that room. Even more obvious, whoever the elusive man was, he was surely baiting her for something. But what?

* ~ * ~ *

ANTHONY AND VICKI crossed the equestrian court in the center of the Arms and Armor galleries in the shadows of the life-size display of crusading knights on horseback. At closing time, faint light filtered through the gallery's clerestory windows. The three-story-high gallery was taking on its usual vesper luminosity, produced by large, circular, medieval-style chandeliers hanging from the ceiling. Several employees passed through the court as they exited for the day. Guards ushered visitors to the main entrance.

They entered a side gallery, where Albert Bennington was standing next to the glass display case containing the saber. Vicki called out his name.

Albert recoiled in a dramatic way. "Oh, there you are."

Anthony clasped hands with Albert and placed his left hand on the frame of the display case. "Tell me something, Albert," he said pulling no punches and looking through Albert's horned-rimmed glasses at his close-set eyes, trying to detect movement. "What's behind this display case?"

"Nothing that I am aware of," Albert replied with a slight flinch.

Content with Albert's reply, Anthony followed up by saying, "Vicki informed me that this particular weapon has a uniquely sharp blade."

"It's one of our prized pieces."

Anthony stared at the saber as he spoke. "I've always wondered if this weapon was made from the Damascus steel that was prized by crusaders?"

Despite the trace of uneasiness in his voice, Albert responded with a collected composure. "I'm impressed by your question, Anthony. Not many people know about Damascus steel. Few indeed, but we believe this blade was forged in Persia in the middle of the seventeenth century."

"Anyone removed it lately?" Vicki asked.

"You mean, remove the saber from this display case? Certainly not."

Vicki examined the saber, contemplating what Albert had said the last time about the mysterious wording in the chamber found underneath the middle emerald. Stepping closer to the display case, she said, "The mount for the top emerald on the scabbard was flipped open when we were here the last time, I believe. Now it's closed."

Albert bumped his fingertips together several times before taking off his glasses. He wiped the lenses clean with the sleeve of his shirt, put the glasses back on, and moved closer to the display case for a better look. "Hmm, I guess someone on my staff must have polished it," he replied in a backtracking tone. "We like to keep them shiny."

"That's understandable, Albert," Vicki said, pondering an ulterior motive.

CHAPTER 22

VICKI AND SIBYL MET IN THE fountain room of the employee cafeteria below a replica of a celebrated painting of a young Dutch woman wearing a blue dress and holding a silver water pitcher.

"I didn't see you this morning," Sibyl remarked. "In early again?"

Vicki hung her uniform jacket on the back of the chair and sat.

"It's been a hectic morning, to put it mildly."

"See the ping that I sent to you earlier?"

"I saw your text, but I didn't have a chance to read it." Vicki covered her mouth and yawned. "Excuse me. We got a shipment for the Georgia O'Keeffe show late last night and I've been at the loading dock since six."

"No worries. It just says that Margarita sent me something from the gift shop at The Cloisters." Sibyl placed a small, black-velvet box on the table and opened it. "It's a charm necklace with an Egyptian ankh."

"It's lovely," Vicki remarked, holding up the necklace.

"Vick," Sibyl began in an advising tone, "I think Margarita sent this to me to set me up. Why else would she send it out of the blue?"

"Set you up for what?" Vicki asked, surprise showing in her sleepy eyes.

"The ankh was an Egyptian symbol for eternal life. See where I am going with this? See the connection?" Sibyl asked, bobbing her head "Listen, I know Margarita well. When I thank her for the necklace, trust me, she'll use that as an opportunity to turn the conversation to the *Crata Repoa*."

"I gave the *Crata Repoa* to Anthony before the gala on Monday. I told her that I was giving it to him." Vicki took a bite of her sandwich.

Sibyl's pink-tinted eyebrows rose above the rims of her glasses. She thought briefly and asked, "What did Anthony have to say about it?"

"He has someone at The Cloisters looking into the matter." Vicki moved her chair in and hunched over the table. "Can you believe it? It turns out that the title of one of the sections of the *Crata Repoa* is uncannily similar to words carved into the Temple of Dendur last week."

"Really?" Sibyl said, staring at the ankh. "That can't be accidental."

Vicki reflected on her trip to The Cloisters. "You know, I found the *Crata Repoa* under the tomb of Jean d'Alluye. I don't think I mentioned that to you before, but did you know that there's a flower etched on his shield? Margarita says the flower might be a representation of Leonardo da Vinci's Flower of Life."

Sibyl sipped her kombucha and swished it around her mouth while contemplating. She pushed up her glasses, her hazel-green eyes showing doubt. She thought for a second, then shook her head. "Not possible. Think about it, Vick. D'Alluye lived centuries before da Vinci."

"Exactly what I thought, but Margarita seemed convinced of it."

Sibyl eyed the replica of Vermeer's *Woman with a Water Jug* on the wall, knowing that most people overlooked the string of pearls on the gold jewelry box. The young woman in the picture appeared so serene, so tranquil. She turned back to Vicki. "You look tired. You're working too hard."

"It's not work. I was up late last night looking into something I found yesterday." Vicki lowered her voice. "This may sound completely crazy, but I think someone may have even wanted me to find it."

"Find what?"

Sibyl wasn't authorized to access the sublevels, so Vicki kept the information brief. "I found a manuscript signed by Count Hompesch."

Sibyl adjusted her glasses again, poked at her salad, and speared a small cube of tofu. "Never heard of him," she remarked, raising her fork to her mouth.

"The name of the manuscript is *La Très Sainte Trinosophie.*"

"*La Très Sainte Trinosophie!*" Sibyl shrieked and gulped down her food with her hand covering her clip-on tie. "That was written by St. Germain."

Vicki took another bite of her sandwich and stared at the fountain in the middle of the room. Nearby conversations faded while auditory senses picked up the gentle dripping sound. Her desire to teach art history was taking a backseat to a growing interest in the art of sleuthing, she realized.

$$* \sim * \sim *$$

WHILE VICKI AND Sibyl were in the cafeteria, Anthony and Paul were behind the museum investigating Humming Tombstone. Anthony had recruited Paul to fill a logistics position in the Security Department several years after accepting the position of director of security. Since that time, Paul rose to the position of second-in-command. His duties varied from overseeing the daily operations of C3 to such things as accompanying Anthony on inspections . . . Humming Tombstone in this case.

The saxophonist filled the Greywacke Arch with notes of 'Tomorrow' from the Broadway play *Annie* as the two walked under Central Park Drive and exited on the west side. Anthony carried a heavy-duty leather bag containing various tools.

Anthony also asked Paul to run a background check on Fabrizio, and he had discovered that INTERPOL put Fabrizio on a list of possible money launderers, though an investigation was never initiated because of rules that prevent INTERPOL from initiating any investigation that could have possible religious implications.

"I just don't get it," Anthony said. "I'm at a total loss trying to figure out why Fabrizio is interested in a painting done for the Jesuit Church."

"Maybe the Black Pope requested it."

Anthony placed the bag down alongside the juniper bushes on the perimeter of the Greywacke Knoll. He removed his sunglasses, eyes squinted.

"For Pete's sake, Paul. You know that's not his real title." The unrelenting heat wave was catching up with Anthony. Never in his sixty-plus years did he recall a summer heat wave lasting so long in New York City. The high temperature and intolerable humidity affected his sleep; he had little appetite for days on end. The investigation of the death in the Temple of Dendur was going nowhere. "I'm sorry. It's just this damn weather."

"You know what I mean, Tony, the Superior General of the Jesuit Order. All Jesuits of high rank are beholden to him. *All high-ranking Jesuits*," Paul stressed.

Anthony contemplated the implications of Paul's statements.

"What's that old Latin saying?" Paul asked. "*Perinde ac cadaver?*"

Anthony's head shook with disapproval. He first heard the rumors about the Jesuit motto while earning his graduate degree at Fordham University. Literally translated, the saying translates as 'in the manner of a corpse', and purportedly was incorporated into an oath taken by Jesuits who vow to possess no opinion of their own or to exercise any free will, but to obey every command received from their superiors. It was a troublesome thought. Anthony shot Paul a look that left little question about his displeasure.

"Look, Tony, I'm just saying –"

"And I think you should stay focused on this Armata guy."

Paul sensibly changed the subject.

"Want to tell me why we left the comfort of an air-conditioned building to come out here in this tropical heat? I feel like I'm back in Nam."

Anthony lifted the heavy leather bag and pointed to the tall box a dozen yards from the path described as Humming Tombstone by David Graham. "Someone suggested that this box is an entrance to a tunnel that goes underneath the museum."

"Through there?" Paul questioned, staring skeptically at the square structure.

"Unlikely, I know, but we should check it out."

Anthony and Paul walked over to the small grassy area on the opposite side of the paved path from Cleopatra's Needle, the site of Humming Tombstone. They glanced at one another and, without hesitation or utterance, stretched their legs, one by one, over the three-foot-high, metal mesh fence surrounding the perimeter of the grassy area.

The limestone-encased box was shaped like any ordinary upright headstone, but it was four times as tall and equally as wide. It sat on a solid, limestone base. The vertical tablet section framed swinging doors.

"Tony, I'm pretty sure this box houses the electrical system for the Delacorte Theater," Paul remarked, pointing at the theater to the west known worldwide as the venue for the summer Shakespeare in the Park evening performances. "That's why there's humming noise inside."

The empty theater to the west basked soundlessly in the rays of the high-noon sun directly overhead. Around the circumference of the public theater, countless black theater lights dangled from a web of aluminum scaffolding. Anthony opened his fist, allowing the leather bag to fall to the grass. He removed the bolt cutters from the bag, approached the tombstone, and effortlessly snipped the lock. "Let's see what's in this thing," he said, opening the swinging doors.

"Make sure you're properly grounded, Tony!" Paul yelled.

"I'll be damned. You're right, Paul. It's just a bunch of wires."

He closed the doors and stared at the box, wondering if his investigative abilities were waning. He knew David was a crackpot. He knew his theories were farfetched. He was now convinced that Cy had sent him to David on a wild goose chase. Why?

CHAPTER 23

FOR THE FIRST TIME SINCE SUMMER started, Vicki felt an invigorating evening breeze as she and Sibyl exited the museum for the day. The lower-setting sun was partially blocked by the south tower of the swanky San Remo apartment building on Central Park West. She gazed at the twilight twinkle flicking from the twenty-two-foot-tall copper lanterns on top of the building's Corinthian temples rising twenty-seven stories in the air. The twin, ten-story-tall temples were designed to replicate the Choragic Monument of Lysicrates, erected in the Acropolis of Athens over two thousand years earlier by the Dionysiac Architects. As she strolled under the spirally American elm trees at the rear of the museum, she realized that the Dionysiac Architects were still in fashion with the wealthy.

Abruptly, Vicki grabbed Sibyl's arm and stopped her from walking onto Central Park Drive as a line of four or five reckless cyclists drafting one another whooshed by with shouts of vulgarities.

Vicki refrained from yelling back but uttered, "Asshole bikers."

Across the drive, they found a shaded bench on the south side of the Jacqueline Kennedy Onassis Reservoir. The steel clock above the reservoir's South Gatehouse declared 5:37 P.M. but ran one hour behind during daylight saving time.

Vicki removed *La Très Sainte Trinosophie* from her purse, placed it on her lap, and scooted closer to Sibyl. A sudden gust of wind skimmed off the smooth surface of the expansive reservoir, blowing her long hair into her face as she examined the colorful cover.

She opened the manuscript and read the poem penned on the inside cover:

Curieux scrutateur de la Nature entière,
J'ai connu du grand tout le principe et la fin.
J'ai vu l'or en puissance au fond de sa rivière
J'ai saisi sa matière et surpris son levain.

J'expliquai par quel art l'âme aux flancs d'une mère
Fait sa maison, l'emporte, et comment un pépin
Mis contre un grain de blé, sous l'humide poussière;
L'un plante et l'autre cep, sont le pain et le vin.

Rien n'était, Dieu voulant, rien devint quelque chose,
J'en doutais, je cherchai sur quoi l'univers pose.
Rien gardait l'équilibre et servait de soutien.

Enfin avec le poids de l'éloge et du blâme
Je pesai l'éternel; il appella mon âme:
Je mourrai, j'adorai, je ne savais plus rien.

The French was dated, but the poem conjured visions of Jean-François Millet's painted scenes of nineteenth-century farmers toiling in a pastoral setting under a rose-colored sky illuminated by the setting sun. The poem was also suggestive of something more profound, particularly the last few verses, which Vicki translated for Sibyl:

Finally, with the weight of praise and blame
I weighed the eternal; it appealed to my soul:
I die, I worshiped, I knew nothing.

She handed the manuscript to Sibyl, removed her laptop from the charcoal-leather sleeve, switched it on, and searched for information on *La Très Sainte Trinosophie*, or *The Most Holy Threefold Wisdom*, translated into English.

Sibyl took out a dainty, silver nose ring from a pouch of her knockoff Vuitton purse and effortlessly slipped the ring through her left nostril, securing the stud on the inside. She adjusted her thick glasses, gingerly opened the manuscript, and methodically leafed through the pages.

102

"This website says that the manuscript was only one of numerous works associated with St. Germain," Vicki said. "The others have been destroyed."

Mouth agape, Sibyl remarked, "The calligraphy is astonishing."

"Another website claims that *La Très Sainte Trinosophie* is loosely based on some long-lost Cabbala manuscript owned by the Vatican."

Sibyl scanned the brilliantly colored drawings of half-dressed men and women engaged in unusual ceremonies strewn throughout the ninety-six, ribbed-textured pages of the manuscript. Some of the drawings depicted ritual objects. Other drawings showed unidentified statues of men and women in Greek or Roman robes. All twelve sections, Sibyl observed, began and ended with odd symbols and words written in hieroglyphics, Greek, Hebrew, Arabic and a variety of unfamiliar or dead languages.

"I can't decipher these images." Sibyl's lenses magnified the squinting of her hazel-green eyes. "Well, this I know," she said, pointing to a strange figure with eight sides. "In fact, apropos to the eight-petaled flower on Jean d'Alluye's tomb that we discussed at lunch, in some ancient cultures, the number eight, or octagonal shapes, represented life and rebirth. You know, Vick," Sibyl said, taking her eyes off the manuscript and staring at the reservoir, "so much has been made of da Vinci's *Last Supper* by people outside the art world, but some say the real esoteric message is plainly overlooked. Do you know the knife that Peter holds?"

Vicki leaned in, staring eagerly at Sibyl. She loved hearing Sibyl's secret little tidbits. "The knife held in an impossible human way?"

Sibyl nodded. "Impossible or not, the placement of that knife is not arbitrary by any means. Nor is what da Vinci did with Andrew's fingers."

"What about Andrew's fingers?"

"In the painting, Peter points the knife at the apostle Andrew, who is, by the way, Peter's brother. Both of Andrew's hands are raised in the air with a gesture of alarm. Though not apparent, the viewer only sees eight of Andrew's fingers. All ten are there, but the pinky and thumb on his left hand are concealed, either obscured into the background or hidden behind Paul."

"Why did da Vinci do that?" Vicki asked.

"Since the left hand only shows three fingers, thus eight in total, da Vinci purposely placed the knife held by St. Peter directly under that hand."

"I'm still not following what you are saying."

"The eight fingers and the knife represent the tension between Peter and Andrew on resurrection. That is to say, Peter is representative of the Church's position on resurrection—in particular, that Jesus was the only person to be resurrected—while Andrew's eight fingers represent the more ancient idea of life and rebirth. Taken another way, it's as if da Vinci was suggesting that Peter is threatening his brother with the knife because of his ideas on resurrection, which makes sense because Andrew's writings don't mention Jesus's resurrection or even the formation of the Church itself."

"And Peter is the founder of the Church." Vicki shook her head. "Where do you learn all these things?" she mumbled, turning back to her computer.

"I've picked them up here and there along the way."

Vicki swallowed hard. "I just did a search for Count Hompesch. Apparently, Count Hompesch was St. Germain. He was known as Count Hompesch when he served as the Grand Master of the Knights of Malta."

Sibyl read aloud the words written on the last page.

"Whoever understands these mysterious images will be transfigured."

Vicki's eyes grew wider as she stared out over the huge reservoir. Large Herring and Great Black-blacked Gulls formed salt and pepper speckles on the surface. Her pulse quickened. "Something just hit me like a tidal wave," she announced. "A French novelist named Joséphin Péladan opened several salons in Paris in the 1890s called the Salon de la Rose + Croix. The salons were popular with certain artists of the time."

"Symbolists painters," Sibyl declared, nodding in unison with Vicki. "And we have some great Symbolist paintings at the Met."

"Many incorporating similar mythological and allegorical imagery from antiquity into their paintings, like the drawings in this manuscript."

"That's brilliant, Vick."

"Just a theory," Vicki said with a self-effacing smile. "I'll take a closer look tomorrow at some of the paintings in the Nineteenth-Century galleries."

CHAPTER 24

ANTHONY ARRIVED AT WORK EARLIER THAN usual to take time out of his already full day with the hope of uncovering some pertinent information about Pulzone's painting.

The provenance file for *The Lamentation* indicated that Napoleon Bonaparte's uncle, Cardinal Joseph Fesch, the Prince of France, was the second owner. The year he acquired the painting was omitted – perhaps intentionally – but the entry noted that Cardinal Fesch hung Pulzone's painting in Palazzo Falconieri, his own provisional palace in Rome.

Anthony contemplated the tumultuous relationship between Napoleon and the pope. At the core of the contentions between the two leaders, he knew, was the lifting of the ban on the Society of Jesus. Napoleon mistrusted the Jesuit Order, convinced they were his rival in his goal to rule the world, the true Napoleon Complex. Anthony also knew that Napoleon's army had looted works of art from the Papal States – though he had yet to learn what Napoleon sought when he invaded Italy and suppressed the papal troops.

He wrote Napoleon's name under the heading 'Possible Thefts'.

* ~ * ~ *

VICKI BEGAN THE day in the Nineteenth-Century Paintings collection.

The museum wasn't open, so there was little activity in the galleries, other than a few employees preparing for the day. Most of the lights were still off.

Paintings from great Symbolist painters like Paul Gauguin, Gustav Klimt, and Pablo Picasso hung with methodical order on the walls of a handful of galleries, though none struck Vicki as analogous to the drawings depicted in *La Très Sainte Trinosophie*.

She entered a dimly lit gallery, and drifted, almost as if guided by an invisible hand, to the other side of the room, and stopped in front of Georges Seurat's huge oil painting *Circus Sideshow*. It was her favorite Neo-Impressionist painting. She had written her graduate thesis on the painting, arguing that *Circus Sideshow* served as the inspiration for Henri Matisse's Fauvism style and was even a precursor for Picasso's Cubism.

Vicki cast an admiring glance as she examined the painting for the thousandth time. The nocturnal scene, *en plein air*, faintly lit by the glow of nine flaring gaslights, portrayed the misty, near-risqué atmosphere expected outside an evening performance at the Circus Corvi, located on the east side of Paris. Lured toward the colorful big top by the sirenic sounds of wind, brass, and percussion instruments, a crowd had gathered. Smack dab in the center of the painting, a scene-dominating trombonist wearing a royal-purple robe and conical hat stares back at the viewer with smug eternalness in his eyes. The trombonist's placement in the middle of the canvas hinted at a possible geometric ratio, but Seurat's use of parallel vertical and horizontal lines clearly mimicked the grid technique used in Egyptian reliefs.

Vicki grinned, knowing there was so much more to the painting than she'd ever know – a hidden mystery. That's why she liked it so much.

Exiting the galleries, she paused to examine Gustave Moreau's *Oedipus and the Sphinx*. The work envisaged the fate of Thebes resting squarely upon the mythical Greek king's ability to solve a riddle posed by a beautiful sphinx with the supple breast of a woman, the hind legs of a lion, and the silver wings of a fabled raptor.

The riddle posed to the mythical Greek king of Thebes: What animal walks on four feet in the morning, two feet during the day, and three feet in the evening? As legend had it, Oedipus answered correctly when he replied that man walked on all upper and lower limbs as an infant, on two feet in his prime, and with a cane in old age.

Vicki then recalled from her reading of the *Crata Repoa* that Thebes was one of the places where initiates had learned the mysteries from ancient

Egypt. She hadn't yet learned that she, too, was to embark on a path of initiation and enlightenment.

* ~ * ~ *

ANTHONY LISTENED AS Lane Merrill convinced herself that no other institution in the world could legally claim ownership of Pulzone's painting. It belonged to the Met.

Interrupting Lane, Anthony said, "Excuse me, please." He knew Paul wouldn't contact him when he was with the president unless it was urgent.

"Come in," he replied, holding his radio to his face.

Paul's voice came through the radio.

"We have another issue in the temple, Tony."

"Again!" Lane shouted, slapping her hands on her desk.

Anthony's face took on an emasculated appearance.

"Mr. Leonardi, the Temple of Dendur is one of the museum's most popular draws. If anything ever happened to it, the museum would lose a ton of money."

Lane rose from her chair and dashed out of her office. Anthony mumbled several expletives and followed her out of the office and into the elevator. Not a word was spoken as they exited the elevator and crossed the shiny, white-and-green marble-clad balcony terrace framing the Great Hall one floor below. Anthony stared over the balcony. The front entrance guards were conducting their daily opening drill. Morning light revivified tall, chartreuse palm fronds potted in five large-marble vases placed in the center of the hall. He redirected his sight to Lane, who motioned to pick up the pace.

"Don't dally, Mr. Leonardi." There was urgency in her voice.

Anthony moved faster, questioning his decision to leave the NYPD.

* ~ * ~ *

A FEW MINUTES after Lane and Anthony passed the top of the Grand Staircase, Vicki climbed the marble stairs and entered the European Paintings galleries. She paused in the first gallery underneath several enormous Giovanni Tiepolo canvases. Nearly twenty feet in height, Tiepolo's paintings brought the world of myths and biblical legends back to life. But it wasn't Tiepolo's large canvases that stopped Vicki in her tracks. Inspired by Sibyl's thought-provoking insight into the hidden message in *The Last Supper*, Vicki took a closer look at Tiepolo's classical murals hung on the opposite wall.

The four towering frescoes, *Geometry*, *Metaphysics*, *Arithmetic*, and *Grammar*, each one related to the others, all contained statues of unidentified men and women standing on top of podiums and placed between large Greek columns. All four were set in an enigmatic location. All four frescoes likewise contrasted architectural illusion with the figures in the frescoes, possibly suggesting a link between secret societies and architecture.

"Architecture . . . architecture," she repeated to herself.

Vicki turned when she heard her name called.

"See you in the locker room after work today?" Sibyl walked through the glass doors leading to the gallery where Pulzone's *The Lamentation* hung.

"Sorry." Vicki shook her head and smiled. "I'm going to do a little probing in the European Sculpture Court after work today."

Sibyl realized that Vicki was looking at Tiepolo's frescoes. She moved closer to the fresco that Vicki was studying. The allegorical statue in the painting was an attractive, bare-breasted woman cloaked in a long, flowing *himation*, a toga-like wrap worn by Greek women. "Ahh," she voiced, turning back to Vicki. "These frescoes look just like the drawings in *La Très Sainte Trinosophie*. How did I not think of this?"

Vicki put her hand on Sibyl's shoulder.

"To be honest, I was just passing through this area and I stopped because of what you told me about the *Last Supper*," Vicki said, checking the time on her phone.

"C'mon, don't be so modest, Vick. You're getting really good at this mystery stuff." Sibyl pointed to the fresco. "Did you know that all four of the Tiepolo frescoes here at the Met come from an Italian palace of a renowned secret society member?"

"You're a walking encyclopedia," Vicki said to make Sibyl feel good.

A visitor held up her phone and took a picture.

"Excuse me," Vicki politely said to the visitor standing to the side. "We don't allow flash or video in the museum."

Sibyl reinforced the rule with an affable shake of her head and turned back to the painting. "Do you see the word, *METAFISICA*, inconspicuously engraved on the top of the marble stand, Vick? Directly underneath the handsome woman?"

Vicki moved closer to the wall.

"That's Latin for 'metaphysics', the study of existence."

"Interesting," Vicki said, again thinking that there was a connection between architecture and secret societies. "Is it true that Tiepolo is considered one of the greatest painters of the eighteenth century?"

"When it comes to murals, he's the da Vinci of the eighteenth century."

Vicki's iPhone buzzed. She took it out of the side pocket of her pants and looked at the message. "I'll see you in the locker room tomorrow morning."

* ~ * ~ *

PAUL DID A double take when he saw Lane walking alongside Anthony.

The two strode around the Nile reflecting pool and up the stairs to the temple platform. Anthony spotted the security manager of the section, talking with several uniformed guards. All fell silent upon seeing Anthony and Lane.

"What happened here, Mr. McDonough?" Lane demanded to know.

"Someone," Paul said hesitantly, unsure what he should or should not discuss in front of the president. "Well, it seems that –"

"Mr. McDonough, anything you say to Mr. Leonardi, you can say to me."

A lot of information was withheld from the museum hierarchy, much of which was censured as a matter of policy. The less the top brass knew about certain matters, all the better for potential legal reasons. It was no different from the unsaid protocol used by corporations around the world and even top military and government officials.

Paul lowered his gaze. "Someone moved a statue into the temple."

"Was anything damaged?"

Paul shrugged. "Cy Hetford is in the temple inspecting the statue now."

Anthony and Lane stepped onto the *pronaos*. Anthony hesitated at the portal to the sanctuary and gestured for Lane to proceed, hand extended.

Lane scurried through the sanctuary and entered the crypt.

"What's the meaning of this, Mr. Hetford?" she asked.

109

"That's what I'd like to know!" Cy bawled, visibly shaken as he inspected the statue of Pharaoh Nectanebo II connected to a falcon.

Paul awkwardly intervened, stomping into the rear sanctuary. "Like I said, Tony. The statue was removed from gallery 126 and brought here."

"128. Gallery 128!" Cy hollered. "For heaven's sake, is there not one employee in this museum familiar with the collection?"

Lane raised both hands in the air. "Excuse me. Is there any damage?"

Cy wheezed and answered. "Fortunately, greywacke is a hard stone."

"Greywacke?" Anthony repeated aloud. *The Egyptians used greywacke stone for their statues? Is that why Cleopatra's Needle was erected on the Greywacke Knoll in Central Park?* His thoughts turned to the importance Cy had placed on Pharaoh Nectanebo II during their conversation in the patrons lounge. *What is he up to?* Anthony wondered, staring into Cy' eyes.

"Mr. Hetford, I am beginning to wonder if the museum's Egyptian Department would be better managed by some new blood."

"My department is in shipshape condition." Cy folded his arms as a show of defiance. "It's the security that's completely lacking. If his camera system wasn't so faulty, we could see everything that is happening in here."

Lane squared off against Anthony, closing the distance. "It's imperative, Mr. Leonardi, that you get to the bottom of this at once. We cannot have these kinds of shenanigans going on in this museum."

Anthony turned his somber gaze to Paul. "Meet me in the American Wing atrium immediately after the closing drill tonight. We should do a thorough inspection of all the doors in the rear of the building. The doors in the courtyard will be a good starting point."

CHAPTER 25

THE GORGON SLAYER, PERSEUS, GREETED VICKI at the entrance to the European Sculpture Court. The eight-foot-tall statue of Perseus, sculpted by Antonio Canova, was a replica of the one that Canova first chiseled for the Vatican. In his outstretched left hand, Perseus, the half-god, half-man offspring of Zeus, held the snake-haired head of Medusa. His right hand gripped the Adamantine sword given to him by his father and used to sever the head of Medusa. The expression on Perseus's face as he stared into Medusa's eyes, undaunted by her power to turn onlookers into stone – an irony that didn't escape Vicki as she examined Canova's stone sculpture – was one of great pride and triumph. But the larger-than-life statue represented much more than just mythical conquest; it celebrated an epoch that witnessed the decline of gender equality and ushered in the beginning of male dominance over the female. It touted patriarchal supremacy.

She glanced at Jean-Antoine Houdon's statue *The Bather* purposely tucked away in a corner of the courtyard. She examined the marble contours of the woman, impressed not only by Houdon's inimitable talent to shape the human form with precision, but also by his ability to capture his subject's emotions, demonstrated by the bashful look of the bather. Houdon even did something with *The Bather* that other sculptors and painters went to great lengths to avoid or to conceal in their work. He depicted her vagina.

Was that so terrible that the work of art had to be tucked away in a corner and out of sight? Vicki asked herself, looking back at Perseus. Even in the dark, it was clear that his protruding, uncircumcised penis was intended to be the focal point of the work. The curatorial arrangement inside the sculpture court, the museum itself, similarly favored phallic symbolism over yonic symbolism, the sun over the moon, male gods over goddesses. *Or did it?*

Vicki sat alongside *The Bather*, feeling a sense of togetherness that only women can share. She looked around. The sculpture court was empty, the lights lowered for the day. Statues of mythical figures seemingly whispered to one another in the quietude of the twilight. Halfway between a state of reverie and semi-cognizance, Vicki finally made the connection between the activities of the founding museum leadership and the Met's architectural developments. A sudden epiphanic sensation similar to an out-of-body experience took hold as she realized that she wasn't simply inside of one of the world's greatest museums, but she was inside a modern-day temple.

She looked through the large glass wall at the far end of the sculpture court at Cleopatra's Needle directly behind the museum. She typed her password into her iPhone and did an Internet search on the functions of Egyptian obelisks. Her suspicions were confirmed. The Egyptians had placed obelisks outside of temples.

"Oh my God," she said under her breath.

EXHAUSTED AND FRUSTRATED, Anthony exited the museum using the street-level entrance at Eighty-First Street. The sun had descended below the horizon hours earlier, but the museum basked in an artificial, nocturnal glow that illumined the features of the iconic façade throughout the night.

He stared over his left shoulder as he headed toward Fifth Avenue and fixed his sight on the four-paired Corinthian columns of the museum's façade. Four discernible pyramids were built on top of the paired columns. Between the columns, three helmeted faces of the Roman goddess Minerva were chiseled into the keystones of the Roman arches. The design was a masterful blend of Egyptian-Greco-Roman triadic symbolism.

The 'Jewel Heist of the Century' crossed Anthony's mind. As it did for all museum security heads since the three robbers turned folk heroes had rappelled from the roof of the American Museum of Natural History and entered the building through a bathroom window. Out of the corner of his eye, he noticed a sedan parked in front of the museum's main entrance. During the day, there was nothing unusual about a car in that location.

Drivers parked, if only temporarily, in the no-parking zone to pick up and discharge passengers. At night, there was no reason for a car to be there.

The engine hummed softly. The tinted window on the passenger side of the car slowly lowered as the car crept toward Anthony. Immediately, he realized that someone had been waiting for him to exit the museum. Out of habit, he placed his hand on his side to make sure he had his SIG Sauer P226 semi-automatic service pistol at the ready.

Slightly on edge, he mouthed, *What now?*

The combination of numbers and letters on the license plate indicated that it wasn't a personal car. The vehicle stopped in front of Anthony. The shrouded face of the man in the passenger side of the car came into view. "Anthony Leonardi?" the man asked.

Anthony didn't answer. Instead, he glared at the shadowy image of the man in the passenger seat, shifting his sight to the driver.

"We'd like to talk to you." The man's voice was hoarse, like a life-long smoker.

"We?" Anthony angled his body, right hand at the ready.

"Special Agent Wilson." The man showed his FBI badge. "This is Special Agent O'Rourke. We have a matter to discuss. I think you'll be interested."

Anthony couldn't see the details of the gold badge in the dark car.

"How do I know you're really FBI?"

"Call Bob Callahan. He says he hasn't heard from you in a while."

A long-lost memory rose to the forefront of Anthony's mind as he recalled the day he had joined New York's finest and replaced Bob Callahan as a lieutenant at the Alphabet City's Precinct when his predecessor left the department to work for the Department of Justice.

Anthony entered the car, leaned back onto the rear seat, and looked into the piercing, dark eyes of the driver, reflected in the rearview mirror.

The interior light softly faded.

"I apologize for the surprise visit, but we couldn't take the chance of being overheard, even on the museum's secured line. This had to be done in person."

"What's this about?" Anthony asked, tensed by Wilson's statement.

Special Agent O'Rourke shifted the car into gear and pulled away from the curb.

"You met with Fabrizio Armata," Wilson said flatly. "What did he want?"

"A painting."

"Painting?" Wilson repeated, surprise in his raspy voice.

"He wants to return it to a Jesuit church in Rome." Anthony stretched his neck and glanced through the front windshield as the car turned east on Seventy-Ninth Street.

"He's been on our radar for some time."

"Because of possible money laundering?" Anthony asked.

"So you know?" O'Rourke said, looking in the rearview mirror. "Are you also aware that most of the money comes from the sale of drugs and banking scams?"

Anthony's right hand covered the gunshot injury on his right knee as he leaned forward in the seat. "Why don't you arrest him?" he asked.

Wilson emitted a huff that signified indignation. "He's got some friends in high places. And as of now, the State Department tells us that he has functional immunity, so we can't touch him, but FinCEN agents at the Treasury Department are keeping a close eye on him."

"Italian law enforcement doing anything?"

"His immunity also works in Italy," Wilson stated with equal frustration.

O'Rourke ran the light and made a left turn on Madison Avenue.

Anthony sat back and stared out of the side window, digesting the information until a well-lit Chase Bank on the corner diverted his attention. His thoughts turned to Aaron Burr and how the disgraced vice president had conned the New York State Legislature into granting a charter for the Manhattan Company Bank under the pretext of creating a novel system to pipe fresh water from upstate into Manhattan.

An intervening notion emerged. The Manhattan Company Bank continued to finance the water system until the bank was acquired by Rockefeller's Chase National Bank, which was incorporated into JPMorgan Chase & Co.

Anthony shook back into the present and leaned forward in the seat. "You said that as of now, Armata has immunity. Does he not work for the Vatican?"

Wilson twisted in his seat and looked over his shoulder. "We're getting indications from contacts in Europe that he may not work for the Vatican Bank, only associated with it somehow."

O'Rourke steered the car to the corner of Eighty-Fifth Street and Madison Avenue and stopped the car in front of Anthony's stylish apartment building. "Seems he doesn't have a good relationship with the pope. And you know what happened to the last pope who interfered with the IOR. This new guy may end up fulfilling St. Malachy's prophecy."

Wilson flicked his card. "If you hear anything further, call us."

CHAPTER 26

"KNOCK, KNOCK," VICKI SAID WALKING THROUGH the open door to Anthony's office.

Anthony took his palms off the corners of blueprints of the museum's underground connection to the adjoining water pipes under Central Park, allowing the blueprints to roll into a long paper tube. He held his gaze on Vicki as he reclined in his chair.

"Got a minute?" Vicki smiled.

Anthony checked his watch, more as a reflex than to convey a message, and waved Vicki in with a gesture. "You're in early this morning," he grumbled, taking off the fancy reading glasses that his ex had purchased from Saks Fifth Avenue.

I'm always the first guard here, Vicki was tempted to say, but instead pointed out that her boss looked good in glasses. "Why don't you wear your glasses more often? They bring out the intellect underneath that rugged exterior, Doctor Leonardi."

Anthony chuckled lowly, then sipped his coffee. "I will take that as a compliment," he said, repressing an impulse to look at the diploma on the wall.

Vicki couldn't let the remark go completely unchecked.

"I would have been in earlier today, but I did two loops around the reservoir this morning at six. It's the only time cool enough for me to run outside."

"That sounds, well, dreadful, to be honest."

Vicki sat in front of Anthony's desk. "Paul around?" she asked.

Anthony shook his head with disapproval. "You're not so fond of him, are you? You know, he's really not such a bad guy."

Vicki adjusted her position in the seat. "Paul is my superior and a longtime friend of yours, so I wouldn't show anything but respect."

Anthony's expression almost reflected Vicki's sophistry. His shoulders rose with a nearly silent chuckle. "Well, I presume you're not here to talk about Paul."

"I did a little homework last night, and I wanted to share something that I discovered when I left the museum."

"Regarding Mr. Miller's death?"

Vicki anxiously bit her lower lip before speaking.

"About the position of Cleopatra's Needle."

"Not more about that damn obelisk," Anthony remarked, noticing an atypical restlessness in Vicki's eyes. He exhaled noisily and said, "Alright, what about it?"

"Before I begin, can you please print a map of New York City? Any map will do as long as it shows Manhattan and the Bronx."

"A map of Manhattan and the Bronx?"

Vicki stood and rounded Anthony's desk, taking the liberty to open a website on Anthony's PC. "This map will do."

Anthony rolled his chair back to the center of his desk with a thrust from his feet, staring at Vicki with a look of confusion in his sleepy eyes.

"Do you know what year the obelisk was erected?"

"I believe 1881. I read the plaque the other day."

She returned to the front of Anthony's desk. "And did you know that eight thousand members of secret societies from the United States and from countries like France, Germany, and Italy marched up Fifth Avenue in October 1880 for the cornerstone ceremony for the obelisk?"

"The same year the museum opened in Central Park?"

"The very same year. And these eight thousand men were under the impression that their organizations had a connection to the obelisk when it was moved from Alexandria to New York." Vicki leaned over the desk. "More interesting, at least I thought so, some say there are several time capsules buried under the pedestal of the obelisk."

Anthony looked at the map of New York City on his computer, thinking he would need another cup of coffee. His gaze reverted to Vicki.

"Time capsules?"

"Most of what's in the capsules aren't of interest. Supposedly, there are items like rare coins donated from the Treasury Department and a facsimile of the Declaration of Independence called a Dunlap something or other."

"Dunlap Broadside copy?" Suddenly, Anthony was fully awake. "That can't be right. The Dunlap Broadside version is extremely rare."

"There was also an anonymous donation of a gold-plated capsule that purportedly contains information on why obelisks were moved from Egypt to Rome."

Anthony peered through Vicki as he spoke. "Obelisks were moved to Italy because the Romans conquered Egypt and took whatever they wanted."

"Maybe, but the information inside the gold capsule may provide clues –"

"Some type of ritual that led to Miller's death. Is that what you're getting at?" Anthony curtly shook his head exactly three-times over, to make a point. "Even if those things are below the obelisk in the park, you'll never see them unless you plan to be arrested for destroying a public monument and committing first-degree larceny."

"May not have to." Vicki took the map off the top of Anthony's printer and placed it on his desk. "This is the other interesting thing I learned," she said, pointing to three locations on the map. "There are three significant obelisks in the city: Cleopatra's Needle, obviously; an obelisk in the Flatiron District; and one downtown."

"You mean the obelisk in the cemetery at St. Paul's Chapel?" Anthony reclined in his chair and rubbed his eyes. "Where George Washington worshipped?"

Vicki's stare projected confidence. "The two obelisks downtown are grave markers. I didn't find anything pertinent about the deceased. Instead," Vicki stressed, "I discovered that all the obelisks are positioned on the same horizontal axis."

"Nothing pertinent about the deceased?" Anthony now questioned, slowly making a mental connection. "Maybe you are on to something. George Washington was a Freemason. The obelisk in the Flatiron District, well, that's not only one of the oldest monuments in the city, second only to

Cleopatra's Needle, I believe, but it sits over General Worth, who was also a well-known Freemason. Now you tell me that the Masons held some grand ceremony at the obelisk in the park." He sat up in his chair.

Vicki placed a legal pad from Anthony's desk on top of the map. Using the edge of the pad, she traced a straight line through the three obelisks with a pen. "As you can see, all three obelisks in Manhattan are located on the same north-south axis. This was confirmed by an English guy who lives in the city by using GPS coordinates."

"GPS coordinates? I'm impressed."

Vicki smiled with contentment. "I noticed something even more curious." She made two small pen marks on the legal pad showing the distance from the obelisk in lower Manhattan to Cleopatra's Needle. She faced Anthony. The apprehension resurfaced in her voice. "If you measure the distance between the obelisk at St. Paul's Chapel and Cleopatra's Needle and continue north the same distance, you end up here."

She pointed to a location in the Bronx and looked up at her boss, now with manifest trepidation in her eyes.

Anthony retraced Vicki's markings.

"The line crosses directly through your alma mater. I double-checked the GPS coordinates for Fordham University. Your school lines up *precisely* on the very same north-south axis as the three obelisks in Manhattan."

Anthony examined the map. "That has to be a coincidence."

"It's possible," Vicki replied, relieved by Anthony's calm response. "But don't you still keep in touch with your college mentor? Perhaps he knows something."

Anthony shrugged. "Nothing to lose, I suppose. He sipped his coffee, and reclined in his seat, contemplating briefly. "And it'll give me a good excuse to say hello to Father Franconi. We haven't spoken in a while. Check back with me at lunch."

CHAPTER 27

EVEN BEFORE LUNCH, ANTHONY AND VICKI were in the backseat of a Chevy Suburban on their way to the Bronx. Malcolm Morris, a retired NYPD officer hired by Anthony to be his driver, had managed to avoid the slower-moving traffic on the FDR Drive in Manhattan and on the Major Deagan Expressway in the Bronx, but he was less successful navigating the always-present gridlock on Fordham Road near the Grand Concourse. Long gone were the days when the Grand Concourse—a five-mile-long thoroughfare designed as the Champs-Élysées of New York City—served as a chic shopping venue for city residents, but the popularity of the numerous discount stores in the area among the people in the neighborhood always resulted in maddening street congestion.

Anthony looked over Malcolm's right shoulder as the car slowed for a red light. "Traffic in this part of the city is always so unbearable."

Empathy and compassion were two qualities that had always surged somewhere in the above-average range in Vicki, and at that particular moment, she felt the need to express both. She sensed the tension.

"I think it's great that you remained so close to your college mentor for so many years."

"Why wouldn't I? He was a wonderful adviser." Anthony looked at the road ahead. "Just a few more blocks and make a right, Malcolm."

Malcolm knew exactly how to get to their destination, even better than the tyrannical voice on the GPS navigational system, but he responded with a silent nod.

The iconic, 10-story-tall clock tower rising above the gothic-designed main building of Fordham University came into view. It hadn't changed one iota since Anthony's college days. A vague recollection of the classes that he sat through in the building in what seemed to be another lifetime rose to the forefront of his mind, alongside feelings of nostalgia.

"Why aren't we meeting the father at the school?" Vicki asked, smiling, and gazing at Fordham University's 85-acre campus, appreciative of all the rolling greenery in such an urban neighborhood of the Bronx.

Anthony settled back in the rear seat. "He prefers to eat on Arthur Avenue because he can't stand the cafeteria food." Anthony thought about some of the ways the father described the campus food: tasteless, unnatural, processed heaps of nauseating dog food. "He also said that he has some confidential information to share. He almost sounded anxious."

"He's probably just eager to see you again," Vicki said.

"Father Franconi was never one to hold his tongue or toe the line. I always admired that." The crow's-feet extending from the corner of Anthony's eyes broadened with expressive facial contractions, revealing hints of his Duchenne – or inner smile – as he examined his Santos de Cartier watch. "You know, he gave me this watch when I finished my PhD."

Stealing a glance, Vicki noted the admiration in his eyes.

"Make a right here, Malcolm, on Arthur Avenue." Anthony leaned forward again and peered between the driver's and passenger's seats and noticed the long line of idling cars a few blocks before the Little Italy of the Bronx, lined with some of the finest Italian restaurants, bakery, butcher, cheese, and pastry shops in the entire city. "What the hell is going on up there?" he roared, now observing the numerous police cars.

Malcolm shifted the car into park.

"Doesn't look like we're going much farther."

Anthony's door was open even before the SUV stopped. He leaped out as a motorcycle sped by in the opposite direction and roared passed after weaving between parked cars, forcing Anthony to lunge back into the SUV.

"Jesus Christ," he uttered, righting himself on the back seat.

Vicki leaned over the top of the rear seat and glimpsed through the tinted rear windshield. "That maniac nearly mowed you down!"

"Forget about him. Let's get moving."

Vicki trailed as Anthony weaved through the crowd and advanced on the aptly-named white-shirt – senior NYPD officers with white shirts and caps brimmed with gold badges – securing the scene and barking orders to the first responders. Police sirens resulted in a wave of anxiousness in the gathering trying to see what the excitement was about, followed by gasps and pointed fingers. An FDNY ambulance slowly weaved through traffic to the scene.

Removing his sunglasses, Anthony stopped in front of the officer and asked, "What's going on here, Lieutenant?"

The officer stood at attention, arms fixed to the side. "Inspector," she called out, with an unbridled tone of surprise and using Anthony's former title. Like mayor or governor, the title of inspector stayed for life. "What are you doing here? Shouldn't you be enjoying retirement in Florida?"

A half grin came to Anthony's face. "Are you kidding? I can barely take the three months of heat in New York these days." The mere mention of the hot weather made Anthony conscious of the sweat under his arms.

The lieutenant pointed up the street.

"Some guy got shot in front of that restaurant about fifteen minutes ago. Paul Castellano–style. You worked that case, right?"

Grim visions of the bullet-ridden body lying in front of a midtown steak house pixilated in Anthony's brain as he raised his neck and gazed ahead at the crime scene. A sudden neural surge rushed down the brain–gut axis. "Let's go!" he yelled and dashed toward the crime scene, removing his jacket and swinging it over his shoulder, pinning down his tie. "Excuse me," he said repeatedly as he scuttled through the crowd and the line of cops. He stopped in front of the Italian restaurant where pointed shards of broken, colored glass littered the sidewalk. A viscous, crimson-like ooze stained a segment of the concrete sidewalk. Near frantic, Anthony bent beside the stretcher.

"Whoa! What do you think you're doing?" a rookie cop asked.

Anthony turned and glared at the young cop in the regulation blue uniform.

"Inspector," the police captain overseeing the crime scene yelled and rushed over. He shot the rookie cop a condemning glance. "Sorry, this guy's still a freakin' boot." He shooed the rookie away. "If he doesn't shape up, he won't last probation. I promise you that."

The rookie's mistake was the farthest thing from Anthony's mind. He examined the black body bag. On closer inspection, the contours shaping the body inside the bag were far too large to be his mentor.

"DOA?" he asked, looking at the captain.

"Real shame. Looks like he was in his early thirties."

Relieved, with heartfelt sadness, Anthony asked, "What happened?"

"Seems the deceased was an innocent bystander. Not even from the area."

"What info do you have on the shooter?"

"Not much so far. Owners of the restaurant won't talk. The people who live in this neighborhood won't talk. I don't have to tell you that."

"Any cameras in the area?" Anthony asked, surveying the storefronts.

"You kidding me? There are no cameras around here. The only person we got information from is him." Captain Lopez pointed to a man on the opposite side of the street talking with two detectives dressed in jeans and dark T-shirts. "He saw a white SUV, said it was a German model, come to a screeching halt in front of the restaurant. Two men got out and dragged an elderly man into the SUV. This guy here," the captain said and pointed to the body bag on the stretcher, "interfered and was shot in the chest."

One fist clenched and the other gripping the captain's shoulder, Anthony held back his anger and asked, "The guy forced into the SUV was an elderly man?"

"That's what the guy talking to the detective said, so this is being handled as a kidnapping. The Major Crime Squad is on the way." Noticing the concern in Anthony's eyes, Lopez said, "By the way, Inspector. What brings you to Arthur Avenue?"

Once more, Anthony scanned the crowd of onlookers.

"I was supposed to meet a friend at this restaurant."

CHAPTER 28

ANTHONY WAS OUT OF EARSHOT OF Captain Lopez, already across the street, and he was moving with bulldog determination. "Excuse me," he said curtly, tapping one of the detectives on the shoulder. "I need to ask you a question. Come with me, please."

The detective flipped his steno closed and did as instructed.

"What did you get from this guy?" Anthony asked.

"He reported a white SUV. He thinks German, with yellow tags."

Anthony's wheels were already spinning.

"Could be New Jersey plates, possibly a rented car. Get the tag numbers?"

The intense rays of the sun seemed to both permeate and reflect off the detective's gold badge. "No license plate number, but an APB has been sent out to all Bronx precincts and state troopers working in the area. Port Authority has also been notified to be on the lookout for a white SUV with yellow plates at all tolls on bridges leading out of the Bronx."

Anthony swayed restlessly. "What else did the witness say?"

"Usual. Everything happened too fast. The car, I mean, the SUV, skidded to a stop. The witness heard a loud noise. Two men in suits jumped out of the SUV and grabbed an old man standing in front of the restaurant. People started screaming. The deceased made the mistake of trying to stop the perps from forcing the old guy into the SUV. Two shots were fired. First shot missed and hit the window of the restaurant. Second shot landed directly in the chest. That's all we've got so far."

Anthony fixed his gaze on the witness.

"Not from around here, is he?" he deduced. "Is he with anyone?"

"B&T. From Connecticut. He came here by himself. Said he was in the neighborhood to pick up some bread and fresh mozz."

"I'd like a few words with him, and I'll send him back to you. When you guys are done talking to him, do me a favor. Make sure he gets to his car safely. I assume he drove here, if he is B&T, like you say." The inflection Anthony put on B&T indicated his disapproval of the abbreviation. He didn't like it. He didn't understand why the detective was using it. The detective was probably B&T, a term used by Manhattanites as a jab to people who come into the city either over a bridge or through a tunnel. Anthony continued. "If the witness took the train, escort him to the train station."

"I'll make a point of it, Inspector."

"Don't forget what I told you. Have someone in uniform stay with the witness after he leaves the area. And don't talk to him here out in the open."

Anthony beelined to the detective who was questioning the witness.

"I'd like a few words with this man," he informed the second detective in a tone that made it clear that he wasn't taking no for an answer. "Mind coming with me?" he asked the witness. "This will take only a minute."

"Alright," the man replied nervously, reluctantly. "Where are we going?"

"Over here." Anthony gestured with an extended arm, instructing the witness to walk into the empty street and toward an unmarked police car. He shouted and waved Captain Lopez over to the car.

"I'm not being arrested, am I?" the witness asked.

"Nothing like that," Anthony assured the man with a smile. Hoping to put him at ease, Anthony introduced himself with a handshake. "My name is Anthony Leonardi. I'm a retired NYPD officer with a personal interest in this matter. I just want to ask you a few questions in private. If that's okay?"

"What's up?" Captain Lopez asked, moving closer.

"I'm going to use this car to talk to the witness."

"Sure, but –"

"Just give me one minute." Anthony opened the car door and prompted the witness to enter the car, then lowered his tall frame into the backseat. He closed the door. "I'm sorry. I didn't mean to be rude. I didn't get your name."

"Robert Offenbach."

"Robert, I know this has been traumatic. No one deserves to see another

126

human killed, but you may be able to help." Anthony paused, making extended eye contact. Assessing Robert's anxious state, he began with a few general questions. "Do you go by Rob, or Bob, or do you prefer Robert?"

"Just Robert."

"Okay, Robert. So, are you in the area to do some shopping?"

Robert rubbed his hands up and down on his jeans. "I was in Manhattan earlier, for work, and I stopped here to pick up a few things on my way back home. Back to Connecticut. That's where I live, in Westport, Connecticut."

Anthony raised his right hand, smiling big. "Say no more, Robert. Best place outside Italy for Italian provisions hands down. Ever try the *pane di casa* at Acilia's? It's fantastic."

"Acilia's? I'm not sure." Robert pointed. "Is that near the end of the street?"

"It's around the corner. I'd suggest you give it a try some time. Now, you told the detectives that the men who forced the elderly man into the car were driving an SUV with yellow plates. Is that right?"

Robert confirmed with a jittery bob of his head.

"Was the elderly man wearing anything notable?"

"What do you mean by notable?"

"Was he wearing a suit? Or maybe clerical clothing? Fordham University is down the street, and faculty members come here for lunch all the time."

"No, he was wearing regular clothes."

Anthony breathed a sigh of relief.

"Okay. You said the SUV was a German model. That's an interesting observation, Robert. What makes you think the SUV was a German model?"

"I'm kind of a car and motorcycle buff, or geek as my friends say, and I know for sure that the SUV wasn't American. It was a foreign make. It's easy to tell the difference between American and foreign SUVs. Even between European and Japanese SUVs. The German SUVs look brawnier, you know what I mean, like German tanks. Don't get me wrong. The Japanese build quality cars, too. That's my car over there." Robert pointed.

Anthony needed the witness to feel more at ease, clearer in mind. Less rambling and bodily movements.

"You certainly seem to know your SUVs. I'd bet dollars to donuts that you're right on the make. Did you see the SUV from the front or rear?"

"The vehicle came barreling down Arthur Avenue from the north," Robert pointed again, hand still shaky. "I think that's north. I was in front of the pastry shop. That's when I heard the loud noise. Actually, at first, I thought it was just some idiot trying to show off. Trying to act cool, you know. Then an SUV came to a screeching halt."

"That's good." Anthony smiled again. "So, you saw the car from the front?"

"The front, yes. Then two men jumped out of the SUV."

"Can you provide a description of the men?"

"They were white, I think, but both had fairly dark complexions."

"Italian? Hispanic?"

"It's hard to say. I just know they were big guys, I mean, big, scary-looking guys. Both guys were wearing suits. In their late forties, fifty maybe, if I had to guess. They had dark hair, that's for sure. Dark and shiny. Definitely had product in their hair."

Anthony nodded acknowledgment and asked, "Did you hear them speak?"

"Come to think of it, I did. They yelled something. Sounded like Spanish, maybe, but I can't be sure. I was too far away."

"Spanish?" That surprised Anthony. The Bronx had the highest crime rate in the city. Murders and violent crime had skyrocketed over the past years, mostly due to the increase in the number of gangs that had popped up in the last decade. There were over eighty different gangs that called one or another Bronx neighborhood their turf. But the few crimes that happened on Arthur, and there were very few crimes, weren't committed by gangs. The crimes resulted over 'family disputes'. Perplexed, Anthony said, "Let's go back to the car. You said you saw the car coming head on. Did you notice the grille?"

"Yes, I did, now that you mention it." Robert leaned forward and let out a gasp. "It wasn't one solid grille across the front of the car!"

Anthony stared into Robert's wide eyes, waiting for the deduction.

"That's right." Robert sighed with recall. "Porsche and Mercedes Benz make SUVs with one long grille in the front of the car. Beamers, or should I say, bimmers, have two separate grilles."

"Very good, Robert. That's helpful."

It was clear to Anthony that Robert felt more at ease, more confident.

"Was there anything else that caught your eye?"

"Nothing that sticks out in my mind, except," Robert continued, but not before a contemplative pause with narrowed eyes, "I do recall seeing a Ducati speeding away as the SUV approached."

"You saw a Ducati?" Anthony asked, thinking back to the motorcycle that nearly took his leg off. "Are you sure it was a Ducati?"

"I know bikes, believe me. It was a Ducati Monster 1200, dual-seater, in their signature red. Awesome bike, and great for city driving because it's as agile as it is powerful. I saw one just like it in their store on Sixth Avenue."

"Ducati has a store on Sixth Avenue?" Anthony made a mental note.

Both heads jerked when they heard a loud knock on the car window.

"A BMW SUV with Jersey plates exited Interstate 95 about ten minutes ago and was headed east on Pelham Bay Parkway," the captain announced.

Anthony opened the door. "Sounds like our culprits." He shook Robert's hand. "Thank you. The detectives may have a few more questions."

Anthony exited the car.

"I'd like to go with you," he told the captain. Unease remained in Anthony's eyes as he scanned the crowd gathered around the crime scene.

"You want to ride with me?" the captain asked.

"I have a car parked on the corner of 189th. Can we get an escort?"

Captain Lopez called the rookie over. "Find your partner, quickly, and get over to 189th. You'll be escorting Inspector Leonardi. Don't fuck this up."

129

CHAPTER 29

VICKI TUNED OUT THE SIRENS AND flashing lights as she stared out the window at the urban scenery to the side of the parkway—unfamiliar and dilapidated apartment complexes, dirty gas stations, fast food joints lined up one after another. After exiting Interstate 95 and veering onto Pelham Bay Parkway, Vicki was more familiar with the area. As a child, her parents often took her and their family dog to Pelham Bay Park during the hot summer months. It felt like she was a million miles away from the hot city every time they went, and the memories remained vivid in her mind. The frothy waves that gently crashed onto the white-sand beaches, rocky coastlines as far as the eye could see, and the invigorating feel of the cool air in her long hair—all evoked joyful reminiscences captured from her youth.

She reflected on some of the locations in Pelham Bay Park where her family regularly visited. The dense, hilly woods of Hunter's Island, the rustic bridge over Turtle Cove in the marshier areas, and Split Rock, the gigantic, split glacial boulder where religious visionary Anne Hutchinson – the colonial American counterpart of Joan of Arc – and her family were scalped and then brutally murdered by Siwanoy warriors.

Malcolm pointed. "Been there lately?" he asked, indicating Rodman's Neck, a thin strip of Pelham Bay Park covered by tall pines that jutted into the Long Island Sound. The tip of the peninsula served as an NYPD firing range. With no response from Anthony, he answered his own question: "I guess not since the museum has its own gun range."

Vicki took her head off the side window and sat upright. Back in the

130

moment, she asked, "Why did the captain say no one in the area would talk?"

Anthony half-acknowledged the question, concern now evident in his eyes. He tried calling his mentor several times, and left two messages, but received no response.

Malcolm shook his head. "Sweet Jesus. You know it's scorching outside when you're driving and notice the hot vapor hovering above the pavement."

Vicki peered through the windshield.

"Looks like some type of desert mirage."

"Dog Days of summer, that's for sure. Do you know where that saying comes from, Vicki?" Malcolm continued talking with the shake of Vicki's head seen in the rearview mirror. "The term began with the Egyptians when Sirius, or what they called Sopdet, rose with the sun in July, and continued to rise with the sun through August. That's when the sun seared the land, and the Nile overflowed with the runoff from the Ethiopian mountains, marking the beginning of the harvest season."

"Nothing to do with dogs lazing around in the heat?"

"That's urban legend, Vicki. Like I said, it's during the Dog Days that Sirius, the brightest star in the sky, rises with the sun. That's why the event is called the heliacal rising of Sirius. In ancient times, the morning star, as it was also known, was the most important star in the heavens, revered by people around the world. Anyhow," Malcolm said, observing Vicki's piqued expression in the mirror, "Sirius is also the brightest star in the constellation, Canis Major, thus the name Dog Days, and the association with the Egyptian god Anubis. Some believed Anubis returned to the living world during the heliacal rising of Sirius. Others, however, simply thought that Sirius was reborn once a year, and therefore it was associated with resurrection."

"Interesting." Vicki leaned forward in her seat.

"But this time of the year wasn't viewed kindly by all ancient cultures. No, sir. Some called Sirius the red star, not because it appears red, but because red was the color of evil. You know, like the devil. The ancient Romans despised Sirius. They believed that evil forces took advantage of the oppressive Dog Days of summer every year, and it was during that time, people were most susceptible to violence and madness."

"Hmm," Vicki sounded, lips closed.

"Did you know that, Tony? Romans feared the Dog Days of summer."

"No," Anthony brusquely answered. He had already heard enough about the heliacal rising of Sirius from David Graham and wasn't interested.

"Pelham Bay Park sure is a *big* place," Malcolm emphasized, changing the subject as he observed the vast tracks of old-growth oak and tulip trees off the shoulder of Pelham Bay Parkway – trees that dominated the region long before the Empire State Building and the Statue of Liberty were built. "It's three times the size of Central Park."

Anthony rose with concern. "Why would the culprits go into Pelham Bay Park?" he asked. "There are only a few areas where you can drive inside the park. Plus, they'd cut themselves off from all the main roads."

"I'm just saying Pelham Bay Park is a big place."

Vicki diverted the discussion.

"The witness told you that the man forced into the SUV wasn't wearing priest clothing. Wouldn't Father Franconi be wearing priest clothing?"

"Then, why wasn't he at the restaurant, damn it?"

"Maybe he couldn't get past the crime-scene barricades and didn't check his phone." She smiled. "You know how old people are with phones."

"It's possible," Anthony said, a bit more calmly, but unconvinced.

"Looks like everyone is pulling over." Malcolm slowed the Suburban.

Anthony stared through the windshield at the wall of cop cars closing off the bridge that connected Pelham Bay Park to City Island. His toes curled in his shoes with anxiety in his gut. *City Island*, he thought. *That can't be good.*

Captain Lopez waved Malcolm to the shoulder of the parkway. Anthony jumped out of the Suburban. Vicki followed closely behind.

"The BMW was found in front of one of the three yacht clubs on the east side of the island. That leaves only a few possibilities of the suspects' whereabouts. The culprits shouldn't be hard to find if they're on City Island, considering it's only a little over a mile long and a half-mile wide."

Anthony nodded in agreement.

"And because this is the only way on and off City Island," Lopez explained while extending his arm and pointing to the three-lane bridge arching over the Eastchester Bay of Long Island Sound, "then whoever kidnapped the man on Arthur Avenue either is still on the island or," he hesitated briefly, "more likely, fled in a boat."

"Do they have Father Franconi?" That was Anthony's biggest concern.

"We mobilized the Harbor Unit and put the Coast Guard on high-alert, but since we don't have any identifying information yet, finding one boat out of the thousands on the sound on a hot day like today will be like finding a needle in a fucking haystack."

"You have guys asking questions at the yacht clubs?"

Lopez gazed over the ear-shaped basin of Eastchester Bay in front of City Island. "They're at the yacht clubs right now getting descriptions, state registration info, and the make of every single boat that left the docks within the last half hour."

Already, Anthony noticed, there was a bottleneck of cars, vans, and delivery trucks on the small island due to the bridge shutdown, and the line of traffic was quickly lengthening, stretching halfway down City Island's central road.

Extending the length of the west side of the island, a hundred, maybe more, motorboats rocked in the boatyards of the less affluent side of the island. Upright masts on sailboats undulated in the air like upside-down pendulums of a clock. On the horizon, across the rippled water, Long Island appeared as a thin line of blurred, green trees.

Anthony lowered his sunglasses and scanned the murky water of the sound. Two of the larger NYPD Harbor Unit boats were now in sight, kicking up tempestuous wakes as they patrolled the deeper waters off the southern tip of City Island. Low-drifting, vapory clouds, formed by the humid air, drifted eastward in the hazy sky, shading Execution Rocks Lighthouse in the middle of the sound. A light pulsed every few seconds from the infamous lighthouse. Anthony tried not to think about the history associated with the lighthouse, but he was finding it difficult to keep his thoughts in check in the searing heat.

Before the lighthouse was built, British soldiers devoid of compunction chained Americans to the henge of rocks protruding above the low-tide line in the location to mete out a slow death as the tide rose. After America gained its freedom, the coned-shape lighthouse was built on top of the rocks, and equally unevolved Americans perpetrated the same heinous crimes against African slaves. A chill of disgust climbed his back.

"I hope the victim isn't swimming with fishes," Lopez blurted.

Anthony visualized the crime scene on Arthur Avenue. The speeding motorcycle came to mind. As he half-stared at the flashing lights of the police cars reflecting off the steely side of City Island Bridge, he concluded that there was a connection between the red Ducati and the BMW SUV. That was obvious enough. He also knew that if they – whoever they were – planned to cement-shoe his mentor and drown him in the sound, it would have been done quietly. Someone was trying to send a message.

Screams rang out from underneath the bridge. "Dear God, no!" Anthony shouted and moved closer to the entrance of the bridge as he stared into the water below. A motorboat with kids wearing bathing suits had just passed under the bridge. The faces of the kids showed shock and disgust. One girl was bent over the side of the boat, dry-heaving into the water.

Anthony scanned the bridge for a way to get underneath it.

"Stay here, Inspector," the captain said respectfully, noticing Anthony's intention to move closer to City Island Bridge. "Let the guys trained for this situation handle it."

CHAPTER 30

WHAT WAS MERELY A MATTER OF ten minutes or so in actual time felt more like a half hour to Anthony. In that time span, a squadron of cops flooded the crime scene. Officers arrived from all directions, their sirens blaring, and pulled from nearby locations like Co-op City, the largest housing development in the world, Westchester Square in the eastern section of the Bronx, and the Eastchester section of the northern Bronx.

Anthony paced heavily. He wasn't accustomed to being sidelined.

"Nantucket of the Bronx, my ass," he grumbled, staring hard at City Island.

Malcolm, who was by Anthony's side said, "C'mon, Tony. You know how these things work. You ran crime scenes for years. Give the guys time to figure it out."

"I want to know this instant what's under that bridge that made those kids scream like that." He squinted, staring harder at the ropes dangling over the middle of the seafoam-green-painted bridge and used by special officers to rappel over the side, but he couldn't see anything beneath the bridge. His sight turned to the choppy water of the sound, reflectively, or so he thought, and out to Execution Rocks Lighthouse.

Captain Lopez returned from a pow-wow with the chief running the scene. His face expressionless. "A body was found underneath the bridge."

"In the water?" Anthony asked, alarmed.

The captain shook his head. He hesitated, looking askance. "Not in the water. An elderly man found hanging from the underside of the bridge."

Gunshots echoed like distant blasts of dynamite from the nearby gun range on Rodman's Neck. Vicki inched closer to Anthony.

"ID the guy?" Anthony asked.

"I was told only that he's an elderly man."

The knot in Anthony's stomach tightened. He tried to remain focused, scanning the area for a vantage point where he could see underneath the bridge, but there was no spot from dry land that would allow him to do so. A trim-lined blue-and-white NYPD boat with powerful twin engines crossed the bay. The police boat kicked up brown mud in the shallow waters as the boat's captain slowed the boat and skillfully maneuvered through the low clearance under the bridge. On the far side, the NYPD Search and Rescue Team of the Scuba Unit drifted effortlessly underneath City Island Bridge in a souped-up inflatable raft with the moniker *Zodiac* painted on the back.

"The guys rappelling off the bridge couldn't get near the man, but they will," Lopez stated, raising his radio and connecting with the Special Ops Chief.

"What are your guys seeing?"

There was a short period of silence before, "The rope used to hang this guy is being cut now. It's tied off with a lover's knot that's too tight to undo."

"Roger that. What's the assessment?"

"DOA. Definitely a murder. There's no possible way in hell that someone can climb underneath this bridge, let alone hang himself, especially someone this man's age."

"Get a positive ID," Anthony stated.

"Can you describe the victim? Over."

"Yeah, give me a second. We just cut through the rope and are lowering the body into the boat." There was another extended pause, "Ah, victim is an elderly man. Probably in his eighties, maybe older, wearing jeans and a T-shirt. Whew. It's clammy under this bridge. Let's get this wrapped up, guys."

"Check that."

"This is odd." Mumbles from Harbor Unit officers sounded through the radio, then, "We just found stones stuffed into the man's pockets."

"Repeat, please. Did you say there are stones in his pockets?"

"Affirmative. They are being removed now."

136

Lopez and Anthony looked at each other, both with expressions of bewilderment. Lopez shrugged.

"Ask what the man looks like," Anthony ordered Lopez.

"Stones, okay, roger that. Can you give a description of the man?"

"Give me a second. I think he's carrying a wallet."

"Stones in the pockets?" Anthony said aloud. "What does that mean?"

Lopez held back for a second. "Maybe to make it look like a suicide?"

"But if the rope didn't extend to the water –?"

"We have an ID. Driver's license says Roberto Franconi. Over."

"Jesus!" Anthony shouted, flailing his arms. Somehow, deep down, he knew it would be his mentor, but that did little to brace him for the news.

"Franconi," Lopez repeated unemotionally, "was your friend?"

Anthony bobbed his head and lowered it on top of his clasped hand.

"I'm sorry." There was a bit more compassion in Lopez's voice.

The sound of his mentor's last words sounded in his ears. *Why did he seem so anxious?* Anthony wondered. *Why was the father wearing regular clothing? Should I have done something different?* These were some of the questions that rose to the forefront of Anthony's thoughts. But he needed to focus. More so than ever. There were now two deaths that he would get to the bottom of. Anthony closed the distance to Lopez.

"Anything else found on the father?" he asked with the unmistakable sound of vengeance in his voice. "I want to know everything he had on him."

"Harbor Patrol. Do you copy? Was there anything else found?"

"Roger. A cross, a few dollars, his watch, keys. That's about it."

Lopez put his hand on Anthony's shoulder out of respect, or support. He didn't appear sure himself. He waved Vicki and Malcolm over. "There's nothing more you can do, Tony. Why don't you head back to the museum? I'll keep you informed of everything going on up here."

The Special Ops Chief's voice sounded through the radio. "We just found a crumpled piece of paper in the victim's pocket, below the stones. Doesn't say much, just has the letters *OTO* and *EGC*, followed by, West 25th Street."

"Copy that," Lopez said.

"We're on our way out. Over."

Vicki observed the scene around City Island Bridge. Red-white-and-blue lights from the light bars of police cars flashed in staccato pulses. New

York's bravest now had its vehicles on the scene, their bright red-and-white lights adding to the display of flashes. People stood on docks and in boats swaying in the bay looking on, eager to find out what had happened under the bridge as the Harbor Unit and Scuba Unit boats emerged from underneath. Daunted – nearly to the point of being tongue-tied – by the scene playing out, Vicki summoned the courage to speak. She had to. The words on the piece of paper found in the father's pocket provided a clue, but only she realized it.

"Twenty-Fifth Street is where one of the obelisks is located," she said to Anthony.

Anthony stared at Vicki in silence. Slowly, his expression changed to one of contemplation. "Let's go," he said to Vicki and Malcolm.

CHAPTER 31

TRAFFIC FLOWED NICELY IN THE BRONX and on the FDR Drive in Manhattan. The congestion from the east to the west side of the island was a nightmare. Not a single word was spoken during the ride back. The unease inside the Chevy Suburban notched several rungs higher as traffic came to a complete standstill halfway down Twenty-Third Street. Vicki avoided eye contact by focusing on the spot where she had stood a couple of weeks earlier on the wide, two-way street alongside a horde of other awed spectators who had assembled to watch the city's summer solstice event as the sun dropped squarely between the buildings on Manhattan's east–west grid.

"Damn it to hell! Why was Father Franconi wearing regular clothes?" Anthony blurted with blatant anger in his voice, breaking the long silence.

Vicki and Malcolm refrained from speculating, eyes fixed on diversions.

Anthony flung his suit jacket into the rear of the SUV. "I can't sit in this maddening traffic a second longer. Let's go," he said to Vicki.

One-by-one, they jumped from the SUV and entered the south side of Madison Square Park, where a long line of tourists stood in front of the park's popular hamburger joint because their tour guides mandated it. The world's once-largest clock loomed over the park to the east and stretched out from the twenty-fifth to the twenty-seventh floor of the building. The pale-green, copper hands formed a near-level plane from the numerals 3 to 9 on the nine-meter long clock dial. More often than not, the time was reliable.

Vicki couldn't hold back any longer. The unyielding heat of the sweltering summer was getting under her skin, making her atypically waspish.

"Are you going to tell me why the captain said he wouldn't get much info from the people on Arthur Avenue?"

Anthony's head snapped left; his eyebrows were furrowed.

"Are you really going to push this?"

Vicki stood her ground. "Why shouldn't I know?"

Anthony exhaled vociferously through his nose; his lips clenched with clutching annoyance. "If you must know, there's a certain presence on Arthur Avenue."

Vicki connected the dots.

"Oh, an Italian neighborhood."

"That's right," Anthony answered before she could put her thoughts into words. "And that presence doesn't appreciate rats or anyone else pressured into talking. Does that satisfy your curiosity?" His head shook. "You were better off not knowing."

No more was said.

Exiting Madison Square Park short of the northwest corner, the two defied the flashing lights forming the words 'DON'T WALK' on the crossing signal and hurried across the street, hopping onto Worth Square, the raised-cement traffic island situated in the busy confluence of Broadway, Fifth Avenue and several cross streets. Large, interspersed, cement planters brimmed with leafy green and maroon coleus. Red-leafed maple trees and sprawling blue-and-red striped umbrellas shaded the café-style seating on the square. The obelisk soared nobly in the upper section.

"What are we looking for?" Vicki asked, not bothering to look at Anthony. Instead, she gazed up at the fifty-one-foot-tall granite obelisk.

Shoulders risen, Anthony replied, "The note said *OTO* and *EGC*."

Anthony and Vicki examined the copper plaque mounted onto the base of the obelisk, displaying a man in uniform on a horse. "Who is he?" she asked, knowing Anthony could provide an answer. He loved to share his knowledge of military history, and that would provide a distraction from the murder of his college mentor.

Anthony hesitated before answering, rubbing an irritated eye.

"General Worth served in several wars during the first half of the 1800s," he reluctantly answered. He wasn't in the mood for conversation.

Tripping a memory, Vicki remarked, "You really knocked Albert for a loop the other day when you mentioned crusaders prized swords made of Damascus steel."

Suspicion ignited in Anthony's mind. "What turned you onto that saber, anyway?" he asked, probingly, turning and looking into Vicki's eyes.

"A Rembrandt painting. Then the replica of a sword on an effigy tomb at The Cloisters." Vicki stared blankly at Anthony, gauging his response.

Straightaway, Anthony knew she was referring to the replica of the distinctive sword on the tomb of the holy crusader Jean d'Alluye. Holding his cards close to his chest, he questioned again whether Vicki had stumbled upon something known only to a few people at the museum. The message left by the senior medieval arts curator also weighed on his mind. She was clearly upset about something that Vicki did at The Cloisters, but Anthony hadn't the time to play phone tag, so he couldn't bring up the matter to Vicki just yet.

He removed his sunglasses, pocketed them, and surveyed the mix of classical and modern buildings encompassing the traffic divide. The yellowy-rays of the summer sun baked the glittery façade of the landmarked Flatiron Building to the south. The wedge-shaped building redirected the light of the western sun to the north, toward Anthony and Vicki. Anthony traced the sunlight until his sight rested on the shadow cast by the obelisk.

"Follow me," he said signaling with his hand, circling the base of the obelisk, and visually tracing the shadow extending across Twenty-Fifth Street. Forcefully, he stopped the cars driving west on the street, and followed the shadow until he reached the very tip, which pointed at the door of the building directly across the street from the obelisk.

Vicki followed close behind, gesticulating *sorry* to drivers as she crossed. Car horns blew repeatedly from the impatient drivers.

Anthony pointed to the sign above a door that read:

Ordo Templi Orientis

Saucer-eyed, Vicki approached the building. It was the most modest building in the area, by far, and the simple brick masonry stood out like a sore thumb among the other buildings, but only after noticing it. *Hidden in plain sight. New York City is funny like that,* she knew all too well with the thousands of buildings in the city. 'Worth Building' was inscribed in large letters on the upper façade of the edifice. She stopped in front of the door.

"The letters *OTO* are written below this coat of arms," she called out, completely amazed at what she believed was happenstance. "Was it pure luck that we're here when the shadow from the obelisk led us to the right place?"

"Considering this is the most distinctive building in proximity of the obelisk, I think it's safe to assume that we would have spotted it one way or another. And that plaque," he remarked, pointing toward the only door to the building, "is a secret-society lamen. This must be some kind of lodge."

"Secret society," Vicki repeated, intrigued, moving closer to the lamen, and examining it. Inside the vesica-piscis-shaped lamen, an acute triangle was painted with an eye in the upper portion, similar to the Eye of Providence on the back side of a dollar bill. Vicki recognized the eye as the all-seeing eye. Below the triangle, the symbols were more esoteric. A bird, possibly a dove, was diving into a chalice with rosebuds and a candle with a Templar-like cross lit with two flames. Lines filled the vesica-piscis.

Anthony pressed the button on the side of the door as he stared trance-like at the wood door. It was an old door, an antique door – the style of door still seen on the brownstones throughout the city, but no longer allowable in the business district areas of the city for fire safety reasons. An outdated mail slot was cut in the lower section. The vintage door released a wave of unexpected feelings of his mentor. Guilt superseded anger as the most painful.

"Think there's someone in there?" Vicki asked.

Anthony buzzed a second time while gazing at the windows one story up. "Someone has to be in there." He buzzed harder.

Vicki squatted and pushed open the mail slot in the lower half of the door. "I see legs," she said.

Anthony pounded on the door. "We know you're in there. We just want to ask a few questions." This time, he hit the door with hammer fist strikes.

"What do you want?" sounded through the slot.

"We'd like to speak with someone in your organization."

"Who are you?" The man's voice was half mumble, half dread.

Anthony lowered and said, "Father Franconi sent us."

From inside, the distinctive sound of locks unlocking.

"Come in, quickly," the man inside demanded. After looking up and down Twenty-Fifth Street, he shut the door and locked it. "Please, remain here. I cannot allow you to come in any farther."

"What is this place?" Vicki asked as she stepped into the unfurnished foyer and tried to glance behind a beaded curtain that led into the lodge.

"Ordo Templi Orientis is an order dedicated to the Law of Thelema."

Anthony stepped closer to the man. "Look, we're not here to pry into your organization. We just want to know why the father would send us to you."

The man swallowed nervously. "I have no idea."

"It may be in reference to the obelisks outside," Vicki said.

"Obelisk?" the man howled. "What's there to know about obelisks? I don't know anything about obelisks." His eye movement verified the lie.

"If you don't start talking, I will get a warrant and have police officers search every inch of your lodge." Anthony showed his retired NYPD identification badge. "You can start by telling us what *EGC* stands for."

"You'll need to speak to the bishop. Please, wait here."

The man twirled, nearly falling over, and dashed through the beaded curtain. His exit produced a swaying of long lines of colorful beaded strands.

"Was it the stuttering that suggested he was lying?" Vicki asked.

"One day, I am going to teach you the Reid Technique."

"Reid Technique?" Vicki commented, instantly distracted by a large, elderly man dressed in a long black vestment with a white collar and a flashy white fascia around his ample midsection. Crosses were stitched with gold thread on both sides of the red stole hanging from his shoulders. Dark eyes beamed as he extended his hand and smiled at Anthony.

"May I help you?" he asked, cordially.

"Yes," Anthony replied, wondering if he should call the man father. "I'm Anthony Leonardi. This is Vicki Lange. We're from the Met Museum, the Security Department, and we have a few questions."

The wide grin amplified the withered lines in the man's weathered face at the corners of his mouth. "Bishop Osbourne," he said, introducing himself. "It's a pleasure to meet you both, I'm sure."

"The pleasure is ours," Anthony responded, smiling humbly.

"The Met, huh? I'm quite fond of your museum. I was just there three weeks ago to see the new Michelangelo special exhibition. Wonderful show."

Anthony couldn't hold back "Pardon my ignorance, but what church are you associated with?" he politely asked, assessing the bishop's garments.

"Did Brother Allen not say?" the bishop remarked with an apologetic tone.

"The Ecclesia Gnostica Catholica is the ecclesiastical arm of Ordo Templi Orientis. I serve as the auxiliary bishop for the New York Chapter, where I've preached Thelemic theology to my loyal followers ever since I left my parish in Boston twenty-two years ago."

"That's what *EGC* stands for," Vicki said aloud.

The bishop leaned toward Vicki. "Pleasure to meet you, my dear."

"What exactly is Thelemic theology?" Anthony asked.

The bishop delicately draped his stole over a velvet hanger, then continued to speak. "Thelema was founded by an English prophet during the nineteenth century," he explained as he hung the stole in the closet. He gently shut the closet door, unlocked the entranceway door, and gestured to Anthony and Vicki to exit the building. The affable smile did little to offset the message that Anthony and Vicki were not welcome inside.

"Ladies first," he said holding the door open.

Vicki and Anthony politely obliged.

Double-checking the locked door from the outside, the bishop picked up where he had left off. "This prophet was entrusted by divine mandate to teach the people of the world that history is divided into three eons. The first was the *Aeon of Isis*, prehistory essentially, when humans worshipped the Great Goddess, symbolized by the goddess Isis. The *Aeon of Osiris* followed, forcing a major change in spiritual direction for our ancestors, who turned their prayers to male gods and revered patriarchal values."

"Like the Abrahamic gods?" Vicki asked.

The bishop nodded, continuing as he walked.

"The third and final eon, the *Aeon of Horus*, is now upon us."

Anthony shot Vicki a veiled incredulous look, and got to the point. "Any idea why Father Franconi might send us to you?"

The bishop abruptly stopped.

"Brother Allen said you know Father Franconi."

"He's no longer with us," Vicki said, tersely. "He was murdered today."

The bishop didn't bother to ask about the details before his head dropped. "That's sad news. Very sad news, indeed." He looked skyward, above the city skyline to the north, at the pointed mask on top of the Empire State Building rising into the heavens. Solemnly, he said, "When it rains, it pours. First, Roberto was removed from the clerical state, then his life taken."

"Hold on!" Anthony barked, realizing that the two events were not unrelated. "Are you saying that Father Franconi was defrocked?"

Vicki gasped. "That's why he was dressed in regular clothes."

The bishop rested a consoling hand on Anthony's shoulder.

"I'm afraid it's true. Laicization began last week."

"Because it's a worse sin to kill a priest?" Vicki deduced.

"In the eyes of the Almighty, the taking of any life is a sin."

"What was your relationship to Father Franconi?" Anthony asked matter-of-factly, facing the bishop and restraining a mounting irritation.

"We did our novitiate together," the bishop explained, eyes tightly shut in recall, and with a mien reflecting sadness. "We worked together for several years teaching in universities in Washington and then Boston before we took our rites of ordination. Roberto went back to New York, and I stayed in Massachusetts. He didn't approve of my decision when I eventually left the Church. Not on an ideological basis, of course, but Roberto felt strongly, resolutely so, that change should come from within."

"From within," Anthony restated with a sardonic tone. "And the next thing you know, you're hanging from the underside of a bridge."

The bishop nearly retched with anguish.

"I'm truly sorry for the loss of your long-time friend, but you may be of valuable help. What do you know about that?" Vicki asked, pointing to the Worth Obelisk on the opposite side of Twenty-Fifth Street.

"I suppose I owe Father Franconi this much." The bishop pointed to the Madison Square Park. "Let's talk in the park. It will be safer in there."

CHAPTER 32

THE ICONIC GREEN 'WORLD'S FAIR BENCHES' strewn throughout New York City lined the circuitous pathways of Madison Square Park. Anthony and Vicki sat on a bench separated from the adjoining bench by an ornate, Victorian-style, cast-iron armrest. The bench was situated in the shadow of the thirty-foot-tall Eternal Light Flagstaff, rising in majesty above the ornamental trees at the entrance to the park. A star-shaped shadow formed by the luminaire on the top of the flagstaff tattooed the pathway in front of the bench.

"Whew," the bishop griped as he patted his large and amply wrinkled forehead with a handkerchief. "This heat is unbearable." He clutched the metal armrest as he flopped onto the adjoining bench with a loud release of breath, shaking both benches.

The park was mobbed. Most of the people visiting the park were tourists exploring the Flatiron District or seeking relief from the steamy streets.

Anthony didn't want to offend the man but felt compelled to ask a question. "Were you a bishop before changing churches?"

The bishop chuckled heartily. "Not many members of the clergy make it to such an elevated level in the Catholic Church, Mr.–?"

Anthony repeated his last name.

"The Ecclesia Gnostica Catholica recognizes different procedures for reaching the Episcopate, Mr. Leonardi, but for those who wish to grasp the transcendentalism of the great priests from the banished age of virtue, there's but one path." He turned to Vicki and stared almost as though he was staring

146

into her soul. "There's a light within a person of light, and it shines on the whole world. If it does not shine, it is dark."

Vicki offered a cautious smile.

"Those are the words of Jesus from the Gospel of Thomas, which is now recognized by many as the actual Q source."

"Doubting Thomas?" Anthony said stridently.

"The significance of the episode, Mr. Leonardi, is not to be found within Thomas's skepticism as we are taught to believe. The more important message, the esoteric significance, is found in the fact that Jesus showed himself to Thomas precisely eight days after he had emerged from his cave."

Vicki sat up. "Did you say eight days?"

The bishop drew the number 8 in the air with his index finger while at the same time saying, "The two circles of life. The top circle descends to the lower circle, then rises again to the top circle."

Anthony had heard enough. "What is it that you wanted to tell us?"

Gasps of astonishment rang out from a small crowd as a Cooper's Hawk dropped with aerial precision from its hidden perch in an American sycamore tree and landed on top of a pigeon, piercing its body with its sharp, curved talons. The more squeamish turned away as the pigeon rolled and thrashed its wings until succumbing. Unfazed by its audience, the hawk fixed its fiery red eyes on its prey, then tore into the pigeon's underside.

The bishop's sight shifted from Anthony to Vicki. "I presume you want to know about the time capsules under Cleopatra's Needle?"

"How did you know?" There was a manifest synchronicity between the perplexed blinks of Vicki's eyes and the angling of her head.

"You asked about the Worth Obelisk, so I naturally assume that you know something about the obelisk behind your museum. Many, actually, know what's under Cleopatra's Needle. Some of those people would also like to get their hands on those time capsules, one of them in particular." Facial lines constricted with a frown. "Dangerous people."

"The gold-plated capsule?" Vicki propped up, readjusting her position on the thin slats of the bench, then leaned forward. "What's the significance of moving obelisks from Egypt to Rome?"

"No one knows for sure what's in that particular capsule. The contents have been secret from the start, but from what I understand from various sources, it's not so much about the relocation of obelisks from Egypt to Rome; rather, it's believed that that particular capsule contains scrolls with detailed instructions to carry out rituals passed from Egypt to Rome."

Visibly vexed, Anthony crossed his arms.

"And what exactly is the source for this information?"

"Several scrolls were removed from the Royal Library at Alexandria only days before the emperor had the library burned to the ground. They were then smuggled out of Alexandria as tensions peaked between Christians and pagans and Christians and Jews. Bishop Cyril ordered monks to destroy all non-Christian temples and to find and kill Hypatia, which they did by dragging her into a church, beating her, and then flayed her alive." The bishop paused for a moment of silence, eyes shut, then said, "Of course, that was the end of the enlightenment in Alexandria, so the scrolls had to be relocated."

Vicki winced. "Hypatia? Wasn't she —"

"The most brilliant woman of antiquity—mathematician, astronomer, and philosopher, who lived at a time when having certain convictions was a dangerous thing to possess." The bishop shook his head. "So many needless deaths, on all sides."

"What about the scrolls?" Vicki asked, leaning forward.

"They were considered lost for centuries. Some say they were hidden on the island of Crete, while others swear to the good lord above that they were sent to Malta. It was even rumored that the Vatican found the scrolls when Pope Sixtus V tried to conquer Egypt." The bishop wiped the sweat from his face with a handkerchief, then returned it to his shirt pocket. "Whispers circulated in underground circles that Sixtus had the Lateran Obelisk, one of the eight Egyptian obelisks, moved to Rome and re-erected to hide the scrolls underneath it, but he never found them. Centuries later, word spread that the scrolls were brought to America, perhaps with Cleopatra's Needle."

Vicki placed her hand to her mouth with an intake of breath.

"And the capsule that you asked about, well, it isn't made of gold. Or, at least not of pure gold, but of a rare metal that the Greeks called orichalcum."

"What's orichalcum?" Vicki asked, in a tone that broadcasted her intrigue.

"A rare copper–gold alloy, used by the most ancient of ancient civilizations for special purposes many centuries before the Roman Empire or even the Greeks. It was a highly-prized metal, and for good reason. Both copper and gold were linked to revivification and eternal life, so orichalcum was known as the ceremonial metal of resurrection."

The day's heat at its peak, Anthony mopped the sweat from his forehead. An anguishing bout of grief forced him to shut his eyes as the thought of the murder of his mentor rose to mind. A fade from conversation allowed for sensory intake. Pigeons cooed below as their purple heads bobbed for dropped morsels of food. Somewhere, a baby cried. Dogs barked commands to one another in the nearby dog run. The bubbling of the park's large fountain was drowned out by the ear-splitting noise of distant jackhammers. The queasy smell of sizzling hamburger grease crested in the humid, thick air.

"I still don't understand how this rare metal can represent resurrection," Vicki remarked, after listening to the bishop's clarification to her prior question, and noticing that Anthony was completely tuned out.

"Long before you were born, young lady, I provided the parishioners in my church with bread and wine to represent the body and blood of Christ. Long before the Church began the practice of the Eucharist, the ancients had their ceremonies."

Anthony slapped his thigh and stood. "You ready to go?" he asked Vicki.

"You strike me as an intelligent man, Mr. Leonardi," the bishop remarked, shifting in a way that suggested he was not ready to depart, "but even the most learned among us may not know as much as he thinks. We are now only beginning to scratch the surface when it comes to our knowledge of ancient times. What has long been opaque, in a manner of speaking, is now more transparent to those who know how to look."

Anthony nearly spat his next words.

"You mentioned dangerous people."

From the start, the bishop had hoped to avoid the subject, at any cost, but he now felt it was imperative to bring up the matter. He owed it to Roberto.

"Mr. Leonardi, I was reluctant to broach the subject of your relationship with Roberto," he said in an almost placating voice, "because I can see the sadness in your eyes. But I must ask. Am I right to assume that you were a student of the father?"

Anthony purposely squinted, tightly. "He was my college mentor."

"May I presume, then, that he felt comfortable enough with you to talk about certain priests who lived in the seventeenth and eighteenth centuries?"

Anthony grimaced at the sight of the mischief of rats scurrying in and out of the park's bushes and swept his glance across Madison Square Park. He rested his gaze on the glass façade of the soulless, modern high-rise on the south side of the park, thinking back to past conversations with his mentor.

Assessing Anthony's reaction, the bishop continued. "I believe, then, that you know I'm talking about Fathers Claude Sicard and Athanasius Kircher."

"Who were they?" Vicki pressed.

"The two never crossed paths, but both men had similar missions. Father Sicard was the first of many Jesuit missionaries who went to Egypt. He also made the first known map of the country. Sicard was sent to Egypt with orders to survey the country. He spent most of his time in Antinopolis, a city named after the boy–lover of Roman Emperor Hadrian." The bishop allowed the information to sink in, then continued. "The boy, Antinous, died in that town, and because of the passion Hadrian felt for him, the emperor named the town after him. But Hadrian had also engaged in the ancient rites of the Greek Mysteries, so Sicard was seeking any possible evidence of the scrolls."

"Father Franconi never mentioned anything about scrolls," Anthony insisted, wiping the perspiration from under his nose with his sleeve.

"Perhaps for your safety." The bishop gazed with sureness. "Sicard had gleaned most of his knowledge of Egypt from Father Athanasius Kircher, also a Jesuit and the world's first Egyptologist. His magnum opus, *Oedipus Aegyptiacus,* in fact, opened up the way for our current understanding of hieroglyphics. Equally remarkable, by studying the secrets of the ancient Pythagorean School, he also learned to decode hierogrammatics."

"That's how Cy described the carvings in the Temple of Dendur," Vicki said, looking at Anthony, then turning back to the bishop.

"You may be interested in knowing, Mr. Leonardi, that Kircher inscribed odd hieroglyphics onto the obelisks in Rome. That," the bishop declared, slowly standing, "is the reason why it was believed that the scrolls were hidden under the Lateran Obelisk. It proved untrue, but the hierogrammatics on the obelisks, many believe, provide clues to the location of the scrolls."

Anthony pictured the hierogrammatics carved into the lintel inside the crypt of the Temple of Dendur depicting Anubis over the words 'gate' and 'death'. Since the death in the temple over a week earlier, he had made little progress uncovering positive leads. Now, his mentor was murdered. He had a gut feeling that the deaths were related, but also realized that he'd never make any progress following preposterous leads or listening to tales of the past. He had to confer with the police commissioner and get down to brass tacks. He put on his sunglasses and pulled out his card from his wallet. "When you're ready to provide helpful information, call me at this number."

THE ANGLE OF the shadow formed from the obelisk pointed more easterly than it had thirty minutes earlier. Vicki focused her sights on the obelisk while exiting Madison Square Park, thinking about what the bishop had said. Anthony, on the other hand, was growing more annoyed by the drivers on Fifth Avenue continuously, infuriatingly, blowing their horns. "It's New York City, for fuck's sake!" Anthony exclaimed. "Do people think they can drive in Manhattan without encountering traffic?"

The ever-present wail of an ambulance blared in the distance.

Anthony used the break in on-coming cars to encourage Vicki and the bishop to jaywalk across the street, hoping to get a fix on the horn blowers. The long line of traffic on Fifth Avenue began to move. Concealed behind a delivery truck, a motorcycle abruptly switched lanes, recklessly swerving around the truck, sideswiping the taxi in the next lane. More horns blew, car tires screeched to a halt. Smoke rose as rubber melted on asphalt and the red Ducati raced head on, bearing down at high speed, motor roaring.

"Vicki!" Anthony shouted, perceiving the head-on trajectory.

"That's the same motorcycle from the Bronx."

"Get down!" Anthony screamed when he saw the rear passenger raise the automatic rifle. Repeated shots rang out, indiscriminately blasting holes in everything in sight as the shooter tried to steady his aim. The bishop froze with an enfeebled fear. Anthony tugged him down to the sidewalk behind a parked car as a second round pierced the body of the car and shattered the windows as an endless onslaught of bullets blasted holes from the rear to the front of the automobile. Screams could be heard in all directions.

Nimbly, Vicki crouch-ran to the rear of the bullet-ridden car and half-rose as the Ducati zipped by with a deafening rumble. Rising with unbridled fury, she racked the slide, took aim, and emptied her KelTec P-3AT.

Anthony dialed police headquarters on his phone.

"Drive-by shooting. Twenty-Fifth and Fifth. Red Ducati. No registration plates. Two suspects. Man down." He stood as he listened for confirmation and watched as the bike ran the light on Fifth Avenue, jumped the curb, and raced down the sidewalk to Sixth Avenue. Frantic pedestrians leaped into building doorways and dove between parked cars. The jet engine-whirl of the Ducati's dual, turbo engine reverberated with a thunderous roar off the buildings on Twenty-Fifth Street, drowning-out the screams of terror.

"I think I got the shooter in the shoulder," she stated, voice shaky.

"Nice job, Vicki." Anthony assessed Vicki's emotional and psychological states. "Holster your weapon," he directed, then surveyed the crime scene.

"Do you think they followed us here?" The high-pitch of Vicki's voice revealed her alarm. She stared down Twenty-Fifth Street. "Maybe they're going up to Twenty-Sixth and will circle back around."

"They aren't coming back." Anthony knew better.

"Is he dead?" Vicki asked, looking at the bishop's large body spread out across the middle of the grimy, concrete sidewalk.

"Stay calm. He's just unconscious."

She braced herself against the bullet-ridden car. "You saved his life."

Anthony gazed at the bishop, splayed on the grimy sidewalk. "I'll stay here until help arrives. Find Malcolm. We'll be here for a while."

CHAPTER 33

THE SUN HAD LOWERED BEHIND THE top of featureless modern high-rise buildings to the west when Anthony finished talking with the commissioner, chief of department, and the chief of detectives. Spectators who had gathered at the crime scene hours earlier were long gone. The increased bottlenecking of traffic in the area waned to the normal level of daily congestion but worsened again with the evening rush hour. Anthony hollered and gestured to Vicki that he'd be another few minutes as he headed to Starbucks.

To pass the time, Vicki found a shady seat under an umbrella in Worth Square and had spent the better part of the past few hours on her iPhone looking into the things that the bishop had said. Right away, she discovered that millions of people around the globe believed in gnostic ideas, most without knowing it.

Gnostic traditions, she had read, had their roots in the mystery schools that had flourished in and around the Greek and Roman Empires, beginning with the Greek Eleusinian Mysteries. Certain accounts claimed that Jesus had learned the knowledge of the Kingdom of God from the mystery schools. Other sources suggested that he had acquired his knowledge of the mysteries from John the Baptist—identified by Jesus himself the reincarnated prophet Elijah—and that Jesus had transmitted the secret knowledge to his closest disciples. Some claimed that his parents belonged to the ancient Jewish Essene sect, authors of the Dead Sea Scrolls, and that the Essenes had long practiced the ritual of giving birth to a prophet. But Vicki was most astonished to learn that the Essenes had been instructed in the Pythagorean ritual of reincarnation, and they had taught Jesus the secrets of resurrection, a claim dismissed out of hand by the Church.

Vicki looked around when she heard her name called.

"You ready?" Anthony said as he approached with two Grande cups of coffee. A plastic bag hung from his hand. "I got you a turkey pesto sandwich. Hope that's okay."

"Two cups? It's been a long day, I know, but –"

"Take it easy. One is for Malcolm." He elbow-pointed to Malcolm, double parked on the south corner of Twenty-Fourth Street and Broadway. The driver side window was down for the occasional extended arm motion, urging drivers who didn't see the blinking hazard lights to pass. "Poor guy has been sitting there for hours." Anthony handed Vicki the sandwich. "Sorry this took so long, and for," he hesitated before saying, "being short with you earlier. I think the heat is getting to me."

Vicki beamed. "Me, too."

"I was sure I'd leave this crap behind when I took the job at the Met."

"Geez, half of the cops in the city were here."

"And only bullets and shells were recovered. It's incredible," he remarked, staring up at the darkening sky and knowing it would be unlikely that the shooters would be caught with every minute that passed. "Aviation had two choppers in the air. Officers are placed at every bridge and tunnel leading out of Manhattan. Hell, New York State and New Jersey authorities were put on high alert, and not a single report of the bike."

Vicki stood. "How can that be?"

"It could mean a couple of things, but one thing is for sure. Those guys on the motorcycle are no amateur criminals." Anthony contemplated as he examined the area around Madison Square Park. Several officers remained at the taped-off scene, standing next to patrol cars with soundless flashing lights. People were going about their business, as if nothing had happened. Anthony took a sip of coffee. "They may also have someone on the inside, someone in a position of authority. You don't just shoot up a place and disappear into thin air, especially on a motorcycle as loud as a corporate jet."

Vicki stared down at the dirty sidewalk in disbelief, shaking her head. "Someone in this city had to see where they went."

"A few detectives are examining the traffic cams within a half mile radius of the scene. Several lieutenants are also asking to see footage from a few stores in the area. When will this fucking heat end?" Anthony unexpectedly shouted, with a release of pent-up rage. "I'm sorry. So, what have you been doing for the past few hours?"

"Just keeping myself occupied. And hydrated." Vicki raised the empty, twenty-four-ounce bottle of water that she had bought from a nearby deli. "It's beyond me how you can drink something hot on a scorching day like this. It's almost sadomasochistic."

Anthony took another sip with an expression of bravado. "Ahh," he voiced, after gulping the coffee. Small beads of sweat began to take shape under the gray hair covering his temples. "Some say drinking hot coffee on a hot day cools you off."

"Others say the industry spent millions in PR dollars."

"Let's go," Anthony said, after scoffing at Vicki's suggestion.

ANTHONY ASKED MALCOLM to drive up Sixth Avenue to the museum, anticipating the heavy evening midtown traffic, but they could divert from the congested streets once they reached Central Park Drive, which was closed to regular traffic during the evening hours.

"Remind me to never drive during rush hour again, Malcolm," Anthony remarked, tapping him on the shoulder. "We've been driving for fifteen minutes, and we've gone from Twenty-Third Street to Thirty-Fourth Street." Through the windshield, he eyed the tiny tree-lined park dividing Sixth Avenue and Broadway at Herald Square. Traffic moved just as slowly in the opposite direction. The clock on Macy's façade read 7:42 P.M.

"Rush hour in New York City," Malcolm remarked and left it at that, but knowing firsthand that traffic congestion was only getting worse with each passing year.

"What's this guy doing?" Anthony pointed to a tractor trailer several blocks ahead. "Vehicles with more than three axles are not permitted on Sixth Ave in the Garment District."

"He knows that, but he also knows that he'll get away with driving in this area nine out of ten times," Malcolm replied. "Worth the risk."

The incessant sounds of the city could be heard through the shut windows of the SUV. Car horns pealed in irksome pitches in every direction. City buses emitted obnoxious motorized whinnies with every stop and departure. An air horn sounded at the construction site on the corner for the next luxury condo marketed as the greatest place to live. A deafening rumble roared from the drum on the back end of a cement truck as the Archimedean screw inside rotated and dispensed cement siphoned forty stories up in the air. Over the grating sounds, the jarring bellow of Rumbler sirens outfitted on NYPD patrol cars sent shockwaves in all directions.

"Are you going to tell us again how empty the streets were when you grew up?" Vicki quipped, unwrapping her sandwich. "Now there are too many people in the city."

Malcolm emitted a stifled laugh, then faked a cough.

"Very funny," Anthony snapped as the tee-heeing sounds filled the SUV. But he realized that Vicki and Malcolm were just letting off some steam after a long and trying day. The remark was nonetheless a poignant reminder of how the city had changed over the past few decades—and not for the better. The ever-growing population was the biggest of the city's many problems. Streets and sidewalks were beyond overcrowding. Taxis, For-Hire Vehicles, and delivery trucks swarmed every neighborhood of the city. Mass transportation struggled ineffectively to accommodate the droves of newly arrived. The infrastructure in all five boroughs was crumbling faster than it could be repaired.

Unlike other great cities around the world where laws were enacted to keep the population at a viable level, New York City didn't have a similar moratorium on the number of apartment buildings that could be built. New luxury high-rise buildings went up every week as brownstone after brownstone was demolished. Two economic classes resided in Manhattan— the well-off and the struggling—and the wealthy were only getting richer. It wouldn't take much, some unforeseen global crisis, to completely tip the scales in favor of the moneyed. But nothing was going to change. Billionaire real-estate developers and politicians were in bed together. Everyone knew it, but it didn't matter. Developers got their way, and the city's politicians assured them of that, while rhetoric spewed from behind podiums about helping those in need ensured political survival.

Anthony observed the sea of cars occupying every single lane as far as the eye could see. "Unbelievable. Six lanes and they're all congested. Six lanes! That's larger than most highways in this nation, for heaven's sake."

To conceal her grin, Vicki gazed out the window. The treads on the large tires of a truck slowly wheeling by were filled with a brown-yellowish gunk. A sculpted Green Man, face covered with vines and leaves, on a corbel of a building came into focus as the truck passed. The ancient god of vegetation was playfully sticking his tongue out at modern society, as if he was saying, "See, I told you so."

"Chaos in Times Square," Malcolm said, getting a hold of his laughter and looking to the west, "but traffic on Sixth should ease up once we pass Forty-Second Street."

"At this rate, we won't get back to the museum until after 8:30."

Vicki's grin vanished.

"Aren't we stopping at Cleopatra's Needle?"

Anthony's dour expression hardened. "What for?"

"Because of what the bishop said. Aren't you the least bit curious to see if there are any signs of time capsules underneath the obelisk?"

The worry lines in Anthony's forehead constricted as he looked out the side window as the SUV passed Forty-Second Street. The crosstown traffic going both ways was also at a near standstill. "I already told you. I poked around the obelisk the other day."

"But you weren't looking for time capsules."

"It'll be dark by the time we get up there."

"Roads looks good once we pass Rockefeller Center," Malcolm injected.

"Wait!" Vicki yelled, sitting up. "I just realized something. I mean, I just made another connection. Cleopatra's Needle was moved from Heliopolis to Alexandria. That's where the bishop said the scrolls were hidden. Then the obelisk was moved from Alexandria to New York. And since there's a correlation between obelisks and the scrolls, the bishop must have been right about the scrolls being under Cleopatra's Needle."

Anthony raised his hands. "Vicki, please."

Vicki placed her half-eaten sandwich on the center console and slouched into the cushiness of the rear seat, twisting her body in a way to release the stress of the day running from her neck and down her spine. Through the tinted sunroof, she perceived the darkening sky. The cosmos above the city

157

was eclipsed by the bright streetscape. New York City was the only place on the planet where artificial lights eclipsed the wonders of the night sky. "Do you think we miss out on something?" she asked, leaning closer to Malcolm, "you know, because we can't see the night sky here in the city?"

"Stargazing is in our very DNA" Malcolm replied, turning his head, before quickly turning back to the road. "Some of the greatest ideas in history were inspired by looking up and studying the night sky."

Anthony didn't stir, so she changed the subject. "What's the next step?"

Hoping to feel more air-conditioning, Anthony adjusted the rear vent and said, "Considering that you're a key witness in the shooting, not to mention you discharged your weapon, you're coming with me to Police Plaza tomorrow to fill out some reports and answer questions for the investigation. Didn't you hear what the commissioner said?"

"I guess I was still a bit shaken up." Vicki mulled over her next question. She had to ask it. "What do you make of the things the bishop said?"

"It was the lack of what he said that bothered me."

Vicki hesitated before saying, "I mean about the religious things."

At that moment, he wasn't too sure what to believe and he was still trying to cope with the murder of his mentor. He gazed out the tinted window at the iconic Radio City Music Hall sign at Rockefeller Center. Though dated, the block-long, gold, blue, and red neon marquee twinkled magically at twilight. A thought arose. He'd kill two birds with one stone.

"Talk to Lauren Perry. I'm sure she can answer your questions better than I can, and," Anthony said, turning from the hypnotizing marquee and shooting Vicki an unequivocal stern look, "she's a little peeved at you for something that you did while you were at The Cloisters."

"Lauren, who oversee the medieval collection? Why?"

"Just do me a favor and give her a call. I'd rather not be involved."

"I'll contact her first thing in the morning and straighten everything out."

Anthony reclined, confident that Vicki could put the matter to rest.

CHAPTER 34

MALCOLM WAVED TO THE TRAFFIC OFFICER at the entrance to the park and steered the SUV around the NYPD crowd-control barriers that prevented cars from entering Central Park. Tourists congested the sidewalk leading into the park, spilling out into the road.

Vicki opened the side window to get a better look at the horse-drawn carriages lining the southern perimeter of the park. The stately, nineteenth–century carriages—both two and four seaters—were freshly painted in bright, attractive color combinations. Red and white. Black and violet. The brindled horses were decked out with tall plumes on their heads and black and brown leather straps with shiny studs crisscrossing thick necks. Groomed forelocks partially covered eyes. Nostrils flared with each exhale. The air was filled with moisture and the scent of horse manure, of simpler times. A bittersweet remembrance permeated Vicki's soul, releasing feelings of longing and joy.

The last of the evening light was fading as the large Suburban zipped up the east side of the park, passing a vintage Carousel, Central Park Zoo, and the Boathouse, with its rear lake awash with rented rowboats oared by jubilant travelers from near and far. Across the street, children mobbed the large *Alice in Wonderland* statue with its whimsical scene.

"Stop here, please," Anthony said after Malcolm drove over the 79th Street transverse, a road that bisected Central Park with a deep gully.

Vicki smiled, appreciative that Anthony conceded on the obelisk.

"Will you need me any more today?" Malcolm asked.

"That wasn't enough?" Anthony said sarcastically, exiting the Suburban.

"Thanks for all your help today, Malcolm. Couldn't have done it without you, as always. Get home safely, please."

He trailed Vicki as she rushed to the Greywacke Knoll. At twilight, the park bustled with people engaged in an array of activities from softball leagues to Frisbee games, to people lazing around on the grass, and even women dressed in belly shirts doing tricks with vibrant, lit hula-hoops. On the tree-spotted, grassy area north of the Greywacke Knoll, Bob White had the extended lens of his camera fixed on a Red-tailed Hawk perched on a branch of a black oak tree with its evening meal – rat shish kebab.

Vicki circled the obelisk, inspecting the four-sided granite pedestal and wondering where eight thousand secret-society members would hide the time capsules. *Eight thousand*, she reflected, again recalling what Sibyl had said about the number eight.

Her eyes lowered to the large limestone-block base that supported the granite pedestal for the obelisk. The pyramidal base was made of six-foot-long rectangular stone slabs, several dozen of them, and all stacked together like Lego blocks, forming three steep steps between the pedestal and the platform for the obelisk. She stopped when she noticed that the cornerstone was topped with a thinner slab of a limestone block, thinking back to the ritual cornerstone ceremonies with Washington and Franklin.

"The time capsules must be under here," she remarked.

"Let's not jump to any hasty conclusions, Vicki," Anthony advised, slowly crossing the platform for the obelisk, panting and wiping the sweat from his forehead. The setting of the sun brought little relief.

Vicki leaned over the protective brass railing surrounding the base of the obelisk and scrutinized the cornerstone.

"How are we going to remove the top slab?" she asked.

"Vicki, I've already told you," Anthony stated with a forceful pitch intended to get the message across. "Unless you get the proper permission, you cannot tamper with anything here. You can get arrested."

Vicki silently lowered her head, perceptibly disheartened.

Anthony exhaled. "I'll put a call into the parks commissioner."

CHAPTER 35

ANTHONY FOUND HIMSELF ALONE IN A desert, uncertain of the right direction. A loose-fitting tunic exposed his left side and the lower half of his legs. The hot sand singed the bottom of his shoeless feet as he frantically attempted to scale the slip-face side of a dune. He crashed into the sand several times as the scorching sand underneath him gave way. The desert boomed with the low-pitched sound of a primeval wind instrument as dunes in all directions violently crumbled. Unable to continue, he collapsed into the sand.

A full body jolt, and Anthony was in a less hostile environment. Meteoric stones protruded above the windswept stretches of desert pleated with rows of long dunes of a more clement environment. Signs of salvation marked the landscape in various directions. *Which way to go? What was the right path?* The blazing sun above obscured clarity.

An anthropomorphic figure—half-human, half-creature—pointed the way to a fertile oasis. Anthony rushed to the lush haven, praying it wasn't a mirage, a reflection of a distant image off the azure sky and deceptively placed onto the vaporous horizon. A remote part of his brain knew that he was in the midst of a dream, but the sleep-promoting regions were actively working to prohibit activity in the wake-promoting areas.

Shriveled, dry hands cupped as they skimmed the silvery water. The blissful jingle of the rattling leaves on a palm tree sounded with a breeze. Yellow sacks bursting with mouthwatering dates undulated within arm's reach from the tree. Anthony splashed the cool water onto his face. The water was revitalizing, baptismal. He bowed his head into the chalice formed by his hands and drank from the life-restoring pool.

Sweat beads cooled his skin, slowing vitals.

Arms extended behind his torso like the legs of a lawn chair, Anthony reclined with a sensation of euphoria. The conical head of a crocodile emerged above the surface of the water. Anthony stared into the green eyes of the crocodile, undaunted, until it transmuted into his mentor's face. "Help me, Tony," he heard right before he realized that his hands weren't touching solid ground.

At once, he was falling backward, tumbling and twirling in 360-degree flips as he descended into a bottomless hole. The sinking feeling of weightlessness experienced during free fall on a roller coaster—a cerebral forewarning for tree-dwelling ancestors passed down to more modern humans and manifested in dreams to signify the loss of control over something—resulted in a gut-wrenching, nauseating, sensation in the pit of his stomach. A part of Anthony's more evolved brain activated enough to shake him from the slumber, but not fully.

He was now in a dark cavern, a primordial womb of Mother Earth.

The air inside the chamber felt misty, ancient, producing a briny taste in his mouth that trickled down the back of his throat. Elongated fingers on stretched arms sought somatic sensation as Anthony staggered in the darkness, searching for what, he did not know. A lapse in time and sequence of events transpired, leaving little recollection of what had happened, but enough information to suggest that whatever had occurred during the gap in the dream was somehow, in some inextricable way, connected to his present predicament – entombed in a dark cavern with tunnels leading off in various directions. At each cave entrance, a flaming torch was affixed to the wall. Anthony grabbed the extended stave of a torch and warily entered a tunnel. The smell of burning wax and kerosene infiltrated his olfactory system. Soft animal-skin shoes now covered his feet and muffled each tenuous footstep. An unearthly voice materialized from the void. WRONG DOOR! Anthony jolted from his slumber.

The red, digital numbers on the alarm clock came into focus.

5:30 A.M.

Fleeting spells of sleep were interrupted by thoughts and reflections normally suppressed during the day. Anthony refused to do the tossing-and-turning thing.

On the bay-window side of the parlor, he pushed aside the ring-topped curtain panels. The streetlights were still aglow, except for one lamp that flickered on and off, heralding civil twilight. The streets were near empty. He looked up. Through the misty glow of the city's amalgamated luminosity, the night sky was transforming into an almost transparent magenta. A singular, magnificent star on the pre-dawn horizon flicked with subtle hints of blue and white, defying the lights of the metropolis. In only a matter of minutes, the sun's hot rays would creep west. Another steamy day.

He pressed the power button on his computer as he thought about his morning cup of coffee. It was a strong-blend day – one that called for a dark roast or perhaps an espresso. Either choice, he would have two, maybe three cups. It was vital that he stay attentive as he further researched the tunnels under the museum and Central Park. The research was imperative, particularly in light of the phone call he had received not less than six hours earlier informing him that several of the museum's strong-motion seismometers had detected irregular activity below the surface of the Met, although such detections weren't out of the ordinary. Past occurrences were clarified by experts who explained that the museum's highly-sensitive machines could pick up many things, such as nearby subsurface construction or even the rattling of an older-model subway train.

Anthony reflected on his one experience in the massive tunnel below the museum. On his first day as director of security, he was led to the lowest subterranean level of the museum, where he was shown the barrel vault, an enormous cylindrical tunnel nearly ten feet in diameter that stretched underneath the entire span of the museum from the northwest corner to the southeast corner. The gigantic pipe was once part of the original Croton Aqueduct water system, completed in 1842. The water system was later expanded to become the largest in the nation, consisting of hundreds of miles of underground tunnels, conveying billions of gallons of water daily from Croton, the Catskill Mountains, and the Delaware River to New York City almost eighty miles to the south.

The link that he made in the backseat of the FBI car between the financial institutions that had financed the water system and their association to the

Met rose to mind; more specifically, the ties between those who had established the financial institutions that backed the water system and their roles in founding the museum and amassing the collection.

* ~ * ~ *

ANTHONY MET PAUL in C3 hours later, and the two devised a monitoring system that Paul could use to track Anthony's whereabouts in the vacant water tunnels. Two-way radios weren't an option so far below the surface, so Paul jerry-rigged a 'real-time' tracking system that allowed him to monitor Anthony's location on a monitor in C3.

The two men took the Wing E elevator to S2, the museum's sub-basement. From there, they descended a steep, square winder-staircase to the barrel vault, gripping the metal railing tightly while shining their high-powered LED tactical flashlights in all directions. Stairs creaked on all four flights as the structure slowly rocked with an unsettling feeling of instability. The staircase had the haunting appearance of a time long past. Each step down felt like a step back in time, down through the strata of time.

At the bottom, Anthony extended the cord on a retractable key chain attached to his belt. He placed his flashlight under his arm as he looked for the skeleton key.

"Phew, it's hotter than hell down here," Paul griped.

"Exactly why I changed out of my suit."

"I don't think I've seen you in jeans since the days on the force," Paul remarked, shining the intense beam of his flashlight on the rusted door to the barrel vault.

Anthony delicately inserted the skeleton key into the keyhole of the centuries-old door and twisted. The lock clicked open. "I guess we shouldn't be surprised," he remarked. "When they built things back then, they built them right." He swung the door open. "Sure is dark down here." There was notable tension in Anthony's voice.

"You going to be okay down here, Tony?"

"If I don't get electrocuted," Anthony nervously responded as he flipped a light switch. The incandescent light bulbs illuminated in a domino effect, starting where the two men stood and continuing, one by one, into the distance in either direction. Both gaped in awe as the filaments in the bulbs increased to a bright white, lighting the entire length of the barrel vault. The circumference of the massive tunnel was larger than Anthony had remembered. In either direction, it stretched at least several football fields in length. He did a quick calculation in his head. The museum was one block wide and four blocks long, which made the barrel vault seventeen blocks long, nearly a mile.

That part would be just the first leg of his journey.

He unfolded the blueprint of the barrel vault, and traced his underground route. Anthony planned to walk in a northwesterly direction to the end of the barrel vault, then continue into the vacant water tunnels hundreds of feet underneath Central Park—that is, if he made it that far.

"Let me come with you," Paul insisted.

"Who's going to look over the security monitors?"

"Same people who are there now. C'mon, this won't take long. I'll walk with you to the end of the barrel vault and let you go solo from there."

Anthony nodded. "Let's make this quick. I want you to get back upstairs before the museum opens."

A march-like stride broke out as the two set off on the wooden catwalk in the center of the huge tunnel. The walls encasing them were built with huge slabs of rusted, concave steel panels, joined by chunky nuts and bolts.

"You know what this reminds me of, Tony?"

Anthony knew exactly what was on Paul's mind. "Cu Chi."

"You guessed it." Paul lit the side of the tunnel. "These walls are ten times the size and made of metal, not earth, but a tunnel is a tunnel. Right? Hell, I'll never forget when we were ordered to clear those goddamn tunnels. I was scared out of my mind. The entire platoon was on the brink of freaking out, but you kept your cool."

"I don't recall you being scared at the time."

"Are you serious? You don't remember how loud I screamed when I nearly got my left leg severed off on those punji sticks? I almost lost my fucking leg."

In the dark tunnel, Paul's sweaty, red hair had the appearance of viscous lava flowing down a dark hillside. More than once, Anthony reflected, Paul had saved his life and the lives of the other soldiers in the platoon. He was a

166

decorated war hero. And once again, Paul was at his side while in the midst of another precarious situation.

"We were just kids back then," Anthony remarked with gratitude in his voice. "Kids lucky enough to be over there at the tail end of the war."

"Kids or not, Tony, we could have saved Saigon if it wasn't for the asshole politicians back in Washington who hadn't a freakin' clue."

Anthony wanted to stay focused on the situation at hand and didn't want to conjure up any bad karma or unnecessary emotions.

"Hey, what's that up ahead?" he asked.

Paul turned his flashlight to the large, square object on the side of the tunnel.

"Didn't you tell me that the more expensive art was stored down here during World War II to protect the pieces from possible Nazi bombing?"

"I was told that option was considered, but I don't think it ever happened." Anthony examined the elongated, narrow box to the side, covered by a worn, canvas tarp. "You don't suppose someone put stuff down here at some point and forgot about it?"

"That does look like the carts the departments use to move chairs."

"Let's see what's under the tarp."

"Be careful, Tony. Probably some monster-sized wolf spiders down here."

Anthony stepped down from the catwalk, onto the steel floor of the tunnel, and flipped the tarp over the top. "Holy mackerel. There must be a dozen or so of those flimsy fruitwood chairs the departments use for events. Are these chairs that old?"

"Look, there's a note." Paul ripped a piece of paper off the side of the cart. He read the note, crumpled the paper into a ball, and threw it on the ground.

Anthony gazed quizzically up at Paul. "What did it say?"

"It just says these chairs are to be moved to the Medieval Chapel for a Christmas concert. And get this. It was dated December 1971. Guess they missed the date."

Anthony flopped the heavy tarp over the front of the cart, and the floor came alive. High-pitched squeaks echoed in the tunnel as rodents dispersed in all directions. "Rats!" he shouted, jumping up onto the raised catwalk.

Paul shined his light on the bottom of the tunnel.

"They're fuckin' everywhere. They must have been under the box."

Anthony shook with a feeling of disgust. "Jesus. One ran over my shoe. I felt its tail brush against my leg. I thought it had crawled inside my pants."

Paul raised his foot. "If one jumps onto this catwalk, I'll stomp the bastard. I swear, I'll stomp the shit out of it. I'll stomp them all if I have to."

"How the hell did they get down here if the barrel vault is sealed off?"

"Rats always find a way."

CHAPTER 36

THE SPACING BETWEEN THE LIGHT BULBS spanning the length of the barrel vault grew wider, providing less light between the bulbs. Loose bulbs buzzed with a low humming sound overhead. A few popped here and there, then disappeared with a fizzle.

With the descent into the ever-darkening tunnel, Anthony felt an increase in his heart rate. His stomach tightened with a wave of apprehension. His breaths were shorter and more rapid. The sogginess inside the tunnel resulted in a sticky layer of perspiration from head to toe, making it uncomfortable to move. It was just a matter of time, he realized, before the wetness inside the tunnel took its toll on his gunshot wound. *How much longer will my knee hold up*? he asked himself more than once.

As a distraction, he looked up at the ceiling and speculated where he and Paul were situated with respect to the museum galleries, guessing they were likely somewhere between the museum's main gift shop and the Egyptian Wing. The two stopped.

"What's this?" Anthony shined his light on the side of the tunnel.

"Looks like a 4x8 sheet of plywood to me."

Anthony turned to Paul with a scrunched phiz. "I can see that."

"Well, if I had to guess, I'd say it's probably a part of the catwalk and removed for some reason." Paul's comment came off as indifferent, and atypical.

"Maybe." Anthony switched his flashlight from his right to his left hand. He leaned over the edge of the catwalk and pulled the board away from the wall, remaining on the catwalk. He wasn't taking any chances this time. "This is strange."

Paul craned his neck. "What do you see?"

"There's a door behind the board." Anthony took note of the polished doorknob. "I didn't see any doors indicated inside the barrel vault when I studied the blueprints. Where do you suppose this door leads?"

Paul shrugged. "Can't record every door, I guess."

"And look at this." Anthony directed his flashlight onto the large board, moving his face closer to it. "There's something etched here. It almost looks like two obelisks. Just like the obelisk in Central Park, but two of them."

Paul jumped down from the catwalk, picked up the 4x8 sheet of wood, and placed it on the catwalk. "I don't see it," he said, studying the surface of the plywood. "It may just be the markings of the wood. It's too dark to tell."

Anthony stared at the door. "I'll have to check this out later. We can't have a door inside the barrel vault and not know what's behind it."

VICKI EXITED THE elevator on an employee-only floor and walked down a short, narrow corridor to Lauren Perry's office. The lights in all the offices in the medieval art employee department were off, but Lauren was presently overseeing the installation of a new illuminated manuscript exhibition, so Vicki knew she was working long hours.

Gently, Vicki knocked on the slightly open door to Lauren's office. In the stillness of the early morning, the knock sounded louder than intended.

A shrieking noise countered, followed by, "Yes."

Vicki pushed open the door. "I'm so sorry."

Lauren reclined in her chair, flipping her ponytail to the side. She was dressed just as Vicki had expected, smartly, but not formal, wearing stylish skinny jeans – a drapey dress shirt, and ankle boots. It was her West Coast protest against East Coast formality. "Vicki, good morning." Lauren seemed surprised, then her facial expression tensed. "Please, come in."

Vicki dialed-down the volume on her two-way radio.

"I'm really sorry," Vicki repeated, barely passing the doorjamb, and trying not to be too intrusive. She stopped, hands clasped at the waist, face slightly blushed. "I was informed that you were upset with me about something, so I felt it was important to come here and talk to you in person."

"Oh, I see." Lauren smiled, enigmatically, trying to conceal her concern. "Whenever I see someone from Security, I automatically think, you know, that there's something wrong, especially when I see someone of your rank."

Vicki hesitantly stepped forward. "I get that often."

Lauren sipped her green tea and placed the cup on her desk. "To be perfectly honest, I find it refreshing that you made the effort to come to my office and not send an impersonal email," she said, graciously. She exhaled through pursed lips. "And I'm enormously appreciative that you found that booklet under Jean d'Alluye's tomb. No one at The Cloisters has any idea how it got there. We're looking into the matter now. But, and this is a huge but, if you do need to investigate something in our department, either here or at The Cloisters, we would appreciate it if let us know beforehand."

"You're absolutely right." Vicki apologized once again. "I guess I just got carried away, but I made a point to put everything back the way it was. To be honest, when Margarita Abran told me that the booklet was in the building, I thought everyone at The Cloisters knew about it."

"Margarita?" Lauren's head tilted. She thought momentarily and said, "The guard with the gorgeous, curly hair?"

Vicki nodded with acknowledgment.

"What was she doing in the building after it closed?"

"She stayed late to work an after-hours concert."

"There was a concert at The Cloisters last Friday night? That's news to me. I didn't hear anything about the concert." Lauren emitted a soft "humph," readjusting her position. "Well, no matter. I'm glad you came to my office to clear this up. Honestly, I wasn't looking forward to having this conversation. These kinds of things are so awkward."

Vicki knew that if she didn't ask her questions right away, she'd lose her nerve. "If you have a few free minutes, I have an unrelated question to ask. A few, actually."

Lauren sipped her tea and smiled. "Of course, Vicki. I'd be happy to answer any questions. Would you like a cup of green tea, first? I have a yummy brand that is picked from trees at the foothills of Mount Fuji. Honestly," hand waved, "it's sensational."

"No, thanks. I had some tea this morning before my jog."

"You ran in this grody heat?"

Vicki repressed the giggle triggered by the colloquialism that she'd only heard in movies starring big-haired, San Fernando Valley socialites that she saw as a girl, and now from a woman with a PhD and well-respected scholar in her field. Nonchalantly, she replied, "Running in the summer isn't too bad if you do it before the daily heat advisory kicks in."

Lauren's head shook with incredulity. "Please, sit."

Vicki grinned, tensely. "Yesterday, I was in midtown with Anthony and we spoke with someone who said that he's from, or somehow associated with, the Ecclesia Gnostica Catholica."

"Oh?" Lauren veiled her skepticism, almost.

Vicki had anticipated the reaction. "This guy was also a Jesuit priest."

Lauren sat up, swiveled in her chair, and crossed her legs. "That's interesting."

"Long story short, this guy, who claims to be a bishop, said a few things that had me up last night scratching my head. I'm not sure what to think."

"Please, do tell." Lauren raised her tea.

"The first thing that he said that intrigued me was that the Gospel of Thomas was recognized as the 'Q source'. Have you ever heard of that?"

"Have I." Lauren placed her tea on her desk. "Though it's unlikely that Thomas is the actual *Quelle*—that is, the 'Q source'—but a few scholars have been working on that question since the Coptic version of the Gospel of Thomas was discovered, which is derived from an older, Greek papyrus unearthed in Oxyrhynchus, Egypt, in the late nineteenth century."

Vicki mispronounced the name of the Egyptian city.

"Oxyrhynchus," Lauren repeated, helping Vicki save face. "I know, it takes some getting used to saying. Anyway, the papyrus was found in an ancient garbage dump outside Oxyrhynchus, along with thousands of other papyri that are being studied at Oxford University. It was a remarkable find, mind you, with fragments written in Egyptian, Greek, Hebrew, Latin, Arabic, Aramaic, and other languages of antiquity. Most scholars believe that the papyri were trashed because of a decree from Rome."

"What makes Thomas so important?" Vicki's head tilted.

"If Thomas is the actual Q source, well, then," Lauren hesitated briefly before saying, "Jesus would have been recognized by his peers as a great preacher, but that's all."

"That would mean —"

"No rise from the dead."

"So, gnostics preached a different message than Christians?"

Lauren bit her lower lip before speaking.

"It's not so much about a different message as it is about the focus on either *faith* or *knowledge*. In other words, those who followed gnostic ideas preached spiritual awareness through knowledge. Christians sought—and seek—salvation through faith. I think it's fair to say, however, that many gnostic and Christian ideas are two peas in a pod. To the extent that either one influenced the other, well, that's not well known."

"But you're saying that there's some overlap?"

"Quite a bit," Lauren remarked. "Some considered in the gnostic camp, like Marcion and Valentinus, for example, preached a Hellenistic, but similar version of Jesus's message accepted by the Church." She clicked on a bookmarked website. "Here's an image of both Marcion and Valentinus."

Noting the men's apparel, Vicki asked, "Were they Romans?"

"Marcion was the son of a bishop who lived in what is today Turkey. He moved to Rome and became a member of the Church, well, that is, until he was excommunicated for his views, but he played an important role in the creation of both the New Testament and the Christian concept of the Father, Son, and Holy Spirit."

"He was gnostic, but a member of the Church?"

"Valentinus was almost elected Bishop of Rome. But let's keep a proper perspective here. People then didn't identify as gnostic or as Christian."

Vicki smiled sheepishly, a little confused.

Lauren rolled her chair closer to Vicki.

"It was a lively time when many different traditions were all competing—battling it out, if you will, for dominance of viewpoints. Preachers in the very same towns preached different messages. Some, like Marcion, believed that God sent Jesus into the world, but not the God of the Old Testament. Other preachers taught more esoteric messages of Jesus, while some didn't subscribe to a literal resurrection at all. Instead, they believed in a more spiritual resurrection, or awakening, experienced while alive."

There were so many questions to be asked.

"I didn't realize that Christian history was so multifaceted, I mean, especially with respect to the history of Jesus," Vicki said, and slowly shook her head.

"Perhaps you'll find this helpful," Lauren remarked, sensing what was on Vicki's mind—a question that she knew from past experience to be on the minds of many people. "The ancient Mesopotamians conducted yearly festivals that celebrated death and resurrection. These festivals began after the first full moon following the vernal equinox, and they continued for thousands of years, extending all the way down to the time of the Roman Empire. Not coincidently, some contend, that Jesus's rise from the dead is consistent with the same lunar calculation, marked by Easter."

Fascinated, Vicki asked, "Where can I get more information on this?"

"I'll put together a list of sources and email it to you." Lauren jotted Vicki's museum email address as a reminder. "But if you're interested in learning more about the past ideas, I'd recommend that you start by looking at the *Greek Magical Papyri*."

"Magical papyri?" Vicki's eyebrows rose. "That sounds intriguing."

"The papyri show that many Christian ideas are a blend of Egyptian, Greek, Near Eastern, and Jewish beliefs. They were also written when the idea of resurrection was ubiquitous in antiquity, so the *Mithras Liturgy* portion of the papyri is quite interesting in this respect because of the similarities between Mithra and Jesus."

Lauren read the Outlook reminder that popped up on her computer.

1 REMINDER(S) X

MEETING

TODAY 11:00 AM

MEETING TIME 90 MINUTES

She looked askance, irritated. "I'm sorry, but I have to run up to The Cloisters for a morning meeting *tout suite*. It's beyond me why they always wait until the last minute to schedule these things."

"What time do you have to be there?"

"Well before I can get there, that's for sure," Lauren replied, standing and gathering her papers. "Why don't you walk out with me, Vicki. I want to show you something in the collection that I think you'll find interesting."

CHAPTER 37

THE BARREL VAULT TERMINATED AT A steel wall with a large oval door. Anthony and Paul were now directly below the atrium for the Temple of Dendur.

"It's jammed," Anthony said, tugging on the door lever.

He examined the oval door in the middle of the wall. The door was made of different steel than the adjoining wall and had the appearance of a prototype of the more advanced airtight doors found in submarines or in space shuttles. Anthony knew the reason for the similarity. The egg-shaped door had been installed when the tunnel was handed over to the museum and had been designed to eliminate any ambient pressure differences between the barrel vault and the connecting tunnel under Central Park.

Unconvinced, Paul said, "Step aside, Tony." With a sudden violent motion, he stomped the lever with the bottom of his shoe, jolting it from a 3:00 o'clock position to a 6:00 o'clock position. From inside the door, a clicking sound rang.

"Just needed a little elbow grease," Paul said. "Or a swift kick."

Anthony heaved a sigh as he swung the oval door on its hinges and then cautiously walked through the opening. Something in the thick air of the adjoining tunnel forced his nose upward, then a deep sniff. "Phew, my God, it stinks in here."

"Where does this tunnel lead?" Paul asked as he stood in the doorway, waving his disproportionately-large hand in front of his nose.

"This tunnel goes under Central Park Drive and leads to the South

Gatehouse." Anthony threw his hands up in the air. "Don't let that door shut!" he yelled.

"I got it, Tony. Why do you think I'm standing in the doorway?"

"Just make sure the door doesn't close." Anthony breathed a sigh of relief. "This particular door is designed to automatically shut and can only be opened from the inside. If it closes, you can't go back into the barrel vault. I need you back in C3 ASAP."

"How are you going to get back?" Paul asked, clutching the oval door.

"I called the Parks Department this morning. I let them know that I planned to inspect some of the tunnels under the park and that I'd pass through the South Gatehouse. The commissioner was kind enough to send someone to the gatehouse to make sure I could exit."

"Are you talking about the gatehouse on the reservoir?"

An utterance of affirmation served as an answer. Then Anthony clarified.

"There's the North Gatehouse on the north side of the Jacqueline Kennedy Onassis Reservoir that controls the flow of water into the reservoir," he explained, "and the South Gatehouse, which once regulated the flow of water out of the reservoir and into several water tunnels that supplied the city's water in the nineteenth century."

"It smells like death in this tunnel."

"I hope it's just the foul water on the floor, not something more."

Paul illuminated the watery floor underneath the wooden catwalk. "Oh, it's more," he said, pointing his flashlight in various directions. "There are decomposed rodent carcasses everywhere. Thank God the catwalk is in here."

Anthony cringed as he gazed into the dark abyss ahead. "I suppose this catwalk was built by the sandhogs who sealed the barrel vault."

"You have to be a nutjob to work in these tunnels. Did you hear the story of that sandhog working under the East River when a pocket of compressed air pushed him through the river bed, all the way through the river, and shot him straight up thirty-feet into the air, only to crash back down into the water. Fuck no, not me."

Anthony continued to stare into the dark tunnel, maintaining his focus. "If my calculations are correct, this tunnel goes only about fifty yards or so."

"What about the next tunnel? Or the next one? You won't have any electricity like we did in the barrel vault." Paul directed the beam from his flashlight into the shadows of the tunnel. There was no end in sight. "I don't like this, Tony. It seems far too risky."

"I checked everything out, thoroughly. Trust me. I'll be okay."

"Alright," Paul remarked, unpersuaded. "Do you have everything you need?"

Anthony patted his pockets. "I have your tracking device, maps, a compass on my watch, and some water." Even the darkness of the tunnel couldn't mask the signs of apprehension. "I even brought my gun. The only thing I need is for you to watch over museum security, and to keep track of me on the monitor in C3."

"How long did you say you would be down here?"

"What time is it now?" Anthony removed the skeleton key from the ring and handed it to Paul. He didn't wait for an answer. "I'll be back in an hour, two at the most."

"If I don't hear from you by then, I'm coming back down, but with a mask for both of us. Can't be good to breathe in this putrid air. This must be what hell smells like."

Anthony winced as he peered down the dark passageway, hoping that his estimate of the length of the tunnel was correct. His heart rate increased. Blood pulsed in his ears. Momentarily, he considered scrubbing his plan, thinking his investigation of the tunnels wasn't worth the risk. But an inexplicable force pushed him forward.

"I'll see you in the museum later," he said tensely.

THE LINK TO the gatehouse was shorter than expected. Anthony exited the tunnel, walked into the lower level – the water bay – of the gatehouse and caught his breath. Sunlight streamed through two steel-barred windows on the east side of the upper level, several stories above, producing honeycomb-like markings on the rusticated retaining walls on the west side of the gatehouse. The design of the granite-brick walls, Anthony observed, closely resembled stone patterns used in mausoleums and in the walls of medieval fortresses.

He wiped the sweat from his forehead and inspected his surroundings.

The water bay of the gatehouse stretched deep down into the earth, far deeper than Anthony had expected. Large steel sluice gates fronted several underground tunnels leading into and out of the water bay. The sluice gates' system was fashioned on the sluice gates used for the Roman aqueduct system that had transported billions of gallons of water throughout the empire. Each granite-lined gate was closed, except for the six-foot-tall gate that Anthony had just ducked under to access the gatehouse's substructure.

Thinking that he wouldn't be able to continue into the tunnels under the park, Anthony ascended a steep, rusted wrought-iron staircase to the upper level of the gatehouse. At the top, he was drawn to an elaborate set of steely gearworks and valves that controlled the sluice gates in the water bay below. He clutched one of the large circular valves that were used to open the gates below as he caught his breath. The valve had the circumference of a car steering wheel. STOPCOCK was embossed on the flange.

Sweat formed above his temples and slowly trickled down Anthony's neck as he bent and examined the apparatus of the sluice gates, pointing his flashlight at each shiny, toothed-gear of the gear train, the perforated metal levers, and along the solid wheel and axle shaft. It wasn't much different than the movement in his Cartier watch that turned the hands, but more rudimentary. Still, the scale and design of the gearworks that controlled the sluice gates of the water bay was heralded as an engineering marvel for its time, designed to regulate the flow of over 500 million gallons of water daily.

It was too hot to wear his L. L. Bean shirt, so he unbuttoned it and draped it on a stopcock. He detached the tracking device from his shirt, clipped it onto the front pocket of his jeans, and stared at the tunnel – more like a large pipe – on the second level that ran through the reservoir. The auxiliary pipe served as the spine of the reservoir and was visible when the water level of the reservoir was low. It was maybe five or six feet in diameter, large enough to traverse, but entering the tunnel was hazardous and would add a substantial amount of underground travel that Anthony hadn't anticipated.

He exhaled his fears. He had to explore further.

* ~ * ~ *

THE SMALL GROUP that had paid a generous fee to tour the museum before it opened listened intently as the tour guide explained that they were walking through the Met's first collection space. She asked the group to stay together as they made their way from the Medieval Hall and walked to the European Sculpture and Decorative Arts galleries. The guide stopped in front of a small, marble statue of a boy known as the *Young Archer*. The statue, the guide announced exuberantly, had been misidentified for centuries, and was now considered by many to be Michelangelo's lost sculpture of Cupid.

In a neighboring gallery, Vicki and Lauren were standing in front of a glass display case containing a Gospel Book. Lauren placed her hand on the glass case. On impulse, Vicki wanted to tell Lauren not to touch, as she did with visitors on a near-daily basis but decided that it would be better to refrain from saying anything.

"I think you'll find this interesting." Lauren removed her hand from the display case. "I don't know if you have seen this yet. It's been on display for only a few days."

Vicki stepped closer and inspected the book inside the case. The illuminated watercolors on the parchment burst in astonishingly well-preserved reds, navy-blues, pink, and turquoise. The leather binding was in pristine shape. A small red sign inside the display case inside verified that the item was a new acquisition. "Is it a Bible?" she asked.

"Close. It's a Gospel Book, that is to say, a bound volume or a codex containing one or more gospels. We were excited when we acquired this particular Gospel Book because it contains various versions of the life and teachings of Jesus."

Vicki grinned. "That's why you showed me this."

"Yep, precisely. This Gospel Book was written in the ninth century, centuries before the story of the life of Jesus coalesced into the account known today."

Though appreciative of the beauty of the book's distinctive art and colorful calligraphy, set between stately Roman columns, Vicki was more intrigued by the history of the Gospel Book. "What's the provenance?"

"Often, we don't know for sure, but we acquired this from Christie's of London, and the trail indicates that it was written in France, Metz, we think. It was likely made for Charles the Great – or Charlemagne as the French say."

"It's written in Latin, I see."

"Um hum." Lauren blinked repeatedly. The gentle transitions of the brown and tan tones of the 'baked' make-up technique applied around her light-brown eyes looked like something straight out of a *sfumato* painting. *Mona Lisa's eyes*, Vicki thought, recalling that the baked make-up technique originated with the ancient Egyptians, brought back by drag queens, and all the rage for women on the West Coast.

"This Gospel Book was written not long after Latin replaced Greek as the language of the liturgy, another reason why we were so attracted to it. If you look closely," Lauren said, proudly, "you'll see examples of Jesus's Latin name, Iesus, an adaptation of the Greek Iesous." Lauren pointed out an example.

"Iesous was Jesus's Greek name?"

Lauren gazed at Vicki with a 'you-didn't-know?' expression.

"Iesous is Greek for Yeshua or Yehoshua, Jesus's actual name."

"Of course, I think I knew that, or heard that once."

Lauren laughed softly, detecting Vicki's confusion. "Needless to say, few people read one of these or even a Bible before the invention of the Gutenberg press."

She stepped closer to Lauren. "Even the literate didn't read the Bible?"

"Goodness, no! Until a few centuries ago, Christians were strictly forbidden by decree of the Church from reading things like this. In England, of all places, the lay person, the everyday person, was killed if he even dared to read the Bible. Bibles and Gospel Books were reserved for the eyes of the men of the Church and high nobility."

Vicki arched. "That seems weird, so elitist."

"I have to run to my meeting at The Cloisters." Lauren grimaced with the thought of having to race around Manhattan in the oppressive heat. "Anyway, it was nice chatting with you, Vicki. Stop by my office any time you have any questions."

* ~ * ~ *

IT WAS PITCH dark, a Vantablack void bordering on the blackness of a black hole in the far reaches of space. The tunnel that presently entombed Anthony was a fraction of the size of the tunnel leading to the South Gatehouse. There was no catwalk. His footsteps echoed hollowly in the tight confines. He had entered the tunnel bisecting the reservoir hoping that he could push through until he reached the North Gatehouse, but the anxiety surfaced from the outset. With each slumped-over step, the tunnel creaked. Putrid slime dripped onto his head. Bodily absorption of the toxic blue-green algae that grew on the reservoir in the summer, he knew, resulted in vomiting, seizures, and even death. His stomach tightened with the realization that he was separated from billions of gallons of water by a rusted, nearly two-hundred-year-old pipe. Slumped over with discomfort, Anthony advanced at a sluggish pace. The nauseating vapors inside the tunnel caused repeated gags. The tightness of his confines triggered all the signs of a panic attack.

He contemplated the reason for the water system in the first place, which resulted in further apprehension. The city's residents had desperately needed the fresh water supply because the island's many creeks and streams had been neglectfully polluted, resulting in the death of tens of thousands of inhabitants from cholera and yellow fever.

The air was hot, and revoltingly clammy.

With no end in sight, Anthony lumbered with physical distress in the direction of the North Gatehouse, shining his light 360 degrees in the crypt-like surroundings. A paralyzing pang shot through a nerve next to his gunshot wound. Nearly toppling, he squeezed his leg and winced in agony. He looked back in the direction of the South Gatehouse, which was completely obscured by darkness. There was no turning back.

CHAPTER 38

WITH THE FEW MINUTES BEFORE THE start of her shift, Vicki scanned *La Très Sainte Trinosophie*, hoping to find a reference, no matter how tenuous, to the mysterious scrolls that she was now firmly convinced were hidden under Cleopatra's Needle.

She slowed her pace as she read a section that caught her interest:

Wrapped in darkness, I seemed to descend into an abyss. I know not how long I remained in that situation. When I opened my eyes, I vainly looked for the objects which had surrounded me a little time ago. The altar, Vesuvius, the country round Naples had vanished far from my sight. I was in a vast cavern, alone, far away from the whole world . . . Nearby me lay a long, white robe; its loosely woven tissue seemed to me to be of linen. On a granite boulder stood a copper lamp upon a black table covered with Greek words indicating the way I was to follow. I took the lamp, and after having put on the robe I entered a narrow passage the walls of which were covered with black marble. It was three miles long and my steps resounded fearfully under its silent vault. At last I found a door that opened on a flight of steps which I descended. After having walked a long time I seemed to see a wandering light before me. I hid my lamp and fixed my eyes on the object which I beheld. It dissipated, vanishing like a shadow.

Without reproach of the past, without fear of the future, I went on . . .

Vibrations from her phone snapped Vicki from her spell. "Darn it," she said, realizing she had been remiss in checking her messages. She scrolled through until she saw the text from Anthony. She read his message:

It's clear that you're on to something regarding Miller's death, but I need you to focus on the WHOs not the WHYs. I'm going into the tunnels under the park, so I won't be around until later in the day.

* ~ * ~ *

THE NORTH GATEHOUSE was nearly identical to the gatehouse on the south side of the reservoir. Anthony sat on a sturdy pipe and unfolded the map of the city's water system. He carefully studied the numerous pipes winding under the five boroughs, each one color-coded to indicate the different systems constructed throughout the nineteenth and twentieth centuries.

The remodeled tunnels of the modernized aqueduct system, Tunnel 1 and Tunnel 2, both entered Manhattan from the north via the Bronx. Tunnel 1 was designed to extend below the Harlem River, supply Manhattan, and then continue out to Brooklyn. Tunnel 2 stretched from Manhattan and into Queens, eventually reconnecting with Tunnel 1 in Brooklyn.

Tunnel 3 was never finished but was designed to be the largest of all three tunnels. Billions of dollars had been invested in Tunnel 3. Dozens had perished during construction. But that was the price tag that accompanied great human achievement. The massive tunnel, after all, was designed to be the greatest engineering feat since the erection of the Great Pyramid.

Salty drops of sweat stung Anthony's eyes before dripping on the map as he studied it, unsure how useful the map would prove in guiding him through the underground passageways. With all the crisscrosses and overlaps in the various pipes constructed over the centuries, getting an accurate fix on his precise route was nearly impossible. The map made the labyrinth of tunnels look more like a pit of gigantic snakes rather than a guide.

But located at the end of Tunnel 3 was a highly-advanced elevating chamber, engineered to control the flow of the water in Tunnel 3, while acting as a state-of-the-art water-pumping system, forcing the water to the surface. It would be a decade, maybe longer, Anthony had read prior to his descent into the tunnels, before the elevating chamber was operational. And he was intent on finding out if unauthorized people could somehow access the tunnels under Central Park through the elevating chamber.

He folded the map and tucked it back into his pocket.

A fey grunt accompanied a body-twitching jolt as he descended several stories down to the water bay of the gatehouse, warily lumbered through an open sluice gate, then entered the next underground passage. The area of orbicular radiance produced by his flashlight extended twenty, maybe, thirty-feet into the dank tunnel. The half-rusted, steel walls reflected variegated shades of black or dark-gray, utterly lacking the colors of life. Rusted, fretted joints gnawed audibly with caution of decay. Already hundreds of feet below the surface when he left the North Gatehouse, Anthony continued to descend with each step farther into the darkness of the tunnel.

A compass check verified that he was descending in a southerly direction, straight into an area that he had hoped to avoid – traversing under an area of Central Park that once served as the burial ground for the eighteenth-century village of Seneca. The City of New York never exhumed the human remains from the village's cemetery when it declared eminent domain and forced the inhabitants from their homes in order to construct Central Park. At that moment, suppressing vampiric thoughts proved nearly impossible.

Knowledge trumps ignorance, Anthony repeatedly reminded himself as he continued with a guarded pace down the dark, damp tunnel.

With each step down into the earth, the temperature became more tolerable. Geothermal temperatures hovered around 55 degrees Fahrenheit, making the remainder of his journey more pleasant. The cooler temperature also triggered fond memories of the time when he and his ex took their daughters to Mammoth Cave National Park in Kentucky, where they searched the cave system. Life seemed much easier back then, he lamented, pushing ahead, though he knew it wasn't. It was just more enjoyable.

Anthony stopped mid-stride, his body completely inert. The unmistakable sound of footsteps sounded in the distance. Something was moving closer.

CHAPTER 39

WOLFGANG AMADEUS MOZART, THE BRILLIANT MASTER Mason, incorporated numerous esoteric themes into his operas. *The Magic Flute*, his most Masonic work, celebrates the themes of knowledge, immortality, and religious superstition. The opera first opened to a backdrop Masonic in design. A sphinx sat on the Nile. Palm trees surrounded a temple. Above the temple, the sun's rays beamed through dispersed clouds. Was it the sun?

Act Two of the opera opens with a solemn and chilling appeal to the Council of Priests of Isis and Osiris. Sarastro, the head priest, informs the council that the handsome Prince Tamino is ready to embark on his long journey toward enlightenment, but he warns of the certain treachery ahead.

Tamino, accompanied by the birdman, Papageno, endures numerous trials and unnerving rites held inside the passages of sanctuaries of temples while on his journey. Priests ultimately separate Tamino and Papageno, and guides armed with long sabers escort Tamino into the heart of a sacred temple during the dead of night. There, the light of knowledge absolves any fear of death. He is rewarded by being united with his true love, Pamina, incarnation of wisdom, who escorts Tamino on his quest toward enlightenment.

* ~ * ~ *

VICKI HAD ADROITLY convinced Paul to provide her with the key to the barrel vault after she found out that Anthony was inspecting the tunnels alone. But she had an ulterior motive. Since discovering that initiates learned the

185

secrets of the mysteries in subterranean caverns and tunnels, she yearned for her own subsurface experience.

How difficult could it be to navigate the tunnels? she asked herself with a brimming eagerness as she entered the barrel vault. Vicki thought about the sacred underground caves around the world where miracles had been reported inside. She contemplated the accounts of Leonardo da Vinci's transformation in an underground cave where he allegedly had acquired his artistic talents and his brilliance. She wondered how such an experience was possible, thinking through the possibilities of how a person might make a life-changing transformation while alone in a subterranean space.

Vicki swiftly traversed the barrel vault to the southeast end, where she found something astonishing. Two large paintings hung on either side of the exit for the tunnel. She lit the more colorful painting on the right, which depicted a gathering of rejoiceful men and women garbed in vibrant tunics and observing a man emerging from a hole in the earth. It was Salvator Rosa's *Pythagoras Emerging from the Underworld*, and Vicki knew it instantly. Her face hovered within inches of the painting as she examined it for signs of *pentimenti*, alterations in paintings that experts look for to determine authenticity. Genuine or not, she knew that placement of the painting in the barrel vault wasn't a matter of happenstance. She was directly beneath the museum's Greek and Roman collection. Nor were the series of events that had set her on the path that led to this particular moment.

She read the plaque beneath the painting:

ASCENT AT THE SACRED CAVE OF IDA ON THE ISLAND OF CRETE,
MOUNTAIN OF THE GODDESS. NURTURER OF GODS.
SANCTUARY OF THE SCROLLS. PASSAGEWAY TO ETERNITY.

"Sanctuary of the scrolls?" she repeated aloud.

A creepier Rosa hung on the other side of the door. In it, the Angel of Death, a hideous, primordial-looking skeleton figure with outstretched pterodactyl-like wings, loomed over a mother with her infant son, reminiscent of an eerie *Madonna with Child*. The message was clear: the boy was destined to die. Vicki centered the beam from her flashlight on the scroll held by the mother and placed in the center of the painting:

Conceptio Culpa, Nasci Pena, Labor Vita, Necesse Mori

She did a rough translation:

Conception is sin, Birth is pain, Life is toil, Death a necessity

Necessity? Then Vicki remembered the Salvator Rosa self-portrait that Sibyl had pointed out and what he had painted on a skull: *behold, whither, when.* Goose bumps raised small, blonde hairs on her forearms as she tried to discern the secret message of the paintings. Why were these two paintings hung together? One conveyed the inevitability of death; the other celebrated the return from death. The themes were wholly juxtaposed, but in some curious way, when taken together, the two paintings exemplified an important message that has resounded throughout the ages.

But there was little time to ponder the more esoteric meaning.

Stepping through the unlocked door, Vicki exited the barrel vault at the southeast end and entered a dark circular room divided in two by wood paneling. She held up her flashlight. The woodworking was extraordinary. Sections of the paneling gave the illusion of three-dimensional imagery, a technique she recognized as *trompe-l'oeil*. A section of darker wood was carved with *faux* cupboards. The lattice cupboard doors were open, revealing an image of a male lion and a cluster of grapes floating on top of a cloud of smoke. Above the scene, the enigmatic source of light beamed radiantly. Hieroglyphics were etched into the sides of the lattice cupboard doors.

She knew that *La Très Sainte Trinosophie* would come in handy. She removed the manuscript from the side pocket of her cargo pants and paged through it, skimming each section, until she came across two paragraphs that sent a chill up her spine.

I LEFT the gallery by a low and narrow door and entered a circular apartment the paneling of which was made of ash and sandalwood. At the further end of the apartment on a pedestal composed of the trunk of a vine lay a mass of white and shining salt. Above was a picture showing a crowned white lion and a cluster of grapes; both rested on a salver sustained in the air by the smoke of a lighted brazier. To my right and left two doors opened, one giving unto an arid plain. A dry and scorching wind blew over it continually. The other door opened on a lake at the extreme end of which a black marble façade could be seen.

I approached the altar and took into my hands some of the white and shining salt which the sages call "the first among the regenerated" and rubbed my entire body with it. I impregnated myself with it, and after having read the hieroglyphics accompanying the picture, I prepared to leave this hall. My intention was to leave by the door opening upon the plain, but there issued therefrom a hot vapor and I preferred the opposite path. I had the freedom of choice with the condition, however, not to leave the one once chosen . . .

Vicki moved closer to the lion and cluster of grapes carved into the wood. The lion was crowned, exactly as it was described in *La Très Sainte Trinosophie.*

Stymied, Vicki contemplated, trying to decipher the meaning of a male lion with a cluster of grapes. The muscular lion in the fresco at The Cloisters zoomed in and out of her mind. She looked around at her surroundings, noticing that the two halves of the secret room formed two crescent shaped chambers, or two semicircles, just like Pythagoras's Semicircle School. And Pythagoras had eventually settled in Crotona, Italy, in 530 B.C., she recalled, where he opened his Semicircle School to a select few men and women, instructing his initiates in the ways of heaven and hell and mysteries of everything in between. A second realization hit home. She was about to enter the Croton Aqueduct. The uncanny similarity in the two names couldn't possibly be a coincidence.

* ~ * ~ *

THE PITTER PATTER of footsteps echoed in the decommissioned tunnel that Anthony hoped would link to Tunnel 3. Senses went on high alert; his breath quickened. Pulsing blood in his ears amplified, rising to a level of distraction from the other senses. Against his better judgment, Anthony called out, but he didn't get a response. Recalling from his war days just how easily the mind can play games when confined in dark spaces for an extended time, he questioned whether he had imagined the footsteps.

Synced with his movement, the footsteps began again. This time, they sounded closer, and they certainly didn't sound like human footsteps. They weren't as heavy and were quicker in tempo. Thoughts of possible animals that could be inside the tunnel immediately rose to mind, like raccoons and opossums, but both animals were too small to make such a noise. He placed his hand over his flashlight, darkening his surroundings but maintaining enough light so that he could see in either direction of the tunnel.

From out of the darkness, a wraith-like shape appeared, dark shadow tailing and growing in size on the concave tunnel wall as the animal approached. The large eyes of the creature were piercing, feral, and distinctly bright yellow-greenish in color. They glowed like spectral orbs in the darkness. A fierce face emerged from the darkness. Black stripes extended from the eyes and down a pointed snout. Ears pointed straight into the air.

The creature stopped, tilted its head in a human way, sniffing the air. At that moment, Anthony could make out the beast. It was a coyote, an emaciated-looking coyote, making the animal look more jackal-like or possibly a hybrid canine.

For several prolonged seconds, man and canine stared at each other, eyes locked, trying to ascertain an intention. Both symbiotically understood that the crossing of paths wasn't simply a matter of chance, but something more, something mortally indiscernible. A connection materialized, one shared by all living things. A feeling of *déjà vu* then connected the moment to the psychopompic dream that Anthony had the night before.

Subconscious and conscious manifestations had crossed.

The canine opened its narrow mouth and began to pant. Then, as if it hadn't seen Anthony, or was uninterested, the creature turned and trotted into the darkness.

CHAPTER 40

THE ILLUMINATED HANDS ON ANTHONY'S WATCH indicated that nearly two hours had passed since he had left Paul at the end of the barrel vault. It didn't seem that long, so he mentally retraced his route, starting with the link under Central Park Drive that led to the South Gatehouse. After crossing the first gate, he traversed the backbreaking tunnel that bisects the enormous reservoir. That took longer than expected, guesstimating in retrospect that the tunnel stretched over a mile. After descending several flights down into the earth inside the North Gatehouse, he passed through the next gate, and entered the tunnel that ran parallel to the western side of the reservoir, which led him under the several-block-span under the burial ground of the colonial town of Seneca. The next leg of his journey took him under the Great Lawn of Central Park in a southeasterly direction.

But Anthony wasn't ready to quit just yet and he continued forward at a steady pace until he reached the junction of two tunnels. His head slowly rotated as he scanned the contours of the grandiose scale of the next tunnel, which easily exceeded peripheral boundaries. Frozen in place, Anthony sensed the universal feeling of individual insignificance aroused by standing face-to-face with wondrous human accomplishments. A feeling of awe welled as he grasped the engineering genius of Tunnel 3. *Humans,* he spontaneously considered, *have certainly come a long way from fearing the underworld to mastering it.* Then, another thought arose.

Has our understanding been wrong? Has humanity's salvation been in the depths of the earth, which has long protected life from the forces above?

Now in a state of a tangled welter by even the most fundamental of knowledge of the past, Anthony pried the plastic water bottle from his rear pocket and finished half the contents, cringing as he swallowed the warm water. His T-shirt and jeans clung to his body as he moved forward and stumbled on the metal railroad tracks bolted to the concrete floor of the massive tunnel. Lurching forward, he managed to keep his balance and avoid a potentially bone-breaking fall.

Continuing in a southeasterly direction, Anthony moved at a slow pace, mouth open, while taking in the practically unfathomable sight of the sheer size of the enormous tunnel. Fears of being entombed hundreds of feet under the surface of the earth dissipated, replaced by a feeling of privilege to be able to experience what surely had to be one of the man-made wonders of the world. The tunnel was at least three-stories tall and wide enough to drive two semi-trailer trucks through, side-by-side.

With each step farther into Tunnel 3, a mounting luminance unveiled details of the inside of the massive passageway. Polished, glossy, steel walls reflected the brighter colors of the visible spectrum. Metallic pipes ran along the sidewalls, extending endlessly, and converged at the vanishing point, a captivating nodal point. The pipes, Anthony guessed, carried the electrical wiring for what had to be an ultrahigh-voltage transformer, but nothing seemed certain, except his desire to investigate whatever lay ahead.

Mesmerized by the intense illumination ahead, he continued, moving with an unavoidable erratic motion, like a moth to a flame. His mind quieted, but he couldn't stop the trembling of more mortal parts as he neared the numinous light. Anthony's eyes filled their sockets; his eyes blinkless, unfazed by the brightness of what could only be described as an astral projection radiating from the elevating chamber. For what felt like time without end, Anthony advanced, staring into a supernova-like spectacle that flared in the far-reaches of space, but up close, and without any trace of harm to his eyes.

The absolute magnitude of the stark light retrograded into an aurora of intermingling, colorful shades. With each step closer to the elevating chamber, the distinctiveness of the colors became more observable to the naked eye. Blues mixed with greens, and contrasted with shades of orange, marigold, and yellow, swirling around, and ultimately fusing into dazzling bursts of varying shades of reds. Now, in a state of tonic immobility, Awed by the sight, Anthony watched the colors blend until the ultra-radiant, colored light coalesced into a kaleidoscope of more familiar, worldly geometric forms, then transformed into what appeared to be divine-like figures with white auras. For an unspecified time, he felt beside himself. His mind floated outside his corpus. He sensed the similar sensation of detachment he experienced when anesthetized. Temporality felt reversed, inexplicably malleable, then wholly devoid of any notion of continuance, only of transformation. Things hidden below the surface now became apparent. Everything that Anthony had ever known in his life was known all at once.

A quick blinding flash forced Anthony to shield his eyes. The pulse from the light shocked him with an electrical defibrillation, causing a cerebral, galvanic sensation. Mind instantly cleared, he looked about, squinting, and thinking—more so, postulating—whether he had just experienced the effects of prolonged sensory deprivation or whether he had actually witnessed a wondrous display of inexplicable lights. He shook his head and walked, zombie-like, through the opening for the elevating chamber. The entrance nearly replicated a lynchgate to a T, but Anthony scarcely took notice of it.

~~*

THE INSCRIBED WORDS 'As Above, so Below' on the hatch door flared with a reddish-gold flicker as Vicki focused her flashlight on the floor of the second semicircular room. She pried open the hatch door, noticing more words on the back side:

Hall of Katabasis.

Flashlight clutched in her teeth, she descended a wooden ladder. More words with inlaid gold leaf, or possibly inlaid with the ancient orichalcum alloy, which the bishop had mentioned, were carved on the rungs in a repeating tenfold sequence:

Ἑρμῆς ὁ Τρισμέγιστος
Mercurius ter Maximus
מחזות תלת חרם
Hermes Trismegistus.

At the base of the ladder, she found herself at the intersection of two well-lit tunnels. Recalling from the *Crata Repoa* that initiates forced to travel dark tunnels always chose the path to the right as the right hemisphere of the brain was the intuitive side, she chose the right passageway. With an uptick in her step, she was heading west, in the same direction in which the sun perishes each day.

With each step farther into the tunnel, it became apparent that the gradient declined at a steady pace. She was heading downward, to where she had no idea, but the tunnel was in good condition for a passageway that had been buried under the earth's surface for over one hundred years. She brushed her fingertips against the red-brick wall of the tunnel, noting that the masonry was similar to brick walls inside the museum.

The steel grid of the walkway seemed sturdy; the untarnished black paint on the handrails on either side hadn't rusted. *Someone maintains this tunnel.*

* ~ * ~ *

ANTHONY PAUSED ONCE inside the elevating chamber, awestruck by the massive size of the cavernous interior of the chamber. Streaked, dark-gray concrete walls rose as high as the walls of a cathedral, maybe higher, and were capped by a sprawling, arched vaulted ceiling. Elongated numbers, alphanumeric ratios, and images of perpendicular lines swirled through his brain as he attempted to apply the Intercept Theorem to assess the actual size of the elevating chamber. He had used the proportionality theorem dozens of times during the war to calculate the length of fields and rivers, or even the deepness of enclosures, but the numbers weren't adding up. The ratios of the line segments weren't calculating, for some reason, in estimating the size of the elevating chamber.

What is so unusual about this place that it defies geometry? he asked himself.

A spontaneous insight sparked through his train of thought: the Intercept Theorem originated with one of the Seven Sages of Greece, Thales of Miletus, to calculate the size of the Great Pyramids. He was also the first to understand electricity. Was there some type of positive–negative or ionic correlation, some type of Gordian Knot? Anthony began to wonder, between the fantastic lights that he had just witnessed and the reason why the theorem wasn't working? Thoughts and senses were superseded by confusion.

The large hyperbaric oxygen chamber on the far side caught his eye. It had the appearance and shape of a space-age, glass sarcophagus, and was used in emergency situations when sandhogs suffered from severe decompression sickness, coming face-to-face with death, but resuscitated back to life inside the oxygen chamber.

A steel grating section of the floor allowed a visual of the cellar ten or twelve feet below. Parts of the cellar floor were covered by dark, but perceptibly shallow pools of water. A rhythmic drip of water sounded out like an idiophone in nature's orchestra, absent other instruments. Hundreds of feet below the surface, the dripping water splashed with a varying resonance, a soothing diapason. Each drop gently resonated with a 'perfect fifth' interval, a mathematical and harmonic *musica universalis*.

He knelt, attempting to get a fix on the location of the dripping, but a more familiar sound interceded. It was the unmistakable sound of a woman's voice.

Straightaway, Anthony was on his feet, looking around, but he didn't see anyone. He hastened toward the sound of the voice, or what became two voices in conversation with each other, one female, and the other male. The bouncy silhouettes of the two individuals slowly came into view. They were headed toward an exit. Anthony started to speak but fell silent. He shifted to the side, until his body was flat against the wall. A metal ladder, affixed to the wall and encircled by a metal safety guard, partially concealed him from sight. Darkness provided the additional coverage.

He peered through the rungs of the ladder and watched as the two individuals exited the chamber. Mystified, he said, "That couldn't possibly be her."

CHAPTER 41

VICKI READ THE WORDS AT THE entrance to the next underground passageway. *Tunnel of Descent*. Tall, golden sheaves of wheat were painted on either side of the words. The name for the tunnel became apparent as Vicki continued down into the bowels of the earth, passing painting after painting depicting evocative scenes of descents into the underworld. To her right hung the portrayals of the journeys of the Roman goddesses Proserpina and Juno through dreamlike underworlds. On the opposite side of the tunnel, Brueghel the Younger's scene from the epic Roman poem *Aeneid* in which the Trojan hero Aeneas, son of Aphrodite, was escorted by the Greek oracle Sibyl through the boscage depths of the underworld.

The vibrant scenes of the redemptive peregrinations of Psyche, Cupid's lover, among those of other once-celebrated females, like Demeter and her daughter, Persephone, artfully bedecked the red-brick walls of the long corridor. Vicki eyed Peter Paul Rubens's passionate scene of Orpheus strumming notes of magic from his golden lyre with all his heart in the abyss of the netherworld to free his beloved wife, Eurydice. The mother-goddess, Ishtar, was visualized wearing the crown of heaven and holding a scepter as she stood at one of the seven gates of death crossed during her descent.

Each visual narrative was softly illuminated by thin, low-wattage LED lamps that conferred a sense of alluring intimacy to the vibrant scenes. Half-robed people reflected with noble sheens in strange though familiar-looking lands. An intrinsic bridge connected the chasm between the worlds of the living and the dead. Each underground pictorial passage stirred Vicki's soul, drawing her imagination in and evoking a longing to participate in the scenes. Desires, some caged up and suppressed deep down, others she hadn't known, unexpectedly rekindled, spontaneously sprung to life.

The *katabasis* scenes of Heracles, Odysseus, Dionysus, Hermes, and the myriad others who descended into the underworld filled the next stretch of the tunnel. With each descending step farther into the recesses of the dark unknown, the *mise-en-scène* inside the tunnel synchronized with now-awoken mental patterns and images. A feeling of wonderment and an accompanying sense of actualization suffused the entirety of Vicki's soul until she reached the end of the tunnel, where she was confronted with a painting of a hellish landscape containing numerous tormented individuals. It was Hieronymus Bosch's *chef-d'oeuvre, Christ's Descent into Hell*. The painting wasn't her favorite. The dark scene portrayed a frightening vision of the fiery depths of hell, replete with sorrowful, naked people being tortured, beaten, and raped, while other poor souls were forcibly drowned in the acidic River Styx or repeatedly speared by the nightmarish and ghoulish creatures haunting the underworld, all because the people lived before Christ.

Vicki continued downward, perilously unaware that she was slipping into a state of semi-consciousness. Odorless natural gas from the earth's subsurface seeped through tiny cracks in the masonry, slowly overtaking the oxygen in the air.

"Victoria," she was sure she heard.

Eyes wide, her heart racing, Vicki looked right, then left, and then back to her right. With her right hand, she gripped the handle of her semi-automatic.

"Who's there?" she blurted in a manner intended to be more forceful.

The creaking of a rusty hatch opening filled the silence.

The beam of her flashlight darted in all directions as she tried to trace the sound. "You're not looking in the right place, Victoria," she swore she heard.

A steel grate covered the hatch, possibly shielding the man's face.

"Show yourself." Vicki demanded, trying to remain alert.

"I'm right here, Victoria."

"Are you the man who has been following me?"

Vicki had a hunch that she'd run into the man in the tunnels, but he was nowhere in sight at the moment. Just an untraceable voice.

"I've been there the whole time, Victoria. You just recently noticed."

"You've been where?"

Blurry-eyed, Vicki looked for an exit door in the tunnel. Glancing upward, she pictured the bust of a man, framed by the circular grate. The bust was particularly reminiscent of a bust sculpted by Jean-Antoine Houdon that was on display somewhere in the museum's collection. Or maybe she had seen it in France. Vicki struggled to maintain her focus.

The question wasn't answered. Instead, she heard, "You have the codex."

Forcing her eyelids open, Vicki's hand shifted from her gun to the side pocket of her cargo pants. She touched the tip of *La Très Sainte Trinosophie*. "Did you leave this to lure me down here?" she asked, slowly moving her hand back to her gun. "I don't see any other reason. Nothing in this book makes any sense. It's totally undecipherable."

The voice took on an uncanny weight, similar to that of a grave voice-over for a *Film noir*. "That rolled-up codex in your pocket contains all the mysteries found between heaven and earth. Treat it with care, Victoria, for what you call undecipherable is in fact knowledge that transcends the limitations of human language and cognition."

"It's full of pictures of people, and animals, and birds . . ." At that moment, Vicki couldn't recall with any precision anything that was in the book.

"Symbolism, Victoria. Symbolism is the language of nature and her mysteries. Look around, and you will see the symbols everywhere you go— on paper, in that book that's in your pocket, on temples around the world, on cathedrals, and even carved into mountainsides. Right there in plain sight, though very few can decipher them."

"Nature and her mysteries?" Vicki silently repeated.

"There are more immediate matters to discuss." The voice modulated to more reverent tones. "There are people performing rituals in your museum."

A facial image faded in and out. Vicki strained, trying to concentrate. She hesitated, unsure how long, and asked, "Do you know something about the death in the Temple of Dendur?"

"The death was an unfortunate inevitability."

"Was a saber used in this ritual?" passed through her lips.

"'Transmutation is the weapon of the Master' are the words written under the emerald over the middle compartment of the scabbard," she perceived faintly, first audibly, then mentally, like a break of a gentle ocean wave.

"Alas, those performing the rituals in the museum have spared no expense to learn the secrets of the ancients, but only the most highly-trained adepts possess the ancient knowledge they seek."

"Knowledge of what?"

"Knowledge to cross the Gate of Death and return."

"Gate of Death?" Vicki's lips parted, her sight further blurred as she contemplated the pantheon of gods represented in the museum's collection who had traveled to the afterlife and returned: Osiris, Marduk, Mithra, Adonis, Dionysus, Serapis, Jesus.

"Many great secrets of the ancients were lost, and by no means accidentally." There was a weight in the voice, a projecting gravitas, which was felt as much as heard, like a rush of wind or a soothing symphony or the calming sound of a cascading waterfall. His words synced with the vision of the blinking of hypnotic eyes. "But a knowledge survives, taught at the innermost levels, elucidating the uniting of the finite with the infinite. A knowledge extending beyond the limitations of the natural world."

Vicki swayed as she spoke.

"Ah! The information in the scrolls under the obelisk?"

"That is correct, Victoria. This knowledge had been passed down from a time beyond human memory, a time before the earliest known civilizations, in an unbroken chain of apostolic succession and has remained in the hands of the initiated until the scrolls were illicitly expropriated by some influential people, wealthy individuals, an inner ring that has not been properly instructed on how to read the scrolls, but believe they can buy eternal life."

The Old Master scenes of the descents into the underworld surfaced in Vicki's mind's eye. The Polish Rider was at the forefront. She wanted to know more. Vicki needed to know more. "Is there really a world beyond?"

"Before planets aligned with stars, a world beyond existed. It has been known by many names by many cultures throughout history—the Duat, Kur, Erşetu, Naraka, Diyu, Hades, Mictlān. Some are considered places of paradise, some thought as fiery realms filled with tests or horrific torments. But nothing can be known that is not experienced."

Vicki stabilized herself before speaking. "They're using the scrolls to attempt to return from the afterlife but failed. Miller wasn't murdered."

A patrician tone delivered the next pronouncement.

"Throughout history many have keenly sought to unravel the secrets contained within the scrolls. Some have even made tremendous fortunes with claims of rightful possession of a resurrection. Alas, the knowledge of the scrolls lies at the heart of humanity's greatest treachery."

A short silence was punctuated by the low, growling sound of a canine somewhere in the dark tunnel.

"Who belongs to this inner ring?" Vicki asked.

"Those who own a disproportionate share of the world's wealth. Shameful, avaricious individuals who believe that they can have whatever they want at a snap of their fingers. But no one can decipher the secrets without the requisite training. Training that you will undertake, Victoria. That is why I left the book. In time you will come to understand those drawings fully."

Near spellbound, she asked, "What kind of journey? Why me?"

"Patience, my dear Victoria, for true wisdom cannot be transmitted from mouth to ear. Your path in life will be one of knowledge and truth, a path that separates you from others—a path that puts your old soul on an otherworldly course of self-discovery and enlightenment."

Vicki shuddered inwardly as she rotated her neck until she felt a soft popping sensation. Visions of the man wearing the conical hat depicted on the cover of *La Très Sainte Trinosophie*, along with the trombone player in Georges Seurat's *Circus Sideshow* levitated above her center of consciousness. Vicki's next words were spoken without deliberation: "A man with a conical hat in Seurat's *Circus Sideshow* looks a lot like the man wearing a conical hat depicted on the cover of *La Très Sainte Trinosophie*."

A laughing sound proceeded: "Many likenesses have been attempted, Victoria, but I'm partial to *La Parade*, or what you Americans call *Circus Sideshow*."

Gold tints twinkled in silvery eyes, distracting from logical thought as her mind drifted into a trance-like state. A sensation of physical weariness intermingled with feelings of spiritual elation, as if she had just finished a large glass of Shiraz.

"But be very careful of others who seek the scrolls."

"Who are they?" she incoherently garbled, drifting into a state of serenity.

"They have operated in the shadows of humanity for many centuries, Victoria. They are men of death, not intellect. They serve higher powers that will never accept or ever realize that it is impossible to suppress the truths of the past."

Dark shades transitioned into one another, producing an indistinct outline around the steel grate and the obscure silhouette of the man. Gradually, the bust lost all detail. Peripherally, then dead on, the scene around Vicki grew fuzzy, lacking in all exactness. Surroundings were reduced to vibrant brush strokes and tiny dots, as her senses went utterly dormant. For once, Vicki genuinely knew what it felt like to be at one with a painting.

The last words she heard: "Someone is in need of your assistance."

As quickly as the apparition appeared, it disappeared.

Fresh air swirled through the tunnel with a life-restoring eruption. In one infinitesimal moment, Vicki was in a near slumber, the next fully awake. Her eyelids snapped wide-open as an abrupt and sudden shake of her head transported her back into a state of normal cognizance. She looked about, fretfully, bemused, trying to comprehend what had just happened.

CHAPTER 42

ANTHONY FELT THE NEED TO COUGH. That wasn't an option. Even a subtle noise would give him away, so he sipped his water as he pursued his targets.

The two individuals exited the elevating chamber and entered the shadows of the tunnel. Anthony trailed stealthily, patiently, keeping his flashlight off and making sure he remained far enough behind so that they couldn't hear his footsteps.

Why was Margarita in the tunnels? he couldn't stop asking himself.

Then he recalled the roguish activities carried out while she worked at the Met. She was often in the museum after hours. She was even captured on camera trying to access restricted areas. Each time, however, Margarita had an excuse . . . excuses backed by powerful people, so instead of being fired, she was transferred to The Cloisters.

Margarita and Darrel hugged the steel wall of the tunnel, walking in single file, making sure to avoid a large puddle of murky water where the wooden catwalk had eroded. With the dogleg in the tunnel, they slowly disappeared.

Anthony guessed that they were headed toward the Met. He grunted and picked up his pace, but without the use of his flashlight, he couldn't gauge the sharpness of the angle of the bend in the tunnel. Arms stretched to the side, he stopped. So did the talking.

Glimpsing around the bend in the tunnel, he questioned why he didn't see or hear them. Then he realized that they, too, must have been stationary. And for some reason had turned off their flashlights. A faint, "Shhhh," sounded in the tunnel.

Knee aching, he contemplated the option of drawing his gun, turning on his flashlight, and rushing toward Margarita and Darrel, hoping they wouldn't run. Perhaps, turn on the flashlight and yell, "Stop right there!" But he wanted to know where the two were going and didn't want to have to pry the information out of Margarita. As in the past, she may be uncooperative.

A beam of light passed Anthony as his body molded to the curved wall of the tunnel. He grinned, knowing that he was hidden from sight, but his expression turned to horror as something with more legs than he wanted to investigate crawled over his hand. Refraining from shouting the expletive that rose with a sensation of revulsion, Anthony grunted as he jumped away from the wall. Flashlights lit. Margarita and Darrel took off.

Anthony uttered the expletive aloud and gave chase.

CHAPTER 43

IN THE DARK DISTANCE, WHITISH GLOWS bounced as two flashlights became visible, but gradually disappeared. This time, Anthony knew the lights had vanished not because the flashlights were turned off, but because Margarita and Darrel had turned into an offshoot tunnel. Flashlight pointed forward, he groaned and pushed forward, despite the burning sensation in his knee, and now perceptible tightness in his chest. His airways were not taking in enough air, or worse, not allowing the release of the carbon dioxide–rich air.

Running at full tilt, his foot stubbed against something hard, something metal, forcing Anthony to lurch forward, nearly toppling over and triggering a shooting pain in his right knee. Bitters from the coffee ingested hours ago regurgitated in his mouth, accompanied by a burning sensation that rose from his chest and into his throat, leaving the taste of bile. Lips puckered with downright disgust, he nearly toppled as he veered into the offshoot tunnel, convinced he couldn't move any further, until he spotted Margarita and Darrel, and it appeared that they had slowed their pace, or had stopped for some reason. Anthony couldn't tell for sure. Everything was blurred. His body throbbed from head to toe. Silhouettes swayed and rippled in the dark distance in the same motions as lateral buoys on choppy water. "Freeze!" His scream boomed inside the corroded tunnel.

The buildup of reflux or lactic acid in his stomach spread into a searing, five-alarm pain that blazed from head to toe, culminating in total debilitation. At once, his body shut down, causing Anthony to crash to the ground with a wretched thud. Breathless and vulnerable, he forced himself to stand, slipping on the watery floor, and falling over once, then twice. With a groan, he summoned the strength to rise halfway, his right hand braced on his knee, his left hand shielding the lights shining in his face. He drew his gun, trying to make sense of the scene. "No one move!" he yelled, racked with pain.

Vicki had her gun pointed at Margarita and Darrel, her flashlight braced on the barrel. She shifted her aim between Margarita and Darrel.

"Got 'em, boss."

Anthony wheezed, coughing fiercely as he struggled to catch his breath.

With a deep-throated emission, he spat, twice, then straightened. He holstered his gun, standing in place, eyes shifting from Vicki to Margarita and Darrel, back to Vicki. Surroundings came into focus as he hobbled closer to Margarita and Darrel, trying not to show any pain, which eased to a level of near-tolerance. Methodically, he circled Margarita and Darrel, legs wobbly, using his flashlight to look in the usual places for concealed weapons.

Satisfied that the two were not armed, his face scowled while looking at Margarita. "Not going to get off this time," he said between breaths.

Margarita whimpered as she lowered her head.

"Give me your cuffs," he said as he removed his Smith & Wesson cuffs from the leather holder. One pair wouldn't be big enough for Darrel.

Darrel held up his hands. "Hey, man, we didn't do anything wrong."

Breathing almost normal, Anthony evaluated the situation while looking at the expression on Vicki's face. He turned his attention back to Margarita. Her white shirt clung to her shoulders, her large breasts expanded and contracted with each breath. "How did you get into the tunnels?" he asked.

Avoiding all eye contact with Vicki, she said, "I can't say."

"You'll just make things harder on yourself," Anthony said, as he had many times prior. This time, he wasn't required to recite a Miranda warning.

Vicki stepped closer to Margarita, gun still in hand.

"Does anyone else know you're in here?" she asked.

"No." Margarita began to sob. "There's no one else."

Anthony knew Margarita was lying, so he tried a different approach.

"Look, we're not dealing with any major criminal offenses here. Things could have turned out much worse. Someone could have been seriously injured, perhaps killed, accident or." He cut the sentence short.

Tears streaked Margarita's chubby cheeks as she turned to Vicki and stared with soulful, brown eyes that shone vibrantly, even in the dark tunnel. Quivering lips solicited sympathy. "I'm not here because I want to be."

"Don't say anything," Darrel commanded.

Anthony pointed the beam from his flashlight directly in Darrel's eyes. "I don't want to hear another word out of you, or the cuffs go on. Clear?"

Vicki lowered her gun. "Tell us what's going on, Margarita."

"You probably won't believe this, but this is the truth."

MARGARITA WILLINGLY CONFESSED that for a generous sum of money she and Darrel had been guiding a small group into the Met at night, using the vacant water tunnels to enter the museum. They weren't permitted to go into the museum, and were sworn to secrecy. The only thing she was told was that the group entered the museum to attend some sort of recital.

"Why are you here now?" Anthony asked.

"To make sure there were no other people in the tunnel."

"What do you mean by other people?"

"I don't know," Margarita replied. "Some other group, I think."

Vicki considered mentioning the man whom she had encountered in the tunnel only ten minutes earlier but decided against it. She hoped Margarita would reveal his identity. Equally important, her recollection of the encounter amounted to slightly more than a dream-like blur. She needed to compute.

"I want names," Anthony insisted.

"She told you," Darrel asserted. "We don't know names."

Vicki shifted her flashlight to Margarita. Her curly, long hair formed a halo around the outline of her head. Strands of gray hair protruded sideways, visible in the flashlight's illuminance. The makeup around her eyes was smudged. Her long, silver earrings sparkled as they swayed.

"Is this why you were looking for the *Crata Repoa* at The Cloisters? Because you wanted to give it to someone in this group?"

"You found that with her?" The timbre of anger and surprise in Anthony's voice crackled sharply inside the hollow of the tunnel.

Vicki redirected her flashlight. "It was in the report I gave to you."

Anthony emitted a grunt of disapproval.

"Vicki, I'm so sorry. I couldn't tell you at the time, but I'd been looking for the *Crata Repoa* for several years," Margarita interjected, head down "I was assured that it was somewhere in The Cloisters. When you showed up, Vicki, I just knew you'd find it."

Anthony put his handcuffs back in the case. "You want me to believe that you are taking a group into the museum and you don't know who they are?"

"Now sobbing, Margarita stated, "They're not exactly strangers. I was asked to do this by someone who had been leading the group into the museum for many years. He told us that people had been going into the museum since it opened, so it was legit."

Anthony pointed his flashlight to Darrel.

"What's his role in all this?"

"He gets us into the tunnels."

"Where?"

"Under the platform for Cleopatra's Needle."

Anthony had a hunch. A good hunch. "If you both cooperate, I'll let the prosecutor know that you will help catch the group that breaks into the museum. You'll get a slap on the wrist, trespassing charges, at the worst."

CHAPTER 44

A HALF MILE SOUTH OF THE museum, a small group had assembled in a converted mansion on Park Avenue, formerly owned by an American oil tycoon. The mansion was one of numerous multi-million dollar manors in the area dubbed 'Millionaire Row' and served as homes for some of the world's wealthiest people, as embassies, and swanky ambassadorial residences—even for representatives from the poorest countries. The four-story limestone–clad mansion still contained the original cathedral ceilings, fireplaces, and crystal chandeliers dangling from the ceilings of all thirty-plus rooms.

The individuals convened for an emergency session in a room on an upper floor of the mansion, seldom used by the Council on Foreign Relations, the entity that had acquired the mansion. The high-powered CFR brokers—made up of diplomats, CEOs, global financiers, and international affairs experts—were not in session, and it was too early in the morning for the support staff other than security to be in the building. But the small group of individuals, whispered to be "a ring within a ring," seated in the Round Table Room – a dark cherry wood–paneled room decorated with paintings of past luminaries over a fireplace mantel – had an agreement with security, bonded by millions in untraceable kickbacks. The group had already been informed of the breach in the underground passages. A strategy was devised. Items were swiftly safeguarded.

* ~ * ~ *

ANTHONY AND PAUL rushed into the museum's main gift shop, where Anthony removed two umbrellas from a circular metal bin positioned next to the cashier. When he had left for work earlier, the forecast had called for a sunny day. It was now pouring.

"We'll bring these back in a bit," he told the cashier.

"I don't think I can allow you to do that." The cashier beamed with a dimpled smile. She was unaware of Anthony's authority.

Incensed, Paul moved closer to the counter. "Do you know who this is!" he roared while slapping his large hand on the countertop. His reply was so vehement, the cashier jumped back, scared out of her wits.

Flushed, she wisely said, "I'm going to hold you to that."

VICKI MET ANTHONY and Paul outside the museum.

They entered Central Park without saying a word. Umbrellas were lowered as they dashed under the Greywacke Arch and into the vacant tunnel.

"The Polish statue is to the south," Paul stated.

Anthony knew the location of the statue. He also knew that the statue, mistakenly referred to as the Polish statue, was the King Jagiello Monument, but he didn't feel like correcting Paul. He was too stunned by the news he had received not twenty minutes earlier. The drop in atmospheric pressure with the wet weather aggravated his gunshot wound.

"How did they get out of jail so fast?" Vicki asked. Thunder resonated inside the Greywacke underpass, squelching the echo from her voice.

"I spoke with headquarters this morning –"

"What did the chief say?" Paul asked before Anthony could finish.

"Both Margarita and Darrel were out on bail in less than twenty-four hours," Anthony said succinctly, keeping the details at that. He was still trying to absorb the information provided by the chief. Reports circulated that secret, elite groups operated behind the scenes of world affairs, but he never thought the rumors were actually true.

Astounded, Vicki asked, "While we were at Police Plaza yesterday?"

A single nod served as an answer.

Umbrellas were raised as they exited the tunnel in tandem and slogged up the incline in the path west of the Greywacke Knoll. All three avoided the deeper water streaming down the concrete path but were helpless against the sideways-blowing rain.

They passed Cleopatra's Needle on the right and Humming Tombstone to the left of the path. To the west, Belvedere Castle, perched on top of the steep cliff of Vista Rock, became visible through the hurricanic conditions. The rain-darkened granite stones of the folly made it appear more formidable than usual. Raindrops crackled like lit rolls of firecrackers on the rippling surface of Turtle Pond directly beneath the castle.

At the top of the path, the word *POLAND*, etched into the marble plinth of an enormous equestrian statue, was barely visible through the sheet of rain. NYPD officers from the Central Park Precinct wearing slickers and hats covered with plastic rain caps were posted in front of the perimeter of the taped-off crime scene surrounding the statue. Crime Scene and Evidence Collection Units were scouring the ground for clues.

All three Met officials winced under tilted, dripping umbrellas, as the grizzly sight came into view. On the top of a ten-foot-high marble base, a larger-than-life King Jagiello was mounted on a feral stallion swathed in thick armor. The arms of the bronze king rose thirty-five feet into the air. Nine-foot-long, piercing swords were held in each hand. Historically, two crossed swords pointing up signified the commencement of a battle. Presently, the raised swords had been used to pierce the bodies of two people—Margarita and Darrel—whose lifeless forms were impaled on the blades of the swords.

"Christ Almighty!" Paul yelled neck craned. "How the hell did someone get them all the way up there?"

Anthony stared at the grotesque spectacle, intently examining all possible angles, and trying to glean possible clues. "Must have been several people," he finally said.

"Very sick people," Vicki remarked. She stared in horror until she couldn't bear it any longer, turning away and wondering how she'd tell Sibyl.

Anthony sloshed across the platform to the rear of the statue, inspecting the king and observing that Jagiello's long cape draped all the way down to the horse's rear, covered by a *croupier*, or buttock protector, for the back of the horse. He noted the scalable slope up the king's back but was perplexed by how the bodies could possibly be raised to the top of the statue. There was no way to physically carry the bodies to the top.

Crimson blood flowed down the king's outstretched, crossed arms, diluted by the rain as it seeped down the huge statue until a salmon-pink runnel trickled off the metal foot. Anthony wondered how many times that had happened during the king's life.

His head turned with a twisting motion when he heard his name called.

"Ain't never seen nothing like this in the park before."

Anthony had met the Central Park Precinct sergeant but had forgotten his name. He stared blankly as he approached the sergeant and said, "Crazy."

"*Sasso in bocca*," the cop remarked, without any sign of emotion.

Anthony did a quick about-face. The usual olive tone of his face blanched as he looked at the statue through the rain and at Margarita's and Darrel's withered, lifeless faces. He still had no idea why stones had been found in his mentor's pockets, but he knew exactly why there were stones in Margarita's and Darrel's mouths. *Sasso in boca*, placing stones in a victim's mouth, was the Mafia's way of saying this person will no longer talk.

"Chief just called in the Organized Crime Control Bureau."

"Who's running this crime scene?"

"Chief of homicide. He's over there." The sergeant pointed.

"We need to get the bodies down immediately. If the rain slows, we'll have people walking around here. The media will follow."

He glanced at Vicki and Paul, knowing that it was with the best of intentions that he had not mentioned who had bailed out Margarita and Darrel. The chief had sworn him to secrecy, anyway, until there was a better understanding of the group that had posted bail. One thing was clear. If organized crime was going to challenge the people who had bailed out Margarita and Darrel, they were in for the fight of their lives.

"You know these guys, Tony?" Paul asked, nearing Anthony and pointing with his nose toward the Great Lawn. "They've been staring this way."

"Come with me," Anthony said without hesitation. Special Agents Wilson and O'Rourke wore identical tan raincoats. Both held bubble umbrellas over their heads.

Vicki and Paul followed. The rain grew in intensity. Incalculable drops pelted the ground with unremitting crackling, while varying winds altered the direction and angle of the downpour, forcing the three to shift the angles of their umbrellas several times.

Anthony slanted his umbrella to the side when he was within arm's length of Wilson and O'Rourke and shook hands. He introduced Vicki and Paul.

Wilson suggested in not so many words that they relocate to the wooden overhang of the Delacorte Theater as powerful gusts flipped flimsier umbrellas inside out. Giant linden trees on the perimeter of the Great Lawn swayed in the howling wind. Limbs and branches crackled and snapped as the tropical storm gained momentum. The apocalyptic sky above rumbled with intermittent flashes of light.

The Shakespeare in the Park season had ended a week earlier, but a billboard announcing the opening of *King Lear* remained nailed to a wall of the theater.

Wilson guided the group in front of the billboard.

"Seems like the police have a messy situation on their hands," he said hoarsely, but in a business-like manner, shaking the water from his umbrella. Wilson directed his sight to Margarita's and Darrel's lifeless bodies hovering on top of the triumphant king. "They were museum employees, right?"

Anthony wasn't surprised that the agents had already investigated the situation. If the surprising information that the chief provided proved to be true, the murders of Margarita and Darrell had multi-state, perhaps even international ramifications, giving the Feds jurisdiction in the matter.

Anthony nodded a confirmation.

"We got some information on Fabrizio Armata," Wilson declared as all five shifted further under the wooden overhang outside the theater with an abrupt crack of thunder. "As suspected, Armata isn't actually an employee of the Vatican Bank. Seems he started his career working as a tax lawyer for a major Italian company. A real wiz, we're told. Organized crime recruited him to skirt taxes, at least at first. The work was easy, and he made a ton of money for the Cosa Nostra. They named him 'Il Predatore', the predator, because he operates like a shark. Not long after, he became involved with heroin smuggling, and was later elected as the chairman of a large Italian bank that funnels drug money through the Vatican Bank. With all the money that he made from the sale of drugs he acquired a sizeable interest in his bank."

O'Rourke delivered the more unexpected news.

"But it just so happens, and not by mere coincidence, that the Vatican Bank is the majority shareholder in Mr. Armata's bank, so he indirectly works for the Vatican Bank."

Anthony withheld his thoughts. He was aware that Italian religious officials and bankers had been accused of smuggling money into Switzerland, but he also knew there were many other players involved in the money laundering. He smelled a false flag.

Wilson figured Anthony had known about the drug trafficking but provided an insinuation to make sure. "Overseas intelligence has been using drug money to fight off Communist expansion in Asia for decades. It's a simple set up, really. Heroin from Asia is sold on the streets of America. Profits are used to help fund the Communist resistance in Asia, but a lot of it stays in the hands of organized crime and held in banks like Armata's."

Anthony finally spoke up.

"Heroin from the Golden Triangle?"

Wilson nodded. "Where Thailand, Laos, and Myanmar all meet. The most productive and expansive opium-producing area in the world." A sharp clap of thunder directly above resulted in a startling chill. Eyes cast skyward momentarily. "We're still not sure what Armata is doing here, but AISI informs us that he came to the States alone, and he may be recruiting others. We haven't figured out what for."

Anthony provided a loose translation of the acronym for Vicki and Paul.

"Italian Intelligence Agency."

"We'll update you as we learn more," O'Rourke promised.

Wet and internally fuming, Anthony thanked the agents. The colorful billboard for *King Lear* caught his eye. He knew that Shakespeare had based *King Lear* on King Leir, the Celtic king of the Britons. He also knew that some construed the scene in which Lear, losing his senses, roves the heath during the deluge as a baptismal conversion from pagan to Christian. He now had a higher appreciation of the tragedy.

To the east, consecutive flashes of lightning irradiated the sky over the museum. Another bone-chilling clap of thunder instantly followed. All five looked upward, to the sky, as if they were about to witness horsemen storming from the clouds.

Through the gray curtain of rain, Anthony noticed that Margarita's and

Darrel's bodies were more slumped over and swollen than they had been a just few minutes earlier. From this distance, the scene jogged his memory. He recalled that King Jagiello wasn't actually Polish, but Lithuanian, and had served as the Grand Duke of Lithuania and pagan ruler of the Baltic region. His greatest victory came with the defeat of the Teutonic Knights, a crusading organization also known as the Order of Brothers of the German House of Saint Mary in Jerusalem. It wasn't long, however, before the Teutonic Knights rose again to wield their swords, along with their devout religious ideas, and completely decimated the pagan Baltic tribes in the bloody Prussian Crusade.

Anthony was now certain that someone was sending a message.

CHAPTER 45

ANTHONY, VICKI, AND PAUL CONVENED IN Anthony's office after drying off. No one, not even Anthony, had ever anticipated dealing with such grim circumstances. All three had taken their jobs knowing that they would encounter thefts, perhaps an attempted burglary, or even a shooting. But a gruesome execution was never even the most remote of possibilities.

Anthony began the discussion with the premise that humans have endeavored to kill one another for one reason or another since the dawn of time. "One of the bloodiest periods in European history," he insisted, circling his desk, "began as a dark mist slowly settled over Europe with the decline of the Roman Empire. The violence that followed grew in proportion to the rise of the Church, coming to a head when crusading armies took up the cause of killing anyone who posed a threat to the Church."

"Crusaders who went to the Holy Land?" Paul asked.

Anthony shook his head. "I'm talking about the second round of crusades, not the First Crusade. Church-sanctioned crusades like the Prussian and Livonian Crusades, perpetrated by Roman Catholic crusaders against people who lived in the Baltic and Slavic regions. Both of those crusades," he explained, disappointment dominating the trace of irritation in his voice, "were just two of the many other religious military campaigns that were part of the larger Northern Crusades, resulting in the deaths of untold numbers of inhabitants of Europe in the twelfth and thirteenth centuries."

"I had no idea," Paul said, tilting back with a surprised expression.

Anthony continued, knowing the following information had been intentionally suppressed. Coming to terms with the past wasn't an essential requirement of religion.

"Then there was the Wendish Crusade, and the Albigensian Crusade, ordered by Pope Innocent III, which lasted for nearly three decades. French men, women, even children were routinely tortured, killed, or burned alive at the pope's demand."

Vicki leaned forward in her seat, astonished by what Anthony had said.

"I knew about the atrocities committed during the Inquisitions in Spain and Portugal," she admitted, "but I didn't know so many other people were killed."

"And the brutality wasn't limited to the massacre of groups who hadn't given up their long-held beliefs for Catholicism. The atrocities were also committed against those who refused to conform to the Church's version of Christianity." Anthony rose with a sudden bout of unease. The cool air seeping through the ceiling diffuser blew on his still-wet hair. He glanced out the window in his office. Rain streaked the glass with long, iridescent trails, blurring the sight of Central Park. "And Margarita and Darrel were murdered in a similar manner as non-conformers, though in a less perverse way."

Paul whistled with surprise and asked, "You mean the victims were stabbed through the –" He ended in mid-sentence, looking at Vicki, then away.

"Impalement was a very common form of murder for non-conformers," he explained, turning to Paul. "Spears and javelins were forced through the underside until they came out of the mouth. The bodies were then put on display for all to see."

With disgust in her voice, Vicki said, "Like piercing Margarita and Darrel."

"I'm confused," Paul remarked, avoiding any direct eye contact. Culpability showed in his face. "Why do you think Margarita and Darrel were killed?"

With a telling look in his eyes, Anthony stated, "The stones in their mouths could mean only one thing. Their deaths were a warning to anyone associated with or helping the people conducting the rituals in the museum."

$$* \sim * \sim *$$

AFTER THE MUSEUM closed, Cy Hetford entered the Egyptian Wing galleries. The galleries had been nearly empty all day. The downpour earlier in the day produced a perceptible drop in the number of visitors, more so than the usual end-of-summer decline.

After putting on a pair of specialized gloves, Cy gently removed a 2.5-inch tall, bronze representation of King Ptolemy II's head from the display case and placed it in a cardboard transporting box. He looked over his shoulders to see if there were any other staff members or night-shift guards in sight. The galleries were empty.

Cy reflected on the life of the Greco-Egyptian king as he slipped into the shadows of the museum. Son of King Ptolemy I, the Macedonian general who had served under Alexander the Great, Ptolemy II ruled Egypt from 285 to 246 B.C. He ordered the construction of the Musaeum and the Royal Library of Alexandria, the first institutions of higher learning, but it was his commission of the Egyptian priest, Manetho of Sebennytos, to list the Egyptian gods and reform idolatry practices that altered the course of history.

Renowned throughout the ancient world as the 'Beloved of Thoth', Manetho served as a historian and as the chief priest of Heliopolis. As a student of the Egyptian philosopher turned god and the founder of the ancient Mysteries Schools, Hermes Trismegistus, Manetho was well versed when it came to Egyptian history. His long list of Egyptian rulers matched the rulers described in the Turin Royal Canon and replicated with pinpoint precision the list of rulers etched into the Palermo Stone.

Aegyptiaca, as Manetho's three-volume history of Egypt was later titled by Roman-Jewish historian Josephus, chronicled the mythic reign of gods and demigods who had ruled in this world and the next. Written in ancient Greek, *Aegyptiaca* was circulated throughout the ancient world, ending up in the hands of religious leaders. Christian chronographer Eusebius praised the work. Jewish scholars pointed to the *Aegyptiaca* to prove their connection to Egypt through Abraham, Joseph, and Moses.

To appease the growing desire to practice the ritual of resurrection, Manetho transformed the worship of Osiris into the worship of Serapis,

217

allowing men and even women of all ranks of society access to rituals of resurrection upon confessing and initiation. Great temples and shrines venerating Serapis sprouted like wildflowers in places such as Memphis, Heliopolis, Carthage, Alexandria, and eventually Rome, where the Greco-Egyptian god Serapis stood out among the many Roman deities.

In like tradition, a Hellenized Isis became the consort of Serapis, giving rise to the cult of Serapis, Isis, and their son. Isis—the giver and restorer of life—became the foremost adored of the Roman goddess. Temples of Isis flourished throughout the empire. Followers of Isis, Serapis, and Christ later worshipped side-by-side. Many Romans regarded Serapis and Christ as interchangeable. Images of Isis and Serapis hung next to Mary and Jesus. Baptismal and communal ceremonies, begun in Egypt and practiced by Roman priests, were associated with Serapis, and later to followers of Jesus, all in the same historical time frame when opaque eyes transformed into shades of brown, hazel, green, and blue.

In more esoteric language, recognizable only to those who had been taught how to glean hidden meanings, Manetho mentioned two scrolls that taught the secret of the ancients. The $κατάβασις$, or *Katabasis Scrolls*, as they are known to a small group of inner-layer initiates, taught the ancient ritual of transmutation of the soul.

THREE THOUSAND YEARS of reverence for Egyptian deities were punctuated by the venomous fangs of an Egyptian cobra into the frail arm of Cleopatra.

To the victor went the spoils. It was the way of the ancient world.

"Without further delay the Emperor put out an edict forbidding the congregations of heretics." *Ecclesiastical History of Theodoret.*

Fearing that the authorities would stumble on the ancient secrets, Ptolemy of Mendes, Alexandrian priest and historian, smuggled the *Katabasis Scrolls* out of the city.

The most recent sanctum was under Cleopatra's Needle.

CHAPTER 46

"MARGARITA SAID THE ENTRANCE TO THE tunnel is under the platform for Cleopatra's Needle," Vicki remarked. She was standing alongside Anthony and Paul, inspecting the platform. The heavier rain earlier in the day had tapered to a drizzle.

"Or maybe hidden in the bushes," Paul said walking to the east side of the platform. He leaned over the railing. "There's a slope over here that goes to Central Park Drive. Maybe the entrance is behind the bushes."

Anthony gazed south, through narrow gaps in the drenched branches of the old-growth oak trees around the obelisk, at the King Jagiello statue. The bodies had been removed, but police officers remained at the crime scene.

The higher elevation from the platform for the obelisk provided a better perspective of the statue. The king's enormous crown was more visible from that vantage point. Anthony contemplated the possibility of a rope strung over the crown and used to hoist the bodies, though that didn't seem plausible. Even the use of a ladder didn't seem probable. The long swords held by the king rose too high into the air. No one could carry a body that high up a ladder. The killers had definitely used a truck with a cherry picker to haul the bodies to the top of the statue, but he had racked his brain over that possibility. Even in the dead of night, someone would have seen the truck and reported the crime. Then it hit him. The area must have been cleared of people when the bodies were raised. Anthony was now sure that someone in a position of authority was involved.

"What do you think, Tony? Maybe the entrance is over here?"

He turned and looked at the area Paul pointed to. "You'd be able to see the entrance during the winter when the bushes are bare." He moved closer to the stairs leading up to the platform. "Makes more sense to hide the entrance under these stairs."

"Hey!" Vicki shouted. "Come take a look at this plaque."

"What is it?" Paul asked as he rushed over.

"Do you see these ruts in the tiles of the platform?"

Vicki squatted in front of a huge, horizontal marble-block placed alongside the obelisk, one of four situated at each side of the square base of the monolith. Affixed to the top of the stone was a bronze plaque – the size of a desktop – that provided a translation of the hieroglyphics etched into the obelisk. She ran her fingers on the ground in front of the plaque.

Anthony approached. "What do you see?" he asked.

"Apparently, the rain somehow made these ruts more visible."

Paul crossed his arms and tapped his foot. "Why would rain make grooves in the ground more visible? If anything," he remarked with an impatient tone, "the water would fill in the grooves and make them less visible."

"Hold on a second," Anthony said, contemplating the reason why he hadn't noticed the ruts in the platform for the obelisk during his past inspections. He bent over and rubbed his pinky finger in the groove and raised it to his nose. "Definite chemical scent," he stated, then wiped the tip of his finger on his pants. "Diamond grinding."

Vicki jumped to her feet. "Diamond grinding?"

Anthony clarified. "Have you ever noticed grooves in the pavement on highways that people refer to as 'rain grooves', though they have nothing to do with rain?"

"They're noisy when you drive over them?" Paul queried.

"Exactly. The grooves are made by machines with diamond-coated saw blades coated with metallurgical powder. They can also be made by hand-held devices."

"What in God's name are you talking about, Tony?"

"It's actually rather simple. There are ways to make cuts into a stone or into a cement surface so that the grooves are not readily apparent to the naked eye. It's why you don't notice the grooves on the highway unless the surface is wet from rain."

An aha moment struck Vicki. "Like an optical illusion."

"Tony, are you suggesting that these grooves are used to help move this enormous plaque out of place? It must weigh a freakin' half-ton."

Anthony nodded, staring down at the grooves in the platform. "Yep, once you put rounded stones or ball bearings in the grooves, the plaque will slide with ease. It's an old masonry technique, dating as far back to the construction of Solomon's Temple. Probably further back in time."

"It's incredible that the ancients had knowledge that only now we understand," Vicki remarked, inspecting the weighty marble-and-bronze plaque. She bent over. "And look here. Ruts have been chiseled out at the bottom of the stone base. This must be where they insert the ball bearings."

"It'd still take a strong person to move it," Paul stated, unconvinced.

Anthony inhaled loudly. "Darrel was a big guy."

Visions of the adventure in the Tombs at The Cloisters with Margarita projected in her mind, conjuring sadness and bitter feelings of nostalgia. Tears welled as she visualized Margarita's beautiful, brown eyes staring into the mirror to check her make-up in the bathroom at The Cloisters. And how Margarita writhed with such excitement when they had discovered the initiation booklet under the stone tomb of Jean d'Alluye.

"I'm sorry." She wiped the tears from her eyes. "I still can't believe they were murdered. What kind of monster would do such a terrible thing?"

Heads bowed in a synchronous moment of silence.

It was now Anthony's turn to be consoling. He inched closer to Vicki.

"I think we can take some solace in knowing the Organized Crime Control Bureau is working on the investigation. They have some positive leads. And those federal agents, the two guys we talked to at the Delacorte Theater, I'm sure they have some positive leads on their end." Anthony nudged Vicki, smiling. "Hey, now that we have the Parks Department's permission to investigate the area, I'd imagine you'd want to check for something."

Vicki's eyes widened. "Are we going to move this plaque?"

Paul balked. "Maybe we should get some ball bearings from the machine shop in the museum before getting a hernia trying to move this plaque."

"Get over here now," Anthony ordered.

Paul waved Vicki away, bent over, and gripped the corner of the enormous plaque with his large hands. Anthony counted to three, and the two groaned as the stone slid a tad out of place. Anthony wheezed and switched positions, securing his feet against the base for the obelisk and pushed, utilizing the power from his legs. Paul grunted, harshly, pulling the stone as Anthony pushed. Vicki grabbed a corner. Steadily, the stone slid out of place. Once fully moved, all three stood, catching their breaths, while gaping at the hole underneath the marble-and-bronze plaque leading to a tunnel.

Vicki unhooked her flashlight and climbed down the ladder.

"What is she looking for?" Paul asked, observing Vicki's eagerness.

Anthony gazed stoically at Cleopatra's Needle as he spoke. "Several time capsules were placed under the obelisk when it was erected. One of the capsules, it appears, contains something that has been sought by secret societies and by world leaders for thousands of years."

"Really?" Paul stated with astonishment. "What's in it?"

"Long-lost scrolls." Noticing Paul's cynical expression, Anthony followed up with, "I was also skeptical when I was first informed of the scrolls."

Vicki resurfaced. "It's gone!" she yelled, ascending from the dark hole at the side of the obelisk. "There are several capsules of various sizes below the cornerstone. They must be the other time capsules. But there's no gold capsule made of orichalcum, as the bishop described it."

"Are we going to investigate the tunnel?" Paul asked.

Anthony moved forward and looked down the hole on the south side of the obelisk. He inspected the ladder descending into the darkness. "No, we know they're using this tunnel, so that won't be necessary. We just need to catch them in the act."

ANTHONY, VICKI, AND Paul spent the next few hours hiding wireless cameras in the trees around Cleopatra's Needle. The cameras that monitored the rear of the museum didn't zoom in close enough to the area around the obelisk to capture clear facial images, especially at night. Experience had taught Anthony that simply capturing culprits in the act was all too easily dismissed by unforeseen loopholes in the law or by crafty, high-priced lawyers skilled in the art of manipulating the system. And the people he wanted to catch in the act had the money and political pull to get around the justice system, so he was hell bent on obtaining the best possible evidence. He needed surveillance footage that would exceed even the broadest interpretations of a reasonable doubt.

"That should certainly do it," Anthony remarked, satisfied that the additional cameras would capture a crystal-clear shot of anyone on the platform for the obelisk. "Now, if only we had a way to get them on camera while in the tunnels."

Paul raised his arms, dumbfounded by Anthony's request. He scratched his scraggly hair. "It's way too dark down there for cameras."

"I thought you said that these cameras worked in the dark?"

"These cameras can do many things, Tony. I can stream the feed live on my phone. I can set them to respond to Alexa voice control. We can even keep them out here during a blizzard in the winter, but they won't be effective in total darkness. It's not like up here where there's some light from the lampposts. Down there, it's pitch-black."

Vicki volunteered to trail the worshippers, but she had a private, more personal motive. She hoped to run into the mysterious man again. She was champing at the bit for an opportunity to turn the tables and use her stealthy skills to catch him off guard. All previous encounters, she realized, had occurred when she was distracted in some way.

"Out of the question," Anthony directed. "I'm not letting you go down into the tunnels alone again. There have been too many fatalities as it is."

"I don't see what else we can possibly do, Tony."

The light of the day was fading. Everything would need to be in place as soon as possible to capture the worshippers, so Anthony wasn't taking no for an answer. He had received a tip informing him of the groups' plan.

"I didn't hire you to tell me there's nothing more we can do."

Paul's copper eyebrows jutted into a v-shape as he stepped back. He turned and observed a police car race up the drive while contemplating, then proposed an alternative, unconvinced himself if the idea had any merit.

"Remember how the Brits used sticky bombs in World War II?"

Anthony reflected on the tactic of applying a strong adhesive to grenades to attach them to their targets, German tanks, mostly. "What about it?"

"I suppose it'd be possible to make a couple more tracking devices and put a very sticky adhesive on them, like the adhesive the Poster Department uses to stick its posters to the backing. We can then put the tracking devices at the base of this ladder," Paul proposed, pointing into the hole leading into the tunnels. Side-eyed, he glanced at Anthony and Vicki. "It's not a sure-fire way, but if one of the devices does get stuck to someone, we could track the movement of the entire group on the monitors in C3."

Anthony patted Paul on the back. "How long will it take?"

"Give me thirty minutes. I'll see if I can come up with three or four."

Vicki stepped up. "I'll get the adhesive. The carpentry shop has a much stronger epoxy adhesive. No need to go to the Poster Department."

"Alright, then let's do this," Anthony instructed, fist clenched.

CHAPTER 47

THE BUYING AND SELLING OF GREAT art began during Roman times with the purchase of Greek statuary. The demand for Greek artwork grew in proportion to the vast expansion of the empire. Statues, bronze and marble, along with frescoes, initially of the gods and then of everyday people, were in high-demand for Roman aristocrats. The acquisitions of works of art, however, waned with the decline of the Roman Empire.

The exchange of artwork flourished once again with the enlightenment that arose with the Renaissance. Great artists refueled demand in the sale of great paintings with an eclectic combination of traditional biblical scenes, along with scenes from antiquity, some of which included cryptic messages.

Clues to the ancient knowledge had been encrypted in Scipione Pulzone's lamentation scene. Above Jesus and the central figures at his death, the True Cross paralleled an obelisk in the far distance. The space between the cross and the obelisk symbolized the timespan of thousands of years before Christianity when the idea of resurrection served as a central religious theme. The Virgin Mary, garbed in an earthly blue dress, was placed directly below the blue water in the painting to reveal the association between her purity and the pureness of the antediluvian waters. The triad of unidentified women behind Mary in the painting – Isis, Artemis, and Diana – symbolized Mary's connection to the older Egyptian, Greek, and Roman virgins.

The reclamation of Pulzone's *Lamentation* was a combative issue among the parties in the trustees' conference room on the fourth floor of the museum. Fabrizio had insisted on a one-on-one meeting with Lane to discuss the return of Pulzone's painting. The discussions were imperative. He was ordered to leave New York City immediately and return to Rome. Lane agreed to the meeting to put an end to the matter once and for all.

Fabrizio had secured the right opportunity.

The two 'seconds' sitting beside Lane and Fabrizio belonged to powerful groups that most people knew nothing about. The seconds were present to bear witness to the negotiations. Except for Lane, the other three at the table knew something very important: that a dangerous schism existed in the world's most powerful groups.

Lane was assisted by a member of the Trilateral Commission, formed a century earlier by the same captains of industry that financed the Met and The Cloisters. The commission enjoyed ties with elite organizations such as the Club of Rome, the Bilderberg Group, Bohemian Grove, the Royal Institute of International Affairs, even British intelligence.

Diametrically across, Fabrizio sat beside his second, an elderly Italian diplomat who had served as an ombudsman and go-between during the postwar years. The diplomat had played a pivotal role in Operation Gladio, a clandestine operation that sprang up in the wake of World War II. Spearheaded by American intelligence in collaboration with NATO and various European governments, Operation Gladio was set in motion for the sole, but secretive, purpose of staving off Communism in the West.

Fabrizio eyed the Trilateral Commissioner with Machiavellian acuity, wondering about the member's ties to the powerful international organizations that influenced world affairs – the World Bank, the IMF, and the OECD, all of which he vilely detested because of their growing expropriation of nearly every facet of international policy. All the more so, perhaps, because of the brazen and far-reaching encroachment by the IGOs on national sovereignty. The shady organizations were corrupt, unchecked, and were leading the human race down an unrighteous and destabilizing path to imminent doom.

There was something even more worrisome to Fabrizio.

Under the guise of fostering international cooperation and prosperity, chosen members of these elite global organizations convened secretly under tight security to shape world policy in a way that he and his associations abhorred—the continual and cunning promotion of a global Marxist agenda that would do away with all religion.

What's their interest in Pulzone's painting? he asked himself.

The answer didn't matter.

Lane had started the discussion and wasn't budging.

"I'm sorry, Mr. Armata, but the museum is not an auction house," she had insisted from the start. "Pulzone's painting stays in New York, and you'll have to inform your superiors that there are no two ways about it."

"But as you can see," Fabrizio asserted, showing Lane provenance documentation for *The Lamentation*, "the painting really should be returned to its proper place."

"Mr. Armata, let me assure you that I've had my people look into the matter quite thoroughly, and there's no question that the museum legally owns Pulzone's painting."

"Perhaps the commission papers for the painting will persuade you." Fabrizio nodded at his second. "If you will," he remarked.

The eyes of the participants widened as Fabrizio's second snapped open his briefcase and removed an envelope sealed with the official Papal Seal.

Instantly unconvinced by validity of the seal, Lane turned to her second, frowned, then back to Fabrizio. "Pulzone was commissioned to paint the lamentation scene for the Church of the Gesù. They'd own the commission papers. And," Lane added, perceptibly, "you're from the Vatican Bank, so why would you have something with a Papal Seal?"

The scowl on Fabrizio's face accentuated his budging platysma muscle as he glared at his second. The fist clenching was also part of the performance. Both men knew in advance that Lane was smart enough to question the Vatican seal. Both men also knew that neither Lane nor her second would figure out the bigger deception.

One last card for Fabrizio to play.

"Surely you must know that the Vatican Bank reports to the Commission of Cardinals and to the pope, himself?" He placed his hand over the envelope, quite confident that Lane wouldn't ask to see the contents, and deliberately brought up a subject sure to get Lane's goat. "Besides, I'm sure the trustees of your museum do not wish to commence a lengthy legal battle with the Holy See. It would be a publicity disaster for the museum."

Lane bought it. "Is that a threat, Mr. Armata? If anything, I would think that the Vatican would want to avoid any publicity at this time, especially after the public learns of the shameless misuse of the Peter's Pence fund by certain cardinals."

Fabrizio leaned his large upper body over the round table, elbows firmly planted. His flint-green eyes radiated righteousness. "People forget what they want to forget. They even forgive. For those who do not forgive will not be forgiven."

Lane reclined in her chair. "Mr. Armata, I don't wish to get into the nitty-gritty, but I'm sure we lawfully own the painting. If you feel that you have further grievances to air, I'd suggest the Vatican take them to UNESCO."

Fabrizio theatrically bowed his head in defeat, slyly shifting his phone into the center of his lap. He pressed 'Send' and released the short text to the Worshipful Master that he had written prior to the meeting: Operation False Flag successful.

~~*

ANTHONY AND VICKI doubled-checked the surveillance cameras used for the Egyptian Wing. They began with the cameras outside the atrium.

"How many fingers do I have up?" Anthony asked, speaking into his radio.

Looking at the monitor in C3, Paul replied, "Peace, brother."

Anthony realized that Paul saw the two fingers, so he gestured to Vicki to move on to the next camera. They entered the museum and stood under the camera over the emergency exit at the rear of the atrium. Anthony held up two fingers and asked again.

"Two," Paul replied.

Cy bleated something inaudible as he approached.

Anthony had called Cy and informed him of the camera check.

"I hope you finally got your cameras working," Cy remarked.

Anthony smiled without saying a word.

Cy followed as Anthony and Vicki checked the cameras monitoring the Temple of Dendur, passing through all thirty-six of the museum's Egyptian galleries, and making sure that Paul saw the two fingers on every camera.

On their way out, while in the galleries located at the front of the Egyptian

Wing, Anthony stopped in front of the main camera of the wing. He asked Paul how many fingers he held up while facing Cy and holding up three fingers. Paul's voice came through the radio with the wrong answer. For his own sense of gratification, Anthony looked into Cy's eyes.

CHAPTER 48

DARKENED IMAGES OF ESCALADES INCHED ONTO a monitor screen in the command center. Men with berets leaped out of the SUVs and investigated the entire bushy, tree-lined area encircling the octagonal platform for Cleopatra's Needle. Several other men inspected the platform itself. When the area was secure, round objects were inserted under the marble-and-bronze plaque and several men slid it out of place, revealing the portal.

The all-clear sign was given with a whirl of a wrist, and the silhouettes of hooded individuals exited the SUVs and stepped onto the brick platform. One by one, a small group disappeared into the hole at the base of the obelisk.

Anthony slammed his fist on the table. "Damn it! Their heads are covered. Why are their heads covered?" He glared at Paul. "Why do you think that is?"

Paul shrugged. "How did you know they'd be here tonight?"

Anthony took note of the shift in Paul's eyes, an indication that Paul was hiding something, something Anthony had recently discovered, but he wasn't ready just yet to call Paul on it. He needed Paul's assistance a bit longer.

"The chief called earlier with the tip," he answered, evenly.

"Really?" Paul fidgeted anxiously. "Who could have tipped him off?"

Anthony let the question go unanswered.

As if on cue, the heads of the security personnel shifted from the monitors on the obelisk to the monitor used for the tracking devices and watched for the blipping dot on the screen to indicate movement. But there was no movement, just blip, blip, blip.

231

"Is the worshippers' security team going to stay parked on Central Park Drive?" Vicki asked with disbelief, stepping back from the computer monitor. She flipped the hair from her face. "In those big SUVs? A little suspicious looking, don't you think?"

"Looks like they aren't taking any chances," Anthony remarked.

"C'mon, you bastards!" Paul yelled, slamming his coffee mug on a table, histrionically. "One of you sons of bitches better rub up against a device."

Anthony sat motionless. His stoic expression affirmed his determination. But something more than just overtones of fortitude reflected in his forceful brown eyes – something about the look in his eyes suggested that the situation had taken on an entirely personal dimension.

A green dot began to move on the monitor. To everyone's surprise, one of the tracking devices had successfully hitched onto the robes of one of the worshippers like a burr on the shorts of a hiker. Anthony's eyebrows cocked as he looked at Paul.

Paul jumped from his seat. "I can't believe it worked."

But the sounds of relief inside C3 were quickly replaced with the ringing of a phone. The heads of the security personnel shifted from the monitor to the red phone on the wall. No one had ever heard it ring, but everyone knew who was on the other end.

Anthony jumped from his chair and rushed to the phone.

"Anthony Leonardi speaking," he said into the phone mouthpiece, holding back his breath as he learned that Fabrizio had received his orders from high-ranking members of Propaganda Due, the half mob, half Masonic order.

"P2?" Anthony whispered, turning his head to hide his expression of concern. He was familiar with the nefarious, ultra-right-wing order. He also knew that the members were as brutal as they were powerful. "What business does P2 have in New York?"

Special Agent Wilson answered by explaining the historical context of the situation, informing Anthony that P2 had been chartered in Turin, Italy, in the early nineteenth century by the Grand Orient of Italy, an Italian Masonic grand lodge established by Joséphine Bonaparte's son, Eugène de Beauharnais, to influence the course of the French Revolutionary Wars.

"Napoleon's wife?"

"His first wife, yes. Napoleon adopted Joséphine's son, and Eugène rose

232

in the ranks of the French army, but when Napoleon fell, the lodge distanced itself from the French aristocrats and took on a new, competing mission."

"I'm not following," Anthony mumbled as a thought arose. Cy had mentioned that Napoleon was searching for something in Egypt. Then he recalled what the bishop had said about the Jesuit missionaries in Egypt.

"Listen closely." Wilson's voice sounded hoarser, harsher than in prior times. "It's extremely important that you know who you're dealing with here. P2 later grew to be a state unto itself. Even now, the order has countless operatives around the globe, and many in high places. Allied forces turned to P2 after World War II to help stave off Communism in Italy. In short order, nearly every left-leaning politician in Italy was killed. With its mission complete, P2 took control of banks, newspapers, courts, even various branches of the Italian military and government. Outside Italy, P2 wreaked havoc in South America—in places like Chile, Uruguay, Paraguay, and Argentina—where its members, once again, were called upon to eliminate anyone believed to be a threat to organized religion."

"Operation Condor," Anthony remarked. He knew that US intelligence had backed the right-wing governments during the Dirty Wars in South America in the 1970s and 1980s, but he was unaware of P2's involvement.

"Make no mistake about it," Wilson emphasized, "P2 is the modern-day Knights Templar, but even more powerful and more brutal. In return for killing those seen as a threat to the Church, government and religious officials looked the other way when the order took control of the Vatican Bank to launder ill-gotten money. That's where Fabrizio Armata comes in," Special Agent Wilson explained. For what seemed to be several drawn-out seconds, Anthony heard nothing on the line. He pushed the speaker of the handset closer to his ear. "As I said before, Armata sits on the board of an Italian bank that launders money through the IOR, the Vatican Bank, and into Swiss and a few off-shore accounts. We also just got word from British intelligence that he was sent to New York under the guise of a representative of the Vatican to reclaim a painting from the museum that was stolen from a Jesuit church. At some point, plans were changed, and Armata recruited a few associates to eliminate people who pose a threat to the Church. Those people," Wilson said, "may have ties to the museum."

Anthony put his hand over the phone.

"Did the device fall off?" he asked.

"No," Paul answered, moving closer. "The change from green to yellow indicates an upward motion as opposed to a forward or backward."

Anthony put the phone to his mouth. "Why are the Brits involved?"

"British intelligence has connections to influential groups and organizations worldwide, and they were tipped off."

Anthony listened to the rest of the information, thanked Wilson, and hung up, contemplating what information could be shared.

"What's up?" Paul asked, battle-faced.

Anthony waved Vicki and Paul to the side.

"Feds got a tip from MI6," he whispered.

Paul's head jerked back. "British Intelligence Service?"

Anthony verified with a tight nod. "It appears there are a few more people involved in this than first thought," he said, visibly annoyed, "because members of some secret Masonic lodge from Italy were ordered to murder the people who are performing rituals in the museum. And if that's not enough," he remarked with his palms up, punctuating his uncertainty on how to handle the situation, "American and British intelligence agencies are involved and are at odds on how to handle the situation."

"This is out of control!" Paul cried, turning and glancing around C3. He stepped closer to Anthony and apologized for the indiscretion. "I'm not sure what to say, Tony. Italian, American, British intelligence. How did it get to this point?"

Vicki closed the distance. "What does all this mean?"

"It means," Anthony responded, a pall of uncertainty in his voice, "that World War III is about to erupt under the museum. If these thugs kill the people performing rituals in the museum, chaos will result. A chain of events not unlike those that followed the killing of Archduke Franz Ferdinand and igniting World War I could likely result." Anthony refrained from saying more, while realizing that not even the Evidence Collection Team could hide the possible aftermath of the near-certain calamity that was unfolding. An incident on this scale would hit the press immediately, revealing a network of world power players who secretly pull the levers of modern society.

CHAPTER 49

VICKI EXAMINED THE MONITOR TRACKING THE worshippers and guessed at their location. She was on the right track. "I know where they are."

"You do?" Anthony blurted.

"When the museum was first enlarged, the entrance was moved to the south side, where the European Sculpture Court is now located."

"And?" he queried, with a rolling hand gesture.

"Remember when we discussed that the museum had opened in Central Park in 1880, the same year eight thousand secret-society members marched up Fifth Avenue and held the cornerstone ceremony for the obelisk?" Vicki hesitated briefly to let Anthony recall the conversation. "The museum was enlarged even before construction was finished in 1880, and the architect of that extension wasn't an actual architect. He was a member of the Board of Trustees and the engineer of the New York City's sewer system."

Anthony's face showed confusion, then comprehension.

"The same guy also worked on the Croton Aqueduct," she said, confident in her knowledge of the museum's history. "And the museum's enlargement included a sub-cellar space on the south end of the museum with several passages that extended down to the water tunnels. That's the route I showed you when we exited the tunnels."

"And that's where the worshippers are now," Anthony realized.

"Wait a minute!" Paul yelled, moving closer to a screen that showed the area outside the museum and observed the figures of three men, two carrying elongated cases. "Tony, come over and look at what's on this monitor."

"What do you have?" Anthony asked as he moved toward Paul.

"I think I just found the hit men. Looks like three of them."

Or intelligence agents, but for which side? Anthony wondered.

He examined the rifle cases held by the two men. They didn't look like the ordinary hard-sided polymer cases. They appeared to be made up of a knapsack-like canvas that wouldn't raise suspicion. "Whoever they are," he remarked, "they're not your usual hooligans looking to steal a purse."

"Judging by the shape of those cases," Paul conjectured while zooming in, "these guys are carrying tactical assault rifles, with plenty of accessory pouches." Paul put his hands around his head, elbows flared. "Tony, these guys are loaded for bear."

Anthony and Paul exchanged telling, extended glances, both recalling from their war days that various types of explosives and incendiary devices could be in those cases.

"Where is this camera?" Anthony was certain of the answer, but he needed verification, if for no other reason than to provide precious seconds to digest and assess all the information. He wasn't ready to get the police involved, just yet.

"Near the rear of the south side of the building."

The armed men were a stone's throw from the security team guarding the entrance to the tunnels at the obelisk, but remained far enough that they must have known that the area around Cleopatra's Needle was being guarded. "Are they going to make a frontal attack?" Anthony asked, thinking out loud as he watched the armed men move toward the obelisk. He knew he'd have some hard explaining to do if an all-out gunfire battle ensued. But as difficult as it was to refrain from taking immediate action, he realized that he had to stay calm and assess how things played out at every step. He could have a hundred police officers at the scene within minutes. In the back of his mind, he also knew, or hoped, there was little chance of a shootout. The thugs had their sights on the worshippers.

Mind overrun with possibilities, he glanced at Paul, knowing that Paul had played a role in the lethal quagmire that he had to discreetly defuse. He refocused on the monitor, studying it closely, and watched as the armed men stepped off the paved path, over a low railing, and disappeared into the trees.

"All three are completely out of sight now," Vicki announced.

"Maybe they know another way into the tunnels," Anthony surmised. A possibility popped to mind. Looking around, he said, "I need the map of Central Park. Does anyone have a map of Central Park handy?"

"A map?" Vicki said, obvious mockery in her voice. "What is it, 1982?" She sat in front of a computer and typed the museum address into the Google search bar, zoomed in on the area of Central Park on the south side of the museum, and hit the satellite view. "A little better, no?"

Anthony grumbled. Vicki was right, though. Not only did the satellite imagery show the entirety of the park, with all the trees and various trails, but it also provided names of locations, landmarks, and structures.

"Zoom in and slide the screen to the south."

"Here's the thick patch of trees that the three men ducked into," Vicki noted, using the mouse arrow to circle a small grove of leafy elm and oak trees not far from the south side of the museum.

Hunch in mind, Anthony examined the computer screen. It was a risky hunch, but he had nothing else, and time was quickly running out. The worshippers would soon be under the museum. The armed men, if he was right, would be close behind. The sense of urgency fueled determination.

"This structure here," he said, pointing to a building on the 79th Street transverse. "I have a feeling this building contains an access entrance to the elevating chamber. My guess is that's where they are headed."

"Elevating chamber?" Paul asked.

"Never mind." Anthony took the mouse from Vicki and widened the satellite image for a broader view of the park. "This is the route that I took the other day when I was in the tunnels. I started right here," he remarked, pointing to the northwest side of the museum, "and then I passed under the reservoir, made a sharp left after exiting the North Gatehouse, and walked in a south-east direction from the west side of the park. At some point, likely here," he stated, making a circle covering the Great Lawn and surrounding are, "I hit Tunnel 3, which took me directly to the elevating chamber."

Vicki scrutinized the route traced.

"You traveled an underground triangular route? Of course," she said, thinking that she was beginning to understand the secrets of the ancient mysteries. "The number three had long been held as sacred. Pythagoras brought the idea of the sacred three from Egypt and introduced the

Pythagorean right angle. There was the Holy Trinity, and the Three Wise Men. Jesus returned after three days." Vicki caught her breath.

Anthony's brain was already functioning on overdrive.

"Stay focused, Vicki, for crying out loud." He zoomed in on the building that he believed contained an entrance way into the elevating chamber. "One of the things I wanted to check while I was in the tunnels the other day was a possible way into the elevating chamber by unauthorized individuals, but I was distracted by Margarita and Darrel."

Vicki regrouped. "Okay, I get it. If the bad guys try to get into the museum without being detected, they'd do it underground."

Engrossed in thought, Anthony stood and nodded.

"What are you going to do?" Vicki asked.

Anthony scrolled through the contacts on his phone until he reached the president's number. "I'm going to put an end to all of this right now."

CHAPTER 50

ANTHONY INSTRUCTED PAUL AND VICKI TO rush to the Egyptian galleries, ordering Paul to stand post at the west entrance, and then telling Vicki to guard the front entrance, but only after doing a thorough sweep of all thirty-six Egyptian galleries. He focused again on the security monitor, momentarily, while he removed his suit jacket, took off his tie, and mentally prepared himself for the danger ahead.

* ~ * ~ *

VICKI TIED HER hair in a bun as Paul provided instructions on how to use the tracking feature that he had installed on her phone. She peered into the darkened Egyptian atrium. The lights were off, but the Temple of Dendur, bathed in a soft golden light, glowed paranormally from the color-filtered LED lights at its base. A faint radiance from the lampposts in Central Park filtered through the glass wall of the atrium, resulting in spectral-like silhouettes cast from the antediluvian statues near the wall.

Exiting the atrium, Vicki passed through the Old Kingdom galleries, noting the group's whereabouts as indicated on her iPhone, which provided the only source of light in the dark maze of galleries. But Vicki knew the layout well. With a poised vigilance, she passed the silhouettes of humans and animals of a bygone age, some dating back four, even five thousand years. The tangential projection of the light from her phone caught the painted eye of the faience hippopotamus statuette anointed as 'William the

Hippo' by the museum. The peaceful eyes of the beloved mascot conveyed approval of Vicki's presence. William knew what was going on in the museum. Ever since Memphis had served as Egypt's first capital, statuettes of hippopotami were placed in tombs to help the deceased reach the afterlife.

After clearing the galleries, and making her way to the front, Vicki closed in on the location of the worshippers as shown on the screen of her iPhone. Completely unsure what she'd do if she encountered the group, she continued, slowing her pace, but eager to get a fix on the group.

At the front of the collection, she stopped and elevated on the balls of her feet as she stretched out her neck and peeked around the limestone blocks of the cyclopean Tomb of Perneb. No one was in sight. She double-checked the group's location on her phone. According to the instructions that she received from Paul, the group should be in close proximity. Momentarily confused, Vicki's jaw dropped with the abrupt realization that she wasn't next to the worshippers, but that she was standing directly above them.

Rushing out of the Egyptian Wing, Vicki slipped through the lofty, marble colonnade at the entrance to the galleries, dashed through the Great Hall, and took cover behind the octagon-shaped information desk in the middle of the entry hall.

She fumbled through several drawers until she found a brochure on the Egyptian Wing. Using the light from her phone, she searched for info on the Tomb of Perneb and quickly understood why the group was below the tomb. For thousands of years, the Tomb of Perneb had served as a house of eternity, and Vicki recalled from her reading of the *Crata Repoa* that worshippers who performed the life-renewing rituals went underground to signify death, passed through a sacred chamber like the Tomb of Perneb, then journeyed the passageway of the underworld and into the ritualistic temple.

"Oh, no. Not him," she whispered, clenching her fist.

Vicki dashed full speed toward the tomb.

CHAPTER 51

ANTHONY EXITED THE SOUTH GATEHOUSE OF the reservoir, where he set in motion a fail-safe plan, if his initial strategy backfired. He had to be careful, not only if he was going to catch the culprits off-guard, but he didn't want the worshippers to divert from their route. He needed them to reach the safety of the museum without any interference.

The two groups were headed toward the museum. Anthony also knew that they would take different passageways to get there. The worshippers would use the tunnel underneath Cleopatra's Needle that led to the rear of the museum. The armed men would have to navigate the same indirect route that he had taken when chasing Margarita and Darrel before they came anywhere near the worshippers.

Anthony had a trick up his sleeve.

He now knew of a secret bypass tunnel that he could use as a shortcut and not have to traverse the lengthy route through the reservoir and under the park, as he'd done the last time. Nor did he have to chance running into the worshippers by using the tunnels that he and Vicki had used to return to the museum. Anthony had uncovered a vital piece of information about the door inside the barrel vault hidden behind the 4x8 sheet of plywood with the two etched obelisks. The door had been added after the tunnel was handed over to the museum, and so had a tunnel leading to the elevating chamber.

He jumped from the catwalk and pushed the 4x8 sheet of plywood with the dual carvings of obelisks to the side. If the door didn't open, he was prepared to kick it in, come hell or high water, but the polished doorknob easily turned, as he had assumed it would. Why lock a door that's hidden in a place that so few know about?

Anthony entered the bypass tunnel, pleased at the sight ahead.

The tunnel, more modern than the barrel vault, was well lit and free of obstacles, allowing Anthony to make good time through the long stretch beneath Central Park and get the tactical advantage on his target.

"I SWEAR, THIS guy is going to spoil everything," Vicki uttered as she rushed toward Cy Hetford, who was entering the Egyptian galleries.

Vicki whispered as she approached Cy.

"I need you to leave this area."

"Why?" he asked almost defiantly.

"Come with me, and I'll explain," Vicki insisted, questioning why Cy was still in the museum at such a late hour. She escorted him to the information desk in the Great Hall and crouched like a baseball catcher behind it. "We're closing in on the group that breaks into the museum. Get down, please."

"Well, it's about time. Where are they?"

"Under the Tomb of Perneb," Vicki whispered, agitation sounding in her muted voice, though keeping her cool. "Please, get down."

"Under the tomb?" Cy muttered under his breath, his face showing confusion. He opened a museum map and placed it on the floor where he put his knees. "That's curious," he remarked, "Perneb was buried fifty feet below his tomb, but no one informed me of a space below here."

"What year did the Met acquire Perneb's tomb?"

"1913. Does anyone here bother to read the information on the placards? The curators in this museum go to great pains to make sure that all two million objects displayed in the collection have a placard."

Vicki put her index finger to her lips, instructing Cy to lower his voice. She reflected briefly, then asked, " While J. P. Morgan was in Egypt?"

"Oh, no, Morgan didn't get this one." Even in the dim light inside the Great Hall, the veneer of annoyance on Cy's face was noticeable. "Morgan was in Egypt alright, but the Perneb's tomb was donated to the museum by Edward Harkness, the son of John Rockefeller's business partner. Both father and son were trustees. The son also donated items in A&A, I believe."

"That explains where the saber came from." Vicki gasped.

Cy was busy listening to himself talk. "Of course, at the time, Morgan was in Egypt looking for something for the Vatican in the El Bagawat Cemetery, the oldest Christian burial ground in the world. I never found out what."

"The scrolls," Vicki said, nodding with certitude.

"What scrolls?" Cy asked. "There are no scrolls."

Staring into the Egyptian galleries, Vicki's thoughts drifted to J. P. Morgan's greatest gift to the museum—Raphael's *Colonna Altarpiece*, an exceptional painting by one of the Trinity of Great Masters. Leonardo da Vinci, Michelangelo, and Raphael. In her mind's eye, she pictured the painting in the altarpiece, which had always struck her as unusual, though she could never quite put her finger on it until now. Mary sat in the center of a pyramid of central figures. An infant Jesus and infant John the Baptist gestured at each other in the exact same manner as they did in da Vinci's *Virgin of the Rocks*, as though they possessed some invaluable secret. What was that secret? More to the point, by what means did the artists know that there were secrets? And how did the wealthy learn of the secrets?

Vicki was getting warmer – Da Vinci, Michelangelo, Rembrandt, Rosa, Tiepolo, Seurat . . . all the great artists' names sprang to the forefront of Vicki's mind as she intuited their many attempts to share their knowledge, which had never been properly deciphered or even understood, but the messages were there, hidden in plain sight.

She visualized the course of the secrets through the ages.

REMOTE PAST → EGYPT → GREECE → ROME

↳ MESOPOTAMIA → NEAR EAST → ASIA

↳ ESSENES → JOHN THE BAPTIST → JESUS

Cy was still carrying on. "Vicki are you listening to me?" he asked, expression tensed. I just informed you that Perneb's name means 'My Lord has come forth to me', and that his tomb comes from the ancient burial ground in Saqqara, the necropolis for the ancient Egyptian city of Memphis."

"Yeah, well, then you'd think the tomb would be better off where it is supposed to be rather than moved for these shenanigans." Vicki peered over the top of the desk, then lowered and faced Cy while making another shushing gesture. "I see them. They're on the move."

CHAPTER 52

EXITING THE BYPASS TUNNEL, ANTHONY ENTERED the expanse of Tunnel 3.

Instantly, he recognized his location inside Tunnel 3, questioning why he hadn't noticed the door to the bypass tunnel the prior time. Only now did he notice the door. Then he recalled the astonishing display of lights. They wouldn't be forgotten again.

In the void ahead, voices were audible.

Anthony wiped his hand on his pants and clutched his SIG P226.

Predatory growls raised hairs. *Same coyote?*

In the distance of the enormous, well-lit tunnel, three men stood outside the entrance to the elevating chamber. One man held a 9-mm. The other two adjusted their assault rifles. Both rifles had extended scopes.

Shit, Anthony said to himself, taking note of the advanced night-vision optics on the rifles. He hadn't planned on this contingency. Unlike regular night vision scopes, which require ambient light to be useful, he could tell by the length of the extended scopes that the rifles were equipped with thermal-imaging scopes that can work in total darkness. He'd be an easy target as he lured the men away from the worshippers and into the tunnel as planned.

Silently back-stepping into the bypass tunnel, Anthony gently closed the door and contemplated his options. At all costs, it was imperative to keep the killers away from the worshippers, even if that meant risking his own life. He turned off the lights in the bypass tunnel and opened the door to Tunnel 3.

Sticking his SIG through the space between the door and the frame, he held the gun at an angle so that the bullet would not project straight, but

244

ricochet from steel wall to steel wall in the wide tunnel, giving the culprits a chance to shield themselves. But the shot would get their attention – and knowing their less-evolved temperament, their goat.

An ear-piercing shot was followed by a trebly, echoing din as the bullet ricocheted off opposite walls of Tunnel 3, ringing out with each strike like a church bell on methamphetamine as it continued. The sulfury smell of gunpowder suffused with, then overpowered, the bog-like scent of the tunnel. With the bullet spent, there was nothing but silence in the tunnel until gruff-sounding, Italian words were exchanged.

A battle cry roared through the tunnel with the advance, but Anthony had already retreated into the bypass tunnel, thinking that his plan of distracting the thugs from the worshippers was working, but his own life was now in jeopardy. At the end of the tunnel, he stopped and aimed his gun knee-high.

The sound of stampeding footsteps stopped, nanoseconds before Anthony fired. An extrasensory feeling of being trained in a scope made the hairs on his arm rise. He scurried through the door of the bypass tunnel.

A man called out. "Who are you?"

Anthony hesitated, catching his breath, while leaning flush against the wall of the barrel vault just outside the bypass tunnel. Wheezing filled the bypass tunnel, allowing Anthony to gauge the distance to his target.

"Someone who'll stop you!" Anthony yelled. He refilled his lungs with air. "Stop you from killing anyone else."

Italian words were followed by, "Signor Leonardi?"

"You killed a priest, for heaven's sake!" Anthony shouted.

A faint snicker. "I'm afraid you're mistaken, Signore."

"*Militari per Dio*!" echoed in the darkness of the tunnel.

"I know it was you, Fabrizio."

"Perhaps you are referring to people, who at this moment, are sailing over the equator, but I'd be rude if I didn't mention that the lovely lady that you were with the other day, the one with the long hair and the semi-automatic, has quite remarkable aim. Tell me, is she a co-worker of yours?"

Fury surged through Anthony's veins, knowing that groups like P2 controlled 'soldiers' around the world who were willing to put a bullet in someone's brain at a moment's notice.

"Go anywhere near her, and I'll make sure you rot in jail for life!"

From somewhere in the bypass tunnel, Fabrizio yelled, "Perhaps this priest whom you speak of veered off the right path. Maybe he forgot that he had taken a vow to be a soldier of God when he became a Jesuit priest."

"You and those goons at your side are living in the past, Fabrizio. There are no more Church mercenaries. Those days ended hundreds of years ago, but ignorant people like you still haven't gotten the message. All those who have blood on their hands have betrayed Jesus!" Anthony cried out, struggling to regain his composure. The muscles in his neck strained as he yelled, "I am going to give you a chance to surrender. One chance only."

"There's no surrender," Fabrizio hollered.

"*Coloro che servono come un soldato di Dio!*"

"*Deus vult!*"

The three men rushed Anthony.

Leaping onto the catwalk, Anthony dashed for his life.

CHAPTER 53

ANTHONY REACHED THE WEST END TERMINUS of the barrel vault and stopped, panting heavily. More than before, the egg-shaped door reminded him of the oval doors installed on submarines and space shuttles.

When he had entered the gatehouse to set up the fail-safe plan, he had looped a chain around the lever of the door and the side rung, locking it with a tautness that kept the door open with a slim gap. That would hopefully buy him some time to climb to the upper level of the gatehouse before Fabrizio and his men reached the water bay. More importantly, he contemplated as he squeezed through the gap in the doorway, the chain would be shot off, and the door would shut after the thugs passed through.

The passageway under Central Park still smelled like death.

"Fabrizio, there's no escape!" he yelled through the gap in the door.

Before he finished, a barrage of bullets slammed and clanged against the submarine-like door with a jolting, eardrum-piercing clamor.

"Holy shit," he muttered as he turned and dashed through the next tunnel.

Inside the gatehouse, Anthony raced up the wrought-iron staircase two steps at a time, adrenaline at the ready, suppressing the pain in his leg. His heart pounded as he peered down into the water bay of the gatehouse several stories below and attempted to catch his breath. He wiped the sweat from his face and neck using the L. L. Bean shirt that he had left on the stopcock, fully aware that if everything didn't play out as he had planned, he'd be inside the gatehouse with Fabrizio and his men.

He said a prayer.

ASTONISHED BY THE sight, Vicki lowered back into a position of concealment behind the Great Hall information desk. "It's them," she whispered. "Maybe a dozen or so, all wearing what appears to be hooded, royal-purple robes and all linked together by a long rope."

"Where are they going?" Cy asked.

"They exited the Tomb of Perneb and it seems that the group is headed toward the Temple of Dendur."

"What should we do?"

Vicki decided to keep Cy involved, if only to keep him from blowing her surveillance. She checked the position of the worshippers on her phone. "Judging by their position, it doesn't look like they made it as far as the temple." She stood up and looked around. "Something's not right here," she whispered. "I'm going in."

Cy stood. "I'm coming with you."

"Fine but stay behind me."

Cy trailed as Vicki entered the Egyptian Wing and concealed herself behind a display case mounted to the wall that contained the museum's oldest human artifacts, some extending back seven hundred thousand years on the branches of the human family tree. She checked her phone. The group was now somewhere between her and the Temple of Dendur.

"Wait here," she instructed Cy, then crept to the west end of the first Egyptian gallery, remaining as close to the Tomb of Perneb as possible.

The score of Mozart's *Magic Flute* filled the gallery.

Then, there was chanting:

O Isis and Osiris! What delight!
The dark night retreats from the light of the sun!
Soon will the noble youth experience a new life,
soon will he be wholly dedicated to our Order.
His spirit is bold, his heart is pure,
Soon will he be worthy of us.

Cy cried out Vicki's name.

"Damn it," she muttered, turning and spotting Cy's slight silhouette in front of the Tomb of Perneb. Vicki advanced on Cy. "I asked you to wait at the entrance."

"I think I figured out how they got into the museum."

Vicki suppressed her desire to wring Cy's neck and decided to take advantage of his knowledge of the collection.

"Is there a door in the Tomb of Perneb?" Vicki asked as she studied the limestone walls of the tomb. All four walls were covered from top to bottom with seemingly endless hieroglyphics, symbols, and elliptical cartouches, all combining to form the sacred instructions of Perneb's pyramid text, the funerary instructions to raise his soul to the heavens.

A plaque provided a translation of a segment:

The gatekeeper comes out to you, he grasps your hand,
Takes you into heaven, to your father.
He rejoices at your coming, gives you his hands,
Kisses you, caresses you,
Sets you before the spirits, the imperishable stars.
The hidden ones worship you,
The great ones surround you,
The WATCHERS wait on you.

Vicki stepped back, staring at the text.

Was the mysterious man a Watcher?

Cy waved Vicki inside the dark tomb. "False doors were an important part of mastaba tombs. In Perneb's tomb, the false door is located over there." Cy pointed to the rear of the offering chamber.

Vicki folded her arms in as she passed through the narrow offering chamber. Perneb's tomb was a fraction of the size of the Temple of Dendur. She pressed on her phone light and pointed the beam at the door at the far end constructed to allow the soul of the deceased to pass to the world beyond. The limestone blocks alongside the door and making up the rear of the chamber were all decorated with colorful depictions of offering bearers carrying bountiful meals to the deceased. "This opens?" she asked.

"False doors in temples are merely representations of doors—a false door, that is to say—but if you look closely, you can see that this false door was turned into an actual door at some point. How did I never notice this before?"

"This is how they are getting into the museum. Very clever."

"It's more than clever, Vicki. It's brilliant. These guys actually made a functional false door," he said, swinging the false door out of position, revealing a pitch-black void. "It's the last place anyone would look."

"They do seem to be cunning," Vicki said. "I've completely lost them."

CHAPTER 54

ANTHONY WIPED HIS HAND ON HIS pants and pulled his SIG from the holster. Consecutive flashes lit the upper level of the gatehouse for a split second as he fired two indiscriminate rounds into the darkness of the lower level.

"No more warning shots!" Anthony screamed.

He shined his flashlight into the water bay several stories below. The three assassins were out of sight, but Anthony knew they were lurking, plotting, somewhere in the darkness below. A single shot heard several minutes earlier indicated that they forced their way through the oval door by shooting the chain that he used to keep the door ajar.

"Law-enforcement officers are outside!" he hollered with desperation in his voice while trying to turn the large circular stopcock. When he had checked the valve before pursuing the killers, it felt loose, but the valve was now stuck in place. Sweat dripped from his hair and chin and onto the metal stopcock, making the valve slippery.

A red beam reflected in Anthony's eyes as he simultaneously dove. The round whizzed by with a blood-curdling hum, smashing into the stone retaining wall of the gatehouse. Even before he hit the ground, Anthony fired two more shots, but the gun slipped out of his wet hand as it recoiled at the same moment he hit the steel floor. With a single bounce, it disappeared inside the gearworks that controlled the flow of water in the gatehouse. A torrent of bullets buzzed overhead like angry killer bees from a disturbed beehive, blasting the wall of the gatehouse and producing a hail of rocks.

Anthony rolled to the stopcock, taking cover.

The shooting stopped. Vowel-ending words sounded in rapid cadence.

Fabrizio stepped into the water bay of the gatehouse, Beretta in hand. In near-exultant fashion, he moved forward, detecting that Anthony was unarmed.

Calmly, he said, "The culturati who oversee your museum proved to be of no interest to me, but there are some dangerous people in your museum tonight."

"I won't let you harm anyone!" Anthony shouted. He stood, concealing himself, while trying to get a fix on Fabrizio's location in the darkness below.

Bile rose with Fabrizio's voice from the depths of the water bay.

"Signore, are you aware that less than ten percent of the people on this planet own over ninety-percent of the wealth? And what do the elite do with their wealth, I ask you? They use it to make more money for themselves, of course. Little goes to charity. When they do pretend to give it away, it's only because they can make even more money."

Anthony felt the same disgust as everyone else about the ultra-rich's control over everything, but he had his priorities straight. He had spent his career upholding the rule of law, and his integrity was not up for negotiation. Not now. Not ever. But he needed to buy more time. "From what I hear, you're well-off yourself," he countered.

Leather-soled shoes squeaked on the hard floor of the water bay. Muffled words were whispered; crocodile-green eyes flickered in the darkness.

"I am speaking of a modern-day *aristocrazia*, Signore—the greedy, elite who hoard the world's wealth and dictate global policies to their liking, manipulate them in their favor, to the detriment of the rest of us. Unless these people are stopped, they'll create a global system no different than the crooked governments in places where they profess egalitarianism, but where a godless few rule over the impoverished majority."

The stopcock gave slightly.

"Sounds like someone brainwashed you, Armata."

"It's a fact, Signore. And if the people in your museum unravel the secrets of those scrolls, the elites of the world will be unstoppable. All three pillars of power will be in their hands. They'll exploit the ritual secrets for their own gain, in this lifetime and in the following, over and over again, and rule this planet like gods. Think of the consequences. The Church you grew up with will be eliminated altogether."

With all his might, Anthony struggled to open the stopcock, but the valve didn't give an inch. It was completely rusted shut. Or, as Anthony feared, his gun may have gotten stuck in the gears and jammed the whole movement.

The two riflemen took their place at Fabrizio's side, standing slightly behind him, forming a tight triangular rank.

Anthony had one option, and only one option.

The first of a sequence of commands was barked: "*Pronti.*"

Assault rifles angled up, butts on shoulders.

Anthony knew the command. "Don't do it!" he shouted.

Fabrizio stepped forward, platysma flared. "*Mirate.*"

Veins in Anthony's body pulsated with coursing blood, climaxing in an imminent sense of relief as the stopcock loosened. "I'm warning you," he hollered, vehemence in his voice, "put down your weapons!"

Coolly, Fabrizio popped the spent magazine from his Berretta and inserted another fifteen-round clip. Night-vision scopes locked in on their target.

"The reign of the gods ended," Fabrizio said, before yelling: "*Fuoco!*"

But the stopcock opened. The sluice gate steadily rose, instantly releasing hundreds of millions of gallons of water into the bay below as Anthony whirled the valve fully open. Screams were drowned-out by the roar of the violent gush of water that ebbed from the reservoir, through the water bay, and into the tunnel under Central Park, ripping the bottom-half of the rusted wrought-iron staircase from the wall, and shredding the catwalk into body-piercing shards of wood. Anthony shrieked and crashed to the ground, securing himself by grasping the grooves in the metal grating as the gatehouse trembled from the rising, churning eddy formed by the rush of turbulence, swishing, and crashing off the walls below. A loud siphoning sound was followed by an explosion that boomed like ten thousand tons of TNT, echoing back from the barrel vault, and into the gatehouse.

Pain shot through Anthony's arm. The gatehouse darkened.

CHAPTER 55

EYES OPENED. CLOSED. SECONDS, MINUTES, AN uncertain time passed. Eyes opened once again, wide, blinkless. Surroundings were framed in landscape, not portrait.

A blurred thought: *Wide, not tall?*

The lit flashlight on the floor next to his face provided the answer. His SIG Sauer underneath the iron-gray gearworks came into view, igniting his recollection.

Jesus. I'm too old for this shit.

Reeling, he yanked himself up to a standing position, gripping the stopcock tightly. Frayed wires on the walls of the gatehouse sizzled and flared with a red burst, lighting the submersed water bay below. The flooding meant only one thing: the tunnel underneath Central Park Drive had flooded. The oval door was shut, and there was no conceivable way Fabrizio and his men could have survived. The force of the gushing water alone should have killed them even before they drowned.

A warm ooze dripped from his elbow. The sight of his blood-soaked arm intensified the burning sensation. A bullet had caught his left arm, entering his biceps and shredded his triceps on exit. He tore off the remains of the sleeve of his shirt with his right hand and teeth and examined the wound as the pain rose to a level of excruciating agony. "It doesn't get any less fucking painful the second time," he muttered, face drawn in agony. He twisted his arm, inspecting the injury. By the grace of God, it appeared that the bullet didn't yaw or oscillate inside his arm in a way to cause any major bone or nerve damage.

Tightly wrapping the L. L. Bean shirt around his wound, Anthony peered through the metal-grated window. The old-style lamppost around the perimeter of the reservoir provided little clarity in the dead of night, but even in darkness, it was clear that the water level was considerably lower.

He raised his two-way radio with his right hand. "Anyone there?"

An extended pause followed the sound of static.

"I'm here, Tony."

Vicki also replied. "I'm outside the Grace Rainey Rogers Auditorium."

Anthony winced as he tightened the tourniquet. "What's going on there?"

"The worshippers are inside the museum. Cy and I watched them go toward the theater, and then all of a sudden, they just disappeared."

"Cy," Anthony snarled. He composed himself. "Vicki, meet me in the Great Hall in five minutes. Stay put, Paul. We'll swing around to you."

"What about the three men who entered the tunnels?" Paul asked.

"I don't care who fishes them out," Anthony remarked, unsure which organization had the greatest interest in recovering the bodies. One of them would get there quickly. Such incidences couldn't be made public.

Didn't have to come to this. He winced extendedly. *But it always does.*

Anthony retrieved his gun, exited the gatehouse from the top floor, and walked into Central Park. Unlike Pythagoras's emergence from the depths of the earth—attended by a cheering and exuberant crowd—there was no fanfare, not one single eyewitness of his ascent. Not a soul was in sight.

CHAPTER 56

VICKI AND CY MET ANTHONY IN the Great Hall. Vicki examined Anthony's arm and suggested that he seek medical attention. Cy was less composed.

Anthony tightened the L. L. Bean shirt wrapped around his arm. "The police and FBI will be here soon, but I want to get these guys now."

"They just magically disappeared inside the theater," Vicki answered.

"I am pretty sure I know where they are," Anthony declared, tentatively, then explained to Vicki and Cy that the millions of dollars donated to the museum to build the atrium for the Temple of Dendur came with strings: namely, that a secret room be built above the Egyptian Wing.

"There's a secret room in my department?" Cy asked, interrupting.

Anthony nodded, pain visible in his face. "But what was long-hidden from the public, and even concealed from the government, was that the gift didn't come from the donor's own personal funds, but from a shady deal that allowed him to buy artwork donated to the museum fifty years earlier at a discount—all masterpieces—and then donate the pieces back at present value and take a tax write-off at current value, making an enormous profit."

Vicki shook her head. "And no tax liability the next year, I suppose."

Anthony nodded confirmation. "And this room had been kept top secret to museum employees. The few who did know about the room were told that the donor used the room to store his own personal collection. Clearly, something more nefarious, more covert, has been going on in the room."

Cy burst into a rant. "All of these hidden rooms and secret passages. I demand to know this instant why no one has informed me of these places."

256

Anthony gazed at Vicki, eyes half shut. "Secret passages?"

"The worshippers are entering the museum by using a shaft below the Tomb of Perneb that leads to a false door inside the tomb."

Anthony couldn't suppress a chuckle, despite the persistent pain. "The surprises never end around here."

Vicki grinned with eagerness. "Can I come with you?"

Anthony squeezed his shoulder and turned to Cy. "You wait here. When the police arrive, I want you to send them into the auditorium."

"I have every right to know where this room is located!"

Anthony glowered at Cy, nostrils flared. "You're staying right here."

Anthony and Vicki rushed through the Egyptian Wing and found Paul standing at his post at the rear entrance to the Temple of Dendur.

"I want you to go to the front of the Egyptian Wing and do two things."

"Whatever you say," Paul remarked, eyeballing Anthony's wound.

"First, make sure Cy doesn't go into the auditorium."

"Got it, Tony. What else?"

"No one is to leave the auditorium until the police get here."

"Tony, I have something important to tell you."

Anthony wasn't ready for Paul's confession. "Hold the thought for now.".

Anthony and Vicki scuttled through the American Wing atrium. The lights in the court glowed softly, as they did every night. The enormous glass wall facing Central Park reflected nebulous golden orbs, caused by the luminescence of the lampposts in the park.

"Where is this room?" Vicki asked.

"You'll see in a second." Anthony stopped, held open the glass door leading from the American Wing to the Arms and Armor galleries, and led Vicki through the darkened galleries. He paused in front of the display case containing the saber. It was missing. He turned to Vicki with a 'you-were-right' expression, eyebrows raised.

Extending the cord on the key chain attached to his belt, Anthony found the right key, pushed aside the curtain on the side of the case, and bent. Fist closed, he struck the baseboard with the side of his hand, causing a small segment of the baseboard to fall to the floor. He inserted the key into the hidden keyhole and made several rotations until the lock clicked. The display case slowly swung from the wall to reveal a hidden door.

"Ingenious," Vicki said with a sudden realization. "Oh? So that is the reason why you asked Albert if there's anything behind the display case."

"I wanted to make sure he didn't find out about the room."

"And that's why you stared at me so intently when I asked you to meet with Albert to see the saber. You thought that I had discovered the room."

Anthony grinned, suppressing his pain. "Reid Technique."

At the top of a short flight of stairs, flashlights were turned off to avoid detection. The security officials groped through a dark corridor until Anthony made a halting gesture. "That's the room," he whispered. A red glow emanated through the space between the door and the floor. The smell of kyphi incense – incense used by the Egyptians in the evening – filled the corridor. Frankincense and myrrh were used only during the day. "I had no idea this area of the museum existed," Vicki quietly said.

"Remind me to show you the video feed of the ghost."

Vicki stopped. "Ghost?"

"We caught something on camera in this area that may actually be a ghost."

"Probably the lingering spirit of the guy who donated the money for the atrium in exchange for the secret room in the museum." Vicki thought back to what the man in the tunnel and said, "Money doesn't buy a ticket to the afterlife." She smiled, thinking of her encounter with the man and hoping that she'd see him again. And see him soon.

Anthony and Vicki positioned themselves on either side of the door.

"Are you ready?" Anthony asked, tightening the tourniquet around his arm.

"I hope the scrolls are in there." Vicki held up crossed fingers.

Anthony inserted a different mortise key into the door and slowly twisted it until he felt the lock open. He forcefully pushed the door open and stepped into the room. Heads under purple-hooded robes turned in unison. The startled expressions were clearly discernible. Ten people were on their knees positioned in two rows of five. Two women, holding long wand-like objects, stood on a marble platform elevated by three small steps. A pedestal in the form of a Greek column stood between them with a chalice on top. A pot of incense and an hourglass were also on the pedestal, alongside the saber, which reflected the misty, red light that faintly lit the small hidden room. Hieroglyphics and depictions of Egyptian rituals covered all four walls. The

Eye of Horus loomed above the depictions. Greek, Latin, and Hebrew words preceded English words that read:

Whoever discovers the interpretations of these sayings will not taste death.

Vicki zoomed in on the altar, hoping to see the scrolls.

"Let's do this peacefully," Anthony demanded, his gun still in his holster. There was little concern of bloodshed. The crimes committed by the individuals in the room were non-violent in nature; crimes that the average person's taxes paid for; crimes that secured the elite's monopoly on the world stage; crimes that assured that the wealthy grew wealthier by the day. Crimes that the average person never hears about.

"I don't see the scrolls anywhere," Vicki said softly, mournfully.

Anthony kept his eyes on the worshippers as he spoke. "Things shrouded in secrecy for thousands of years don't just fall into your lap. I'm sure these guys moved the scrolls out of New York City at the first sign of trouble." He tapped Vicki with his elbow. "Take them down the stairs they came up. The police should be in the auditorium by now. I'll meet you in the Great Hall."

"Where are you going?"

Anthony looked at his Santos de Cartier watch.

"To put in a call to Rome."

"At this hour?" Vicki asked.

"And to meet Lane Merrill. Both parties may be interested in knowing that Fabrizio was falsely operating as a member of the Vatican."

Vicki stepped forward. "Folks, if you would follow me, please."

One by one, Vicki guided the worshippers down the stairs in the back of the room known to only a handful at the museum. But all great museums were manipulated by the invisible hand of the ultra-rich. It was the way of the great art institutions – a modern-day irony, considering that most of the objects in museums around the world were painted, crafted, sculpted, and constructed by people who cared little about riches.

Anthony exited and locked the door, hoping that no one would use the room again. But he knew that it would be used again, just not on his watch.

CHAPTER 57

WHEN ANTHONY AND LANE MERRILL APPROACHED, Vicki and Paul were in the Great Hall watching as the group was being taken out of the museum. The worshippers were handcuffed, hoods lowered. Lane asked how the group had moved around the Egyptian Wing without being caught on camera.

"There's an old Roman saying, *Quis custodiet ipsos custodes*? Who will guard the guards themselves?" Anthony turned to Paul, arms folded. "Would you like to answer President Merrill's question?"

Speechless, Paul's eyes widened, projecting remorse.

"I'm very disappointed," Anthony said, looking at Paul. "I had someone look into the monitoring system. You know what she found?" he asked rhetorically. "The feeds from some of the cameras in the Egyptian Wing were rigged so that they looped the image of an empty gallery after closing."

"Listen, Tony," Paul pleaded, looking back-and-forth between Anthony and the president. "I had no choice. Do you know who those people are who just walked out of here? Do you know the power they wield in this place?"

"I want to see you in my office first thing tomorrow morning," Anthony said soberly, then called Cy over. "As for you."

"As for me, what?" Cy folded his arms.

"Did you really think you could move museum items around without being seen?" Anthony asked, knowing that Vicki would love to give Cy an earful on the proper procedures required to move museum objects. "After I informed you that something was wrong with the cameras in the Egyptian Wing, I also had my technician place additional cameras in hidden locations. She did one hell of a job because I caught you moving the statue of Nectanebo II into the temple. I also watched you remove the statue of Ptolemy II from the collection. How's my knowledge of the collection now?" Anthony asked sarcastically."

"Even if I did, I certainly didn't do anything improper. I'm the head curator of this museum's Egyptian Department. I don't need permission from security or anyone else to move objects around in my collection."

Anthony turned to Lane, uninterested in Cy's rationale. "I had Cy accompany me on an inspection of the cameras earlier tonight. I purposely kept the main camera off-line momentarily. I wanted to see his reaction when he noticed it wasn't working. He certainly seemed rather pleased by it."

"Why did you do it, Mr. Hetford?" Lane pressed, her hand fastened to her hips, tips of her python-skinned boots protruding beneath twill trousers.

"I'll tell you why. I did it because there was a lot of funny business going on in this museum. I informed both of you of that as soon as I saw the hierogrammatics in the temple, but no one realized the inherently dangerous nature of the matter. It was incumbent upon me, for the sake of Egyptology, for the sake of everything we know about the past, to force the issue."

"Why send me to talk to David Graham?" Anthony asked.

"Because you needed to hear first-hand just how outrageous these new theories about the past are. How damaging they are to the conventional historical record, to all that's been established over the years."

"Outrageous or not," Anthony remarked, staring at Cy with a new-found feeling of sadness for him and for all of those who are unable to transform their understanding of the past, "we just apprehended some very real people."

Lane stepped closer to Cy, staring at him squarely in the eyes.

"I want your letter of resignation on my desk first thing tomorrow."

A lieutenant approached Anthony with several EMS paramedics. "Hey, Anthony, let these guys take you over to Lenox Hill Hospital."

Anthony was ready to go.

"Need me to fill out a report?"

The officer pointed to the individuals being loaded into the police van in front of the museum and said, "Cap informs me that the Feds are handling these guys? Why would you need to file a report?"

Anthony shook his head. "Feds are investigating others who wanted to kill them," he said, knowing that the worshippers were certain to get off with a light fine, if that. Whatever they did, they did with impunity to the law.

"Who wants to kill these guys?" the officer asked.

Anthony stared at the lieutenant. Solemnly, he said, "One of many groups that operate behind the scenes and influence the course of human affairs."

Confused, the officer squinted at Anthony. "Well, it's over now."

"It's not over. There will always be those who suppress the past and those who look to benefit from it. It's been going on ever since the dawn of time."

"Now you're just talkin' in riddles."

Vicki moved closer to Anthony. "See you in the morning."

$$* \sim * \sim *$$

IN THE AUSTERE Cappella della Passione inside the Church of the Gesù, the Superiore Generale studied the painting of the Madonna and Child that had long ago replaced Pulzone's *Pietà* as the altarpiece.

Would have been nice to have Pulzone's painting out of the public eye, he thought to himself. *And to once and for all do away with those troublesome scrolls. If the ancient secrets hidden in the scrolls are unlocked, it will be the end of the world as we know it.*

Irritated by the heat, he removed a silk handkerchief from an inside pocket of his black cassock, wiped the perspiration from his brow, and entered the main nave. It was another one of those sweltering days when it was too hot to exert any more energy than necessary, so he sat on a bench in the empty church, pressed on his smartphone, and reread the headlines of the story on the front of every major Italian newspaper:

WORSHIPFUL MASTER, CAPO DI TUTTI, CHARGED WITH MURDER

No one false flags the Vatican. The Generale recited Mathew 28:18:

All authority in heaven and on earth has been given to me.

CHAPTER 58

VICKI BEGAN HER MORNING ROUNDS IN the atrium of the American Wing. She stared pensively through the glass windows facing Central Park as she entered. The courtyard was filling with the sound of excited visitors and the arousing smell of coffee.

It's certainly nice to have things back to normal, she ruminated.

The sundry white-marble, bronze, and gilt bronze statues glistened cheerily in the early-morning light. Unlike in the other sections of the museum, the collection of statues in the American Wing glorified women, not past male figures who presided over a deceitful and violent era of human history. "It's a reassuring feeling," Vicki said aloud.

She entered a gallery that contained a dozen or so Hudson River School paintings, pausing in front of Thomas Cole's *View on the Catskill – Early Autumn*. The imagery transported the viewer's mind to the verdant Hudson Valley; it necessitated a connection with nature. The painting also displayed the artist's depiction of nature itself as the true manifestation of God. More than ever, she appreciated the Hudson River School's condemnation of the destruction created by the prevailing masculine order.

"Didn't know you liked American paintings so much."

Vicki spun around and smiled. "How's the arm?"

"Doctor said it isn't too serious." Anthony moved closer to an adjacent wall. "This is a nice painting," he said, turning back to Vicki.

"That's *Autumn Oaks* by George Inness," Vicki replied, realizing that Anthony didn't want to talk about his injury. He wasn't one to complain.

263

"I like the fall colors of the leaves on the trees."

"You mean you like the way the light reflects in those colors. It's called luminism, which was a popular style used in nineteenth-century American paintings." She pointed at the painting. "You can really distinguish the autumn browns and burgundies, mixed in with the more brilliant shades of yellows and greens."

"Very informative, Professor Lange." Anthony closed the distance to Vicki. "But I'm glad you are not at some university saying that in front of a class of students."

Vicki smiled wider.

Anthony pointed to Inness's painting. "Is this a real place?"

Vicki nodded. "He painted the scene in upstate New York, not too far from here."

"I bet there are some trees in the park starting to turn about now." Anthony looked at his watch. "What do you say we go to the park for a walk at lunch?"

Vicki smiled. "Only if you promise not to tell my boss."

ANTHONY AND VICKI exited the museum's main entrance, descended the stairs, and walked onto the stately front plaza. Fewer people were sitting on the entryway stairs than had been just a few weeks earlier. There was less overall congestion on the sidewalk. Every year, the autumn season produced a noticeable dip in visitors to the museum, but the holiday season always brought them back, and brought the crowds back in droves.

The bitterly cold wind that gusted down Fifth Avenue during the winter, currently disguised as enlivening fall breezes, persistently blew Vicki's long, brown hair into her face as she and Anthony entered Central Park at Seventy-Ninth Street.

"I saw Paul exiting the museum earlier. Did you?"

"Yes," Anthony replied curtly.

"I'm sorry. I know you have been friends for a long time."

Anthony fell silent as his sight fixated on the grayish-marbling of the cement path. A shake of the head, and he said, "Not as long as the friend I lost the other day."

People streamed into the park alongside Anthony and Vicki, taking advantage of the break in the hot weather. Locals chatted on the green benches that lined the paved path. Sunbathers were out in full-force, taking in the last of the summer sun and occupying the entire grassy area of Cedar Hill on the opposite side of the 79th Street transverse. Above and below the hill, groups in varying numbers sat on blankets, picnicking, and sipping wine.

Vicki broke the pause in conversation.

"I still can't believe Paul manipulated the cameras. To be honest, I can't believe people had the audacity to use the museum for their own secret purposes all these years."

Anthony exhaled. "Well, in time you'll learn there are two immutable truths in our line of work. First, there are different rules for different people."

Vicki shook her head. "Doesn't seem fair."

"Second, people get angry when you question why two sets of rules exist."

"Why does it have to be that way?" she asked, knowing the answer. Money.

Anthony felt the sense of contentment shared by those who better understood the ways of life. "We're a flawed species. Unfortunately, we haven't been able to fix our imperfections, so we go about our merry way in denial of them." He looked at the museum, knowing it was filled with extraordinary marvels from all civilizations in recorded time. "Maybe one day, we'll appreciate that it's just as important to come to terms with history as it is to understand the human mind. There's likely a correlation."

Vicki knew she wasn't going to get an answer, but she had to ask the question. "You did a good job keeping the authorities out of the picture until the last moment." She turned her head and met Anthony's eyes. "Was that to protect the Met or the Vatican?"

Anthony grinned with satisfaction, thinking, *I taught her well.*

"I'll just presume both," she said.

At times, unspoken understandings were the most effective.

The saxophone player at the Greywacke Arch was swaying and playing something atypically upbeat. Anthony couldn't quite put his finger on the name of the tune, but he liked what he heard. He reached around to pull out his wallet and cringed.

"Let me get that," Vicki reached into her pocket and pulled out a single dollar bill. She bowed and respectfully dropped it into the musician's case, smiling.

Bob White had the large Canon lens aimed directly at a Red-tailed Hawk in an oak tree just north of the tunnel. Anthony spotted the large bird, observing how the sunlight brought out the red-brick color of the square tail, while also highlighting the white lacing of the silky feathers. *They are majestic birds*, he now understood.

Following the bend in the path at the Greywacke Knoll, neither bothered to look at the obelisk. It was a beautiful day, and both wished to keep it that way.

Neighborhood families were back from vacation. Over the sound of the playing children, Vicki heard someone calling out her name. She looked up at the museum's rooftop café, overlooking Central Park. Sibyl waved exuberantly. Vicki waved back.

"Is her post on the rooftop?" Anthony asked.

"No, she must be on her break."

"How long has she worked at the museum?"

Vicki brushed back her hair. "Longer than me."

"Maybe it's time that she was promoted to Security Manager."

"You can ask, but she probably won't be interested. She's much more interested in her artwork than she is with promotions."

Anthony sat on a bench bordered by a grove of apple trees.

Vicki picked a ripening apple and polished it on her cargo paints. She watched as the runners on Central Park Drive trained for the New York City Marathon. Her line of sight shifted when she heard the clatter of horse hooves galloping on the hard pavement. The elaborate horse-drawn carriage that came into view from the south appeared to be transported from nineteenth-century Europe. "That's weird," she said, gazing at the stately carriage. "The horse carriages usually stay at the south end of the park."

She noticed on closer inspection that the man inside the carriage was staring back her way. Gold tints twinkled in his silvery eyes. "Oh my God!" Vicki uttered, completely transfixed on the man. He was dressed peculiarly, in attire reminiscent of clothes worn by the past princes of Europe, just like the man in the Rembrandt painting.

"See you soon," Victoria, she heard.

An incoherent sound passed through her lips as the apple fell to the ground.

Anthony's head jerked up. "What's the matter, Vicki?"

A silver streak twinkled in absorbed eyes as she watched, almost utterly mesmerized, as the carriage continued north on Central Park Drive. The loud clacking sound of shoed hoofs on asphalt faded as the carriage followed the westward bend in Central Park Drive. Vicki snapped back to the present. The carriage was gone.

She shook her head and sat next to Anthony. His face slowly came into focus, his brown eyes staring back with concern. "Every year," Vicki began with a tone indicative of reflection, "I pick an apple off one of these trees. Not long after, the trees go into a long slumber, but always bloom beautifully again the following year."

Anthony nodded his head, somewhat baffled.

Vicki leaned closer to Anthony. "Do you think reincarnation is possible?"

"I'm not sure what to believe anymore." Anthony slowly shook his head.

"Have I got news for you!"

CPSIA information can be obtained
at www.ICGtesting.com
Printed in the USA
FSHW011254011220
76481FS